ELIZA'S DAUGHTER

A SEQUEL TO JANE AUSTEN'S
SENSE AND SENSIBILITY

D1057160

JOAN AIKEN

SOURCEBOOKS LANDMARK
AN IMPRINT OF SOURCEBOOKS, INC.®
NAPERVILLE, ILLINOIS

Published by Sourcebooks Landmark an imprint of Sourcebooks, Inc.
P.O. Box 4410, Naperville, Illinois 60567–4410
(630) 961–3900
FAX: (630) 961–2168
www.sourcebooks.com

Originally published in 1994 by St. Martin's Press, New York

Library of Congress Cataloging-in-Publication Data
Aiken, Joan
  Eliza's daughter : a sequel to Jane Austen's Sense and sensibility / Joan Aiken.
     p. cm.
  ISBN-13: 978-1-4022-1288-8
  ISBN-10: 1-4022-1288-7
  1. Young women—Fiction. 2. England—Fiction. I. Austen, Jane, 1775-1817. Sense and sensibility. II. Title.
  PR6051.I35E44 2008
  823'.914—dc22
                          2008014209

Printed and bound in the United States of America
CHG 10 9 8 7 6 5 4 3 2 1

To Julius

Chapter 1

I HAVE A FANCY TO TAKE PEN IN HAND AND TELL MY STORY, FOR now that I am arrived, so to speak, at a favourable hilltop, a safe situation above water level, I may look back on such mires, floods, tempests and raging tides as I have encountered with a tolerably tranquil eye; besides, my history should serve as a guide (or at least afford some diversion) to those who may be at present less favourably placed.

While, as to the dark that lies ahead, who can chart it?

In short – and without further preamble – I'll begin.

I have no information as to the circumstances of my birth, or even in what county that event took place; indeed I doubt if there is any record of it.

My first memories are of the year 1797, when I must have been, I believe, about three or four years of age, and, from the circumstances of my life, already a shrewd and noticing child. As an infant I had been, I heard, somewhat frail and puny, and with the unlucky blemish that caused me to be scorned by some and feared by others. My foster-mother, Hannah Wellcome, having at that period several boys in her care greater in size than myself, and fearful that, among them, I might receive some fatal injury (thus depriving her of my foster-fee) daily dispatched me with a halfpenny, from the time that I could walk, to the vicarage and the decidedly questionable custody of the parson, Dr Moultrie. With the halfpenny I bought three cakes at the village baker's for my dinner; and Dr Moultrie, to keep me from plaguing him with questions, for he was a slothful old party given to drowsing away many of the daylight hours in his chair, lost no time in teaching me to read, and turning me loose in his library. There, having run through such tales of *Tom Hickathrift, Jack the Giant-Killer* and *Gold-Locks* as remained from the days of his own children (long since grown and gone), I was obliged to munch on more solid fare, Goldsmith's *History of England,* volumes of the *Spectator,* the plays of Shakespeare, and much poetry and theology, besides Berquin's *Ami des Enfants* and some simple Italian tales (in consequence of which I acquired a readiness and taste for learning foreign tongues that has later stood me in good stead).

There was one volume that I read over and over, *The Death of Arthur* it was called, and I found the tales in it of knights and battles, Sir Beaumain, Sir Persaint, Merlin the enchanter and King Arthur himself, most haunting; they held sway over my mind for weeks together. But alas! one day, absorbed in the tale of the death of King Hermance, I dropped a great blob of jam from the tart I was eating on to the page of the book. When Dr Moultrie discovered this, he gave me a terrible beating, after which I could hardly crawl home, and he locked the book away; I never laid eyes on it again.

However, to his credit, it must be said that finding me an eager pupil Dr Moultrie was prepared to emerge from his torpor for an hour or two each day to instil in me the rudiments of Greek, Latin and Euclid, besides a thirst for wider knowledge.

But I run ahead of my tale.

Hannah Wellcome, my foster-mother, appeared good-natured and buxom: round red cheeks and untidy yellow ringlets escaping from her cap would predispose a stranger in her favour. I believe a certain native cunning had incited her to marry as she had done, thereby endowing herself with a propitious name and the status of a matron; Tom, her husband, kept in the background and was seldom seen; a narrow, dark, lantern-jawed ferret of a man, he scurried among the lanes on questionable pursuits of his own. But she, smiling and curtseying at the door of their thatched cottage, her ample bulk arrayed in clean apron, tucker and cap, might easily create an impression of kindly honesty, and had, at any one time, as many small clients as the house would hold.

The house, whitewashed and in its own garden, lay at the far end of a straggling hamlet sunk deep in a coombe. Our muddy street wound its way, like a crease through a green and crumpled counterpane, between steeply tilted meadows and dense patches of woodland, close to the border of Somerset and Devon. There were no more than twenty dwellings in all, besides the small ancient church presided over by Dr Moultrie. He had, as well, another village in his cure, perched high on the windy moor seven miles westwards. This was Over Othery. From long-established use and local custom, *our* hamlet, Nether Othery, was never thus referred to, but always, by the country folk round about, given the title of 'Byblow Bottom'.

I write, now, of days long since passed away, when it was still the habit amongst all ladies of the gentle classes no matter how modest their degree, even the wives of attorneys, vicars, and well-to-do tradesmen, not to suckle their own infants, but always to put them out to wet-nurse. The bosoms of ladies, it seemed, were not for use, but strictly for show (and indeed, at the time I am recalling, bosoms *were* very much in evidence, bunched up over skimpy high-waisted dresses and concealed by little more than a twist of gauze and a scrap of cambric; what with that, and the fashion for wearing dampened petticoats and thin little kid slippers out of doors, very many young ladies must have gone to their ends untimely, thereby throwing even more business in the way of foster-mothers). Whatever the reason, it was held that the babies of the upper classes throve and grew faster when fed and tended by women of a lower order, and so the new-born infant would be directly dispatched, perhaps merely from one end of a village to the other, perhaps half across England to some baronial estate, to be reared in a cottage for two, three, or even four years, while its own mother, if so minded, need never lay eyes on it for that space of time. Of course I do not say this was the rule; many mothers, no doubt, visited their children very diligently, very constantly; but many others, I am equally sure, did not.

Be that as it may, our village had for many years past been distinguished for the number and excellence of its wet-nurses. Perhaps, too, the superiority of the West Country cattle, the abundance and richness of their cream and butter, bore some share in this good repute. Also, during the last twenty years, an additional fame had attached to Nether Othery: that of a retreat, remote and secure from gossip or corruption, possessed of a balmy climate and healthy, unspoiled surroundings, where those random, unsought, but often interesting and well-beloved *accidentals* – if I may so term them – the natural offspring of public persons (who may bear great affection towards such issue, yet wish to avoid the disclosure of their existence) could be reared in wholesome, bracing privacy.

Lord S———, for instance, who fathered fifteen children on his lovely and obliging mistress Mrs R———, dispatched them all, one after another, to be reared in Nether Othery. So did the Duke of C——— and Mr G——— H———, and many another that I could mention.

As a consequence of this custom, the village boasted at all times a floating population far greater than any rural census would have recorded, and by far the larger part of this population would be under the age of twelve years.

Those infants respectably born in wedlock were, as a general rule, removed by their parents at around the age of three or four; while the bastards were seldom reclaimed under eleven or twelve, when the boys would mostly be dispatched to public school, and the girls, depending on their station, might be apprenticed as milliners, or sent for a few years' schooling in Bristol or Exeter, in order to fit them for a career as governesses in great households.

By the time that I was three or four – the period when I commence my history – I had seen many such migrants come and go. I was already, as children may be, tolerably aware of the hazards and hardships that, for most of us, lay ahead. Among the youthful population of Byblow Bottom there was a certain freemasonry; we compared our hopes and fears, such scanty knowledge of our own parentage as we might possess, and such information as might drift back to us regarding the subsequent fortunes of our mates.—And when I say *mates,* I do not deny that sexual congress, among the older members of our group, was not infrequent: feeling themselves to be, as it were, cuckoos in the nest of Nether Othery, they were not greatly trammelled by the rules of a society which as yet had afforded them no benefits.

The fifteen side-slips of Lord S———, who frequently over-lapped in their periods of residence, corresponded regularly one with another, and the elder ones, departed to London, sent back to their cadets cheerful accounts of the unorthodox existence of S——— House in Grosvenor Square. Here the owner's wife and his mistress lived side by side in harmonious proximity and few distinctions were drawn between bastards and legitimate children, who all consorted together freely and gaily. But of course such good fortune was not to be expected by most of us.

As to my own progenitors, I held only the vaguest and scantiest notion. My mother, I was given to understand, had died in giving birth to me; and this (I was also given to understand) was the greatest piece of mercy that she might have hoped for, since she had run away from her friends at the age of sixteen, and had been heart-lessly abandoned at seventeen by her seducer. And who might *he* have been? was the question over which I pondered for many, many hours of my childhood, watching the rain float by Dr Moultrie's casement, until he summoned me to an hour's Latin exercises; or as I walked alone in the mist over the Brendon Hills.

For, although there was always plenty of company in Byblow Bottom and, on the whole, a rude camaraderie and good-fellowship prevailed between the transient youthful population and that minority of children born in the place who had a right to be called natives – yet I felt in myself, at all times, a longing, a craving, if not for solitude, for a different kind of discourse from any that my mates could provide. And walking over the steep and blowy landscape by myself served, if only in small measure, to appease this craving.

My tale commences on a day in early autumn. The leaves, though they had not yet changed colour (and, in our salt-ridden, coastal country, would only fade to a rusty and tarnished brown), hung limp and melancholy on the trees, the sun gave out a mild warmth, the birds cheeped very softly to themselves and the sea lay hushed, as if autumn gales were a thing unheard-of.

Gross Dr Moultrie, suffering from a recurrence of the gout which every two or three months rendered him speechless and motionless with agony, had dismissed me with instructions not to return for three days. Of this edict I had not informed Mrs Wellcome who would, I knew, find copious occupation for me about the house. Small as I was, she already employed me to pick beans, feed the chickens, pull out weeds, chop suet for pie-crust and mend the boys' stockings. There would be enough work to keep me busy until bedtime, which I regarded as wholly unfair, since the boys (Will, Rob, and Jonathan at the present time) were never put to such labour, but might fish in the brook, roam the moor, or go a-swim-ming at the shore, just as they chose. In fact they most often went off poaching with Tom Wellcome and were learning such arts as, probably, their families had never dreamed of. Intermittently, they attended the village school, since Dr Moultrie had rejected them as being too noisy and fidgety for his services.

Pleased with my liberty, I turned away from the village and struck off over the hill towards Ashett, the little fishing port which was our nearest town. There I planned to pass the rest of the day, idling on the narrow quay, watching the lobster-fishers mend their nets and the ships unlading. I had heard a tale that a Spanish vessel had been brought in, under suspicion of piracy or smuggling, and I was eager to see it.

Arrived at the quayside I prepared to take my station, perched on an upside-down fish-hamper but, to my disappointment, the Spanish ship had already been given its quittance and departed. The tide was low, and I observed Will, Rob, and Jonathan, with some fisher-boys, running and splashing naked on the muddy foreshore that lies eastwards from the harbour bar. Not wishful to join them, I wandered away westwards and loitered for many minutes on the high, hump-backed bridge that spans the rocky little river Ashe, at the point where it takes a steep plunge into the harbour, and its waters transmute from a clear topaz brown to a salt and cloudy green.

This bridge was always a favourite vantage point of mine; here I have spent hours together, gazing, sometimes upstream at the river threading its way through the quiet little town to the steep moor above, sometimes downstream at the tossing waves and lively harbour.

Today, as I stood tiptoe, so as to rest my elbows and chin on the stone parapet, I became aware, gradually, of two voices conversing above my head.

At first, single words began to filter into my notice – *remarkable* words, of a kind that I had never expected to hear spoken, but only to discover and pore over between the pages of Dr Moultrie's books: glittering, blast, challenge, cataract, meditation, tyrannous, spectral, the star-dogged moon. . .

These words were to me like a spell, an extraordinary incantation. Indeed for some few minutes I entertained the mysterious impression that they had arrived from the depths of my own mind, as bubbles come sliding to the surface in a moorland marsh. But then I realized that two men were, like myself, standing at gaze upon the bridge, occupied partly by the scene before them, but more by the talk that ran between them even faster than the current of the little river below.

Both of the strangers were tall; so tall that I had to twist and crane my neck to study them. Who could they be? I was quite sure I had never seen them before; they certainly were not natives of these parts. Indeed one, the taller, conversed with a curious northern gruffness, which made it quite hard for me, at first, to comprehend some of his language.

The other man, the shorter (yet even he was by no means short) spoke with a more homely accent; his tones had the warm friendly burr of Devon or Somerset; but he was by far the more striking in appearance. In truth, I thought him wonderful! Not handsome, no; his complexion was pale, he had a wide mouth and fleshy lips; but his forehead was tremendous, and his eyes flashed with power. Long, rough, glossy black hair hung nearly to his shoulders. He and his friend were clad in the kind of jackets and trousers worn by the gentry; yet their garments were shabby and ill-fitting, decidedly so. Their neck-cloths were loosely tied, not over-white, their shoes were worn; both carried satchels of papers and their pockets bulged with books. The taller man, whom the other addressed as 'Will' or 'Bill', was gaunt and stringy and bony; he had a nose so enormously prominent that it seemed likely at any moment to over-balance him and topple him forwards on his face. There was also – these were my first impressions – something a touch self-satisfied about his air; his mouth was small and pursed above a receding chin; yet he too had a noble brow, and his eyes, though less dark and flashing than those of his friend, were bright with comprehension and intelligence. Like his companion he seemed filled with such fervent enthusiasm that, for a few moments, I wondered if both men were in liquor; but no; this, evidently, was their accustomed mode when together as I was soon to understand.

'It is not from the *metre,* it is not from the order of words, but from the *matter itself,* that the essential difference must arise,' the man called Bill was proclaiming in a loud assured tone. Indeed, he trumpeted through his large nose.

His friend laughed. 'I put my hat upon my head, And walked into the Strand, And there I met another man, Whose hat was in his hand!' he suggested.

'Precisely so! Or, on the other hand, "And thou art long and lank and brown, As is the ribbed sea-sand."'

'*Hey!* Will, my dear fellow! That has it to a nicety! You singular genius – pearls flow continually from your lips! A moment, if you please, till I set that down.'

And he pulled a notebook from his satchel and wrote vigorously.

His friend, also laughing, observed, 'Take care, my dear Sam! Our faithful Home Office follower is busy marking our actions from afar through his spy-glass; without the least question he now suspects you of making observations about coastal defences, so as to facilitate a French invasion.'

'Oh, devil take the silly fellow. Pay no heed to him.—But, listen, Bill, now here is a point that has been troubling me; tell me, how in the wide world are we to get the ship home again? With all the crew perished and gone? This, I must confess, has me quite in a puzzle. What can we do? You are so much more ingenious than I at solving these practical problems.'

Bill said: 'I have two thoughts about that. But let us proceed on our walk, or the day will be gone. Besides, my mind always operates more cannily when I am in physical motion.'

They left the bridge, strolling, and took their way westwards.

I could not help myself; I followed them as if drawn by a powerful magnet.

Up the steep cliff path I pursued them, and squatted nearby when they paused at the top to get their breath and admire the light on the calm blue autumnal sea. Far across the channel the mountains of Wales dangled like a gauzy frill bordering the skirts of the sky.

'Hollo!' said Sam, noticing me. 'It seems we have a follower.'

'A little cottage girl.'

'Are you a Home Office agent, my little maid?'

'No, please, sir. I don't know what that is.'

'Never mind it. How old are you, child?'

'Please, sir, I don't rightly know that either. I am an orphan.'

'No parents?' inquired Sam.

'None, sir. I'm a bastard, do you see, from Byblow Bottom.'

'And who provides for you, then?' asked the man called Bill, bending on me a sad, solicitous look. 'I, like you, was orphaned when young. It is a hard fate.'

'Please, sir, a gentleman called Colonel Brandon provides, but he never comes to see me, only writes letters, not very often, telling me to be a good girl and read my prayer-book.'

'And *do* you read it?' put in Sam.

'Oh, yes, sir, and a deal of other books besides.'

'Such as what? *Cinderella?*'

'Oh no, sir, but Cicero and Sir Roger de Coverley.'

At that both men burst out laughing and gazed at me, I suppose, with astonishment.

'And who gives thee such reading matter, thou little prodigy?' inquired Will.

'Dr Moultrie, sir, he teaches me, but he has the gout at present. So, please, sirs, may I come along of you?'

'But we walk too fast, my child; besides, it is not well advised that a little maid of your tender years should roam at large all over the country with two great grown men.'

'Oh, bless you, sir, I've always roamed; Mrs Wellcome don't care a groat, so be as she don't want me to feed the chicken. *Please* let me come, sirs; I won't hinder or plague you, *indeed* I won't.'

They looked at one another and shrugged. 'She will soon fall behind after all,' said Mr Sam.

But I knew I would not. Sometimes I joined the boys at hare-coursing. And although I always hoped that the hare would get away, it was the sport of theirs that most pleased me, because I could outrun nearly all of them. At a steady jog, over the moors, I could outlast all, even the biggest ones.

'I won't pester or ask questions, truly I won't. Dr Moultrie won't have that,' I offered. 'It's just, sirs, that your talk do be so interesting to I. 'Tis better far than looking at pictures.'

'Whose heart could remain unmelted at that?' said Mr Sam, laughing. So they let me follow.

And indeed it was true that their talk – specially that of Mr Sam – was like nothing I had ever heard before, or have since, up to this very day. So many subjects were covered – Nightingales, Poetry, Metaphysics, Dreams, Nightmares, the Sense of Touch, the differ-ence between Will and Volition, between Imagination and Fancy – on, on, flowed the talk of Mr Sam the black-haired stranger, in a scintillating torrent of only half-comprehensible words. Sometimes his companion, Mr Bill, would put in a rejoinder; his contributions were always very pithy and shrewd. And sometimes they would be tossing back and forth some project that they were hatching between them – a plan for a tale of a ship, it seemed to be, and a ghostly voyage.

Now and then, for a change, they asked me questions.

'Is it true, child, that in these parts hares are thought to be witches?'

'Oh yes, for sure, sir; why, everybody knows that. Only last August the boys coursed and caught a black hare over there on Wildersmouth Head; and that very same week they found old Granny Pollard stiff and dead in her cottage with her dog howling alongside of her; she'd been the hare, don't you see?'

'Hmn,' said Mr Bill. 'It seems odd that a woman who spent half her time as a hare would keep a *dog;* don't you think so?'

'I don't see that, sir; every witch has her familiar. So why not a dog, just as well as a cat?'

Mr Sam asked me about changelings. 'In a village where so many children lack parents, is it not supposed that one or another might be a fairy's child – yourself, for example?'

I answered readily enough. 'Nobody would take *me* for a fairy's child, sir, because I am so ugly, my hair being so red, and because of my hands – you see.' I spread them out, and both men nodded gravely. 'But yes, Squire Vexford as lives in the Great House up on Growly Head – 'tis thought his granny was a changeling.'

And I told the tale, well known in Othery, of how the nurse, all those years ago, had been giving suck to the Squire's new-born daughter, when a fine lady came into her cottage carrying a babe all wrapped and swaddled in green silk. 'Give *my* pretty thing to suck also!' says the lady, and when the nurse does so, she vanishes clean away leaving the child behind. And the two infants were brought up as twins, and when one of 'em pined and dwined away, no one

knew whether 'twas the human baby or the elf-child that was left
lonesome. But from that day to this in the Vexford family, each
generation there's allus been a girl-child that's frail and pale, fair-
haired and puny, unlike the rest of 'em that are dark-haired and
high-complexioned, like the Squire hisself.

'That is a bonny tale, my hinny,' said Mr Bill. 'And is there such
a girl-child in the Squire's family at present?'

'No, sir, but Lady Hariot is increasing, and they do say, because
she carries it low, that the child will be a girl.'

Mrs Wellcome's daughter Biddy was also with child, and I knew
it was hoped by both women that the honour of rearing the Squire's
baby would be theirs; and I hoped so too. The Squire's great house,
Kinn Hall, up on Growly Head, with its gardens and paddocks and
yards and stables, was forbidden ground, but most dearly I wished
to explore it, both inside and out. If Biddy Wellcome had charge of
the Squire's baby, I foresaw there might be comings and goings
between the village and the Hall, there might be errands and
messages to run and a chance to get past the great iron gates. This
was my hope.

I cannot now remember for how many weeks or months I had the
extraordinary joy and privilege of accompanying Mr Bill and
Mr Sam on their rambles and explorations. I believe that the space
of time might have extended over as much as a year. The memory
of my first meeting with the two men remains sharp and clear, like
a picture in my mind, but later events blend together in a gilded
haze. I was not – by any means – invariably successful in my efforts
to escape and join the two strangers on their walks. Nor could I

always find them. Their houses lay some distance apart, and they did not go out together all the time. Mr Sam had a wife and babe, Mr Bill, a sister. Sometimes the weather proved my enemy and northerly gales lashed the coast and kept me housebound. Sometimes Dr Moultrie was exigent. But, despite these hazards, it seems to me that I succeeded in accompanying the two men on at least seven or eight occasions, and these were long excursions – for both men were prodigious walkers – along the coast to Hurlhoe, or over the moor to Folworthy, or up the twisting Ashe Valley to Ottermill. Both friends doted upon rivers and brooks and cascades; they would at any time go substantially out of their way if beguiled by the sound of falling waters, and were always ready to sit or stand for hours together gazing at spouts or sheets or spirts of spray. Indeed our very first walk – which I do remember clearly because it *was* the first – took us along the steep wooded cliffs for several miles to a little lonely church, St Lucy's of Godsend, where I would never have ventured to visit alone as it was reputed to be haunted. And such a tale was easy enough to credit, for the church stood at a most solitary spot, in a deep coign of precipitous and forest-covered hillside, with tall oaks all around it, and a stream which splashed down between high and fern-fringed banks to empty itself into a narrow cove, far, far down below. Because of the trees, the sea was not visible, and yet its restless presence could be felt; the sough of the tide like a heart-beat, and, from time to time, a deep and threatening boom or thud as a larger wave than usual cast its weight upon the rocks at the cliff foot.

'A fearsome place,' said Mr Sam, when the two men, removing their hats, had stepped inside the tiny church (I have heard said that it is the smallest in the whole kingdom) and come out again to admire the saw-toothed shadow which it flung, in the noonday sun, across its cramped little graveyard.

'Here there would be no need to pray,' said Mr Bill. 'The sound of water would say it all.'

'But at night,' I objected, 'the sound of the brook would be drowned by the voice of Wailing Sal.'

'And who, pray, is Wailing Sal?'

'She was a girl that used to meet her sweetheart here in the grave-yard. But her father forbade her. And why? Because, unbeknownst to her, her sweetheart were the Wicked One. But she met him none the less, and gave him three drops of blood from her finger, and that made her his for all time. But after she done that, he never came to see her no more and she pined and dwined away. So they buried her under gravel, and they buried her under sand, but still her ghost comes out, lonesome for her lover and bitter angry with her father because he forbade her. So, 'tis said, her ghost is moving slowly up the hill, back to her father's farm, at the rate of one cock's stride every year.'

'Merciful creator!' said Mr Sam, pulling out his notebook. 'One cock's stride every year? And what happens when she gets to the farm?'

'I don't know, sir. Maybe 'twill be doomsday by then.'

'And what about Wailing Sal's father?'

'Oh, he died many years agone; when Good Queen Bess were queen. Since then they've had six parsons with Bibles to try and lay the ghost, but Wailing Sal won't be laid; not one of them could do it.'

'What a sad tale.'

Mr Sam wandered away from us and leaned on the churchyard wall, staring down at the white water racing below in its narrow gully.

'Sam!' called his friend after a while. 'It is high time we were on our way back. The sun is westering. And we promised not to be late. And this little maid's friends will be growing anxious about her.'

'I know, I know,' said Mr Sam.

But still he lingered.

Lady Hariot did bear a daughter in the spring, little Thérèse. And Biddy Wellcome, being brought to bed about the same time, was given charge of the child, which she reared along with her own Polly. Biddy, like her mother, was a lusty, well-fleshed, red-cheeked woman, and of the same hasty temper. Polly's father had been a Danish sailor (or so it was said; he never came back to contradict the tale). Biddy, again like her mother Hannah, earned herself a sufficient living as a foster-mother and had in her keeping just now two lads from an attorney's family in Exeter, besides the misbegotten daughter of the Dean of Wells. This poor lass, Charlotte Gaveston, was touched in her wits (believed to be a result of the desperate efforts her mother employed to be rid of her before she came to full term); so she could never be left to mind the babes if Biddy went a-marketing. Nor could the boys; they were far too heedless. Therefore it became Biddy's habit to step next door (for she lived just up the lane from us) and deposit her two infants in their rush baskets with her mother for safe-keeping, while she went to the mill for flour, or down to the shore for fish, if the men had been out after pollock. In consequence of which, on most occasions, the care of the two children devolved on me, and many and many a time have I sat rocking and hushing them in Hannah Wellcome's back kitchen, or out among the cabbages and gooseberry bushes, as the new year began to open out and the weather to grow warm again.

Both babies were girls. But whereas Polly Wellcome was pink-cheeked and yellow-haired, like her mother and grandma, with round china-blue eyes, Lady Hariot's daughter Thérèse had lint-pale flaxen hair, fine as thistledown; her cheeks were pale, her eyes had a glancing light in them, like the sea itself, so that you could never say if they were green or grey. She was a small-boned, slight little being; looking at her, it was easy to believe the bygone legend of the faerie visitor and her child from elf-land all wrapped in green silk. Yet though so small and frail in appearance she seldom cried (unlike fat Polly, who would bawl her lungs out on the least occasion); little Thérèse lay silent and thoughtful in her crib, with her great melancholy eyes apparently taking in every slightest thing that passed. From an early age she seemed to recognize me, and smiled her faint smile when I came to lift her, or wash her, or do what was needed. And I myself came to love her dearly.

Where was Lady Hariot, meanwhile? Why did she never come to visit her daughter? Poor woman, she had been brought down after the birth, as many are, by the womb-fever, and lay for weeks between life and death, but with death, so said old Dr Parracombe, much the likelier outcome. For weeks he rode daily to Kinn Hall, and would sometimes call at our cottage to see how the babe throve; and seemed no little astonished, given the difficulties of her birth, that she prospered as she did.

'But indeed, Mrs Wellcome,' he always pronounced, 'you and your daughter are a pair of notable foster-nurses.' And Hannah Wellcome would curtsey, and beam at him, and say, 'Ah, 'tis the love we give them, sir.'

Even after she had escaped from the danger of death, Lady Hariot was confined to her bed for many months, and was so terribly weak that it was thought the most dangerous folly for her even to be permitted to see her child – conducive to over-excitation and strain upon the faculties. And after that she was taken abroad to some island, Madeira, I believe, where she stayed with her sister, for the warm sun there to bring back her health. So, for months we heard no more of her.

Once in a great while, Squire Vexford might stamp in to inquire after the child. He was a hasty, hard-featured man with thin lips and small angry eyes; it was known in the village that the Vexford property was entailed on a male heir, so he was sadly displeased that the outcome of all Lady Hariot's trouble was a mere daughter, and even more so when told that his wife might be unable to bear further children. He consequently paid scant heed to the child's progress or welfare, but would thrust his head in, cast a brief glance at the cradle, snap out a question or two and then stamp on his way, after the otter-hounds or along the track to the salmon pools in the upper windings of the Ashe river. More often it would be the Squire's man, Willsworthy, who called; and he was a close, silent customer who at all times kept his thoughts to himself. Only, once in a way, when his eye lit on Biddy Wellcome, a queer sudden glow would come into it, like the glimmer on a piece of fish that has lain in the pantry too long.

My frequent duty in minding the two babies meant a decided curtailment of my liberty to roam out and hope for a meeting with Mr Sam and Mr Bill; but, with a child's sober-minded realism, I believe I had long since understood that my outings with those two men were not to be looked for as something I might depend on; they were not for human nature's daily food. I was lucky beyond all deserts and expectation to have had them at all. And – I later understood – they had fed my mind with such thoughts and pictures and imaginings as would stand me in good stead through many troubles to come.

There remains one more singular event that is connected in my mind with those happy rambles. It was after I had returned from one such outing – I think to the Cain and Abel stones, high up on Ashe Moor, which stones prompted Mr Sam to tell me a queer story about Cain and his little son Enos, a tale of the boy asking his father the reason why the squirrels would not play with him. Mr Sam's stories all had some element of puzzle about them; I had to think and think, to ravel out their meaning.

I returned home late and, as was my habit on such occasions, crept in as quietly as a mouse through the kitchen door, for I knew that, on principle, if she heard me come in, Hannah Wellcome would give me a slippering. It was not that she greatly cared where I had been, but on account of all the tasks she had been obliged to undertake herself, lacking my services. Luckily I could hear that she and Tom and Biddy were in the parlour, fuddling themselves with green cider. I therefore crept up the narrow stair to the little crevice under the eaves which was my sleeping-place. It had no window, but plenty of fresh air came in through the thatch.

On the way, I passed the boys' room where I could hear them tossing, thrashing and teasing one another, as they would continue to do for half the night.

'Hollo? Is that you, Liza?' whispered Rob, as I tiptoed by their door.

Rob was Rob Hobart, my chiefest friend among the boys. Hob, or Hoby, or Hobgoblin, I called him. His father, I believe, was the

Post-Master General, his mother had sold cockles on the Strand in London. He was a lanky, freckled, yellow-headed fellow with a nimble tongue and bright wits; he was for ever leading the other boys into trouble, but then as often extricating them from their difficulties by some combination of bold inventiveness and shrewd sense. As a companion, if he was ever on his own, I liked him very well; but he seldom *was* on his own, being sociable and popular with the other boys. And in their company he descended to their level of teasing and abuse, would address me as 'Liza Lug-famble', or 'Funny-fist', or 'Mistress Finger-post'.

However on this evening he seemed mild and friendly enough, slipping out to join me on a kind of landing-shelf at the top of the steep little stair below my closet.

'A lady came driving through the village this afternoon in a chaise and pair,' he whispered. 'And she asked if you lived here.'

'Oh, Hoby! And I not here!' For the first and only time I regretted my wanderings with Mr Bill and Mr Sam. 'Who in the world can she have been?'

'She left no name, she would not stop, she was with a fine gentleman, and he was wild to get on, or they'd never reach Bristol before dark –'

'Bristol? They were fair and far out of their way, then. But who can it have been?'

'Blest if *I* know,' said Hoby. 'All I can say is, she was fine as fivepence, with feathers in her hat and rings on her fingers. She said she'd have liked a glimpse of you and sorry it was not to be. She said, from the look of me, she could see that I was a trustable lad' – he chuckled at this, and so did I, thinking how wide of the mark the strange lady had been in her judgement, even farther than from the road to Bristol – 'so she handed me a keepsake to give you and here it is.'

He passed me a smallish object, long and thin, swathed in a wrapping of what felt like coarse silk, tied all around with many threads.

'What can it be? And who, *who* was she? Did she leave no name? What did she look like? Was she handsome?'

'Umm. . .' Hoby began, but I knew he was no hand at making a picture in words. And just at that moment, the passage door opened to the front parlour, letting out a shaft of lamplight.

'What be all that mumbling and shuffling?' bawled an angry voice.

'Mizzle!' hissed Hoby. He fled back to his own quarters and I scrambled off with haste to mine, as a heavy step started up the stair. I thrust the mysterious token, whatever it might be, into a cavity of the thatch where I was used to hide apples or cakes if ever I was given one.

Tom Wellcome stood breathing heavily at the top of the stairs for a moment, letting off sour fumes of cider, then plumped back down, but left the parlour door open so that I dared not stir.

Naturally, after this I lay wide awake on my pallet for at least an hour, tormented by curiosity as to the identity of the strange lady. Could she be the wife of Colonel Brandon who paid for my upkeep? Was the strange gentleman Colonel Brandon himself? But if so would he not have stopped and asked to speak to Hannah Wellcome? Often I had wondered why he never came to see me; other guardians and protectors did, once in a great while, visit Byblow Bottom, but he, never; nor did he ever write or send a gift. Only the money arrived regularly from some bank in Dorsetshire with a regular exhortation to me to be a good girl and mind my books. So this small object, whatever it might be – it was the size and shape, perhaps, of a comb or a pair of scissors – would be the very first gift I had received in the whole of my existence. Palpitating with excitement I fingered and felt it, over and over, but could not solve the problem of the many threads that bound it round. So my curiosity must wait, unassuaged, until first light.

Long before cockcrow I was awake, gnawing and nibbling at the threads with my sharp child's teeth, until at last they gave way and the white silken wrappings unfolded to reveal an object which I had seen pictured in the *Gentleman's Magazine* at Dr Moultrie's, but never in actuality, for it was not the kind of article made use of by the women of Ashett and Othery. It was a fan made from delicate strips of ivory, rubbed fine as threads and jointed together, I knew not by what means. For some time its beauties and intricacies eluded me, since I was unable to solve the mystery of the opening clip.

Later, after breakfast, I was able to catch hold of Hob, behind the chicken shed, and ask for his help.

'Here, Goosey! It works like this,' he said, easily pushing back the catch with his thumb and flipping the fan expertly open. He then wafted it to and fro, giving me such languishing looks over the top, raising and lowering his brows, eyeing me sideways under his thick, sandy lashes, that I was soon reduced to helpless laughter.

'Oh, Hoby, you are so funny! Where did you ever learn to do that?'

'Never you mind, young lady.' Deftly, he snapped the fan shut and restored it to me. 'That is how the gay ladies of Bristol go on, and it is no business of yours, not for another ten years.'

Hoby's father occasionally toured the western counties in the course of his duties, and would then carry away his son for a few days' pleasuring.

'But I say,' he added, 'you owe me a good turn, little one, for if Biddy Wellcome had been in the house you'd never have laid a finger on that fan. You had best keep it well hid.'

Since I dared not conceal the fan anywhere indoors, I stowed it in the hollow of an oak that grew in a little coppice where we used to gather firewood. Here – if nobody else was by – I would luxuriously fan myself, raising my brows, lowering my lashes and glancing sideways out of the corners of my eyes in faithful imitation of Hoby's performance.

I did not show my treasure to Mr Bill or Mr Sam. Young as I was, instinct told me that such a toy as a fan would be of no interest to either man. They were absorbed by matters of the spirit, or of the wilderness, cataracts and tempests, rocks and rainbows; a fan, a trivial feminine trifle, would be to them an object of indifference, if not scorn.—Thus early, I taught myself to divide life into compartments, turning a different countenance to each person with whom I came into contact.

The next event worthy of record came at the season of Michaelmas when I had achieved, I suppose, my seventh or eighth year. Mr Bill and Mr Sam, deeply mourned by me, had quitted our neighbourhood and sailed to foreign lands; Germany, I believe. In my childish heart their absence was a continual ache; at each street corner, if I went into Ashett, I looked for Mr Sam's floating black locks and flashing eyes, Mr Bill's Roman nose and lofty height; I could not truly believe that they would never come back, and I made endless forlorn plans for the celebration of their return, tales that I would relate to them, secret wonderful places I would show them; I do not know how many years it took me to understand that none of these plans would come to fruition.

Meanwhile the two babes, Thérèse and Polly, had grown into small, fair, curly-headed children, wholly unalike in their natures, but resembling each other in one respect, in that both were unusually late in learning to talk. Biddy Wellcome, as she slopped about her careless housework, never troubled to address them except to bawl out a command or prohibition; that, I suppose, may have been one reason for their lack of linguistic facility. And Polly, like her mother, was naturally stupid, slow at learning anything, even when it was to her advantage to do so. Thérèse (whose awkward foreign name had long since, by everybody in Byblow Bottom, been abbreviated to Triz) was, conversely, very far from stupid, but she remained delicate and somewhat listless; would sooner forgo some treat than be obliged to take trouble for it. So she did not bestir herself to speak, seeing no advantage to be gained thereby. When I was with them, I defended and protected Triz a great deal of the time from the overbearing greed and selfishness of Polly, who could be quick indeed to grab any good thing for herself once she had become aware of it. And as a result of this, little Triz had become, in her quiet way, very attached to me.

She had a word for me: 'Alize,' she would murmur, smiling trustfully as I approached. 'Alize.'

As I say, it was the festival of Michaelmas. Dr Moultrie had gone off, grumbling very much, to officiate at the funeral of an Over Othery parishioner who had been so inconsiderate as to die just then. So I had a holiday. Down at Ashett, a hiring fair, a three-day annual event, was in full swing. Shepherds, farmhands and dairymaids would come there from all over the country to offer themselves for employment, in hopes of bettering their condition. Also, I knew, there would be jugglers and peepshows, music and dancing, gypsy fortune-tellers, toys and fairings for sale. But I had no heart for Ashett; the streets where Mr Bill and Mr Sam were no longer to be expected made me feel too sad; and in any case I had no money to spend.

All the boys from Byblow Bottom, whether bastard or born in wedlock, planned to go junketing; they had saved money, mostly ill-gotten from poaching, and looked forward to a day of pleasure.

'You can come along of us, little 'un, if you like,' said Hoby to me good-naturedly. 'I'll give ye six pence to spend.'

His mates growled very much at this offer. 'Wha'd'we want with *her?* She'd be nought but a trouble.'

Regardless both of them and of Hoby, I shook my head, though I had a lump in my throat big as a Pershore plum.

'No. I don't want to come.'

'Not want to see the fair? But Hannah and Tom are going down to buy tools and calico. *Everybody's* going.'

'I don't want to.'

'Ah, she's cracked. Bodged in the upper storey,' said Jonathan disgustedly. 'Besides being faddle-fisted. Who wants her? Come on, leave her.'

Hoby still tried to persuade me. 'You'll like it, Liza. Indeed, you will.'

But I shook and shook my head, more obstinate as he became more pressing, and at last simply ran away from the boys and hid myself in Farmer Dunleigh's haymow until they were well out of sight. In truth I had some regret at missing the fair, but knew full well that, although Hoby meant kindly *now,* after they had drunk a fair quantity of cider, as they were bound to do, the boys would grow wild and silly and their company would be worse than none.

I wandered along the deserted village street. Tom and Hannah had left already, in hopes of picking up early bargains. Biddy also was gone; along with them, I supposed; at all events her door was locked; I felt faintly surprised that she had not left me in charge of Polly and Triz. Given this freedom, I took myself off in the direction of Growly Point, past the horsepond and the Squire's orchards of gnarled, wind-twisted apple trees.

Growly Point was one of my favourite spots. The Squire's house was perched on top of the headland, along with a chapel and a stable block; behind it huddled a stand of wind-slanted beeches, and before it the gardens rolled down the hillside in steps and ledges, with a small brook meandering among them, which lower down formed the boundary alongside the public footpath. This was a stone track that led through a wishing-gate and on, past meadow and plough-land, to a dip in a low cliff.

Passing through the lych-gate I made my usual wish 'that Mr Bill and Mr Sam come back', then hurried on, glancing up to the left where some of the gardens were in view filled with great drifts of late daisies and roses, and pink-and-white tall-stemmed flowers, their name unknown to me; but most of the garden was screened by high evergreen hedges. Until I reached the cliff top and looked back, the house itself was not visible. Then it seemed huge and menacing, with two great twisted brick chimneys like wolves' ears, and all its windows glaring at the sea.

On the footway I was not trespassing, I knew, yet the spread of those wide, watchful windows gave me, as always, a prickle on my shoulder blades. I sped round a corner of the path. Here it led steeply, through a cleft in the cliff, down to the shore. But I turned westwards and made my way farther along the cliff top until I reached a kind of den, or nest, where I had been used to come after the departure of Mr Sam and Mr Bill. In this sheltered nook, among thistles and dried grass, and sloe and bramble-bushes, I could with luck spend hours peacefully doing nothing but watch the comings and goings of the tide.

And the tide here was worthy of attention. A track led along the shore from Ashett, but natives of the place took it only with discretion and a number of incautious strangers were drowned every season, despite being warned. For the shore here, beyond the point, was treacherous, formed not of sand, but from curious strips of flat striated rock running in mazy patterns, many of them so regular that they appeared to be the work of man, others so irregular that they seemed like the distracted jottings of some giant pencil. Mr Sam had loved to study them from the cliff top and try to describe them in his notebook. Among these rock ledges it was all too easy to be caught by the incoming tide, for it rushed into the bay very fast, and the channels between the strips of rock varied greatly in depth and the water gushed through them in wayward spurts and torrents.

Down below the spot where I sat, the rock strips ran in huge concentric curves like the markings on a giant oyster. Blue crescents of water showed where the tide was turning; gulls and oyster-catchers whirled and swooped and cried and paddled, feasting on the mussels and whelks and barnacles before they should be covered by the incoming water.

. . . I sat and longed for the company of Mr Bill and Mr Sam. I remembered those words – 'long and lank and brown, as is the ribbed sea-sand'. Perhaps Mr Bill had been looking at this very beach when they came into his mind; the curved formations could easily be the ribs of some great beast. Over the next headland a great pale lopsided hunter's moon sailed upwards, and I remembered how dearly Mr Sam loved the moon. 'She is the only friend,' he said, 'who can accompany you without walking.'

When I am grown, I vowed, I will go in search of those two men. When I am a woman and have money of my own, I will travel, I will find them. And I made great plans for earning money; I would write plays and tales and verses, as the two men did; I would have my tales published and make a fine name for myself. And besides that, I would be very beautiful, so that people would love me and never notice my hands.

So I sat and dreamed. And the afternoon floated by like a wisp of cloud, like the soaring moon. As for the boys and the fair, I never gave them another thought, although before I had felt no little pain at being obliged to refuse Hoby's offer and hurt his feelings. Sometimes he came here to Growly Head with me, and when we were alone together he seemed like a different person. Yet he would soon forget his offer and my refusal, I knew, and simply dismiss me from his mind as a queer little body, full of wayward fancies.

'Child! How still you sit!' said a voice above me. 'I have been watching you these two hours and you have never shifted a single inch, I do believe, during the whole of that time!'

I gave a violent start of surprise, almost, in my confusion, tipping myself over the edge of the cliff.

'Oh, ma'am! How you startled me!'

'Hola!' she said, laughing. 'Don't fall down on to the rocks! Now I am sorry that I took you unawares. That jump you gave when I spoke made up for the whole two hours' inactivity.'

She must herself have been sitting equally motionless. For now I saw her plainly – a lady seated quite still in a hammock of grass, up above me and on the opposite side, as it were, of my little gully. The dress and shawl that she had on were thinly striped in straw-colour and grey, and she carried a green lacy parasol; her whole costume might have been designed, and perhaps was, to melt into her background and render her almost invisible. Her face was thin and brown, very tanned; her hair, plainly dressed in bands, was fair, almost grey. She seemed faintly familiar; I thought I must have seen her in the village, but not for some time. Around her neck, on a velvet ribbon, she carried a little pair of field-glasses.

Her eyes were very strange.

'Don't hurry off, my child,' she said, as I began to scramble to my feet. 'You have as much right here as I . . . perhaps more. Are you from Ashett?'

'No, ma'am. From B-Byblow – from Nether Othery.'

'I believe I may have seen you there. Do you – are you an orphan?'

'Yes, ma'am. I live with Mrs Wellcome.'

A light came into her eyes at that. She made a move as if she would have questioned me; but then changed her mind.

Inquisitively, as a child will, I studied her eyes.

They were a beautiful dark grey but one of them, the left, was cast or twisted sideways, so that while the right one met my own gaze, the left stared away over my shoulder. This gave a queer effect; as if the whole of her mind was never, at any one time, fully upon oneself or upon what she was saying.

'I have been watching the birds,' she said, smiling, touching the field-glasses. 'Like you, I take great pleasure in sitting and observing what is to be seen. But in future I shall have less leisure for doing so.'

'I – I am sorry for that, ma'am,' I said politely. 'If so be as you enjoy it.'

'Oh no. Oh no, it has been an enforced holiday. Tomorrow begins a new era.'

I liked listening to her. Her language, her low musical voice reminded me of my two lost friends. But all the time, at my back, I felt the great house with its pricked ears, its staring eyes. As she rose to her feet I scuttled hurriedly up the slope. She sighed.

'Goodbye, my child.'

'Good evening, ma'am.' I curtseyed and fairly ran off up the hill towards the wishing-gate, wondering where the lady came from.

Back at home chaos and consternation reigned. Hannah and Tom were returned from the fair. (I noticed a stout bundle of calico, and so knew what the next two years' dresses would be made of; no doubt Tom's tools were in the shed.) The boys, all three, lurked in the back kitchen. Some neighbours were in the parlour. All attention was trained on Biddy, who sat enthroned by the hearth. She was in tempests, in storms, in floods of tears.

'*My little Polly!* Oh how, oh how could such a calamity have happened? Oh, oh, I'll never be happy again.'

Others besides villagers formed her audience, I noticed: Mr Willsworthy from the Hall – why was he here? Also Dr Moultrie, back from conducting his funeral at Over.

'I was gathering mussels on the shore – to make a mussel pie –'

Why in the world would Biddy Wellcome do that? I wondered. She never gathers mussels. She never ever makes a mussel pie. The only thing Biddy ever does in the kitchen is make herself a cup of tea, and tell the foster-children to gobble down their taties and be off to bed.

'I was gathering mussels – I was carrying little Tirrizz, bless her heart, so she wouldn't cut her little tender feet on the sharp mussel shells –'

And when did you last carry little Tirrizz? I wondered. And where had all this happened?

The mussel beds were all on the beaches east of Ashett.

'Did you inform the coastguards?' asked Willsworthy in his hoarse rasping voice.

She whirled on him.

'In course I told them! Or – leastways – I sent a message by Frank and Charley Tedburn. Oh, my poor heart! Oh, my little Polly. Shall I ever, ever see her more?'

She lapsed into hysterical sobbing.

'In the midst of life, God moves in a mysterious way,' said Dr Moultrie.

I stole into the back room. Nobody was paying any heed to me. All eyes were on Biddy. In the kitchen I found the boys, Hoby, Will and Jon, lugubriously contemplating a single rush basket in which slept a child.

With my heart crashing painfully against my ribs, I tiptoed across the floor and inspected the occupant. There slept Polly Wellcome, in heavy, red-cheeked, open-mouthed slumber which suggested to me that she had been given a few drops of laudanum in her Daffy's Elixir (a mixture to which Biddy sometimes had recourse if she wished to go out of an evening).

'Wh-where's T-Triz?'

My teeth chattered so much that I could hardly utter.

'That *be* Triz,' said Will. He was a large, fat, stupid lad, who, although nearly twelve, had not yet succeeded in learning his letters. 'Polly's drownded,' he added.

I met the eye of Hoby.

He explained: 'Biddy, you see, keeps saying that it was Polly who drownded. And you better not give her the lie; old Willsworthy would be down on you like a chopper.'

'But - but –'

'Well, Biddy ought to know her own child, didn't she? If she says it was her own little 'un got drownded?'

That was Jonathan, whose mind moved sensibly enough, but he was, I knew, amazingly short-sighted, could hardly see more than a yard away from his nose, always came last in the games when the boys shot arrows or played at marbles. He had never looked closely at either child, I was sure of that.

'Hoby – what *happened?* What does Biddy say?'

'Why,' said Hoby, scratching his head and frowning, 'Biddy says she was out gathering mussels with the pair of kinchins, down on Growly Point rocks – and that the tide came in extra fast, and Polly was swept away down one of the wynds.'

That was what the local people called the rock channels.

'But,' went on Hoby slowly and thoughtfully, 'I don't say but what that tale has me in a puzzle.'

'Why, Hoby?'

'Well, this is why: Biddy was at the fair until three; I saw her then, with my own eyes, colloguing with an old rapscallion wearing gold rings in's ears. So how the pize would she have had time to get down to the shore? The tide would have been flooding afore that; the mussel beds would have been covered over. And she warn't there earlier, for after dinner the lads and I saw her start off to Ashett with both the kinchins; didn't we, Will, Jon-o?'

'Ay, that's so,' they said.

'But –'

Then I began to think.

'What is Willsworthy doing here?'

'Why,' Hoby explained, 'this very morning, it seems, a message came down from Kinn Hall that Lady Hariot is better now, come home from Madery, cured of her sickness, back on her pins, and wants little Triz took up to the Hall, right away tomorrow, so as to be with her rightful ma.'

'Oh, my heart alive . . .'

'So Triz is to be sent off tomorrow.'

'Biddy is going to send *Polly* – being as how she's lost Triz –'

None the less, something about the story seemed to me to be wholly wrong. And queer. Why, suddenly, would Biddy take Triz down to the shore and lose her – just when this summons had come? Why should she send off her own child to the Hall? Biddy was not a devoted mother, certainly, but she did show a kind of animal affection at times, when she would suddenly pluck Polly from the ground and give her a few smacking kisses. Towards Triz she had never displayed the slightest feeling. So – what was behind this? Did she want to part with her own child? And would nobody notice that an exchange had been made? Nobody guess?

'Where does she say she was gathering mussels?'

'On Growly Rocks.'

'She never was there,' I said with confidence. 'Never. I sat up on the cliff head the livelong afternoon, and there was not a soul on the rocks all that time. Not a single soul. And there was – there was another lady on the cliff, who would say the same.'

'You going to go in that room and give Biddy the lie?' said Hoby with his wicked sidelong grin, eyes bright under sandy lashes.

'What do *you* think she did with Triz, Hoby?'

He shrugged. 'Sold her to the gypsies? Triz was like a liddle elf-maid, anyway. Maybe they'd want her.'

'Oh, no!' But after a moment I said, 'Do you really think Biddy might have done so?'

Hoby cast up his eyes and shrugged again.

I said, with a stiff tongue and a dry mouth, 'I shall go over to Ashett. I shall find those gypsies. If they knew – if they knew the whole story –'

'You are going to the *gypsies*?' Jonathan looked at me in stupefaction. 'Do you want your tripes cut out, girl? Firstly – how will you find them? And I wouldn't care to be in your shoes when Biddy and Hannah come to hear –'

'I don't care.'

I thought of little Triz, alone and terrified among the gypsies.

In fact, I knew nothing about gypsies, whether they were cruel or kind. Among the natives of Othery they had a wild reputation. Some of it might be deserved, some not. It was said they stole or bought children. Why? Nobody knew. They had plenty of their own.

'Well, I'm going,' I said, more stoutly than I felt.

Just then there came wails from the back door. It was poor Charlotte Gaveston, the lack-wit, and Biddy's two foster-boys, Charley and Frank, crying for their supper. Under cover of the commotion, I slipped away on the path to Ashett. After a moment or two I heard footsteps.

'I'm a-coming with you,' Hoby said. 'I reckon you are wholly daft, crack-brained, dicked in the nob; and there will surely be Old Hokey to pay if you do find Triz; but you do stand by your friends and I like that in you, liddle 'un. And you may need a bit of help.'

I was immensely glad of his company. Night was beginning to thicken as we crossed the ridge and dropped down into Ashett; but the fair was still going full tilt, with torchlights, and flares, and music and dancing, pipes and tabors and drunken yells.

'Where were the gypsies?' I asked Hoby.

'When I left, they were all grouped together on the Folworthy Road, starting to pack up their gear.'

But when we had made our way with some difficulty across the fairground, between half-dismantled stalls and groups of drunken revellers, and reached that area, I was dismayed to find it empty and dark; the gypsies had already moved on.

'Ay, ay, they went up Folworthy way,' a man said when we asked him. 'Likely they'll make their camp up on Folworthy Moor. They Romany travellers never wants to bide too long near a town.'

I was nearly crying with disappointment, and Hoby made a strong case for turning back.

'Liddle 'un, Liza-loo, see, we've come far enough; 'tis fair and late, and we'm never going to catch 'em now.'

'Oh, Hoby! Let's go another mile or two. Maybe the gypsies will camp just outside of town. Or, you go back, if you are tired, and I'll go on . . .'

But he would not let me go on alone, and so we walked two, three miles westward from Ashett, across Hoe Bay and up the steep hill on to Umberleigh Down. My feet ached, and the night was beginning to be very cold; a huge pale sparkling moon soared overhead – the same moon that had looked on me kindly so much earlier in the day.

Mr Sam would like that moon, I thought. Mr Sam would give his endorsement to my quest.

Hoby was very patient. He walked quietly beside me. He did not complain.

And at last we found the gypsies.

They had made themselves an untidy camp, with their wagons in a circle and a few shabby tents. A fire burned in the centre. Pale-coloured lurcher dogs glided about, and nimble tabby cats.

A noble smell of cooking came from the pot on the fire. Rabbit stew.

'What do *you* want, *gadscho* children?' asked a dark-haired woman, seeing us hesitate at the edge of the circle of firelight. She gave us a sour, dismissing glance.

I thought of Mr Sam; thought how he would comport himself at such a moment. 'If you please, ma'am, I wish to see the – the main person. The head person here.'

She looked at me frowningly. And, I suppose, I extended my hands in appeal.

From that moment, all changed. The woman seemed immeasurably different. She nodded. She led us to a wagon that was somewhat larger than the rest. Here, on the steps, sat a man not old but thin and weathered, sharp-featured with a hooked nose and very bright eyes, gold rings in his ears. A shock of grey hair.

''Tis the same cove as I saw Biddy a-colloguing with,' Hob whispered in my ear.

'What is it, then, *gadscho* children?'

'Sir,' I said – I thought it best to be very respectful, as if he were a magistrate or a parson – 'is there – did a woman leave a child with you today? A very pale-haired little child – like an elf-child?'

'What is her name?' he said, looking at me very intently.

'Her name is Thérèse.'

Upon impulse then, I called aloud – in a high shrill voice that I hardly ever made use of, except very occasionally to call home the cattle or pigs – most people had never heard it.

Triz had, though; sometimes I would do it to make her laugh.

'*Triz?* Ohee, Triz? Are you here? Can you hear me?'

In a moment she came bundling out of another wagon, flung herself tumbling down the steps, hurled herself across the firelit circle and into my arms.

'*Alize! Alize!*'

'There was a mistake made,' I told the earringed man. 'She was handed over to you by mistake. You can see that, can't you?'

'And the money that passed?' he demanded, rather grimly. 'Can you pay it back?'

I spread out my hands. 'I don't know anything about money. We have no money.'

Hoby helpfully turned his ragged pockets inside out.

But the earringed man, like the dark-haired woman, was staring at my hands.

He murmured something to her rapidly, in a foreign tongue. And they both made a gesture, as if to ward off the Evil Eye.

'And you can sing?' he said to me.

'*Sing*? I don't know. Why?'

'Sing after me.'

He sang a queer spread of notes; almost a tune. It began very low, and ended very high. 'Sing that now,' he said. So I sang it.

'Again.' I sang it again.

'Very well,' he said. 'We forget about the money. You are a –' And again that foreign word.

He took hold of my hands (Triz was terribly unwilling to let go of the one she clung to) – and held them for a moment between his own, which were rough, greasy, gnarled like the bark of trees, but surprisingly warm and kindly.

'Go in peace then, *gadscho* children. You have a long walk home.'

It was indeed a long walk. My feet ached more and more. The moon became ginger-coloured and trailed down the sky. We took turns carrying Triz, who weighed amazingly heavy, considering her fairylike stature.

And when we did get home, what a rumpus!

Hoby had been perfectly right in his forebodings.

Biddy had remained in Hannah's house, and a kind of wake was being conducted. They had been drowning their grief and mourning the dead in tankards of green cider with smuggled eau-de-vie added; a most perilous mix of liquors. Nobody was at all grateful to have Triz returned; quite the contrary. Biddy reviled me as a wicked little viper, always ready to do somebody an ill turn.

'Making out as how that's Triz! *That's* not Triz! How do we know that's not some gypsy's brat? Bringing her here! The idea! What next, I'd like to know?'

However this argument was wholly undermined when Polly woke up, roused from her drugged slumber by all the shouting, and mumbled out, 'Tiz! Tiz!' and with, for her, a quite unusual demonstration of enthusiasm, went to hug her foster-sister.

But I noticed Triz flinch away when Biddy approached her, and wondered whether her infant mind had absorbed the fact that her foster-mother had planned to dispose of her as one might part with a puppy or a kitten, turning her over to an alien group without the slightest compunction.

In the end everybody was too tired and too drunk, I daresay, to pursue the argument further that evening. Dr Moultrie and Mr Willsworthy, figures of authority, had left, and I did not think it was the time to fire my main salvo, the fact that I had been on the cliff all afternoon and knew that Biddy never went anywhere near the shore. (Or that the lady with the odd eyes would be able to corroborate my story; if I could ever find out who she was.) In the meantime I said, 'Triz can sleep with me; if you don't want her,' and carried her off to my cubbyhole, where, twined together – for there was scarcely room for one, let alone two – we passed the rest of the night, she in a sleep of utter exhaustion with her threadlike arms tight around my neck, while I lay awake for hours in a fever of worry.

Being but a child, and only too well aware of the great and incalculable powers of adults, I feared that next day might bring yet worse troubles; that Biddy might find some means of repudiating Triz and sending her back to the gypsies; that somehow her tale would be preferred over mine; that evil and injustice would triumph, as I had seen them triumph many times before.

Next day, however, matters turned out very differently from my expectations. (As they almost invariably do; but I am never prepared for this.)

For a start, we all overslept, worn out with exertion, dispute, green cider and brandy.

I was roused from my slumber by a thunderous rap on the door, and shouts.

'Open up there! Where's Mrs Wellcome? Where's t'other Mrs Wellcome? Show a leg, show a leg! Here's Squire's lady a-waiting for her babby!'

Stupefied with late, heavy sleep, I stumbled downstairs and opened the door. Behind me I could hear the grunts of Hannah and Tom as they staggered about, trying to make themselves presentable.

Outside the door was a pony-chaise waiting. A groom stood at the horses' heads, and another – I knew him, it was Jeff Diswoody, head groom at the Hall – was the one who had been banging and shouting.

'Damme, what's to do? I'd have reckoned ye'd all be up at cock-crow making the little maid ready – here's my lady come her own self – iss! – to welcome home her nestling – who you'd think 'ud be a-waiting wreathed in roses like a May queen – what do we find? Not a soul astir!'

I looked past him to the chaise – and there was yesterday's lady of the cliff! Today she was dressed fine, in yellow silk and gloves, and a silken sunshade, but I knew her at once by her swivel eye – and also by the smile she gave me. She was Lady Hariot! Of course, I should have guessed it. Who else could she be?

Here was my chance and I took it like lightning.

'Only a moment, my lady!' I gulped, hasted back up the stairs to where Triz, like a scrawny fledgling, was blinking and rubbing her eyes in my tumbled nest.

'Come quick, Triz, here's your lady mother waiting for you, all in silk-satin, and two grand white horses ready to pull ye home!'

I lifted and carried her down the stairs. Poor little thing, she was still half-asleep, and, I daresay, mazed from all her adventures of the previous day; she burst out a-crying and buried her head in my shoulder, clinging to me frenziedly as Jeff Diswoody tried to take her.

'Alize! Alize!' she cried.

'Now, now, what's all this to-do, don't want to go to your own mam?'

Of course she didn't.

'Poor little one,' said Lady Hariot seeing at once how matters lay. 'No wonder that she does not like to leave her friends. But I have a solution: why do not you – what is your name, my child?'

'Liza, so please you, ma'am.'

'You, Liza, come up with Thérèse now to the Hall – then it will not seem so strange to her. For I can see she is very attached to you. And then, after she is settled in, one of the grooms shall drive you back.'

'Law bless you, my lady, I can walk back from the Hall easy as fall off a brick,' I said, enchanted at this solution to my problem, and I hopped up into the chaise, still clasping Triz in my arms. 'I am sorry, ma'am, that you should see her all of a muss, like this, but – but Biddy and Hannah were both late back from the fair last night –'

'It does not signify, not in the least,' said Lady Hariot absently. 'I have clothes waiting for her.' With one eye she was thirstily, eagerly studying her daughter, while the other one strayed to the cottage where Hannah, who must have made one of the speediest toilets of her existence, was curtseying, bobbing and beaming, now arrayed in a clean cap, tucker and apron.

'Oh, ma'am! Oh, my lady! Oh, 'tis such a joy to see ye well and back home and bobbish again!'

'Thank you, Mrs Wellcome. And thank you for taking care of my daughter. I am not standing on ceremony, as you say. Good-day!' she called, as Jeff cracked his whip and the ponies broke into a trot. Hannah's face was a study as we bowled away down the village street. I rather dreaded to think what my reception would be when I got home, but to have Triz safely settled, *and* this chance of seeing the Hall, would amply compensate, I felt, for whatever trouble lay ahead.

Over details of what befell after our arrival at the Hall, memory begins to fail me; I can recall that Squire Vexford was there, gruff and crusty: 'I have brought our daughter home, Godric, as you see,' says Lady Hariot. 'Is she not exactly like the portrait of your aunt Tabitha at the head of the stair?' And he: 'Humph! It would be a deal better if she resembled my uncle Thomas.' At which Lady Hariot sighed and bade me follow her to the nurseries, a set of rooms which looked down to the bay and had been equipped with every plaything that the heart of a child could desire. A smiling nurse-girl waited with a bundle of clothes on her arm.

'There!' said Lady Hariot, lovingly studying Triz who stared all about her in silent wonder. 'There, my lambie, now you are at home and all this will be yours, all your own!'

And she showed her daughter a toy – I forget what it was, a wooden horse, perhaps. Never having possessed such an article, Triz was puzzled as to what to do with it, and I felt it not my part to show her, so Lady Hariot went down on her knees and demonstrated its use. Triz watched in silence, her eyes very wide and solemn.

'I will leave you now, my lady,' I said. 'For sure, Triz will soon be happy in these fine rooms.'

But again, when I made to go, Triz wept and wept and clung to me and would not be comforted.

'Massy me, dearie!' cried the nursery maid. 'Why you be in your own room now, with all your things about you. Never mind the lass, she's from times gone by.'

But Triz evidently did not feel so.

'Alize, Alize!' she wept, stretching out her arms to me.

I stood silent, thinking of the strange contrast between most of the orphans in Byblow Bottom, who were never likely in their whole lives to inhabit such rooms, such furnishings, as these; and poor little Triz, who wanted none of it. I thought of my fan, my treasure, hidden away in the hollow oak; Lady Hariot probably possessed a dozen such; and so would Triz in the course of time.

I did not like to go and leave her crying so bitterly.

'Listen, my darling,' said Lady Hariot, soothing and fondling the little thing. 'Your Liza, your Alize, do you call her? She shall come back tomorrow – how about that? And shall take you for a walk in the gardens, and you shall show her all your new toys. Will that content you?'

My heart leapt up as Triz thought about that for a while and then nodded, seriously, twice, knuckling the tears from her eyes.

'She shall come in the morning – after you have had your breakfast.—Can you do that, child?' Lady Hariot asked me.

'If Dr Moultrie will give me leave – I study my lessons with him, you see, ma'am.'

'Do you indeed? Well, I will see that he gives you leave.'

She nodded to me to slip away now, and I did so, for Triz had at last begun attentively studying the toy she held in her hands.

I ran back to the village, down the gravelled driveway, peering most eagerly all along the vistas of terraced garden, none of which were visible from road or footpath. I would have liked to loiter and gaze, but knew that this would not do. Never mind; I could explore the gardens tomorrow with Triz; and with luck the visit might be repeated. My feelings on the way home were a mix of triumph and deep apprehension. This last was well justified, for when I reached Hannah's house she received me with a very black and stormy mien.

'So, Miss: what have you been telling her? What did you tell Lady Hariot?'

'Tell her? I didn't tell her *anything.*'

'A likely story! When you told those boys all about sitting on the cliff top and never seeing Biddy!'

Bother the boys, I thought. Why could they not have held their tongues? Since Triz was now safe at the Hall, I could see no gain in teazeling out the full story of what Biddy had done, or planned to do, or why she had done it. To me it seemed fairly plain that, taken by surprise when Lady Hariot suddenly returned and sent for her child, Biddy had been tempted to plant her own daughter in lifelong security, and meanwhile quickly get rid of the other child so that nobody should have a chance to query or make comparisons.

But by now the gypsies would be well away; there was no proof of what Biddy had done; people in the village might be puzzled by the fact that an apparently drowned child had turned up alive and well; still, such things did happen.

'Well, I *did* sit on the cliff top yesterday,' I said. 'And I didn't see Biddy. But I never told Lady Hariot that. Why should I? Lady Hariot was there, sitting on the cliff top, her own self, all yesterday afternoon. I saw her there. I didn't know then who she was, but she spoke to me.'

Hannah stared at me, for once completely dumbstruck. Presently she went away to her daughter's house, and what passed between them I never heard. But next day we suddenly discovered that Biddy was gone; gone silently and without a word to anybody.

At first the care of the deserted Charlotte, Charley and Frank devolved on Hannah, but she very soon farmed them out to neighbours.

'Where do you suppose Biddy has gone?' I asked Hoby, when it became plain that she was not coming back.

He replied enigmatically, 'To ask sailors how they do for soap.'

'And where would she do that?'

'At Exeter or Plymouth, maybe. Or – perhaps – she has gone to try her luck in London town.'

'Are there sailors in London town too?'

'Fine gentlemen, if not sailors.'

'Why would *they* want soap?'

He burst out laughing. 'Oh, Liza, you are green! You don't know anything! She has gone to be a whore, of course.'

'Oh well, why didn't you say so?' I was affronted. 'I know all about whores.'

'Well, you shouldn't.—What do you know about them?'

'Fanny Huskisson told me.' (She was a girl who had lodged for seven years with Mrs Pollard at the Green Man Inn. She had left last year.) 'She told me they lie with men for money.' Fanny, a jolly girl, had been in some sort my friend.

'They don't just lie with men. They fornicate.'

'I know! And in spite of that they don't bear children, because they swallow ergot of rye. *I* think it is a paltry way to make a living – to have to be with men all the time.'

I had a very poor opinion of men – except for Mr Sam and Mr Bill.

'I could tell you a great deal more than that,' said Hob.

'Well I don't wish to hear it.'

As a matter of fact I could have told *him* a great deal more. But I did not want to do that either.

Chapter 2

HITHERTO I HAVE RECORDED IN DETAIL SOME EVENTS OF MY early childhood, for they may have a bearing on what came to pass later; but I do not intend to proceed at such a leisurely pace over the following period of my life; that would be to tax the reader's patience too highly.

Moreover I suffer sometimes from uncertainty. Did such an event really occur, I wonder, or did I imagine it? I know that I do, from time to time, envision whole episodes as if they were stories that befell me. And I reserve the right, when I so choose, to keep my own counsel over certain occurrences.

Triz, or Thérèse, as she was now called, soon settled contentedly enough with her own family up at Kinn Hall. Heaven knows she had not been particularly well used or had much affection bestowed on her while she was in residence with Biddy Wellcome; there were few reasons why she should object to the change. And now, among these new friends who continually talked and sang to her, asked her questions, played games with her, she rapidly learned to talk. But she continued very attached to me and would demand my company every few days. So by degrees I came to spend the greater part of my time up at the Hall, Whether, growing older, Triz had any recollection of that strange episode at the Michaelmas Fair – whether she remembered being handed over to the gypsies – I do not know; she never alluded to it. Perhaps it was sunk deep down in the mists that obstruct our recollections of infancy and early childhood. But my arrival and intervention on that occasion, whether consciously recalled or not, I believe must have played its part in her great devotion to me.

Some mothers might have been jealous of such an attachment to a stranger in their newly restored child. But Lady Hariot was not of that kind. Her nature was just and considerate, and because of her protracted illness she had had time to think long and deeply about matters which are, by most people, accorded little attention. Anything that brought comfort or interest to her child, she welcomed; and so she welcomed me. I may say that she was like a mother to me – certainly a better mother than Biddy Wellcome had ever been to her own little Polly (who was now relegated to her grandmother's fitful and fluctuating care; if sober, Hannah treated the child kindly enough, but her sober periods were becoming more widely spaced. Very often, these days, she was to be found incapably drunk).

Lady Hariot, indeed, made the suggestion to me that I should come and live entirely at Kinn Hall. Nether Othery she thought to be a less than satisfactory haven for me. She even went so far as to write a letter to my guardian, Colonel Brandon, having obtained his address from Hannah in one of her lucid intervals, asking if he would have any objection to my removal to the Hall.

But after a long lapse of time a reply came back, not from Colonel Brandon himself, but from some lawyers in Dorchester, to the effect that Colonel Brandon had last year rejoined his regiment, the 33rd Foot, under the command of General Wellesley, and that he and Mrs Brandon also were now in Seringapatam, letters to and from which place must necessarily take many months. In his absence the lawyers were not empowered to permit such a change in my situation.

'Never mind it, please, dear ma'am,' I said to Lady Hariot. 'It is kind in you, but we go on very well as we are.'

In fact I was myself in two minds about such a scheme.

'*Let us, you and I, be best friends always,*' Fanny Huskisson had once said to me urgently, before she left Byblow Bottom. But I could not give my agreement to this. Apart from the fact that Fanny was a stupid, foul-mouthed girl (though cheerful and very good-natured), I did not feel able to commit myself to such a promise. And by the same impediment in my own nature I had been held back when Hoby invited me to go to the fair; a desire to keep apart, not to be at anybody's bidding, to move alone and freely, never to be bounded by the dealings of others. My fondness for Hoby did not blind me to the fact that he and his cronies had many ploys in which I did not at all wish to share. And though Fanny had always felt that she was my particular friend, I, for my part, felt that we had hardly anything in common.

So now it was the same with my life at Kinn Hall.

Firstly, I was at all times well aware that the Squire looked upon me with a sour and most unfavourable eye. Neither an affectionate father nor a loving husband, he never entered the nursery world and paid little heed to it; but the dullest intelligence could not but be aware that, beyond this indifference, he bore towards me an active dislike and, if he came across me in the grounds or garden, leading

Triz's pony or playing with her at bat and ball, would screw up his mouth in a bitter line and cast upon me a glance of evident repulsion. This dislike, I knew, was fostered by his man Willsworthy. If ever Triz and I fell into some minor misdoing, as children must at times, if there was a trampled flower-bed to be reported, or a broken rose bush, or a toy left forgotten in the rain to rust, be sure the tale would reach Mr Vexford as fast as Willsworthy could seek his ear. And I think Lady Hariot had her work cut out to defend my position.

But defend it she did.

Then also, though Lady Hariot was so kind towards me, so amazed at the quantity of learning that I had already contrived to acquire from Dr Moultrie, so desirous of assisting me to other attainments, to the end that, when little Triz began to have masters to teach her music and dancing and French and Italian, I must share all her lessons (and indeed that was a sovereign advantage to the poor little thing, for she was by nature a slow learner and many times found it easier to understand or to recall what she had been taught after I had gone over it with her) – yet, despite these benefits, I felt a constraint up at Kinn Hall which I was mortally glad to cast off when I ran home at evening-time, back to the squalor and freedom of Byblow Bottom. Pray do not mistake me. I perfectly understood what inestimable gifts I was daily receiving. Under the impartial, affectionate eye of Lady Hariot I was learning the way that high-born folk speak and move and comport themselves, and quite quickly, at will, I was able to discard the rustic airs of the village.

I soon came to realize that Lady Hariot's birth and blood were superior to those of the Squire.

'I married him, you see, because I had no other choice,' she told me calmly one day, when we were watching Jeff Diswoody instruct Triz in the art of managing her pony.

A moment before the Squire had ridden by, scattering gloom and despondency about him as was his usual habit.

I watched him out of earshot and then said: 'No choice, ma'am? How could that be, so kind and beautiful as you are?'

But, of course, I knew full well what she meant. How could I not?

'I was one of five sisters,' she explained. 'And my father, though an earl, was not a wealthy man. He could not give us large portions. And no man in his right mind is going to offer for a girl with a squint like mine. Why, in many countries – just across the Channel, even now, in poor peasant communities – a cast such as I have would be sufficient to get me burned as a witch.'

'Yes, I do understand, ma'am.' And I did. I remembered the gypsies.

'So, in fact, I was fortunate. The lot of an unmarried woman is bleak enough. To be a spinster aunt, a poor relation – that is bad, even without a physical handicap, causing one to be despised and sneered at. In consideration of my excellent connections, Mr Vexford was prepared to overlook my unsatisfactory appearance. But now, I fear, he reckons that he has made but a poor bargain.'

She sighed, watching the stocky, angry figure canter off down the driveway to join a meeting of otter-hounds at Folworthy. Such sports took him farther and farther afield.

'This house is nothing but a nest of cripples and misfits!' I had heard him shout furiously at his wife. 'Damme, a man might as well live shut up in the Dunster Asylum. All I can do is get out!'

It was true that Lady Hariot had a large-hearted proclivity for selecting to serve her those who also suffered from some disadvantage and thus might otherwise have fared badly. Her maid, Prue, walked with a severe limp; Mrs Lundy the housekeeper stammered when she spoke; my own odd hands, I felt sure, played no inconsiderable part in the Squire's dislike and Lady Hariot's favour. Even Jeff Diswoody was deaf, due to a fall in infancy.

I think she had noticed my hands on that very first afternoon.

'They are a most unusual feature, perhaps unique,' she said sighing, when Triz and I commenced lessons on the pianoforte and the music master, Mr Godfinch, made some nervous and startled comment. 'To have one hand so much larger than the other, *and* the sixth finger, I have never encountered anything so – so out of the common way. When playing the piano, I daresay it may be a decided advantage; but otherwise, my poor child, I imagine that it must have caused you some grief and abuse?'

'Oh, bless you, yes, ma'am, all the children in Othery call me names, such as Liz Lug-fingers, and they used to sing: 'Three six nine, the goose drank wine, six fingers on your hand, your mother came from mermaid-land.' But I pay them no heed; some of them are frightened of me and think I could put a spell on 'em, but the rest are friendly enough.'

With the hard knowledge of experience though, I was well aware that no man was likely to take me to wife; indeed, Hoby and the rest had often said so. Who in the world wants a girl with odd hands? Or children probably cursed with a similar blemish? Even if the girl were as beautiful as Venus? For which reason, when Dr Moultrie told me about the Roman gods and goddesses, Venus was never my prime favourite. I guessed that the Goddess of Love and Beauty would never look favourably on me. Rather, for my patron, I chose Athene, the Wise Lady, and asked for her help in any new enter-prise. And she had often given it.

However my extra-large right hand and surplus finger did, as Mr Godfinch had suggested, serve me well in playing the piano; stretching an octave was no problem at all, whereas the fairylike hands and fingers of little Triz were Mr Godfinch's despair, and her singing voice was but a faint thread of sound like the sigh of a kettle.—Here again, my voice proved a surprise to Lady Hariot and the music master.

'Five octaves! It is unparalleled!' he cried out in astonishment. 'The voice itself, I grant, is of no particular merit, though strong and clear and of good pitch – but what a range! We should make an opera singer of the child, Lady Hariot, she is wasted otherwise.'

But to this suggestion Lady Hariot was utterly opposed. Opera singers, she held, were little better than whores; no proper person would commit a decent girl to such a life. And I came, after all, of gentle stock; Colonel Brandon, my guardian, was a gentleman greatly esteemed by all who knew him, both in Dorset and in London. He had married a Miss Marianne Dashwood, a young lady of excellent family (though not wealthy) from Sussex; Colonel Brandon himself was a most upright character, owner of a comfortable property, Delaford, in Dorset . . . No, no, it was quite out of the question that I should become an opera singer. What my precise connection with the Colonel was, no clue had revealed; but simply the fact that there *was* such a connection must serve to guard me from any such disreputable future.

– Nevertheless Mr Godfinch trained my voice painstakingly and thoroughly; he was a zealous and practical little fellow who taught dancing also, in Exeter and Taunton; he had a great red birthmark, poor devil, right across one cheek; I reckon he rated my prospects of matrimony quite as low as I did myself, and concluded that he had best supply me with a practical means of earning a living.

Lady Hariot continued to worry about my place of abode.

'I have heard questionable tales of Dr Moultrie,' she said. 'He is a lazy old wretch, that is sure. I doubt if he can be a good influence on you, child – and he tipples disgracefully; only last Sunday, at the rail, I was scandalized by the smell of eau-de-vie. Can his teaching really be of any further benefit to you?' Now that you are acquiring manners and deportment here at the Hall, was her unspoken corollary.

But I made haste to reassure her. 'Truly, ma'am, he is very clever, and I learn a great deal from him of – of literature, and Latin, and ancient history, and much else besides. I do believe he could answer any question that I thought to put.'

And he would, I knew, be furiously angry at any suggestion that I might discontinue my visits to the parsonage; in fact when I first began going up to the Hall he had become very morose, threatening and choleric; much pacification and blandishment were required before he would accept that I was not to be wholly reft away from him and would not blacken his character to the Squire. His enmity was not to be thought of; indeed it was a terrifying prospect.

Lady Hariot sighed. 'Learning and superior character do not always go hand-in-hand, I know. And certainly learning is never to be despised; especially in such a remote neighbourhood as this, where we have to make the most of our advantages.'

I daresay she was thinking of the Squire, who fell asleep nightly over the first page of the newspaper and never progressed to the second.

So I was suffered to continue my lessons at the rectory, where, indeed, I learned far more than Lady Hariot reckoned; and which lessons were by no means unalloyed pleasure; but, as with

Mr Godfinch, I esteemed that my safest plan was to acquire all the knowledge that came my way, by whatever means, and trust that some part of it would, in the future, repay any evils or inconveniences encountered during its acquisition.

Thus my chequered life proceeded; the happiest times were when, up at Kinn Hall, Triz and I had leave to wander in the grounds or the gardens, or ramble down to the shore. (Though in the latter case we were subject to countless warnings and prohibitions; Lady Hariot understood vaguely that in the past some child from the village had been drowned by the incoming tide, and we were therefore never permitted to go down to the beach save when the tide was on the ebb.)

Triz, even by the time she reached the age of six, remained small and delicate in stature, with a gossamer fairness of hair and complexion; she ate like a bird and was sadly susceptible to colds and coughs. She must be watched at all times with the utmost vigilance lest she take a chill from damp slippers or stockings; so our excursions had to be confined to the warmest, mildest, most windless days. (Sometimes I used to sigh, recalling the immense walks I had undertaken with Mr Bill and Mr Sam, striding on for miles on miles, regardless of rain or wind.) But my outings with Triz had a charm all their own.

She loved me to tell her stories. At first I related all of those most clearly remembered from Dr Moultrie's little chap-books, of *Gold-Locks* and the tale *Jack the Giant-Killer,* and that of Mr Philip Quarll, the English Hermit. But I soon ran through these and, Triz still demanding more, I bethought me of the strange tale that Mr Sam and Mr Bill had put together between them (though Mr Sam did by far the greater part); so, recalling as best I could and half-chanting such of the verses as returned to me, I took her through the adventures of the mariner and his unlucky mess-mates who sailed to the Southern Polar Regions, and how the hero killed the great sea-bird and of the fearsome fate that befell him. This tale kept her spellbound, and she asked for it over and over again. Then, as the addict calls for his laudanum, she demanded more and yet more, so I was constrained to fall back upon history, real or invented, and tell her the sagas I had read of Saxons and Normans, of Hereward the Wake and Robin Hood, of Joan of Arc and the British queen who fought the Romans. But her favourite amongst all these were the stories of King Arthur and his Knights of the Round Table, which I had found in a book of Sir Thomas Malory among Dr Moultrie's volumes. (This was the book I had soiled with jam, after which episode Dr Moultrie had never permitted me to lay fingers upon it again. But still I had such a vivid recollection of the stories – for I loved them as much as Triz did – that I was able to pass them on to her with every detail still burnished in my mind.)

Over and over I told her of the arm rising from the lake to catch the falling sword, when the wounded king lies dying on the field of battle, and how the ladies arrive in the magic barge to rescue him, and how he promises Bedivere that one day he will return to rule once more.

This was the part that Triz found full of such haunting appeal. And so did I, for that matter.

'I wonder what Sir Bedivere did after the barge had rowed away?' she would sigh. But that I could not recall; if I had ever known. 'I wonder where he went? I wonder if he ever did see King Arthur again?'

Not very far eastwards of Nether Othery, as the crow flies, lay the great hill of Glastonbury, under which King Arthur is supposed to sleep, until the summons arouses him to come back to the help of his people. Mr Sam had once told me about this, and I told Triz.

'Oh!' she breathed. 'If only we could go there! How I wish that I might see that place!'

In the meantime, we often played a game; that one of us was King Arthur and one Sir Bedivere. She, as Arthur, would give me her sword (a bulrush, plucked from the side of the pool in Kinn Hall garden) and I would promise to fling it into the pond, but would fail twice to do so because of the value of the jewels in the hilt; but at last, after bitter reproaches from the dying king, I would cast it out into the water. Then we would pretend to see the magical barge approaching, with seven queens all robed in black. (Here I clung to the stated number of three queens, but Triz insisted on seven.) Then she would pretend to climb, groaning, into the barge, and turn to say, 'I will into the vale of Avalon to heal me of my grievous wound.' And I would fall a-weeping on to my knees and call, '*Come again, my dear Lord King Arthur, come again!*' Meanwhile Triz, since there was no magic barge, would hide herself among the bulrushes. This play we acted over and over again, to our great satisfaction, alternating the parts.

I suppose Triz must be the only person with whom I have never felt impatience. When we played, I always took the lead – except in this play of Arthur. Whatever I told her, she received as gospel. She would have given me any of her possessions in a moment, if I had asked for them. She was like my younger sister – a gentle, fragile being who must be treated at all times with cherishing care.

I was never hasty or sharp with her. All she asked, I performed. When she must have the lesson explained, or the way to work out a sum demonstrated, or the lines repeated, or the passage in the book found and marked for her, I did it at once, calmly, however many times it might be required. Over and over.

Is it any wonder then, at the end of the day, when I ran down the driveway and back to Byblow Bottom, that my feet, of their own accord, went faster and faster, my breath came quicker and quicker, that I flung myself into the untidy village like a fish diving back into its native element?

The end of my sojourn at Othery came with dramatic suddenness.

The season once more was autumn. I must have been twelve or thirteen, and Triz seven or eight, still pale and frail but pretty as a primrose. Matters at Kinn Hall, I was aware, went badly; the Squire displayed open animosity against Lady Hariot while she, silent and reserved, kept her own counsel, never alluded to him in his absence and spoke to him only on matters of domestic necessity. It was not a happy household. Yet we children, like birds or small woodland creatures before an approaching storm, kept to our normal ways and went about our humble affairs, busy and self-absorbed, without paying much heed to what took place above our heads.

One day the Squire had gone off to join a meet of the stag-hounds at Ottermill, high on the moor. We, therefore, assuming him away for the day, breathed more easily and, once our French and Italian lessons were done, roamed out into a sparkling world, for night storms had dashed many leaves from the trees, and the air, cleansed by rain, was wet and fresh.

'The scent will be very good for Papa's hunting,' said Triz.

Strangely, for he never regarded her and spoke to her only to reprimand, she seemed to feel a kind of sorrowful affection for

Mr Vexford; I think she perceived that he was a weak and not very intelligent man, who must be aware that his wife had him at a disadvantage and could always best him in argument if she chose; his only recourse was to rail and shout at her.

Lady Hariot was lying down in her bedroom with a headache – there had been furious words at breakfast, I gathered – so, after we had played in the garden for a while, we told Prue that we were going down to the cliff top to gather blackberries.

'Don't ye goo down on the rocks, now,' warned Prue. 'Tide's a-making. 'Twill be high just after noon.'

Knowledge of the state of the tide came as naturally as breathing to the people of the coast. We promised that we would go no farther than the cliff top.

So, carrying baskets, we ran down the path of worn slippery rock, between meadows, to the rough clumps of bush that fringed the cliff top where I had first met Lady Hariot. I wondered what had become of Biddy; no news of her ever came back to Othery.

I was feeling melancholy, because Hoby that morning had received a letter from his father informing him that he had been secured a scholarship at Eton College, and was to transfer there at once.

''Tis very advantageous,' Hoby said hopefully. 'For sure I'll get a King's College Fellowship and can go on to Cambridge, and then I've a chance of a seat in Parliament or some public position. After all, a fellow can't rusticate in Byblow Bottom all his life.'

'That be true enough – ' when I was down in the village, I naturally reverted to its language – 'but, oh, Hoby, I'm feered that at Eton they'll larrup and ill-use ye sore. Remember Dickie Chester.'

Dickie, one of the fifteen children of Lord S———, had gone to Eton and wrote many most miserable letters back to his sisters about the hideous conditions in the Long Chamber, the dormitory where all collegers slept together, locked in without ushers or masters, from eight at night till seven in the morning, where debauchery and tyranny and evil practices went unchecked. And how Ascot Heath, the Master, would beat seventy boys at one time, each as hard as the one before.

'Well, I can stand up for myself,' said Hoby stoutly, and clenched his fists. It was true he had grown tall and lanky enough, already as tall as a grown man, more likely due to a diet of poached pheasant and salmon than from Hannah's haphazard housekeeping.

I knew that I would miss Hoby sorely and worry about him. Though he teased me, and did things that filled me with fury, and others of which I deeply disapproved, yet we were good friends and kept each other's confidence. I was afraid that at Eton he would be held in very low esteem, because of his rustic manners. Unlike me, he had never been given the chance to learn the ways of gentlefolk – except on his father's brief visits – and had often scornfully rejected my offers to correct his speech.

'What the pize do it matter how a fellow talks?'

Thinking these anxious, melancholy thoughts about Hoby, as I dropped blackberries into my basket, I suddenly saw him run at speed over the broken ground at the head of the little coombe, or dingle, on the southernmost lip of which stood Kinn Hall.

Half a dozen boys from Byblow Bottom followed him, and they soon came panting up to Triz and me. She gazed at them with wonder and apprehension, for now she never had any dealings with the village children, and as a rule they kept out of her way.

'Such fun!' gasped Will. 'Th'owd buck's a-making this way, heading for the watter, see – any minute now I forecast ye'll get a glim of mun.'

'There!' shouted Jon. 'There mun be! Racken a'll goo up the track to Ashett! No – a waint! A be a-coming this way! And theer be Squire, hard ahind him! How a ridth! Squire be raring mad, a rackon. What be tu? Tryin' to head the buck?'

A huge stag was bounding across the meadows with a mixed pack of hounds in full cry close behind him, crying and yammering in a frenzy of excitement. The stag carried his head high with a desperate air as if, once he looked down, the weight of the massive antlers would cause him to trip and fall. The dogs' tails threshed like branches in a gale.

'Oh, the poor thing!' cried Triz. 'What will he do?'

'A be makin' for the watter,' explained Will. 'But ol' Vexford be a-trying to cotch mun first.'

The Squire, galloping his grey cob as if seven devils were in pursuit, had taken a circle westwards and was now coming up along the cliff edge on the left hand side of the stag who, ignoring him, made full tilt for the break in the head of the cliff.

The rest of the hunt, far away in the rear, hallooed, shouted and blew on horns.

Everything happened at once, very fast.

The stag leapt out unhesitatingly from the cliff edge and fell down, down, twenty feet, into the tossing waves which were now at the tide's highest point. But they were not deep enough to save the poor beast; we saw him crumple among rocks, and then his body was washed to and fro among them, still feebly struggling.

'*God dammit!*' shouted the Squire, galloping along the cliff edge.

At the same moment, the grey cob lost his footing on a treacherous bit of loose overhang. Man and horse plunged over the edge and fell, as the stag had done, down on to the barely covered rocks below.

'Fegs! Look at that! Owd Squire be done for, I reckon!' gasped Hoby. 'Come on, lads! We'd best goo down and haul 'un out.'

He and the other boys scampered down the roughly cut steps that led to the beach. The rest of the hunt coming up, dismounted with cries of consternation. Some followed the boys. Some ran to the village for ropes, brandy, hurdles.

But nothing they did could benefit the Squire, who had dashed his brains out on a rock; or his poor grey nag, who had broken two legs and had to be shot.

The Squire's younger brother, Frank Vexford, inherited the manor; he was a needy man who had hitherto lived in a precarious way, farming at Moretonhampstead, and he made his appearance up at Kinn Hall to claim his inheritance before the flowers had withered on the grave. Apart from the entail, the Squire had had a little money of his own (half of it Lady Hariot's) but, because of the bad relation between them, every penny of this was left away from her, to other kindred, as he explained in a vengeful letter lodged with lawyers in Taunton.

'Because my undutiful and blameworthy wife Hariot has absented herself from my bed and refused me my lawful rights of wedlock since the birth of her daughter, I hereby disinherit them and declare that they do not deserve any consideration whatsoever from me.'

'Ah, the spiteful old bugger,' said Hoby, when this news percolated about the village, as of course it very soon did. 'What'll the poor lady do?'

'Go and live with her own kinsfolk, I suppose.'

I hardly dared go up to the Hall until a message came from Triz beseeching me to do so.

When I went, I made my way, as had become my usual habit, through a pair of french doors that led into what had been Lady Hariot's favourite drawing room, where we children had been used to take our piano lessons. Since nobody was to be seen, I sat myself down at the pianoforte and began playing a soft, melancholy little sonata by Haydn, for I thought that this was the best way of advertising my presence to Triz.

A voice exclaimed: 'Deuce take it, that's a pretty tune! And *you* are a pretty little fairy – with your rosy cheeks and your copper-red hair – far prettier than my wan little tadpole of a niece! But who the blazes *are* you?'

The man who said this was staring at me across the top of the piano. I could guess in a moment who *he* was, by his red complexion, small mean mouth and close-set eyes; he was as like the old Squire as one pea to another, and must be his brother. I jumped to my feet, saying, 'Excuse me, sir! I did not know anybody was at hand; I will leave at once,' nervously enough, but he came quickly round and caught me by the arm, fondling me in a very unwelcome manner.

'Not so fast, not so fast, no harm done, my pretty –' and then his eye fell on my right hand, and he retreated as if he had picked up a viper, exclaiming, 'Devil take it, what's *that*?'

I could have burst out laughing, the change in his demeanour was so sudden and so marked. But I made my escape and ran upstairs to the room that was still called the nursery, while behind me he was stamping and bawling, 'Who is she? Get that monster out of my house!'

I found Triz and Lady Hariot hard at work packing clothes in boxes.

'Oh, *dear* Lady Hariot! Where shall you go?'

She gave me a small, wry smile.

'Well, my dear, we must just walk our chalks, as they say. I am lucky that my sister, Anna Ffoliot, in Lisbon, has always said that she would take us in if matters – if matters chanced to fall out as they have done. So – to Lisbon we must go.'

'Lisbon? In *Portugal*?'

'Yes, my child, and there's the advantage of studying the use of the globes! A Spanish vessel is due in Ashett this Thursday, and we must board her at break of day. Indeed it is a piece of good fortune for us that she calls this week, for funds are decidedly low – I won't deny – and my brother-in-law Francis wishes us out of his house as soon as may be.'

My throat was tight with woe. I could hardly speak.

'But – but – but – but this is your *home*.'

'Not any longer, my poppet. Women build nests, but men make bequests, and scatter them. Heigh-ho!'

Lady Hariot, I could see, was trying to be as cheerful as she could in order to distract Triz who seemed utterly shocked; white, trembling and tearful.

I, too, was inexpressibly outraged that after somebody had taken such pains to make a home and run it justly as Lady Hariot had, they could, all in a day, be dispossessed. Lady Hariot was a fair, thoughtful mistress, I knew; she was well-liked in the village.

Triz finally found her voice. 'Can't – can't Alize come with us? To Portugal?'

'No, my dearie.' Lady Hariot's tone was very gentle, but the message in her eye to me was unmistakable. A faint hope crumbled away within me. 'You and I have so very little money between us that it will only just suffice to take us overseas. We could not ask Aunt Anna to accept another guest. And Liza has her own friends who might not wish her to go gadding abroad with such a ramshackle pair as we shall be. Liza – if she will follow my advice –' Lady Hariot briskly folded a shawl and tucked it into a basket trunk – 'Liza will take her own way now, to her own friends, and not remain here any longer at Nether Othery.'

Tears began coursing silently down Triz's cheeks. I put my arms round her and held her close.

'Don't leave me, Alize – pray, pray don't!' she whispered in a choked voice.

'My dearie – I must; don't you see? We are children, we have no choice. But I will write to you – long letters – as soon as you send me your direction in Portugal – I will write you often. And you will be happy there – the sun will be so warm, and you will catch no more nasty coughs or colds – And when we are both grown I shall travel out and find you – '

Lady Hariot's eye, meeting mine steadily over her daughter's head, sent me a message of approval.

'And now,' she said briskly, 'Liza must go back and tell Dr Moultrie that his lessons are to terminate. Give the good doctor this, my dear' – she handed me a guinea – 'that will sweeten the blow. And you, my dear child, take this' – another guinea – 'go into Ashett and reserve yourself a place on tomorrow's stage-coach to Dorchester. And put these letters in your pocket, and give them to Colonel Brandon's lawyers. Tell them that you should go to your connections at Delaford.'

'But Lady Hariot – can you spare –'

'My dear girl – you have done so much for and *with* Thérèse that I only wish it could be twenty times more! And I hope, like you, that some day – when it is possible – we shall all meet again. But now I urge you – most sincerely – to lose no time in doing what I suggest. Lacking our company – lacking the influence of this household – I must impress upon you that Othery is no fit place for you. And, for her sake' – she placed a gentle hand on her daughter's head – 'I think we should make our goodbyes speedy.'

I could see that this was wise advice. Triz was nearly dying of woe. I gave her a last hug, gulped out a 'Goodbye' and ran down the stairs even faster than I had come up them.

When I gave Lady Hariot's message to Dr Moultrie, and told him that I was about to leave the village, he fell down in some kind of fit. It was no great surprise – he had been red-faced, short of breath and dropsical in his constitution for a long time. But it was dismaying to see him writhe snoring and gasping on the floor. I cried out for his housekeeper, blind old Mother Fothergill, and ran for Dr Parracombe, who bled him and purged him and leeched him.

Disobeying Lady Hariot's instructions, I waited until Thursday to take the Dorchester coach. Meantime I wandered the country, saying goodbye, in my own fashion, to all the places that I had visited with Mr Sam and Mr Bill. Hoby was gone off to Eton already; there was nobody else that I minded leaving. I washed and darned my clothes to the best of my ability, and tried to neaten my appearance. I retrieved my fan from the oak tree and tucked it at the bottom of my small bundle, wondering again about the lady who had left it.

I had never mentioned her to Lady Hariot.

'I suppose you know what you're a-doing of?' Hannah Wellcome said sourly, in one of her sober intervals. 'Sposin' they won't have ye at Delaford? What then? Sposin' they cast ye off? *I* won't have ye back, don't think it.'

'Then I'll have to find some sailors and ask how they do for soap.'

On Thursday morning I rose long before it was light and walked in to Ashett. There, hidden behind a great pile of fishermen's nets, I secretly watched the sad little procession of Lady Hariot, Triz and Prue, with their bags, clambering aboard the Spanish vessel.

I do not choose to tell whether I wept or not; that is of no importance.

As I said earlier, there may be incidents or matters which I am not prepared to discuss; they are my own affair, and nobody else's.

When the Spanish ship – her name was *Santa Maria* – had weighed anchor and made sail, I walked away from the quayside and took my place on the coach to Dorchester. With a tolerably heavy heart.

Chapter 3

THE COACH SET ME DOWN IN DORCHESTER AND I INQUIRED MY way to Colonel Brandon's lawyers, Messrs Melplash, Melplash and Grisewood, in South Street. They, needless to say, were aghast at the arrival of a rumpled girl with a soiled bundle proffering a letter To Whom It May Concern from Lady Hariot Vexford.

There were two partners in the office, an old one and a younger one. Mr Melplash and Mr Grisewood.

They deliberated over Lady Hariot's letter.

'Lady Hariot – who, I must say, indites a very proper and conformable missive – seems to suggest here, that Othery is no longer a fit domicile for you.' Mr Melplash peered at me over the tops of his spectacles. 'I gather that you have spent much time in Lady Hariot's house, with her daughter.'

'Lady Hariot has been so good to me!' I declared fervently. 'But now she is obliged to go abroad to Portugal. Squire Vexford died and his brother inherits the house.'

'Hmn. Hmn. Yes. I have heard of Vexford of Othery.' Nothing to his advantage, suggested the tone. 'But now, child, what in the world is to be done with you?'

'Why, sir?'

'Why, you see, we have learned lately that Colonel Brandon intended to return from India to England with his regiment; but it may be many months yet before he arrives in this country.'

'Oh, I see.' My heart sank. 'Perhaps – until then – could I go to school?'

This had been one of Lady Hariot's suggestions. It sounded respectable.

The two partners looked at one another. Mr Melplash, the elder, had a neat little flaxen wig above his glasses, and a grey worsted suit with a flapped waistcoat. Mr Grisewood, the younger, wore so very tiny a wig that it seemed more like an odd snippet of cotton material that had fallen from above and lodged on the top of his head. Beneath it his brown hair could be seen, tied back with a bit of ribbon.

'Girl wishes to go to school,' said Mr Grisewood. 'Not unreasonable, hmn?'

'Lady Hariot here says that the girl has been well taught already and can also sing and play. Pity to waste that, hmn, hmn?'

'And she ain't old enough to earn her living.'

'She is certainly not old enough for that.'

I thought of Fanny Huskisson. I thought of sailors and soap.

'Thing is,' said Mr Grisewood, tilting back his head so that, if *he* had worn glasses, he would have been looking at me over the tops of them, 'thing is, no funds authorized for sending you to school.'

'And we shall be unable to communicate with the Colonel, now, until his arrival in this country.'

I said timidly, 'Is there no one who could act for him in the meantime?'

The two men looked at one another thoughtfully.

'Girl speaks well for her age,' said Mr Grisewood.

'Sensibly, too,' said Mr Melplash.

'Perhaps we should communicate with Mr and Mrs Ferrars?'

At this I pricked up my ears, for who were Mr and Mrs Ferrars? Could Mrs Ferrars be the lady who left the fan?

Grisewood explained: 'Mrs Ferrars is the sister of Mrs Brandon.'

Melplash amplified: 'Mr Ferrars is the vicar of Delaford. In Colonel Brandon's absence, matters of business are referred to him.'

'In that case,' I said hopefully, 'perhaps *he* would agree to my being sent to school?'

The two men communicated non-verbally. Melplash consulted his turnip-watch.

'Too late to ride out to Delaford this evening,' said Grisewood.

'*Indeed* yes. *Far* too late,' said Melplash. They peered at me again, with disapproval this time, for I was presenting them with a tiresome problem. At last Melplash said, 'I suppose she may as well lodge overnight in my house. Mrs Tasker can look after her, I daresay.'

'That *would* resolve the difficulty,' said Grisewood in a tone of relief.

So when the two men left their office, as they shortly did, I was instructed to follow Mr Melplash to his house in Durngate Street, where his elderly housekeeper, not unkindly but very much astonished, gave me a meal of cold beef and bread-and-butter and tea, exclaiming in a loud whisper to herself all the while, 'Dear, dear! What are things coming to, I should like to know?' and then led me off to a little narrow attic bedroom where, all night, I could hear the church clocks of the town chiming the quarters. Never to my knowledge having passed a night away from Othery before, I slept very ill; the parting from Triz and Lady Hariot, from Hoby, from all the places I knew, from the last reminders of Mr Bill and Mr Sam, created an ache in my heart and made me feel like a snail that has had its shell stripped away.

In the morning Mrs Tasker, who had taken away my tucker overnight, presented it to me, washed, starched and ironed; she also combed and plaited my hair with such ferocious tightness that my eyes felt pulled to the edges of my face.

After breakfast Mr Melplash informed me that he had ordered a chaise, and that Mr Grisewood was going to escort me to the village of Delaford which, I learned, was about twelve miles to the southwest.

'And it's to be hoped that Mr and Mrs Ferrars will have some idea what to do with you,' he said in a gloomy tone. Evidently during the night he had been afflicted with severe doubts as to the wisdom of having taken me in hand.

Mr Grisewood, on the other hand, seemed quite cheerful today; perhaps at the prospect of a pleasant ride on a warm autumn morning.

'Delaford House is a grand, old-fashioned manor house,' he told me, as we jogged along. 'Pity 'tis all shut up at present, the Colonel being abroad. It has the best fruit trees in the country, a fine old mulberry and a handsome dovecote. But the parsonage ain't bad either; it is by the canal, and there is some very fair fishing in the river also. Were you never out of Othery?'

'Never, sir, I reckon.'

'Ay; well, I've heard of Othery.' Nothing that was suitable to be passed on to me, his silence indicated. But after a few minutes' rumination, he resumed, 'And do you know anything about your parents, child?'

'No, sir; only that my mother r-ran away from her friends; and that she died when I was born.'

'And you know nothing about your father?'

'Nothing at all, sir.' After a pause, I said timidly, 'It was not – my father is not Colonel Brandon?'

'Oh, good gracious me, *no!*' cried Mr Grisewood, greatly shocked and most emphatic. He repeated, 'Good *gracious,* no! I should think not! The idea! Colonel Brandon is a man of – of the most unblemished probity. The very *thought* of – Mercy on us, what a notion!'

'I am very sorry, sir. I did not mean – The thing is, you see, I have never met Colonel Brandon – so far as I know. He never came to Othery.'

'Ah, no. So I understand.'

There followed a pause. The horses trotted on, through Toller Valence and Winterbourne Cheney. It was a pleasant country, with low green hills, narrow valleys and little fast-running rivers. Very different from ours around Othery. Milder. Tamer.

'I wondered *why* Colonel Brandon never came,' I said in a low voice. 'To see me, you know.'

At length Mr Grisewood answered me. 'You must understand, there were difficulties. There were objections. That is to say – a close connection of Colonel Brandon had – ah – very strong reasons for wishing to avoid any – any re-opening of former – ah – *connections.*'

I found it almost impossible to make head or tail of this.

'Colonel Brandon did not want to come to Othery? Was that it?'

'No. Not that precisely.'

'Somebody else didn't want him to come?'

'Ah. In a manner of speaking,' Mr Grisewood allowed cautiously.

'I see.'

I did not see, really. But it was quite plain that no further explanations were going to be given by Mr Grisewood, so I concluded there would be no sense in putting any more questions. Besides – having turned off the turnpike road – we seemed to have reached our destination. We had entered a small pretty village, not so large as Othery but a great deal neater, of grey thatched cottages set comfortably – if rather low-lying – among handsome trees, with a river and a canal twining between them, and a larger house perched a short distance away upon a slight eminence. The church was by the canal, and the parsonage was by the church: a modest-sized brick gentleman's residence.

'Perhaps it would be best if, for the moment, you remain in the carriage,' reflected Mr Grisewood. 'Just in case – well, perhaps it will be best.'

So I remained in the chaise, while the driver walked his horses back and forth.

In about ten minutes Mr Grisewood reappeared at a white gate, and called, 'Ah – Miss! Miss Eliza! Will you come in, if you please?'

So I went into the house, which was small and cold and smelt of pot-pourri made of roses and lavender. The front door opened directly into a little parlour, square and panelled. I could see immediately that this was not the abode of rich people: the curtains and furnishings were tasteful, but extremely worn, and of Spartan simplicity.

In this room two people were waiting nervously to receive me: a man and a woman. They were, I suppose, in their early thirties; the man stocky, fair-haired but already turning grey, with a long, careworn, weather-beaten countenance – the face of a country clergyman who spends most of his time on horseback; the woman had once been handsome and still possessed good features, but also had a worn, spiritless air. Her hair, too, was streaked with grey. Her clothes were shabby and she looked haggard and anxious. When she saw me, a curious quiver passed over her colourless countenance, like a squall of wind over a calm sea. I noticed that she plaited her fingers together and drew a deep breath.

The husband and wife had stood up defensively as I entered. There was a round table in the room and some upright chairs. On the table stood three tiny glasses, empty.

'Mr and Mrs Ferrars,' said Mr Grisewood formally, 'this is the young person I spoke of; this is Miss Eliza.'

Mrs Ferrars spoke, clearing her throat a trifle. 'Have you no other name, child?'

'I am called Eliza Williams, ma'am; but I am not quite sure if I have any right to that name.'

Mr Ferrars said, quite kindly, 'And how old are you, my child?'

'I am not quite sure of that either, sir; but about thirteen years, I believe.'

'And you wish to go to school?'

'Yes, if you please, sir, I should like to be put in the way of earning my living. I believe I could pay back the fees by and by. I can play and sing quite well, sir, if you please.'

Without thinking, I spread out my hands, and heard Mrs Ferrars give a little hiss of distress. Quickly I put my hands behind my back again; but I noticed the lady became somewhat more friendly from that moment, as if she were sorry for my affliction. Before, I had felt as if the mere sight of me made her angry.

I wondered why.

Mr Ferrars said gravely, 'Why don't you go and play to us, child, while we consider this matter. You will find a pianoforte in the next room, and some music on it.'

I noticed that his wife gave him a quick glance, not wholly agreeing with his suggestion, but, as she did not raise any objection, I curtseyed politely and walked into the next room, which was even smaller and contained little more than bookshelves round the walls, a desk and the instrument. Needless to say, I would far rather have studied the contents of the shelves, and did in fact eagerly run my eyes over their titles as I crossed the room. They were essays and theology. On the music stand by the piano I found a sonata by Paradisi which I had practised with Mr Godfinch, so I played that, softly, meanwhile stretching my ears (but to no avail) to try and catch anything said by the quiet voices in the next room.

After ten minutes or so Mr Ferrars walked through to summon me back.

'You seem to play well, my child,' he told me calmly. 'I wish my sister-in-law might hear you – she is a great proficient herself –' then he cut himself short with an odd, wry expression on his face, and said no more.

In the parlour, Mr Grisewood was standing as if about to take his leave.

'Well, Miss Eliza,' he told me with an air of relief, 'I leave you here in excellent hands. Mr and Mrs Ferrars have very kindly agreed that you may be sent to Mrs Haslam's school in Bath, which – but they themselves will tell you all about that. Mr Ferrars authorizes that the fees may be paid from a fund left by Colonel Brandon for – ah – unexpected contingencies. And Mrs Ferrars will see that you are properly fitted out and – ah – made pre – ah – prepared in every way for your new life.'

I was profuse in more curtseys and thanks.

My face had begun to grow tired and stiff from so much politeness, and because of the hair dragged so tightly behind my ears.

Mr Grisewood bowed, shook hands and left, adjuring me to be a good girl and do credit to my benefactors. I promised him that I would do so.

As soon as he had gone, Mr Ferrars looked at his watch and said, 'Elinor, I must be off to see old Goodman Boyce; I had a message from his wife that he is sinking fast. I should have been there an hour ago. I know I can leave you to – to settle the arrangements for Eliza.'

'Of course, my love,' she said calmly, and, turning to me as he strode out, measured me with her eye. 'Clothes are the main item; is that bundle *all* your possessions, my dear?'

Shamefacedly I said yes.

'It is fortunate that I have it in my power to remedy the deficiency. Mrs Haslam expects her pupils to have a plentiful supply of clothing, though it must be plain, rather than fine. But my daughter Nell has already attended the school for two years – she is there at present for the Michaelmas term. She has been growing fast and though she is younger than you, I believe her outgrown things may serve you well enough. I have them upstairs, laid up in woodruff.'

With a small crooked smile – the first I had seen – she added, 'Nothing goes to waste in this house.'

And so this was how Mrs Ferrars and I spent the rest of that day: stepping upstairs she fetched down a drawerful of neat grey woollen gowns, besides calico petticoats, chemises and other items, most of which required some alteration before they would fit me. Nell Ferrars, I gathered, was a tall girl. There was a cloak, a bonnet, even stockings and gloves, many of which had already been carefully and exquisitely darned.

I was set to work turning up petticoats; Mrs Ferrars, herself a most superior needlewoman, evidently thought but poorly of my stitchwork. I struggled to improve it under her critical gaze. Meanwhile we talked: she asked me about my life at Nether Othery, and I supplied her with a carefully edited version of the doings there, but gave a fuller account of Lady Hariot's story, which she heard with considerable sympathy.

Then I ventured to inquire: 'Ma'am – can you tell me anything about my parents?'

She turned on me a startled eye, as if this were not a question that it was at all proper for me to ask.

After a moment's reflection, she replied, 'Your mother – I understand – was a cousin of Colonel Brandon. Of your father – I am able to tell you nothing.'

I sighed, and said, 'Thank you, ma'am.'

With a comprehending look she said, 'Why do you not call me Cousin Elinor? And my husband Cousin Edward? We are not, in fact, related – Colonel Brandon is my brother-in-law – but perhaps that will make you feel more comfortable with us.'

Poor lady: I could see that she was not at all glad to have me, but was making the very best of the situation.

I said, 'When shall I go to the school, Cousin Elinor?'

'I think we may have your clothes ready by next Saturday. On that day every week I send a package of fruit and vegetables to Bath on the carrier's cart; you can go with it and my maid Cerne shall accompany you. That will incur the least expense for Colonel Brandon.'

Incautiously I remarked, 'I thought he was a rich man.'

'So he is. All the more reason why we should take pains to see that his money is used carefully. And', she added scrupulously, 'it would not be appropriate to say that he was *rich*. Comfortably circumstanced would better describe him.'

Care with money, I soon discovered, was the main element of life in the parsonage at Delaford. Everything spoke it: the darned curtains, the worn rugs, the plain and not very plentiful food. When Mr Ferrars came back from his pastoral visit, I noticed that he turned aside, at once, into the garden and set to work among his rows of vegetables.

Presently, in walked two people from the street, a maidservant with a shrewd, resigned, humorous face, and a little old lady in a silk mantle and handsome bonnet. She was dressed much finer than Mrs Ferrars – though untidily; she had a vacant and wandering eye.

'Well, Mother!' Cousin Elinor greeted her. 'Did you enjoy your walk?'

The maid gave a sharp nod. 'Walked as far as the turnpike, we did, mum; she'll have a rare appetite for her dinner.'

'Cerne was very impertinent,' snapped the old lady.

'She would go into Ford's and order a forequarter of pork and eight pounds of sausages,' explained Cerne with a grim smile.

'I *like* pork,' cried the old lady peevishly. 'You know I do, Elinor! I should fancy a dish of fried pork for my dinner.'

'Pork is far too rich for you, Mother; you shall have some nice mutton stew. (This is my mother, Mrs Dashwood),' Mrs Ferrars added to me.

Now the old lady's eye lit on me. '*Marianne!*' she exclaimed in a tone of rapture.

'No, Mama. That is not Marianne, though a little like her in feature. But look again! Her hair is quite a different colour. Your Marianne will return home, all in good time, and then we shall be very happy to welcome her. And you will return to the Manor House. But in the meantime this is Miss Eliza Williams, who spends a few nights with us, and then she will go off to school in Bath, with Nell.'

'I don't like Nell. Nell is a very rude and unkind girl. Sometimes she gives me a push. And she always takes the biggest piece of cake. —But are you *sure* that is not Marianne? Somehow – somehow – her face makes me think of Marianne – when we were all living at Barton – when we were so happy – so happy – ' Mrs Dashwood's face crumpled. She began to cry a little.

'Come, ma'am,' said Cerne, not unkindly. 'Let's get your bonnet and cloak off. And then you'll be wanting your eggnog.'

They went upstairs slowly, with much urging from the maid.

I could hear the old lady crying, 'There's a bird in the house! There's a bird!'

'No, ma'am, there is no bird.'

'There is a bird, I tell you! House! House! Where have you hidden the poor bird?'

'There is no bird, Mrs Dashwood.'

A door closed, upstairs.

Cousin Elinor explained, rethreading her needle: 'When my sister Marianne (Mrs Colonel Brandon) is at home, my mother resides with her, up at the Manor House. It is more comfortable for her there than with us. And Marianne was always her favourite daughter. (I am explaining these things to you, Eliza, because in many ways you seem remarkably sensible and older than your years.)'

'Thank you, Cousin Elinor. When will – will Cousin Marianne come home?'

'In about a year, we hope. I have missed her a great deal since she has been in India – and Colonel Brandon also. They are our dear friends and neighbours. But – for various reasons – he thought it best to rejoin his old regiment and commanding officer, although it meant such a long journey. And it was thought best – my sister was happy to accompany him. She is of a – of a very adventurous temperament.'

'They have no children?'

'No.' Cousin Elinor sighed. 'That has been . . . a grief to . . . to the Colonel. But – as matters turned out – perhaps it was fortunate. I only hope that when they do return my brother-in-law will decide to sell out and settle down at last. But I am apprehensive that if General Wellesley is sent to fight Bonaparte in Europe, the Colonel will think it his duty to remain on active service. And in that case I don't know *what* Marianne will do. She is so extremely devoted to her husband.'

Cousin Elinor frowned, knotting her thread. It struck me that Elinor Ferrars was a very lonely lady. I supposed that she missed having her sister to talk to and was using me as a substitute, inadequate though I must be. Mrs Dashwood was plainly touched in her wits; Mr Ferrars seemed to be out of doors nearly all the time, visiting his parishioners or digging in the garden. Very different from Dr Moultrie! – (Though, when together, the pair seemed affectionate enough, in their mild way, a great contrast to the Vexfords.)

To turn Cousin Elinor's thoughts, which seemed melancholy, I asked about the school in Bath.

'It is not a very big one, fifty pupils only. But of very high standing. Most select. Colonel Brandon, very kindly – he is the kindest, most generous man in the world – pays for our daughter to be a parlour boarder there. And my other sister, Margaret, is one of the teachers. But, in the meantime – Eliza – I hope you will not think this unfair on our part – '

She paused, visibly embarrassed, biting her lips, plaiting together in folds the linen chemise that she was hemming.

I waited in polite silence.

'We have not entered you as a boarder, you see – Mr Ferrars did not think it right to render Colonel Brandon accountable for such a large expense in his absence – so I have written to Mrs Haslam explaining your – your circumstances, and entering you as a day pupil.'

I must confess that my heart rose up at this information. I had not expected such a possibility. Indeed I had looked forward, with no little dread and dismay, to five years' penal incarceration. But I kept my voice and expression carefully blank as I inquired,

'With whom then shall I be lodging, Cousin Elinor?'

'Your cousin Edward and I have an aunt residing in Bath – well, she is my mother's aunt in fact – Mrs Montford Jebb; she is a widow and lives in – in somewhat straitened circumstances; she will be happy to give you lodging, and she is in New King Street, so that will not be too far for you to walk to and from the school in Queen Square every day. (Mr Ferrars is going to provide you with money to buy yourself an umbrella, for it rains a great deal in Bath.)'

'You are both excessively kind to me, ma'am.'

'Oh, no, child; not excessively; indeed – ' she paused, appearing troubled, and murmured something about her sister Marianne which I did not catch. Then she added, 'We do no more than our duty, as your nearest connections. Your *only* connections.'

I said politely: 'I shall look forward to meeting my cousin Nell.'

At that she seemed a little dubious.

'Nell is about two years younger than you, my dear. She will be in a different class. Perhaps it may be best to wait until – to let her make the first overtures. Nell has – ' Cousin Elinor considered, delicately working her way round a buttonhole, then said, 'She has been used to be the only child of the house, you see. Her only brother – very sadly – died of a fall from his pony when he was five.'

'Oh, how dreadful,' I said sincerely.

'Yes. Yes it was. Really, Mr Ferrars has never – has never got over it. And so Nell – so Nell – well, we shall have to see.'

Thus leaving me with no very buoyant expectations of my cousin Nell.

Later that day, after a frugal meal of pease pie and whey, and stewed apples, and water to drink, I was occupying myself usefully in the garden, sweeping leaves when, unaware of my proximity just outside the window, Edward Ferrars said to his wife: 'It is best she not be in this house too much. Better if she spends the holidays with Aunt Jebb.'

'Because of the resemblance? You think *he* might come to hear?'

'There might be talk. The resemblance is so curiously strong. If you recall, Brandon first observed it in Marianne. That was why he – And then your mother, you say, also –'

'Hush! *On croit que la petite est au dehors, pas loin d'ici,'* said Cousin Elinor, unaware that my French was probably better than hers.

This overheard snatch of conversation suddenly filled my mind with the notion that perhaps I was the child of Marianne Brandon. If so, no wonder that Mr and Mrs Ferrars did not want me in their home. But – on the other hand – no wonder they thought it their duty to see that I was provided for.

So who was my father?

On the whole I found it a decided relief to set off for Bath, humbly, in the carrier's cart, on the following Saturday, accompanied by two hampers of vegetables and the box containing my remade wardrobe. I felt very much as if I myself had been unpicked and made over in a new design. But the real self was still there, watchful, underneath.

On the journey I talked a good deal to Cerne, the servant, who proved not unfriendly.

'Best give a wide berth to Miss Nell,' she advised. 'If ever there was a spoilt, marred young 'un! And proud! She'd not give you the time of day if you had a diamond tied to every hair of your head. I can tell you, there was plenty about the village breathed easier when Miss Fine Airs went off to school. The only friend she ever made was young Ralph Mortimer over the valley. And he got sent away to Harrow. Mind – what young Ralph ever saw in her –'

I asked about Mrs Jebb. 'Is she a kind lady?'

Cerne screwed up her nose reflectively. 'Well – she's a mortal deal different since she went to prison.'

'*Prison?*'

'Didn't Mrs Ferrars tell you?'

'No, she certainly didn't. Mr Ferrars started to say something – but then he was called away to a sick person. Cousin Elinor said nothing at all.'

'Well, I'll tell you how it was.' Cerne settled to her task with relish. 'For you did ought to know, 'count you'll say something okward to the poor lady. Five years ago, 'twas, when Mr Jebb was still alive, and he stood by her through thick and thin most faithful, poor gentleman, but it cost him his health, and he was never the same after. He was out with his lady one day a-strolling, and she bought a card of lace at a draper's shop near the Pump Room, and the next thing, the shopman came a-running after them declaring that Mrs Jebb had slipped *two* cards of lace into the packet, 'stead of just the one she'd paid for. And Mr Jebb said, no such thing, but let him look to satisfy himself, and so he looked, and – would you believe it – there 'twas! So the constable was called, and the poor lady was committed to jail, till Taunton Assizes. In Ilchester Jail, she was lodged, and the gentleman, her husband, along of her, for he said he'd never desert her in her troubles. And, mind you, *if* she'd a been found guilty, she could a been hanged! The lace was worth five shillings, you see. Or, at the very least, transported to Botany Bay. Eight months, she continued in Ilchester jail, and then at the assizes, they brought in Not Guilty. In no more than fifteen minutes! They reckoned it was just a wicked try-on by the shop people, they'd slipped it in the parcel. And they'd expected Mr Jebb – who was a warm, and a well-respected man – would pay them hush money, so as to buy them off. But not he! Mr Ferrars reckoned he spent over two thousand pound in legal doings. Oh, there was *such* a crying and a kissing and a hoorooaring when the poor lady was brought in Not Guilty. But it proved the death of him, poor man, he was never the same again, and his business failed, and he died; and after that she was obliged to live very quiet, for although found innocent, some of her former acquaintance fell away from her. She sold up the big house and moved to New King Street.'

'Poor lady. What a terrible thing to happen.'

I had found the frugal, punctilious and high-minded atmosphere at Delaford Rectory rather tiring and decidedly hard to live up to; I could not help wondering what life with Mrs Montford Jebb held in store, and looked forward to it with a good deal of interest.

Chapter 4

Mrs Montford Jebb occupied a small house in New King Street.

'Of course when my late dear husband was alive, matters were very otherwise,' she told me. 'Then we resided in far more spacious and handsome premises, a large house in Paragon. But such accommodation would be sadly unsuitable for a lone, lorn widow.'

To me, Mrs Jebb appeared neither lone nor lorn. Almost every evening three of her particular friends, Mrs Langley, Mrs Chamberlayne and Mrs Busby, came in to play whist, or she went to their houses; during the day, also, she went out a great deal, either on foot or in a chair, to take the waters, visit the shops and meet her acquaintance in the Pump Room or at circulating libraries. She lived comfortably, and kept two maids and a manservant.

As soon as I had been led into her parlour, Mrs Jebb ordered me: 'Take off your hat, child, and let's look at you.'

The bonnet was a straw one that Mrs Ferrars had given me (hitherto my only headgear had been a ragged broad-brimmed hat woven of sedge, which Elinor had condemned as uncouth and fit only for the garden bonfire). I took off my hat and placed it carefully on a chair. It was trimmed with white ribbon and I was extremely proud of it.

Meanwhile Mrs Jebb studied me and I studied her.

She had once been, I thought, a massively built woman, but was now somewhat shrunk, perhaps by age and calamity. But her voice and manner were still commanding. Her face was very large and square, pale-complexioned, rather ugly, the lips much pursed and puckered, the nose bony. Her hooded eyes, light-grey, had a most unblinking, steady regard. Her hair was scanty and plainly dressed and her attire less stylish than what I had observed on ladies as we drove along the streets of Bath; but still it was evident that all her things were carefully chosen and of good quality. She wore handsome jewels.

'Well, now, Pullett,' Mrs Jebb suddenly demanded of the servant who had admitted me. 'Look carefully at the gal. Does she have a colour? A ring? What have you to say about her? Does she give out light? Or darkness?'

Much startled at these obscure questions, I turned my eyes on the maid Pullett, who bore an almost simple-minded appearance, with brown bulging eyes, long narrow face, clouds of soft dark hair beneath her cap and half-open mouth; I would, from her look, have put her down as slightly wanting in wit, but she answered at once quite sensibly (only I had not the least idea what she meant), 'Oh, yes, ma'am, she've a ring. A good one. Blue, quite bright.'

'In that case she may stay,' briskly rejoined Mrs Jebb. 'Take her things up to the back bedroom, Pullett. And you, child, sit down – on that chair, there – and answer my questions.'

'Excuse me, ma'am, but may I first go somewhere and relieve my-self? It has been a long ride and there was nowhere along the way – '

Mrs Jebb nodded slowly, twice. I saw with surprise that I had surprised her, too, and in some way exceeded her expectations of me.

When I returned to the room, she was reading the note that Cousin Elinor had given me to deliver to her.

'Humph, you certainly seem to be a well-educated young gel.—Are you looking forward to school?' she pounced.

'No, ma'am, not very greatly. But I know that it is needful. I have to earn my living.'

'Humph,' she said again. 'Let's see your hands.'

I showed them. There need be no false shame or pride with Mrs Jebb; she was wholly straightforward.

'Yes . . . Unfortunate. *You*'ll never get a husband. However my niece informs me that you are a capable performer on the pianoforte and have a tolerable singing voice. At Mrs Haslam's they will give you lessons on the harp, and other instruments too, I daresay. No doubt there will be an opening for you later as a music teacher.'

I assented politely, without troubling to inform her that I would sooner jump off a cliff.

'Ma'am?'

'Yes, child?'

'What did your maid mean? When she said that I had a blue ring?'

Mrs Jebb nodded again. 'I could see you thinking that Pullett must be a zany, touched in her wits. But she is not. A trifle slow, she may be, but about people she has unerring instinct. She comes of mixed stock: gypsy blood two or three generations back, I don't doubt. She sees people in colour – as you have just been given proof. Blue – your colour – is a good one. Fortunately for you.'

'If I had a bad one, what would it be?'

'Black – or purple – or some reds. No one but a gaby would invite such a person into their house.'

'Are you serious, ma'am?'

'Indeed I am, gal.'

'If I had had a red ring, what would you have done?'

'Turned you out directly into the streets of Bath.'

I suppose I gaped at her, and she looked back at me, half smiling, half scowling. I wondered whether there might be any sailors in the streets of Bath, and how they were provided for soap. I wondered if Mrs Jebb, as well as Pullett, could be slightly mad, have a gap in her thatch, as they put it in Byblow Bottom. But I had received no such intimation from Mr Ferrars or his wife. And Mrs Jebb did not behave like a mad person. She was perfectly brisk and businesslike.

'However,' she went on equably, 'as Pullett vouches for you, I expect we shall deal together well enough. I cannot be bothered with young people around me for a great deal of the time. You will keep to your own quarters, except when I invite you in here, or at meal times. You will run such errands for me as you have time for, along with your school duties. You must find your own way about Bath – my servants have enough to do without attending you through the streets.—You have been used to take care of yourself, I conclude?'

'Indeed I have, ma'am.'

'Humph, yes, here it says – Lady Hariot and that dolt Vexford,' she muttered, reperusing the letter. 'At some other time you shall tell me all about them. Not now. Tomorrow is the Sabbath, no classes at your school; you will of course accompany me to Divine Service in the morning. And in the afternoon you may as well plan your daily route to the establishment in Queen Square. It is no great distance. And I shall expect you to be well-behaved, polite and entirely truthful at all times.'

'Of course, ma'am.'

'Pullett *always* knows when someone is telling a lie,' Mrs Jebb remarked, giving me an exceedingly sharp glance. For the first time I remembered about her arrest by the constables, and the affair of the packet of lace. Which party in that episode had spoken the truth?

It behoves me to get on to good terms with Pullett, I thought. For I was as used to lying as to breathing, and saw no benefit to be gained from discontinuing the practice.

'Shall you accompany me to the school on Monday, ma'am, or shall I go there by myself?'

'Which would you prefer?' she surprised me by saying.

I thought. 'By myself, ma'am – if you do not think that would be improper?'

'No, why? Mrs Haslam is expecting you; she has a letter from Elinor Ferrars. Of course you will have to find your own level in the place. I do not think you will receive much assistance from your cousin Nell; (if she is your cousin, that is). But I daresay your cousin Margaret may be friendly enough.'

Mrs Jebb gave a sniff.

'That will be Miss Margaret Dashwood? Mrs Ferrars' sister? She teaches at the school?'

Another sniff. 'History and literature. Of course the poor thing hoped – when she came to Bath ten years ago – that she would soon secure a husband. But what man in the world ever married a history teacher? Let alone one as silly as Mag Dashwood. She has been at her last prayers for years.—Run to your room, now, child. You have tired me. I must rest before meeting my friends.'

'Thank you, ma'am.' I turned at the door to say, 'I am very obliged to you for having me to live in your house, Mrs Jebb,' and met her disconcerting regard.

'Have you any idea who your father was, gal?' she suddenly rapped out.

'No, ma'am. Not the least in the world.'

'Oh. Very well. That is all. You may go.'

Up in my room I found that Pullett had unpacked my modest belongings and arranged them neatly in cupboards and chests. Quite unused to such a service, I thanked her heartily and received in return a beaming smile, which completely transformed her thin hare's face.

'I daresay you'll find it sad here, at the start, Miss, being used to the country as Missis tells you are,' she said kindly (for the first thing I had done was to run to the window, open the casement and hang out. There was a view across city roofs to a handsome wooded hill – Beechen Cliff, I later learned – and far away, where the sun was setting in the distance, I could fancy I saw the hills of Somerset).

Pullett's sympathy almost undid me. To me, Bath was a huge black ugly place. I had never conceived that a city could be so large. Byblow Bottom, Growly Head, Kinn Hall, Hoby, Triz and Lady Hariot all seemed unbearably distant, lost already in the past.

'I come from a small place myself, Emborough. It took me a mortal time to get accustomed to all the houses and the paved streets, and all the folk everywhere,' Pullett went on. 'But you've a lucky colour, Miss Liza. I won't say you're certain of a smooth passage, for that beant so, but there's allus likely to be *one* as loves you. So try not to fret, and if you'm low-hearted, and in need of a friendly word, why, come down to me and Thomas and Rachel in the kitchen, and we'll try to cheer ye.'

'But what will Mrs Jebb say?'

'She'll never know,' said Pullett simply.

On Sunday morning, wearing a black stuff dress (too long, too loose) which had been discarded by Nell Ferrars, I accompanied Mrs Jebb to the Abbey and sat through what – after Dr Moultrie's skimped offices at Othery – seemed like an interminable desert of prayers, chanting, music, more prayers and long periods of declamation. Once, Mrs Jebb had to prod me sharply because I had fallen asleep, exhausted after a long, sad and wakeful night listening to the hum and clatter of the town outside and the regular cry of the watch.

On the Abbey Green, after the service, I was made known to various of Mrs Jebb's acquaintance, who were all elderly ladies in widows' weeds, or aged gentlemen walking very lame with sticks, or pushed by attendants in Bath chairs.

To my surprise, Mrs Jebb introduced me as 'Miss FitzWilliam' to these people.

On the way home, as she was carried in her chair along Monmouth Street and I walked beside, I said,

'Ma'am, I thought my name –'

'Hush, be quiet,' she said sharply.

And when we were back in the New King Street parlour, she told me, 'Mr Ferrars and I have agreed to expand your name to FitzWilliam. Firstly, it sounds better.'

'But why, ma'am? And what is secondly?'

'Never mind about that now. Just hold your peace and accept what your elders decide is best for you.—Now you had better take Pug for a walk. The way to Queen Square, where you will find

Mrs Haslam's school, is up Chapel Row. It will be as well for you to know how long the walk takes you, since you must be at school by nine o'clock tomorrow morning.'

And so Mrs Jebb turned me loose in Bath, with Pug and my new name. I rambled around, at first dolefully enough, for it was a damp, misty and gloomy afternoon, but by degrees I became fascinated by the city, which was most majestically situated, up and down a steep hillside with many handsome houses. The streets, some of them in the form of circles or crescent shapes, were pleasing to the eye, and peopled with elegantly dressed strangers, sedan chairs and glossy carriages. There were arcades and stores, and a great market building (closed for the Sabbath) wholly unlike anything I had ever seen before. I discovered a few pleasant gardens, luminous at this season with fallen leaves. There was a wonderful bridge, which had shops and houses along it on both sides, and a rushing torrent below. And on the far side of this bridge a noble street led away into open country.

I wondered what Mr Bill and Mr Sam would make of this place. With their abiding passion for sounding cataracts and wild country, I concluded, they would not think highly of it. But they would enjoy the bridge and the river.

'Bunch of hips 'n' haws, Missie?' whined a beggar-girl at a street corner, proffering a dismal posy of a few berries made up with some dead beech leaves. I told her in Byblow Bottom language where she could put her posy, and received a look of startled respect. She had believed me to be a nob.

Pug began to whine – evidently he was not accustomed to such long promenades – and I retraced my steps to New King Street.

Next morning, tidily and correctly dressed, equipped with my umbrella, I presented myself at Mrs Haslam's Seminary for Young Ladies in Queen Square.

What can I relate about the period of time I spent at this school? It was of some value. But by far the greater part of the information I acquired there was nowhere written down on the school syllabus. Lady Hariot had already acquainted me with the manners of good society. What I learned at the school was society's hypocrisies, concealments, rancours and enmities. I learned how neat, sweet-voiced, trimly dressed young ladies are able to conceal in their bosoms the hearts of hoydens and the dispositions of street-girls. I learned how battle can be joined over the needles and thread-bobbins, how darts of malice and snobbery can pierce through the armour of muslin, lace and jaconet.

From the very beginning I understood how fortunate I was, in that I could escape from the compressed and hectic atmosphere of the school each evening and repair to the calm precincts of Mrs Jebb's house. Of course the boarders and parlour boarders at the school heartily despised the day girls who went home at night (and who paid lower fees); taunts and gibes were exchanged between the two parties; the boarders were known as Queensers and the day girls (for some reason) as Pillihens. But, as well as this division, there were many, many exquisitely fine distinctions between the better-off and the worse-off pupils: at the top of the school scale were those whose parents paid the full fees, who attended the school for five or six years in order, it was assumed, that they should acquire enough ladylike accomplishments to equip them for matrimony – and also to keep them out of the way of their friends and families until it became time for them to be presented at Court, attend assemblies at Almack's, endure the ordeal of a London Season, and hope to emerge from this with the necessary nuptial prize. Below them were those whose friends, for various reasons, paid reduced fees, either because they were acquaintances of Mrs Haslam, or taught at the school; below *them* came the ones who, like myself, were not considered eligible candidates for matrimony, and so must learn enough to prepare them for teaching others; and at the very bottom of this melancholy ladder were to be found a group who were paid for by public subscription or some charitable organization in Bath. They were despised by *everybody,* and, indeed, to some degree, served as handmaids to the elevated young ladies in the top levels.

Mrs Haslam, the founder of the school, had long since ceased to play any active part in its functioning. She appeared at daily prayers, a vague old creature, nodding and bemused, pink and powdered, much swathed in shawls. After that she was seen no more. The real administration of the establishment lay in the hands of her deputy, Miss Orrincourt, who interviewed me upon my first arrival there. She was a thin, dry, bracket-faced woman, who walked lame with a stick, and wore an enormous garnet brooch, holding together a great many folds of lace.

She scrutinized me with half-closed eyes, and said, 'All the young ladies in this seminary, Miss FitzWilliam, are very *genteel* young ladies. I could never accept or keep here any that were not. The tone of my establishment is particularly high, and it is my intention to preserve this. Your hand – let me see it; ah; most unfortunate . . .'

Annoyance spurred me to retort: 'I was born so, ma'am.'

'I did not invite you to speak, Miss FitzWilliam.' Each time she pronounced my name she laid a heavy accent on the *Fitz,* as if to remind me of its inauthenticity. 'Ah – you appear to have been well educated in – ah – *bookish* concerns. We have now to see if you can adjust yourself to the ways of polite society – ah – gentlefolk.'

I said that I would try to do my best.

'Scholastically – ah – you appear to be on a level with the top class. But they – ah – being, all of them, considerably older than you, that – ah – would not be satisfactory. You may therefore, for the moment, take your place with the young ladies of the middle group, under the authority of Miss Bush. Yes. Hmn. Miss Bush will tell you how to go on. The room at the end of the hallway. I wish you good-day, Miss FitzWilliam.'

As I was curtseying, about to leave, she called me back. 'Your – ah – aunt, Mrs Montford Jebb – she is well?'

I said yes.

'And your – ah – guardian, Colonel Brandon?'

I said that he was at present on his way back from India; I was not informed concerning his state of health.

'Ah – yes. In this establishment, Miss FitzWilliam, it is not considered at all polite to – ah – discuss – or allude to – the connections of other students. To gossip is *wholly* unladylike.'

Later, I was to ponder this piece of direction. For in fact the case was exactly the converse. At any moment of liberty, when the girls were in the garden, or walking two by two to concerts, or between classes, or on the stairs, or in the hallways, the prime, the *only* topic of conversation was people's family connections. Whose uncle the Duke was arriving to stay at the White Hart; whose aunt the Countess had rented a house in Paragon; whose parents were coming to take their daughter driving to Wells; whose dashing brother was betrothed to a West Indian heiress. So I supposed that what Miss Orrincourt really meant was that *I* should not talk about *my* connections.

Not that I had any intention of doing so.

My first encounter with Nell Ferrars was not propitious.

Mrs Jebb had told me that for its day pupils Mrs Haslam's establishment did not supply luncheon and I must therefore take care to provide myself with my own noontide refreshment each day (from which I understood she did not wish to see me back in New King Street for this meal). On my first day Mrs Rachel the cook had furnished me with a pear and a piece of bread-and-butter, and I had betaken myself to the school garden, a largish pleasant area with a few flower-beds and some trampled gravel paths at the rear of the house. Here I had perched myself on a low wall bordering a rose-bed, while I munched my pear and sighed for the peace of Growly Head, when I was approached by a pair of young ladies. One of them, large, long-faced, fair and plain, I instantly guessed to be the daughter of Edward Ferrars; she was remarkably like him, but the features that made his countenance open and authoritative were too large and pronounced in hers, and gave her a heavy, overbearing aspect. She was tall, like her mother, but had none of Cousin Elinor's fine, worn distinction, evident always despite her shabby attire. Nell was far better dressed than her mother; I could guess at what cost to the latter.

'You must be the new Pillihen – are you not? Eliza FitzWilliam,' she announced, and then both she and her companion (a slender, elegantly dressed girl with very narrow hands and feet) exchanged a number of tittering, low-voiced witticisms concerned with my choice of site for a picnic. I answered yes, composedly, to her question, finished my pear and wiped my fingers on the square of butter-muslin in which Mrs Rachel had wrapped my luncheon. Then, standing up, I walked away to rinse my fingers in a small fountain beyond the rose-bed. This (I heard later) greatly disconcerted Miss Ferrars, who had expected me to ask some questions in return, which would have given her the satisfaction of snubbing me, by informing me that new pupils must not speak unless invited to do so.

Thereafter Nell took pains (when it lay within her power) to hold me up to ridicule among her cronies; my ignorance of dancing, of fine needlework, of most card games, of London gossip, of fashion, of nearly all the common topics of talk among my fellow-pupils, each in turn was sneered at and made fun of; and I passed several irksome and tedious months before acquiring sufficient proficiency in these areas for the mockery to die down.

Needless to say, this contemptuous usage spurred me on to exert myself, so as to pick up the necessary knowledge as speedily as I could. Furthermore, it soon became plain to me that Miss Ferrars was herself obliged to work hard – exceedingly hard – to curry favour with the set of well-to-do young ladies to whose company she aspired; being less well furnished than they in departments such as clothes, school materials, work-box, dancing shoes and the like, she must continually run errands for them, contrive to be in attendance at all times, and supply a regular feast of tattle, jokes and gossip.

I never grew to like Nell; she was too earnest a self-seeker to be likeable; but in the end I grew to feel sorry for her, since her great wish for popularity seemed to receive so scant a reward, and all these matters appeared so desperately important to her. I myself had few friends at Mrs Haslam's, but this never dismayed me, because I so mightily preferred my own company to most that was offered.

– Some young ladies, by degrees, despite my odd hands and my dubious origins, made overtures; but compared with the friends of my past, Mr Bill and Mr Sam, Hoby, Triz and Lady Hariot, they seemed of little importance, and while not rejecting their company I never went out of my way to solicit it. This attitude of independence did me no harm; indeed I believe that by the end of my sojourn at the school I was reasonably well-liked.

The teaching was tolerably good – for those who cared to apply themselves; and, especially in music and singing, I could feel that my time was being usefully employed. But to what end? I still had not the least intention of becoming a music teacher, and I feared that my physical abnormality would preclude any operatic or stage work.

Of course I had looked about the school for Nell's aunt, Mrs Ferrars' younger sister Margaret, and was not a little disappointed by my first encounter with her, which occurred a week or so after I had entered the establishment.

Miss Dashwood taught literature to the senior girls, and one morning – my own class had, for some reason, terminated early, and I was on my way to eat my nuncheon in the garden, as remained my habit until it grew too cold – passing the half-open door of the senior classroom, I was thunderstruck to hear the girls all together chanting familiar lines:

> The Ice was here, the Ice was there
> The Ice was all around
> It crack'd and growl'd and roar'd and howl'd –
> Like noises of a swound.

I stood spellbound in the doorway of the classroom until the teacher, espying me, exclaimed, 'Heyday, who have we here?'

'That is the new young lady, Miss Dashwood,' somebody said. 'Miss FitzWilliam.'

'Well? And do you like our poem so much, child?' Miss Dashwood asked.

'Oh yes, ma'am, thank you – but I know it already.'

'You do? But how can that be?'

Just then the clangour of a great bell drowned my reply, but later on Miss Dashwood had the curiosity to seek me out in the garden, and to interrogate me. I told her of my acquaintance with Mr Bill and Mr Sam.

'You lucky, lucky little thing! What a great piece of good fortune for you to have been acquainted with such a pair! Their works have now been published in a volume,' she told me. 'It is called *Lyrical Ballads*. Would you like to read it?'

'Oh indeed, ma'am, I should.'

Miss Dashwood was a dark, intense-looking lady of, I suppose, twenty-seven years; her features were too lumpy and irregular for her ever to have been considered handsome, which, I supposed, was why, unlike her sisters she had never married, though she appeared good-natured enough. However there was something whimsical, freakish, over-emotional about her, which made me slightly mistrust her; I thought she looked unreliable. I would never entrust a secret to her. But at least she in no way resembled her niece. I believe there was little affection between them; Nell, as was her habit, made fun of her old-maid aunt.

Miss Dashwood asked me for descriptions of Mr Sam and Mr Bill and listened with keen attention to all I had to relate, interjecting, at frequent intervals, cries of astonishment at my good fortune and eulogies of these men.

'A pair of poets such as this country has not seen in many years!' Then, impulsively, she exclaimed, 'Poor child! And you have never met your own father, I conclude? For he was a wonderful man also – a wonderful, wonderful man!'

'Good heavens, ma'am!' I was utterly astounded by this declaration, coming so unexpectedly. '*You have met my father? You knew him?*'

'Oh, indeed yes, child! At one time he was a great, great friend of my elder sister, Marianne.'

Then, suddenly recollecting herself, she clapped a hand across her mouth and stared at me over it with huge eyes. 'Oh, good God! Mercy on me! What have I done? I was instructed never, ever to mention a word of the matter.'

'By whom, ma'am?' I quickly asked.

'By my brother-in-law, Mr Edward Ferrars. A most right-thinking, sensible man. He said – he wrote – Oh, how dreadfully unfortunate! Pray, pray, forget what I said, my dear. I had no business to be saying it – none, *none*. It was wholly improper in me. I am a fool – I blurt things out. Excuse me – I must make haste to seek out Cecilia Castleforth and hear her recitation.'

She went off at blundering speed, fairly running away from me, and took with her, to my great chagrin, the volume of poems I had so eagerly looked forward to reading. Thereafter she sedulously avoided me outside of classes and, it seemed to me, took pains to leave a room if I should chance to enter it. The next I heard of Miss Dashwood was that she had temporarily quitted the school, in the company of Miss Helen Smythe-Burghley, who had left the senior class in order to commence her first London season, and whose parents, urged by their daughter, had requested the services of dear Miss Dashwood to act as *dame de compagnie* to Miss Helen during the succeeding months, for which function she would doubtless be paid a great deal more than she received as a teacher at Mrs Haslam's. It was believed that she might return in due course (presumably if Helen received a proposal) but nobody expected that would be very soon.

It may well be imagined how utterly transfixed I was by this brief and tantalizing exchange. Had Miss Dashwood actually quitted the school for fear of inadvertently letting out more information to me, and incurring her brother-in-law's wrath? Or was it sheer misfortune that had taken her away just then?

Ever since I commanded the power of coherent thought I had, very naturally, wondered from time to time about my father, what kind of a man he might have been; but as I grew older and more sceptical, and accepted the usages and standards of Byblow Bottom, I had grown also to accept that a man who would deflower and then abandon a young girl of seventeen was no kind of character to look up to with admiration or affection; on the contrary, he must be the most despicable scoundrel, and it would afford me no pleasure or benefit ever to meet him. If, indeed, he had not long ago perished in some affray, or died in a debtors' prison, or been transported to Botany Bay. So – although curiosity pricked me every now and then – I had devoted no serious thought to him for years past.

But now – how was this long-established, half-consciously formed portrait of my father as a dissolute, callous, feckless ne'er-do-well to be conjoined with Miss Dashwood's description – 'a wonderful, wonderful man'? And 'a great, great friend of my sister Marianne'? All my previous suspicions boiled up again; was I, in truth, the daughter of the said Marianne, now Mrs Colonel Brandon, in India? (Or wherever the Colonel and his lady presently were, halfway back to England, presumably.) Could this be the fact at the bottom of all this secrecy, the things that must never be mentioned, the haste to get me away from Delaford, the interdict on Margaret Dashwood telling me what she knew?

What had Edward Ferrars said: '*He* might come to hear'? *Who* might come to hear? My father? They spoke of my likeness to somebody – to whom? There was a miniature hanging in the parlour at Delaford Rectory – 'my sister,' Mrs Ferrars had said when I admired it. It depicted a beauty, brown-skinned, with brilliant dark eyes and raven ringlets. A charitable friend (if I had one) might describe the colour of my red-brown hair as auburn, and the colour of my eyes as grey; but the youthful denizens of Byblow Bottom, when not addressing me as Lizzie Lug-fist, commonly called me Copperknob, or simply Ginger; and it seemed to me highly improbable that I could be the daughter of that dazzling brunette. But – it was true – our features, the shape of our faces, did show a considerable similarity. I had noticed it.

While staying in the village of Delaford I had made cautious inquiries about my guardian Colonel Brandon and his helpmeet, the lord and lady of the Manor. Everybody agreed that he was a fine, excellent landlord, serious and grave in aspect but considerate and benevolent; and she was a lovely young lady, only eighteen at the time she wed the Colonel, less than half the age of her bridegroom, but wonderfully devoted to him, and, though very different in character – for she was as lively, spirited and talkative as he was sober and silent – yet they got on so well together that their mutual fondness was the admiration of the whole country. And when he rejoined his regiment, nothing would serve but she must pack up and accompany him to India, despite the wicked climate, and the ferocity of the natives, despite the warnings of her friends, and the fact that she had seemed very happy at Delaford; and she had thrown herself with vigour and enthusiasm into many schemes for the welfare of the villagers. And although it was a pity that she did not show any signs of conceiving – yet it was early days still, she only just out of her twenties, and just as well she should not bear a child while off in foreign parts.

Could she have borne me before she married the Colonel?

But no – for she could hardly have married the Colonel so soon after I was born. It had been told me that my mother was only seventeen when she gave birth to me. That only a few months later she had become Brandon's bride seemed in the highest degree improbable.

So my mother must have been somebody else – but who?

Nell Ferrars had no information about my parentage, of this I was certain, for if she had any clue as to my origins she would indubitably have made use of it to tease and taunt me. She always addressed me as *Miss FitzWilliam* with satirical emphasis, as if she entirely questioned my right to use that name; but she could never have withheld a real fact, if she had been armed with one, any more than she could have addressed an inferior person with civility, or a superior without sycophancy.

Mrs Jebb, I suspected, knew somewhat more than she communicated; but there was no prying information from Mrs Jebb; one might as well put questions to the statues of Peter and Paul on the Abbey front.

If I were ever to discover anything about my parentage – and dearly did I wish to – it must be by my own unaided efforts.

The years of my attendance at Mrs Haslam's school crept by – slowly enough – marked only by the dogged, painstaking acquisition of more knowledge and more musical proficiency; until another accidental encounter placed further information within my grasp.

But I anticipate.

Previous to my first Christmas in Bath, on learning that the school closed for a week, I had wondered if there was any possibility of my being invited to pass the holiday at Delaford Rectory. I knew that Nell expected to return home. But I was soon disabused of such a notion.

'Taking all the circumstances into consideration,' wrote Elinor Ferrars in a letter delivered by the carrier; 'my mother's precarious state of health, the inclemency of the weather, the expense of the journey, the bad condition of the roads, and the value set by Aunt Jebb upon your company, we think it best you remain in Bath over the Christmas holiday.'

Most of this was news to me. That the weather was inclement and the roads bad, I thought, need form no greater impediment to my visiting Delaford than it did for Nell; and that Mrs Jebb set such particular store by my company I took leave to doubt, though we got on comfortably enough. But still, on the whole, I was quite content to remain in New King Street. A whole week in close proximity to Nell's hostility would be no treat, even with the opportunity to walk in green fields and breathe country air.

'Please convey our warm seasonal greetings to Mrs Jebb,' continued Cousin Elinor's spiky writing, 'along with this pincushion which I made her. It is stuffed with coffee grounds, sovereign against rust. If you can inform me of any other small token that would be acceptable to her – thread-cases or card-racks – or any hand-knitted garment that would be of use to her, which I could make, I should be obliged to you for the information. And

I hope, my dear Eliza, that you yourself have been able to procure some small but appropriate seasonable gift in acknowledgement of your obligations to her . . .'

Obligation be blowed, thought I, reverting to the usage of Byblow Bottom; Mrs Jebb gets paid for my lodgement, does she not? And further to that, I walk Pug for her twice a day, I read aloud the paper and the works of Mrs Edgeworth, I sing to her, I play the harp to her snuffy friends four evenings out of five, I write and deliver her notes, I buy her cakes at Sally Lunn's shop and fetch her novels from the circulating library, besides trimming her black satin cap with new feathers and hemming her a great square muslin shawl. In fact I might, if I were Miss Margaret Dashwood, expect to be paid a substantial wage for my services as *dame de compagnie*.

(And pray that this will not be your occupation for the rest of your life, said an inner voice.)

When I presented the tatting-trimmed pincushion 'with the compliments of Cousin Elinor Ferrars' Mrs Jebb looked at me very sharply and shrewdly over the rims of her spectacles.

'Humph, gel! So they employ you as a messenger? To enlist my goodwill, hey?'

I said mildly that it was the season of goodwill.

'Ho! But I notice they do not invite you back to spend the holiday with whey-faced Miss Nell?'

'I am happy to remain in Bath, ma'am.'

'So I should think! The only night I passed in that parsonage I was nearly brought to my terminus by lumbago and spasmodic bile – I never entered so cold a house in my life and do not intend ever to do so again. So: I know how it is; the poor creatures are expecting to come in for something handsome in my will. And – if at any time

---

they should ask you (though I daresay they are too genteel to come flat out with it) – you may inform them that you have no information as to my testamentary intentions. But they may as well know they can have no claims on my future consideration. Nor, my child, can *you* – supposing they should have encouraged you to entertain any such notion.' Another sharp look over her glasses.

'No, ma'am, that they never have. Nor, indeed, would I dream of such a thing.'

Though Nell had, in fact, oftentimes hinted about 'expectations.'

'I am happy to hear it,' she rejoined drily. 'So all you do is done for love, eh?'

'No,' I said calmly, 'not for love. But from – from friendship, and because you are kind enough, ma'am, to supply me with a comfortable, respectable home.'

. . . Which was true enough. I did feel a sober regard, a tolerant comradeship for the stoic, gritty quality which I recognized in the old lady. And, though I could not say that I felt a warm welcome when I entered the door of Number Two New King Street, I had come to understand that a place had been established there for me as part of the household.

If Mrs Jebb wished to be alone with her whist-playing cronies, I retired to my bedroom with its view of far-away hills; or I descended to the kitchen. Here Pullett and Mrs Rachel the cook were always ready to tell fortunes with cards and tea-leaves.

– 'Shall I ever find my father?' was always my first question at these sessions. But that was a question Mrs Rachel was never able to answer satisfactorily.

'There's two figures here, dearie – an old king and an old queen. Neither of 'em's going to bring ye much in the way of fortune. But there's a building. And there's a little tiny child – like a dwarf – and here's a fellow looks like as he's had the pox – never did I see such a pitted front, maybe he's a coal-miner – and a whole heap of money sliding about – like water on a ship's deck. That man have it in his power to do ye a plenty good or a plenty harm, best keep the right side of him, dearie –'

'If I knew who he is.'

'All in good time ye'll find that out. Hark! There's Mistress's bell a-ringing. Tom, go see what she wants . . .'

'So!' said Mrs Jebb, scowling at me as was her way when she wished to conceal any deeper feeling. 'I know as well as any what it means to be isolated and have no refuge in the festive season.—Now run along, child, and take Pug with you, or he will make water on the Turkish rug.'

So on Christmas Day I accompanied Mrs Jebb twice to Divine Service, and then was given my liberty to amuse myself and escort Pug into the Sydney Gardens. It was a damp, misty freezing day, not a soul stirring in Bath except myself.

Later I ate beef and Christmas pudding solemnly with Mrs Jebb, and remembered how little attention had been paid to the festival in Byblow Bottom. Seldom did Hannah serve any meal at all, by noontide she would be incapably drunk, half of her condition left over from celebrations the previous night.

Stealing up to my cold bedroom I wrote a couple of long letters, one to Lady Hariot and Triz at Lisbon, in care of Lady Anna Ffoliot. I had heard from them once or twice, briefly, I knew they were there. But now there was talk that Bonaparte had sent Junot with an army into Portugal, as he had already spread his armies over Europe. Portugal was our ally, but such a small, helpless country. Would my friends be safe there? Would they return to England?

Then, without much more confidence, I wrote a letter to Hoby. (A girl in my class at school, Tilly Percival, had a brother at Eton; she had furnished me with the address.) I asked Hoby how he was, and told what I thought might interest him of my own doings . . .

Then I sat, dejected, for an hour longer, listening to the pat of rain on the casement, until summoned downstairs to sing ballads to the old ladies.

Chapter 5

IN MY FOURTH YEAR AT MRS HASLAM'S SCHOOL I BEGAN GIVING music lessons to some of the younger pupils. And in my fifth year the lessons were extended to pupils of my own age, and singing was added. This was an occasion of considerable spiteful comment on the part of Miss Nell Ferrars, who had never become my friend; indeed as we grew older our mutual dislike increased. Nell made it her business to propagate the story that my advancement in the school was due solely to the partiality of Mr Tregarron the music master, a handsome and melancholy-looking man. This, in fact, was not so, though he and I were excellent friends and I was to some degree in his confidence. When I was seventeen he became involved in an affair of honour which terminated in a duel; Mr Tregarron was shot in the thigh, inflammation ensued, and for some time his life was despaired of; and even when that anxiety was allayed, it was still considered needful that his leg must be sacrificed.

Miss Orrincourt, naturally, was outraged and shocked by this episode. If Mr Tregarron had not been such a particularly well-liked and capable teacher, with very superior connections among those of the highest consequence in Bath, he would certainly have been given his marching orders. But since the school's high reputation depended largely on the excellence of its musical curriculum, of which he was the prime buttress and support, she found herself obliged, not precisely to condone the disgraceful affair, but at least to turn a blind eye, like the noble Nelson.

Mr Tregarron's connections had procured the young ladies of the school choir a series of engagements in the weekly winter concerts held at the Assembly Rooms, which must add substantially to the prestige of her establishment; she therefore swallowed her indignation and contented herself with transferring many of his duties to myself. Indeed, I foresaw with gloom that in years to come, if I did not soon make some move to alter my prospects, I should find myself fixed for life as Senior Music Teacher at Mrs Haslam's.

Fate, however, decreed otherwise.

A few of us were to sing solos at the concerts, and I was one of those so chosen. 'Not,' as Mr Tregarron kindly told me, 'that your voice is anything out of the common, my dear Miss Fitz, but it is loud and clear and well-pitched; and that is all that the dyspeptic old grumblers in our audience will care about.'

You may be sure that Miss Nell Ferrars had plenty to say about this preferment, also; but just then, very fortunately for me, she received a greatly prized and much-laboured-for invitation to accompany her chiefest crony, the handsome but sour-tongued Lady Helen Lauderdale on a visit to the latter's parents in London. Nell's absence was, I must confess, no small relief to me and I heartily hoped (as no doubt she did too) that she might catch the eye of some eligible *parti* while under the Lauderdale roof in Berkeley Square.

Some of the young ladies chosen to sing alone were in a rare fright about it, others were as proud as peacocks; but I had no strong feelings in the matter, either way.

A childhood passed in Byblow Bottom carries this benefit: it engenders great fortitude and a wholesome indifference to mere social anxieties. Taking part in a public concert would be no especial ordeal compared with some episodes in my past; or, for example, with the indignities and misusages that poor Hoby had been suffering these last four years at Eton. (I had received some information about these, for he had in due course replied to my letters, not very often, but once or twice a year; and the tales he had to tell of dire doings in the Long Chamber, even conveyed in Hoby's blotched, ill-written and mis-spelled orthography, were enough to make any normal person turn faint with horror.—Yet thanks to Fortune, Hoby seemed to be surviving, and even learning to give as good as he got. He wrote his approval of my being so creditably established in Bath. This interested me as of old he would probably have despised such a humdrum existence.)

Mrs Jebb and Pullett, on learning that I was to make an appearance at a public recital went into conference, and came to the unsurprising conclusion that my wardrobe was inadequate.

'She has to do New King Street credit,' Mrs Jebb declared. 'Which, as matters stand, she emphatically does not. You cannot sing in public, child, wearing a five-year-old cast-off Sunday gown that once belonged to Nell Ferrars.'

'The difficulty is, ma'am, that I have nothing better.'

To me, my wardrobe had never been a matter of much concern; so long as my things were not in actual holes, I was satisfied; and this was just as well, for it seemed that the funds assigned by Colonel

Brandon, which had been used for my education and support, had begun to run low and had recently dwindled away altogether.

'It appears that my brother-in-law quitted India, after he suffered a severe wound at the Battle of Gavilghar,' wrote Elinor Ferrars. 'But we are still wholly uncertain as to Colonel Brandon and my sister's whereabouts. It seems most likely that they have been obliged to make a stay somewhere on their journey back to Europe, perhaps in order for him to undergo further medical treatment, or to pass some months in rest and convalescence.'

Or perhaps he has just died, I thought . . .

At the same time I had a letter from the lawyers.

'We deeply regret, Miss FitzWilliam,' wrote Mr Melplash, 'that we cannot continue to authorize the allocation of funds for your educational requirements since the sum allotted for contingencies has been used up, and lacking any further direction from Colonel Brandon on the matter.'

Since by now a good three-quarters of my time at Mrs Haslam's seminary was passed in teaching, my position at the school was not in jeopardy; Miss Orrincourt found me too useful for there to be any suggestion of her dispensing with my services. And, as I had begun giving a few private singing lessons in the city, I was able to continue paying Mrs Jebb a small amount for my board and lodging. New clothes I simply managed without; since I had arrived in Bath my height had not greatly increased, and the substantial wardrobe of cast-off clothes supplied by Mrs Ferrars, all the garments which were of heavy and durable stuffs, had survived being patched, let out, darned and periodically made-over by Pullett and myself. Nell Ferrars had long since grown bored with her own witticisms about them. But my only superior gown, a skimpy sprigged muslin with a blue trim, sadly worn and faded, though doubtless well-enough for evenings spent playing and singing to Mrs Jebb and her whist-minded cronies, would be but a poor advertisement for Mrs Haslam's school.—Indeed Miss Orrincourt had expressed concern in the matter. She hoped I was provided with 'something unexceptionable to wear, some suitable toilet', and I had hastily assured her that this would be no problem.

'If, ma'am,' I said to Mrs Jebb, 'you would be kind enough to wait for your week's lodging money until Saturday – I understand the performers are to be remunerated for the concert –'

'Tush, child, never trouble your head about that. Funds will be found.' And she added drily, 'I shall enjoy an excursion to Wetherells'. There no doubt we can find some suitable stuff and Pullett shall make it up for you.' Catching a gleam in her eye and detecting also a faintly anxious look on the face of Pullett, I recalled that, when Mrs Jebb had been accused of stealing lace, Wetherells' had been the draper's shop in Stall Street where the alleged misdemeanour had taken place. No doubt my hostess enjoyed returning there at intervals to tease them.—Mrs Jebb, though she very seldom smiled, had her own bleak and dour sense of humour.

The trip to Wetherells' began uneventfully enough. A piece of India muslin was chosen and purchased. It had a small black dot and a fine black trim.

'In view of the colour of your hair and your complexion,' Mrs Jebb observed with her usual dispassion, 'you will do well never to indulge in bright or gaudy colours.'

'So I have always understood, ma'am.'

Some pairs of gloves were inspected and discarded. Gloves were always a problem for me. 'I daresay I can find an old pair of my own to lend you,' said Mrs Jebb, who was never, at any time, lavish in her disbursements. 'And your feet, at least, will be out of sight behind the piano, so we need not worry about shoes or stockings unduly.'

On the way home from Stall Street, Mrs Jebb stalked ahead with Pug. She had a curious, stately gait, setting each foot very firm and flat upon the ground, as if to prevent the paving-stones from rising up in rebellion against her. Following behind with Pullett, who carried the bundles, I murmured in her ear:

'Pullett, the man from the draper's shop is coming after us. Do you not think that is rather queer?'

Pullett looked round, and her hare's eyes started in fright.

'Oh, Miss!' she breathed. 'What ever can he be after?'

Now Mrs Jebb turned round.

'What are you two mumbling about?'

She twitched on Pug's lead, he set up a yapping, and she dropped the muff which she carried as well as an umbrella, for the usual chilly Bath drizzle infused the atmosphere. I caught up the muff, brushing off a little mud, and restored it to Mrs Jebb just as the man from the draper's shop came alongside of us and blocked the footway.

'Well, sir, well?' said Mrs Jebb. 'What is this about? Why, pray, do you impede our passage? Did you perhaps discover that you over-charged me?'

'No, ma'am' – Mr Wetherell was a tallow-faced, nervous fellow, given to thrusting his hands in and out of his pockets, then rubbing them rapidly together; he did so now – 'No, ma'am, but being uneasy in my thoughts I made so bold as to run after you, besides calling Mr Sunwill the constable of the watch' – another man appeared, as if by clockwork, behind him – 'being, you see, Missis, uneasy in my mind, I couldn't think it right or proper to allow – er, that is to say, ma'am, *not* to allow –'

'Not to allow *what,* you tiresome man?' demanded Mrs Jebb impatiently. 'Will you kindly stop jabbering at us, here in the wet, and permit me to proceed on my way?'

Mr Sunwill the constable, in top hat and shabby frock-coat, now spoke up. 'Mr Wetherell, you see, ma'am,' he said in a tone of apology, 'he tells me that he reckons he saw you tuck a pair o' black silk gloves into your muff – when it was laid down upon the counter of his shop back there, do you see. O' course, maybe it was done quite accidental-like, these little occurrences *do* occur. So, you won't raise any objection to our just taking a look, ma'am? In the muff?'

'That is a wholly nonsensical and outrageous accusation,' replied Mrs Jebb with total calm. 'And I *do* have the strongest possible objection to your making any such search.'

After which we all remained gazing at one another, at a stand, in the drizzle, entirely blocking the footway.

Pullett, casting me an anxious, frantic, imploring look, then addressed her mistress: 'Ma'am, wouldn't it just be simplest to do as the man says? In order to save time and bother, like?'

I judged that it was the moment for me to intervene.

'There is unquestionably some foolish mistake here,' said I. 'Certainly we did look at a pair of black silk gloves in the shop, I remember them well' – which I did, for I had tried them on; the left was a tolerable fit but the right one too small. And, of course, there was the finger difficulty – 'but this person here, Mr Wetherell, then himself removed them from the counter. In fact, I seem to recall seeing him put them in his pocket.'

'A likely story!' said the constable. 'Why in the world would he do that, Miss?'

'I cannot imagine why, it struck me as very odd at the time.'

'Ma'am, why not *let* them look in your muff, where's the harm?' implored Pullett. 'It will save us all standing here any longer in the mizzle.'

Which by now had increased to a regular downpour.

So, with the utmost ill-will, Mrs Jebb handed the grey squirrel-fur muff to Sunwill. He with his large gnarled hands explored inside it – I observed Mrs Jebb give this process a distasteful glance – but he discovered nothing, save a small paper of brandy-balls.

'Now,' I said briskly, 'perhaps Mr Wetherell will be so obliging as to turn out his own pockets.'

To which Mr Wetherell responded with a most indignant outcry.

'A fine notion! Why should I do any such thing? It is *my* goods that were pilfered.'

'Nay, but I think you should,' remonstrated the constable. 'After all, the lady allowed us to look in her muff. And no one's said anything about pilfering.'

'It ain't right! It's as good as making out I bore false witness –'

Without more ado, I stepped up to him and thrust my hands into his pockets. Sure enough, in the right-hand one was a pair of black silk gloves, fastened together by a short twist of black silk cord.

'There, what did I tell you?' I remarked mildly, handing them to the constable. 'We all commit such absent-minded acts at one time or another. Without being aware of it, the man put them in his own pocket. Now, I trust, we can all be on our way.'

I moved past Mr Wetherell, contriving, as I did so, to kick him pretty sharply on the shin – a manoeuvre I had perfected years ago in Byblow Bottom where it was a necessity of life to conduct one's attack unobtrusively and then remove oneself with the greatest dispatch.

I saw him turn white with pain and outrage as our little convoy proceeded smoothly on its way.

Afterwards, I was to regret this piece of foolish self-indulgence.

Mrs Jebb did not ever allude to that incident, then or later. But she lent me a handsome cashmere shawl to wear over the pretty black-and-white muslin dress which Pullett and I fashioned from the material we had bought. And Pullett herself crocheted me a pair of black net gloves, taking great pains to construct them with two fingers joined together, so that my deformity need not be too obvious.

My performance, on the first night of the recitals, was nothing out of the common way – or so I considered, and Mr Tregarron confirmed my opinion – (he, poor fellow, lacking a leg, had to be wheeled to the Assembly Rooms in a Bath chair) – but, for some wayward reason, I satisfied the public fancy, and was encored over and over. I had begun by singing a group of folk songs, and some verses from Shakespeare: 'Come away, come away, Death', which I had set to an air of my own. For my last encore, since the audience of richly dressed valetudinarians continued to cry, 'Bis! Bis! More! More!' I chose a song greatly beloved by Mr Sam and Mr Bill, in which I had joined with them a hundred times:

> Oh, *she* looked out of the window, as white as any milk,
> And *he* looked into the window, as black as any silk.
>> Hollo, hollo, hollo, hollo, you coal-black Smith
>> Oh, what is your silly song?
>> I never shall change my maiden name,
>> That I have kept so long . . .

It was plain that many of the audience knew it too, and all joined in. As the *Bath Echo* said next day, 'It was an event unprecedented in the annals of the Winter Concert Season . . .'

Mrs Jebb grumbled, 'I never bargained for this! All these old fellows coming to call – Lord Glastonbury, Lord Frome, and now the Bishop! Where am I to find biscuits and Madeira wine to feed them all?' But in fact she was quite amused. For her it was like a return to the old days in Paragon. And besides, when the gentlemen came calling, I was generally off at my duties in Queen Square. This I did not in the least regret. Lord Glastonbury and the Bishop – a pair of whiskery seventy-year-olds – reminded me a little too forcibly of Dr Moultrie.

But soon I was to have an adventure of my own.

After several of the concerts I had noticed a group of young men staring at me very attentively, as if they would have liked an introduction. But this was not to be: Miss Orrincourt had been most stringent in her decree that the young ladies who took part in the performances must be escorted away from the Rooms the very moment that their part in the entertainment was concluded. Back to Queen Square we rolled in a hired conveyance; and from there, once the young ladies had been dispatched to their hard beds and their Napoleon blankets (with tapes attached, so that they could be worn as outer garments in the event of a sudden French invasion taking place in the middle of the night), I was graciously permitted to make the best of my own way home to New King Street.

Sometimes a party of young gallants would assemble near Mrs Haslam's school to applaud our return there after a concert, but they were prevented from approaching us too closely by the school porter. And since I did not choose to walk the streets of

Bath alone at night, being concerned not to endanger my hitherto unblemished reputation in Bath society, I had persuaded Thomas, Mrs Jebb's manservant, to meet and escort me home on these occasions. This he very obligingly did for a weekly fee of sixpence, unknown to his mistress who from the outset had made it plain that I must not expect such services.

I was accustomed to slip away from the garden gate, where Thomas would be waiting for me, and had not so far been detected.

Of course the young ladies of the school giggled and sighed and languished over these fashionable admirers.

'They are a group known as the Bath Beaux,' explained Miss Cleone Artingstall. 'Oh – they are all so handsome! Lord Edward Weatherspill, Augustus Link, Daniel Dane-Fotherby – but especially Lord Harry ffinch-ffrench!'

'Come, Miss Artingstall, sing your scales,' I suggested.

'Nay, how can I be expected to sing scales when I think of Lord Harry? Have you looked at him, Miss FitzWilliam?'

'No, I cannot say that I have.'

'He is so romantic – with his tangled elf-locks and his flashing dark eyes! So like Lord Byron.—Oh, Miss FitzWilliam – *have* you read "Hours of Idleness"?'

I had, and considered Byron's verses inferior in every way to those of my two friends.

'The scale of C major, Miss Artingstall.'

'He is the younger son of the Duke of Flint.'

'C major.'

'Oh, bother C major!'

'Miss Orrincourt says that no young lady can expect to shine in polite society unless she has a mastery of the rudiments of music.'

So at last, sighing and grumbling, she applied herself.

'I don't know how you can be so hard-hearted, Miss Fitz. When I think of Lord Harry my heart melts inside me.'

My defence was not so much hardness of heart as lack of interest; the distant group of young beaux, with their smirks and murmured innuendoes, making eyes at the young ladies from the seminary, impressed me not at all. But one day I chanced to encounter Lord Harry on his own, and that proved a very different matter.

The series of winter concerts had ended: spring, rainy, tardy and reluctant, was beginning to creep through the streets and gardens of Bath. I had resumed my habit of taking Pug for an evening stroll in the Green Park. There was a small iron gate leading to an inner garden, which, I suppose, had once belonged to a private house. Here I used to ramble with Pug (now becoming aged and asthmatic) because the early flowers in this sheltered spot, crocuses and snow-drops, made a poignant reminder of the gardens at Kinn Hall where, between deep banks, the little brook dropped from level to level, and there would often be spring flowers in January, or even December. I wondered, walking here, how Triz and Lady Hariot were faring, whether they were still in Portugal. It was long since I had heard from them. The French had reached Oporto now, and were all over Spain; Napoleon had set his brother Joseph on the throne in Madrid. Perhaps my friends were safe enough in Lisbon; British troops were there, still. And now there was talk of Sir Arthur Wellesley being sent out to the Peninsula to do battle against the French forces under the command of Soult and Ney. Colonel Brandon, I knew, had served under Wellesley in India; perhaps (if healed of his wound) he too might have decided to rejoin his old commander, if Sir Arthur should take command there? But, in that case, what would Mrs Brandon do? Would she accompany her husband? Or return to England?

All these speculations were sad and fruitless. I had heard nothing from Mrs Ferrars as to the Colonel's whereabouts. My only news of the war came from Mrs Jebb, who, on her regular excursions to the Pump Room, devoted at least half an hour each morning to careful perusal of the newspapers; she had been bitterly disapproving of Sir John Moore's retreat to Coruña. 'Trust a man to make such a botch-up of the business! If a female had been in command there would have been no such retreat. We would soon have sent that Soult about his business, and Bonaparte also!' (Boney-party, she pronounced him.)

'You should be at the Horseguards, ma'am,' I said, teasing her, and she seriously replied, 'You are right, child. Wars – and utterly stupid, costly wars, at that – will continue, no question, until government lies in the hands of females. And that will not be in my lifetime, nor in yours, neither.'

Quitting the little garden, in the February dusk, I caught a finger of my glove in the rusty latch of the gate and stood trying to disentangle it without breaking any of the silk and worsted threads. In this I was much hampered by Pug, who wheezed and twitched impatiently at his lead.

'Allow me to assist you, madam,' said a courteous voice over my shoulder, and a large male hand appeared, which skilfully detached the twisted strands from the rough latch. 'Quiet, sir!' the voice admonished Pug. 'Can you not see your mistress is in difficulties?'

Startled and subdued, Pug desisted from his pulling.

'I am very much obliged to you, sir,' I said, glad that my left, or better hand had been the object of his solicitude. The right one, holding on to Pug's leash, I tucked well under my mantle.

'There can be no obligation in the case. I have been longing for such a chance to introduce myself ever since I heard you sing. Miss FitzWilliam, is it not? I am Harry ffinch-ffrench. I know all about you, Miss FitzWilliam, because I have a cousin, Maria Glanville, at Mrs Haslam's school. And she tells me many wonderful things about you, Miss FitzWilliam, including the fact that you are a great devotee of poetry – which I am too! I cannot tell you how eagerly I have longed for an opportunity to discuss with you all my favourite authors and their works!'

His voice was extremely agreeable, warm and cajoling.

Oh, me! How readily we may be deluded, if the delusion should chime with some pet vagary of our own! Harry ffinch-ffrench could not have hit upon a subject more attractive to my taste; and in no time, recrossing the Green Park, we were deep in discussion of Mr Scott and Lord Byron, of whether it was permissible to compare their work, and whether Scotland was as suitable a location for tales of chivalry and drama as the more romantic Italian or Turkish mountains and valleys.

I ventured to inquire whether he had come across the works of my friends Mr Bill and Mr Sam. He expressed surprise at my being acquainted with them, said he himself had not read them, but understood their verses were crude peasant stuff and imbued with dangerous revolutionary notions, to boot. At which I laughed very heartily and urged him to acquaint himself at once with the works in question, before he revealed such an ignorant misconception to any other interlocutor.

My new acquaintance seemed quite startled at this, and turned to peer at me inquiringly in the dusk. His looks, I could see, fully lived up to Miss Artingstall's panegyrics; and – what did more to recommend him to *my* favour – he bore a certain resemblance to dear Mr Sam, in that he had large deep-set eyes and glossy black locks which were swept back in picturesque disorder. (He was in truth somewhat handsomer than Mr Sam, who had thick lips and a habit of letting his jaw hang open when excited; but no qualities could ever excel those of my dear Mr Sam, or not in *my* estimation.) Still, as I say, the resemblance, superficial though it might be, recommended this new acquaintance to my goodwill. Also I was happy to encounter someone, and a member of the male sex, at that, with whom I might discuss matters that were of interest to *me*. I had spent so many hours, days, weeks and months, uncountable periods of time, it seemed to me, during the past few years, listening to trivial conversation on supremely uninteresting topics.—At least in Byblow Bottom when we talked, it was on subjects relevant to our life: somebody's wife had died, somebody's pig had escaped, somebody's roof had collapsed. Means of dealing with the situation were canvassed. But here in Bath, conversation was, it seemed, an end in itself. Materials for it were collected like kindling wood, but then used in an artificial and prodigal manner, merely to generate a flame. But to what end? Simply to make a sound, to fill a silence, to pass a period of time. Time which, it seemed to me, could in a thousand ways have been more profitably spent. Mrs Jebb's aged friends, the girls at the school, the teachers there, made themselves acquainted with books, attended dramatic performances, not because they cared about the book or the play in question, but simply in order to be supplied with topics for chat.

'You *must* converse, young ladies!' Miss Orrincourt admonished her charges over and over. 'The gentlemen – your husbands, fathers, suitors – always require to be entertained. Always. When they are not hunting, shooting, governing, making laws or fighting wars – then it is your task to provide them with entertainment. So you must at all times have a fund of conversational topics ready to divert your company.'

Be hanged to that, I had often thought, remembering Lady Hariot and her unique knowledge, wit, intelligence, all lavished and wasted on the Squire; *I* shall look for a man who can interest *me*. And if I do not find him, like the lady in the ballad, I will go to my grave unwed.

Which is more than likely to happen in any case.

But now here, for a wonder, seemed to be a man who *was* prepared to interest me. Who walked beside me talking of Crabbe and Cowper and Sir Charles Grandison. As we parted at the park entrance, he suddenly drew out from the breast of his jacket a paper and handed it to me. He said beseechingly, 'I have long, as I told you, Miss FitzWilliam, been seeking an opportunity to meet you and I have not come unprovided. This paper – somewhat warm and creased as you may see – has accompanied me for several weeks through the streets of Bath in the hopes of such a lucky encounter.'

How many weeks? I wondered in parenthesis. For he had told me that he was a student at the university of Cambridge and I had wondered no little at his apparent liberty to leave his studies so freely in order to flit away and disport himself in Bath.

'I have been so eager for your eyes to rest upon these lines, Miss FitzWilliam! And I shall do my utmost to procure an early opportunity of hearing your comments.—Do you often walk here at this hour?'

I replied cautiously that I did now and then but that my time was not at my own disposal, etc., etc., and he bowed, with much grace, sweeping his hat from those artlessly disordered locks – would have pressed my hand – only it was still holding the paper he had given me – and then vanished into the dusk.

The light being by now insufficient for me to be able to read what was written on the paper, I had to suppress my natural curiosity until I was back in my bedroom in New King Street.

There, I am obliged to confess, I felt a certain disappointment.

> I long to be
> My lady dear
> The drop that sparkles
> > In your ear
> I'd share your pillow
> All night through
> I'd hear each gentle
> > Breath you drew
> If not the jewel
> Then I'd be
> The glass wherein
> > Your face you see
> Ah! joy! for then
> > You'd smile at me!

I could not help regarding this verse and the various others that accompanied it as sad trivial stuff, surely unworthy of my new friend's intelligence – and decidedly inferior to my expectations. It seemed curious that one who could talk with warmth and admiration of Cowper or Scott should produce such indifferent work himself.—Not only that but it seemed to me that I had come across something very similar elsewhere. Also I felt – and here I must confess a touch of impatience entered my critical attitude – that, if the lines were supposed to be addressed to me personally, it was unobservant of Lord Harry not to have noticed that, unlike most of the young lady boarders at Mrs Haslam's, I wore no earrings. (Mrs Jebb had a pair of silver-and-jet buttons which she had sometimes appeared almost on the point of offering to lend me; but the point had never quite been reached and I had no great expectation that it ever would.)

Still, I told myself, there was a world of difference between an intelligent appreciation of literary works and the ability to create such works; there had been many shrewd critics of poetic style who could no more compose verses themselves than they could fly to the moon. And if Lord Harry showed a generous appreciation of other talent, then that was as much as could reasonably be required of him, and he would rapidly learn to know his own limitations. Was I to be the one to disillusion him as to his lack of genius? I hoped not. The harsh world would enlighten him soon enough.

These thoughts, and others of a similar nature, ran through my mind that evening as I sang some operatic airs by Mademoiselle Duvan from her *Suite de les Génies* for Mrs Jebb and her friends, and played on the harp a set of variations by Handel. The hours seemed to pass rather more smoothly and speedily than usual on such evenings, and when I retired to bed it was to hear again, in echo, that warm and engaging voice: 'I know a great deal about you, Miss FitzWilliam,' he had said, and I wondered what else Maria Glanville had told him about me. Nothing very flattering, I could be sure; she was a hen-witted girl, unable to distinguish one note from another, who fell into a paralysis of fright when asked the simplest musical question. She had probably told her cousin that I was a dragon. It would be amusing to disabuse him . . . So thinking, I fell asleep.

I need not retrace here in day-to-day detail the progress of my acquaintance with Lord Harry ffinch-ffrench. Suffice it to say that, isolated and somewhat off my guard as I was at that time, I found myself looking forward to our next encounter with unaffected eagerness and made my way to the Green Park as often as daily circumstances permitted. Or as the weather permitted: that was an unusually rainy spring.

– He was not always there. And now the evenings were beginning to lengthen, and more people came to stroll and enjoy the favours of the season, our chances of a private encounter grew fewer and fewer, unless I took my promenade at a late hour, which suited neither Pug nor Mrs Jebb.

I found myself reluctant to tell Mrs Jebb about my new acquaintance.—It was not precisely that our encounters were clandestine; but I knew by instinct how much Miss Orrincourt would disapprove if one of her instructresses should be regularly meeting a gentleman, however innocuous the circumstances, however respectable his intentions and antecedents; and although Lord Harry appeared the pinnacle of respectability – and eligibility – the gulf between our stations sufficed, in itself, to cast a shadow of doubt and discredit over our acquaintance. I tried not to devote too much thought to this aspect of our friendship, I must confess; that we *were* friends and liked to talk about books, was, at that time, sufficient for me. If he asked questions about my background I returned evasive answers; I never suggested that he come and present himself at Mrs Jebb's house, for I felt sure that she would not wish to receive him; and he himself never suggested a meeting anywhere else.

– Just occasionally I seemed to hear Fanny Huskisson's voice at my ear: 'A rare cheapskate he be, dearie, if you ask me! Not to offer you so much as a cup of chocolate at a pastrycook's or an apple from a coster-monger! Why, I'd think it a shame to be acquainted with such a skin-flint, and he the son of a dook with all his millions at command.'

But then Fanny Huskisson, a thoroughly vulgar girl, had no notion of any such thing as the interplay of two intelligences.

Learning that Lord Harry had passed his schooldays at Eton I did consider, at one time, asking if he had ever encountered Hoby, but on second thoughts refrained. That might lead to revelations. Next time I wrote to Hoby – now entered at King's College, Cambridge – I would ask him if he knew Lord Harry. His opinion might be of interest.

I wondered sometimes what had become of the rest of the Bath Beaux, Lord Harry's friends. Once I alluded to them in a casual manner; where were they now? I asked. Oh, he said vaguely, he had seen them the other day; they had all been to a race-meeting together. They were shocking, inveterate gamblers, his friends, he told me, laughing; if there were no steeplechases to bet on, they would wager on the colour of the first dog to come out of the market, or the number of swans along the bank by the Parade Gardens. 'Ned Weatherspill and Gus Link once staked five hundred apiece on the number of hairs in the blacksmith's beard at Corsham,' he said, laughing even more heartily.

'But – good God – how would they ever discover which of them was right?'

'Ned paid the fellow to have his beard shaved off.'

'He was willing to *do* such a thing?'

'No; not at all willing; but they made him drunk and it was done. And Ned won his bet. They obliged the barber to count the hairs three times over.'

I pondered over this story, which somewhat shocked me. Not that it exceeded in outrageousness various pranks perpetrated by Hoby and the others back at Byblow Bottom; but I had assumed that these gently reared young sons of lords would have higher standards.

'But now the other fellows have all gone back to Cambridge – and I ought to return there, too,' he added in a somewhat languishing tone. 'But I have fallen into shocking bad habits here of sinful self-indulgence. Can you guess what keeps me lingering and procrastinating?'

He threw me a slanting look from his large dark eyes and repeated, 'Can you guess! Are you not going to ask me what I mean?'

I felt suddenly ill-at-ease. An exquisitely fair evening after a week of rain had tempted us beyond our usual limits, and we had persuaded the protesting Pug up Beechen Cliff, which, because of its noble hanging woods, always reminded me of the walk I had taken along the coast to St Lucy's of Godsend with my two dear friends. By myself, I could not have come as far as this; for it was not considered a suitable walk for a young lady on her own. And few of the girls at Mrs Haslam's cared to ramble so far, even in each other's company.

'Lord Harry,' I said hesitantly, to break the silence which all of a sudden seemed to envelop us like a cocoon, 'there is something I have been wishful to say – no, not at all wishful, but it needs to be said –'

'Ah!' he exclaimed, laying his hand upon my arm. I was much struck by the warmth of that hand, and by the fact that it quivered violently. 'Ah, surely,' he went on, 'by this time we need not be quite so formal? 'Lord Harry'! Can you not venture to call me Hal, as my friends do? And may I not – pray – address you as *Eliza*?'

I glanced about us. We were now in a little clearing of the beech wood, where a seat had been erected, commanding a majestic panorama of the city of Bath, roofs and spires and the winding river far below us.

He led me to the bench and invited me with a gesture to sit on it, then sat down himself, facing me, with an arm hooked over the back rail.

I felt both nervous and resolute. For the last few meetings I had been evading him, practising with an adroitness of which I had hardly known myself capable Miss Orrincourt's art of leading the conversation away from a risky area into a more innocuous region. But now I felt our intimacy had reached a point where the truth could be postponed no longer.

'Very well then – Hal.'

'Ah!' he exclaimed in a throbbing tone. 'How exquisite – how truly interesting that word sounds upon your lips! Hal! It has a grace – a resonance – hitherto undreamed-of! I shall for ever like the name better – from this day on – now that I have heard it from your charming voice –'

'Well – I hope so. Perhaps you may not think that when you hear what I have to say. For, my dear Hal, I am obliged to tell you that – sadly – I do not believe your gifts lie in the realm of poetry. Your true genius, perhaps, may be situated elsewhere – as critic, perhaps essayist – philosopher – man of letters –'

He was staring at me intently, his mouth somewhat open – like Mr Sam's, I thought – his eyes dark with urgency. There were numerous beads of sweat upon his forehead, though the evening was not warm, and he had all of a sudden grown so pale, so very pale, that I felt – I must confess – considerable compunction for being obliged to dash his poetic hopes.

But then he stammered out: '*Eliza* – there is something else also that – that I have to say – dammit, this is hard for me – I have never been in such a devilish predicament before –'

His face was working strangely, as if he were in a fever; he seemed to be in a curious medley of fright, frantic excitement, regret and embarrassment.

But the fear predominated.

Fear of what?

Of me?

My senses are very alert. It has always been so. Whether these faculties were inborn, or developed from early habit in Byblow Bottom – where such vigilance was daily required for survival – I know not; but eyes and ears, even my sense of smell, were acute as those of a fox or hare. Now, three such messages assailed me simultaneously: I heard a crack in the bushes, and what sounded like a stifled chuckle; I saw Pug turn his head sharply, and observed a telltale twitch in Lord Harry's hessian pantaloons; even more strongly, I smelt the sweat on him, of fear, of shame, of bodily excitement.

I sprang to my feet, snatching up Pug.

Lord Harry, too, jumped up, and now his physical state was even more apparent.

'Don't – my dear creature – oh, pray don't go!' he gasped, and made a clumsy grab at me, snatching my shawl from my shoulders. I dealt him what, in Byblow, would have been rated a mild buffet on his ear and, abandoning the shawl, darted off into the underground. Instinct prompted me to avoid the track, and the quarter from which the sounds had come; I made uphill for a shadowy grove of young bushes and stopping there, crouched low, stifling Pug, and remained very still.

Now I heard sounds in plenty, shouts, footsteps and curses.

'God dammit, where has the bitch fled to?'

'I thought Hal had her all to rights –'

'Deuce take the jade! She's gone to ground –'

'Hollo, hollo, sweet one? Where are you hiding?'

Lord Harry's friends, the Bath Beaux – as I readily guessed – were crashing and stumbling about, searching for me and blaming their comrade for mismanaging the tête-à-tête.

'Devil fly away with you, Hal, why were you so slow with the wench – why not broach-to directly? What need for all that argy-bargy? A pox on you! Now here we are up non-plus creek –'

Hal defended himself.

'I had to talk her round! I was doing capitally until you –'

'Talk her round? Begad, you talked to such purpose that the vixen smelt a rat and has given us the go-by –'

'Oh stap me, look here, there's a cursed bramble round my leg which has torn my stocking –'

'Mistress! Mistress Fitz! Where are you hid, my charmer?'

'Come out, sweetheart, and let us see you!'

'Tally-ho, tally-ho!'

There was a strong odour of liquor. Several times one or another of them nearly stumbled over me. Luckily they were fairly fuddled with drink, it seemed. Grumbling and blaming Hal, they finally gave up the search and doubtless concluding that I must have made for the city they themselves proceeded quarrelsomely in that direction.

'I talked poetics to her, did I not?' Harry ffinch-ffrench was declaring in peevish, injured accents as they tramped in single file along the path, still thrashing hopefully at the brambles with their canes. 'I led her on finely. I talked poetry for days on end, until I could barely order dinner but it came out in rhyme – and now all my application and hard labour is wasted because you stupid dunderheads could not lie doggo in the bushes for ten minutes at a stretch – '

I heard their trampling and cursing fade into the distance. Some allusions to 'the stake money at the White Hart' were the last words to come back to me.

When the voices had quite died away, I returned to the bench hoping to reclaim my shawl. But they had taken it with them.

So, cold, angry, dishevelled and heartsore, I took my own way back to New King Street, carrying Pug, who made his displeasure very plain by snoring at me in a gloomy and censorious manner.

But his gloom and censure were nothing to what I encountered on my arrival.

By now it was late.

'We were about to notify the watch!' Mrs Jebb told me, stroking and pacifying Pug. I noticed a strong odour of brandy in the parlour. Even stronger than in the woods. 'Poor old fellow, then! Did he get taken for a long disagreeable cold walk in the dark? And where is your shawl, Miss? And what – pray – have you been up to?'

The shawl was a Norwich one she had given me; old, worn and darned, but still handsome.

'Ma'am, I have had a misadventure. There's no getting away from the fact. I'll tell you the whole story.'

I did so.

Pullett, who had come in to bring me a hot drink, remained to listen with starting eyes.

Mrs Jebb sucked in her breath at the finish.

'They did not, then, violate you?'

'No, ma'am; though plainly that was their intention. And,' I said with satisfaction, 'I dealt Master Harry a sharp clip on his ear which will, with luck, leave him a fine black eye in the morning.'

'You stupid child.'

Mrs Jebb did not berate me. She spoke in her customary harsh, measured tone. 'Those men are in possession of your shawl. And now they will make it known all over Bath that, in those woods, they had you at their mercy and enjoyed you each in turn.'

'But that would be a lie.'

'How could you prove so?'

'I suppose – I could go to a medical man – ' but my voice faltered as I thought of the ensuing indignities, the difficulties. 'Miss Orrin-court will no doubt give me notice,' I said dejectedly.

'Not if she is a woman of sense. And such I believe her to be.' Mrs Jebb glared at me. 'You are a *very* stupid child. I had believed you to be dowered with sense and discretion beyond your years. But I see that I was wrong. Let this be a lesson to you, my girl! Never, *ever*, pay the slightest heed to a man who says that he shares your tastes, your interests. It will be a black falsehood, told inevitably in order to gain his own ends. Which are always, and unalterably, the same. So at least you have learned what will stand you in good stead.'

She scowled at me and continued, 'In the circumstances, this letter comes very apposite.' She produced a paper from her reticule. 'It is a request from Edward Ferrars, which I had been on the point of refusing. (Why, pray, should he think himself entitled to favours from me?) But, as matters stand, it will be as well to indulge him, and poor Cousin Elinor will benefit.'

'Mr Ferrars?'

She unfolded the paper.

'They have had severe floods in Delaford. It is a damp, unhealthy spot – always was. Low-lying, in the Levels. A week's rain, and the canal overflows its banks. Half the village down with a putrid fever. Several women died. And your cousin Elinor (I call her cousin because Edward Ferrars, now that he finds a use for your services, employs that term) your cousin Elinor laid down upon her bed, deathly sick; and nobody but a half-wit to nurse her.'

'Good heavens, ma'am! Poor Mrs Ferrars! And they want *me*? But' – here commonsense set in – 'why does she not send for her own daughter? For Nell?'

'Hah!' A spasm of sour laughter shook Mrs Jebb. 'As well hope to enlist the help of the constellation Andromeda! Of course Nell's father wrote to her first – but it seems she was about to set out for a northern tour with her fine friends. No help to be had from that quarter.'

'Well – if I can really be of use,' I said a little doubtfully, 'naturally I will go. Cousin Elinor – Mrs Ferrars – is by no means an easy person to help. But it is the least I can do. And –'

'And it will take you out of Bath while this little *scandale* dies down. Tomorrow is Saturday – you had best go directly, on the carrier's cart. The last thing we want is for people to make connections.'

'Make connections, ma'am?'

But Mrs Jebb broke off and would not continue.

'Run to bed, child, I am tired.'

Indeed she looked it. She looked a hundred years old. Now I felt remorseful that I had brought this anxiety on her.

'Ma'am I am indeed sorry that – that any action of mine should cause you trouble or worry. I thought – I thought no harm. I thought I had found a friend.'

The hooded eyes surveyed me impatiently. Her visage was all down-dragging lines like some seamed and puckered rock face, deeply chiselled with water-courses.

'Child: we all think thus, and it is our undoing. If you find *one* friend in your whole life, you will be luckier than most. If you do, you should thank heaven fasting and cherish that person as best you can.—Now, leave me.'

In my bedroom, later, when I was gloomily taking stock of my bruises and scratches, Pullett came creeping in with hot water and compresses.

'Don't you worry, dearie, I'll write that one's name on a piece of paper. And I'll drop it in the brook. And then we'll see what we shall see!'

'What *do* you mean?' I asked wearily.

'Never you mind, Miss Liza! We shall see what we shall see.'

And she tiptoed away, nodding her head.

Chapter 6

BEHOLD ME THEN, IN A TOLERABLY DISCONSOLATE FRAME OF mind, travelling towards Delaford on the carrier's cart.

I had dispatched a note to Miss Orrincourt, explaining that Mrs Ferrars was gravely ill and that I was obliged to go to her assistance. It seemed unlikely that any rumour of my misadventure would yet have reached the school. And indeed I had a very amiable and approving reply, delivered by the school boot-boy, before I set off. They would feel my absence keenly (Miss Orrincourt wrote), but it was clearly my duty to hurry to the bedside of my kind benefactress; she hoped that my withdrawal from my classes need not be of long duration. And she sent all manner of cordial wishes to Mr and Mrs Ferrars.

No mention of Nell, nor yet of Margaret Dashwood. Perhaps Miss Orrincourt felt that even if either of them did present themselves at Delaford they might not be of much use.

Along with this note I received another, on pink paper, folded into a cocked hat.

'What's *this*, Davey?'

Could it be an apology from Lord Harry ffinch-ffrench? I eyed it with some aversion, as if it might fly open and discharge a poisoned dart at me.

'I dunno, Miss. A lady left it at the school. She reckoned as you was there. Miss Orrincourt said, best bring it to ye, along with hers.'

A lady? Then it was not Lord Harry; not unless he had a female accomplice.

> Dear Miss FitzWilliam:
>
> I heard you sing the last concert at the Rooms, and was hugely affected! Not only by the brilliancy of your voice, but also by your exceedingly strong resemblance to a long-lost, long-yearned-after acquaintance of mine, Miss Eliza Williams. I feel convinced that you must be a connection of hers! When I was younger she was my greatest, my most-loved friend and confidante. This was some years ago – many years ago. (My name in those days was Clara Partridge. Now I am Mrs Jeffereys.) I should be so very happy to make your acquaintance, and perhaps hear news of one so long missed, so greatly cherished.

The lady wrote from an address in Walcot Street.

Needless to say I was not a little chagrined that this message came *now,* at a time when I could not respond to it. But I resolved to write to Mrs Jeffereys from Delaford, and go to see her as soon as I returned to Bath. For it did appear as if she must be able to give me information about my mother, and perhaps about my father also. This new hope for the future came as a very welcome distraction, since otherwise I found myself shamed and low-spirited enough, aware that in Mrs Jebb's eyes – and in my own also – I had shown myself as a great booby – *I!* who esteemed myself so shrewd! – and had fallen to the lure like any seminary miss. I felt both anger and mortification; and my sore-heartedness did not abate until we reached Delaford, when the melancholy condition of this pleasant hamlet caused all such thoughts to be swept from my head.

It was plain that the flooding had been severe, as water marks high on the walls of the whitewashed cottages bore muddy witness. Branches and weeds and dead animals lay at random where the water had carried them, and a fetid stink hung over the whole place. The flood had not as yet wholly retreated; the horse and cart that conveyed me were splashing through a couple of inches of water along the cobbled roadway.

Not a soul was about. No one was to be seen out of doors. The whole place was deathly silent.

''Tis a proper kettle of eels,' said my driver, looking gloomily about him. He set me down at the parsonage, which had fared a little better than its humbler neighbours, being set up on a slight rise; here the waters had evidently flowed over the lintel, but had not risen as high as the windows.

I picked my way through ankle-deep mud to the front door and plied the knocker, but no one answered. The door was never locked, I remembered, so without more ado I pushed it open and walked in.

The small parlour inside was as I recalled it, but looked dirty and uncared for. A thin layer of mud lay over the brick floor. The single rug was sodden. The house stank.

'Hilloo?' I called. 'Is anybody about?'

No answer. I made my way, slipping and sliding, along the short passage to the kitchen. Here I found an unlit hearth, dirty dishes strewn everywhere and a dismal miasma of mud and decaying vegetables. A small sluttish figure stood listlessly with her back to me, staring vacantly out of the window. She turned slowly at the sound of my step. I recognized a village girl called Sal, little better than half-witted, who had sometimes come up to the house to assist Cerne the maid in rough tasks, scrubbing floors or washing curtains.

'Good day, Sal,' I said. 'Do you remember me? Where is Cerne?'

She looked at me uncomprehendingly and shook her head. I remembered that she could hardly speak.

In a state of no small alarm I turned and began to mount the stairs.

'Cousin Elinor?' I called.

A faint sound of reply came from the main bedroom. I pushed open its half-closed door and found a state of disorder similar to that below-stairs, with used soup bowls and plates, soiled towels flung over chairs and a sour smell of illness and filthy linen. On the bed lay a figure which I had some difficulty in recognizing as Mrs Ferrars, so clay-coloured and sunken were her features, so lank and greasy her hair, so emaciated her limbs.

A feeble croak came from her again.

'Drink – drink –'

I looked about. There was none in the room, only empty vessels. Gathering up as many of these as I could carry – everything I picked up felt slimy – 'I will be back directly, Cousin Elinor,' I promised, and ran down the stairs.

'Is there any water in the house? Water?' I asked Sal, who had not changed her position in the kitchen. She shook her head, gesturing vaguely towards the garden, which could be seen through the window. The parsonage derived its water from a well, I knew, but I could see that the well-head, which lay at the bottom of the garden, was still submerged under six inches of flood-water. The water in the well would be filthy, I had no doubt.

Under the stair, I recalled, Edward Ferrars kept a few bottles of wine, reserved for very rare and special occasions (of which there had been none on my former visit); also a barrel of cider; this indulgence he sometimes permitted himself after a hard day's work around the parish.

I found a corkscrew, opened a bottle of claret and carried a glassful upstairs to Cousin Elinor. Supporting her with my arm, I held the glass to her lips and she was able to drink a little. The heavy lids rose from her sunken eyes and she looked at me in perplexity.

'Nell?' she murmured. 'Nell? . . . No . . .'

'Never mind,' I said gently, laying her down again among the grubby sheets.

During the ensuing three hours I worked and made poor Sal work, as seldom before in either of our lives. The kitchen fire was lit, after a severe struggle with damp kindling and sodden wood; water was boiled on it in a pail, and linen washed; a great purging and scouring of dishes took place; a scrawny fowl, from the flock miserably pecking about at the damp upper end of the garden, was ruthlessly slaughtered, plucked and set to simmer. The water I used for this latter purpose was procured from the well of the Manor House which, being set up on a knoll, had escaped the flood. And I set Sal to fetching more pails of water from the same source, as she seemed fairly useless for any other purpose.

Meanwhile, every ten minutes or so, I persuaded poor Elinor – now more comfortably established at least in clean bed-linen and night-apparel – to take a few more sips of wine. At the end of three hours she had drunk close on two tumblerfuls and was visibly the better for it; a trace of colour had come into her face, and she had slipped into what was probably a somewhat drunken slumber.

By now the daylight had begun to wane. I had not troubled to question Sal about Edward's whereabouts, for it was plain that she had not the least notion and, if she had, could not answer. I assumed that he was out on parochial affairs; and so it proved for presently I heard the tired clip-clop of his elderly cob and, through the kitchen window, saw him dismount and lead the beast into the building which did duty as stable, barn and hen-house.

After a few minutes he came into the house. He had aged by ten years from the man I remembered; his hair was greyer and scantier, his face more gaunt; the severity of his expression lightened not at all at sight of me or at the changes which had been wrought in his house. These he took for granted. Plainly, he was at the very extremity of exhaustion.

'My wife – Mrs Ferrars – how does she go on?' he croaked in a voice ragged with fatigue.

'She is asleep; I have rendered her a little more comfortable.'

He nodded – made as if to sit down, then recollected himself and climbed upstairs with a slow, heavy step. His visit to the bedroom lasted but a moment; when he came down again his long face wore a look of severe displeasure.

'You *opened a bottle of wine!* You had no leave to do that!'

'There was no water in the house fit to drink.'

He started a long harangue about the need for economy and respect for other people's property. In the middle of it I simply walked away; I have never seen any value in argument with obstinate fixed ideas, and if ever there was a man with set ideas Edward Ferrars was that man. You might as well try to shift a granite gatepost.

So, instead, I brought him a basin of chicken broth and a bannock which I had baked over the fire. (Fortunately the pantry, where the sacks of flour were stored, lay up two stone steps at the back of the house, and had escaped the flood; *un*fortunately it had become a refuge for mice.) There had been no time, as yet, to set dough a-rising.

Mr Ferrars ate without comment for a while. Then he said, 'But this is *meat* broth. Whence had you the meat?'

'I killed a fowl.'

'You *killed a fowl?* Were there not potatoes – turnips – carrots – in the store?'

There had been; many of them rotten; these I had flung out to the dejected poultry, along with seventeen little pots of rancid dripping, and various crocks of sour milk and hideous mouldy lumps, nature unknown.

I contented myself with saying that Mrs Ferrars needed the extra nourishment. Even in Byblow Bottom, where living was scant enough, I had never seen anybody closer to death from hunger, thirst and neglect.

He gave a defeated sigh, passing his grimy coat-sleeve across his forehead, then stood and said, 'I will retire now.'

'I have made you up a bed, sir, in Cerne's room; I believe Cousin Elinor will do better if she is alone and can sleep undisturbed.' Ignoring his frown, I continued, 'Where *is* Cerne, by the by?'

'She went to nurse her sister – who had the fever – Cerne took it as well. I have just come back from burying them.'

(Later I learned that he had also conducted two more funerals that day, and had sat at three death-beds.)

'That is bad news,' I said. 'I am very sorry. Cerne was a kind person. Cousin Elinor will miss her greatly.'

To this he made no reply, but said: 'I must be at the church at five minutes to seven tomorrow to conduct the early service. Will you see that I am called in good time?'

I nodded, and returned to the kitchen to set oatmeal and water in a pot over a banked-up fire, which I hoped would stay in all night. Sal had long ago trailed away homewards; I had made myself up a bed in Nell's room, which was where I had slept on my previous visit.

Next day, by great good fortune, Mr Grisewood the lawyer chanced to visit Delaford on business connected with the Manor House estate. He called at the parsonage, asking for Edward Ferrars, who was miles distant at the time, by the bedside of a stricken parishioner.

Mr Grisewood made no attempt to conceal his dismay at the desolation in the village. 'Merciful heavens! I had heard about the flood but had no notion it was half so bad! I must write to the Colonel directly. He would wish to be informed.'

'Oh sir! Do you know where Colonel Brandon is at this present?'

He hesitated. 'No, my dear Miss FitzWilliam – it is true that we are not precisely certain. But we did have a communication, some months ago – it had taken that long again to reach us – announcing the Colonel's intention to break his voyage and make a stay at Lisbon, before returning to this country. I shall write to him at Lisbon in care of the British Envoy there. He should know about matters here in the village. He may wish to return without further delay.'

'That had not been his intention?'

'No, I believe he had thoughts of rejoining his regiment.'

'In the meantime, sir, do you think some funds might be advanced to provide assistance for people in the village?' I had been through the village that morning, to find if any help might be procurable for the stricken parsonage. But I had found all other households in the same condition, or worse. I said to Mr Grisewood: 'Their need is very acute. All their provisions were carried away in the flood, or rotted in the water. And the fever has killed many.'

I did not add that Mr and Mrs Ferrars were almost as needy as their parishioners, but, on his promising to provide help, resolved to see to it that the occupants of the parsonage received their fair share of whatever was forthcoming.

The Colonel, it seemed, had made provision before his departure in case of some such disaster (floods here were not uncommon, though this one was unusually severe); Mr Grisewood promised that coals, clothing and a stock of food should be sent from Dorchester directly.

'Is it permitted to see Mrs Ferrars?' he then asked.

I said I thought this might be possible. Today she was more collected; had recognized me, after a few puzzled moments, had submitted to be bathed, and have her hair combed, had eaten a spoonful or two of porridge.

Mr Grisewood came from her bedside looking shocked to death.

'I must say – good gad! – it is fortunate, Miss FitzWilliam, that you arrived here when you did. Otherwise – I hardly like to think – why in the world did not Ferrars apprise me of the situation?' he muttered to himself.

'He has been worked almost to a standstill – out on his visits all the hours of daylight. And,' I said moderately, 'he has a great deal of pride.'

'Stupid fellow,' muttered Grisewood.

He looked as if he expected to be offered some refreshment. I remembered the tiny glasses from that former visit. I said, 'Can I offer you a glass of cider, sir? – Mr Ferrars has very little wine left, and what there is he – he reserves for emergencies.'

Mr Grisewood's expression suggested that he had tasted that cider before. 'No, I thank you, my dear. I must be on my way. Perhaps I may chance to come across Mr Ferrars on my ride.—By the way, where is old Mrs Dashwood?'

'I understand, sir, that she had gone to stay with a connection of the family – Sir John Middleton – very fortunately some weeks before the flood, and Sir John sent a message to say that she should stay with him until matters were in better train.'

He nodded. 'Ay, ay, Sir John is very good-hearted, he'll keep the old lady as long as necessary.—I wonder, Miss FitzWilliam, if I might entrust you with the key of the Manor House at this time? I had meant to leave it with Mr Ferrars but – burdened as he is with so many cares at present – and you seem like a young lady with her head on her shoulders. (Indeed, it is most fortunate that matters have turned out as they have.)'

I thought of Lord Harry ffinch-ffrench and my tarnished reputation in Bath. I did not allude to Bath, but said civilly that I would be happy to serve Mr Grisewood in any way that was required.

'The Colonel plans to sell a piece of property. Since he has no heir, he has decided – well, that need not concern you. But I may need some estate maps, which are kept in his business room at the Manor. If I send a messenger out from Dorchester, could you be so obliging as to look them out for me if it becomes necessary?'

I promised to do so, if given specific directions; Mr Grisewood bowed, appeared inclined to pat my cheek, but thought better of it and merely said, 'I am very glad that you are here, Miss FitzWilliam,' and took his leave.

Mr Ferrars did not make any allusion to Mr Grisewood's visit until two or three days later, when the stocks of coal and food had arrived and been distributed. Then he said coldly, 'I understand that Mr Grisewood entrusted you with the key of the Manor, Miss FitzWilliam?'

'Yes, sir, since you were out at the time. It hangs there, on the hook over the kitchen mantel.'

– That Mr Ferrars did not at all like me, I was well aware. His dislike seemed to increase daily, but he kept it most thoroughly within check. The manifold and complex causes for this antipathy I did not try to disentwine. He was a difficult, disappointed man; something had gone badly amiss far back in his life; he seemed to have warm feelings for nobody, except his wife, to whom he was attached by a strong, gloomy, longstanding bond; in all other areas he steered his course by the star of Duty. The villagers, I had found, were not particularly fond of him, but they did very completely trust him and respected him as a good, if not a likeable man.

'Oh,' he mumbled now, looking at the key. 'Um. Well. Yes, I daresay it may as well hang there.—Have the families at Crouch End been supplied with coals and fodder?'

'Yes, sir. Amos Pollard carried them down in the farm cart.'

Amos Pollard was the old man who took care of Edward Ferrars' three emaciated cows.

'How is my wife this evening?'

'She finds herself a little better. She is able to read.'

'Read . . . She would be better employed at her devotions.'

'She has time for them as well,' I said shortly.

In fact for the past twenty-four hours, on a sustaining diet of eggnog and broth, Elinor Ferrars had been far more alert.

'Where is Cerne?' was one of the first questions she asked, and I saw no profit in concealment. Elinor, I judged, was a strong character; and so it proved. She sighed, and said she hoped that Cerne had gone to well-deserved joy and rest in the hereafter; the household had been undeservingly blest to have had her for so long.

Little by little, as the days passed, I disclosed to Elinor the full state of affairs in Delaford. Luckily, by now, matters were on the mend; in the March breezes the mud was drying; those who were going to die of the fever had done so, and the rest, like Elinor, were slowly on the way to recovery. Edward Ferrars' daily duties were not quite so arduous, or so painful. But still, he was out of the house during most of the daylight hours, and Elinor and I had time for long, meandering conversations. I grew, in those days, to have a considerable affection and respect for her. She, like her husband, was activated by a strong sense of Duty, but this was modified by a certain dry humour, apparent only now and then in brief subterranean murmurs – and never in the presence of her husband.

'Do you –' she asked tentatively, one day, while I was holding wool for her to wind – 'I assume you must, since you have remained with her for over four years – do you deal comfortably with my aunt Montford Jebb?'

I considered.

'Comfortably? I am not sure. But reasonably, decently – yes. She has her quirks. And I respect them. She is not a tyrant. So long as the household runs according to her taste.' After a moment I added, 'And it is her household, after all.'

'Are you warm enough? Well fed?'

'Yes, yes,' I said, and thought, warmer, better fed than you, poor devil.

Very awkwardly, reddening a little, without raising her eyes from the wool, Elinor asked, 'Do you by any chance know – has my aunt ever given you any indication – as to how she – as to her testamentary dispositions?'

And I know who put you up to *that* question, thought I; it is not one that you yourself would ever in this world have asked; it is the voice of Edward Ferrars that I am hearing.

And in some pity for her embarrassment I answered quickly, 'No, Cousin Elinor, Mrs Jebb has never given me any firm indication of her intentions.' Suppressing memories of various sour allusions to 'folk spending their lives in expectations of dead men's shoes,' I added, 'But her way of life is tolerably frugal. I do not believe that she has a large fortune.'

Elinor made no reply. Perhaps she was hoping that a miserly way of life might denote handsome savings. I wished I could repeat to her in so many words Mrs Jebb's statement, 'They may as well know they can have no claims on my future consideration.' But that seemed too harsh in her present state of enfeeblement. I said, 'I think – I think you would be wise not to base any strong hopes on her goodwill.'

A sigh was Elinor's only rejoinder. She said irrelevantly, 'It is queer, I talk to you so much more, and more easily, than I have with Nell.'

'Well,' I said, 'you have lost the habit, perhaps. Nell seems to be at home so seldom.'

'Never if she can avoid it.'

Nell, I thought, prefers a snug berth.

It seemed to me that Elinor missed her sister very much. More than her daughter. So many reminiscences, stories, illustrations coming from her began with 'Marianne says –' or 'Marianne always used to –' From these I constructed a picture of a lively, passionate, poetic person, quite different from Elinor herself.—And this Marianne had married a man almost twenty years her senior and had gone to the Indies with him. Why?

It also, by degrees, became clear to me, during this period, that Edward Ferrars, although he went to great lengths to suppress the emotion in himself, nourished a decided resentment against his brother- and sister-in-law up at the Manor. Again, Why? Because they had so much and he so little? Because they were able to go off to the Indies, leaving him to look after the village, deal with floods and disasters and sickness, on a barely adequate stipend? – And yet Colonel Brandon, by all accounts, was a benevolent, well-disposed man – surely he could have made better provision? I noticed that if ever Edward Ferrars found himself obliged to refer to 'the Manor' he did so with a wry mouth and disparaging tone.

When, after four or five days, Elinor began to appear more like the person I remembered, she surprised me, one afternoon, by asking me to look in a box in her clothes chest – for which she produced a key – and pass her out a bundle of papers.

'No, not that one,' she said, giving me back the bundle I first handed her. 'It is tied with green ribbon and has the name *Charlotte* on the first page.'

I found it – there were half a dozen in the box – and carried it to her – she still in bed but now propped up against pillows. The package was several inches thick. All the pages were covered in her spiky handwriting.

'Is it a novel?' I asked, curiosity overcoming good manners.

'Yes,' she answered – sighing, smiling, musing. 'As you may see, I have written several . . . *Charlotte* was the second. I still think it the best. And it occurred to me that now, while I am laid by the leg, might be a good time to revise and make a fair copy.—Not that I entertain very high hopes of publication. But oh, a little extra money would be so *useful!*'

I was immensely impressed by her industry and inventiveness. And somehow, in Elinor, it seemed so unexpected.

'Does Mr Ferrars know? Has he read them?'

'Good gracious me, no! He never reads novels. In fact he considers them vulgar, trivial things.'

Indeed, I had noticed that as soon as we heard his characteristic slam of the front door she would slip the page she was working on under a sheet of blotting paper and replace it with a half-written letter to her sister, mother or daughter.

'Do you know the names of any publishers, Cousin Elinor?' I asked her.

'If only my brother-in-law were at home! He is a reading man, a literary man, he would advise me. But my sister used to read novels and had several up at the Manor. I thought that I could take the address of one off the title-page. Chapman & Hall are names that I remember.'

I asked if I might read the manuscript, and took it away to my bedroom, where I devoured it in a couple of evenings.

'– Cousin Elinor, I think you are so clever! How did you invent such a tale, all out of your own head? The people are so alive – and their talk is so amusing! Those two dreadful vulgar sisters, who put upon poor Miss Charlotte so – and the funny old lady – and the stupid coxcomb, who thinks of nothing but his snuffbox – and the miserly couple, always resolved not to part with a single penny! You must have been in society a great deal, to strike them all off so shrewdly?'

'No – no,' she said, sighing. 'Just the once.—But that was enough. You may meet such folk anywhere – not just in society.'

I realized that this was true. There were plenty in Bath.

'But truly, Cousin Elinor, I do think you should have it published. It is so *very* entertaining. Much more so than many of the novels that Mrs Jebb reads.'

'Well,' she said, 'in our present straits – which I will not deny are exceptional – any addition to our income would certainly be an advantage. Even Edward might be brought to agree.—I believe you intend to visit the Manor today, to find some maps for Mr Grisewood?'

'Yes, I had planned to go this afternoon, after the flannel petticoats have been distributed.'

'In that case,' said Elinor, 'I would be greatly obliged if, while you are there, you would walk into my sister Marianne's boudoir (which is the room at the east end on the first floor, overlooking the rose garden), take a look at the books on the shelf, and write down for me the addresses of some publishers. That would not be a nuisance?'

'Of course not!'

On my visits to the kitchen in New King Street I had by degrees absorbed various of the culinary arts of Mrs Rachel the cook. These I was now imparting to Mrs Ashcott, a poor woman who had lost her husband and son in the recent fever epidemic, and was glad enough to have some work and distraction. After she, under instruction, had made a nourishing broth for the noon meal, and after Edward and Elinor had partaken of it, and he had ridden off to admonish various widely distributed parishioners, I made my way up to Delaford Manor.

I had, I will not deny, long been curious to visit the abode of Colonel and Mrs Marianne Brandon, for several reasons, not least because a lofty brick wall and many clumps of trees protected the Manor from casual view; only its roof could partially be glimpsed among the treetops. Walking up the driveway that ascended to it, I found that it was a large, old-fashioned residence, built at least two hundred years ago. An orchard lay to the right, an enclosed garden to the left. The windows were mullioned, the brick-arched doorway was low and massive. The front door, however, opened readily enough to my great key, and I stepped inside with all those breathless feelings of awe, hesitancy, the guilt of being an uninvited trespasser, that accompany such a penetration into the abode of strangers who are not themselves present.

The place was dusty and deathly cold. A caretaker had been appointed but he, like so many others, had perished in the recent epidemic, and no successor had yet been found. I ran up the broad, shallow oak staircase, hoping that the upper floor might not be so chilly, and found my way along a wide passage-way to Marianne's sitting room. This had been made inviting with modern furniture, chintz curtains, shelves of books, many watercolours on the walls (chiefly by Marianne herself, I guessed, recognizing local scenes) and a piano. The windows looked out over the enclosed garden, which contained a great mulberry tree and a yew-arbour. It was a pleasant room, and I imagined how the sisters must have spent many hours here together, on spring mornings or autumn afternoons, talking, reading, perhaps playing duets or singing. More and more I began to realize what a loss Marianne's company must be to her sister. Somehow, hitherto, I had found in myself a prejudice against Marianne Brandon; she possessed so much, and her sister so little; but now I began to feel a sympathy for her, wondered if she was homesick, if she missed Elinor, how she had occupied herself in the Indies, or, now, perhaps, in Portugal? Did she not long for her books, her piano, her sheltered rose garden with the mulberry tree in the corner?

Hurriedly, feeling like an interloper, I jotted down the addresses from the title-pages of various novels. (Why did not Elinor borrow some of them? Surely Marianne could have not the slightest objection?)

As I closed the first volume of *Evelina,* a paper fell out from between the pages.

It was a drawing – a pencil portrait by the same hand that had created many of the pictures on the walls.—It was a portrait of a man, a young man with dark hair, brilliant black eyes, a sensitive mouth and a handsome, lofty forehead partially concealed by a soft windblown lock of hair.—I found myself studying this unexpected trove with a strange intensity. The fact that it had been tucked away between the pages of a book, rather than displayed in a frame on the wall, seemed to suggest that it had a special significance for its owner. Could it be Colonel Brandon? But no, his likeness, along with that of his wife, hung in the rectory parlour; Colonel Brandon's hair was brown, not black, and somewhat receding; his eyes were of a greyish tint, not dark and sparkling; so this could not even be a portrait of him at a younger age. Besides, Marianne had not *known* him at a younger age; he had already been five-and-thirty, Elinor told me, when her sister met him. And I was sure the likeness had been taken by the hand of Marianne, it resembled the portraits of Elinor and Mrs Dashwood on the walls.—No, this was certainly not Colonel Brandon. I peered more closely at the drawing, to see if any further clue to the identity of the handsome stranger might be discovered, and was almost able to convince myself that I detected a hastily scratched letter W among the ruffles of the cuff at the foot. Had the Dashwood sisters any acquaintance whose name began with a W? I would ask Elinor, if I found a suitable opportunity. I found in myself a strange, an eager curiosity to know the identity of this person – among other reasons, because he bore a certain resemblance to my dear Mr Sam.—Then I laughed at myself, returning the portrait to its hiding-place. Descrying a resemblance to Mr Sam had put me in trouble once already.

Running downstairs, hastily, like a thief, I made for Colonel Brandon's business room. It was here, Edward Ferrars had told me, that maps were kept.

On my way I passed the cellar entrance. 'You might,' Edward Ferrars had observed, stiffly, 'you might, if you are up at the Manor, be so obliging as to check the cellars, to ascertain that flood-water has not seeped in. Do not omit to provide yourself with a candle.'

So – provided with candle – I checked the cellars. No flood-water, but wall after wall, rack upon rack of dusty bottles up to the brick-vaulted ceiling. Port, claret, Malaga. Constantia. Cognac. Diabolino. Why in the world, I wondered, when the village was dying from the effects of drinking filthy water, had not Edward Ferrars availed himself of this plenty?

I had half a mind to carry a couple of bottles back for the comfort and benefit of myself and Elinor. In the old Byblow Bottom days I would have done so without a second thought.

What prevented me? Some buried prohibition. I could not analyse it.

Up the stone steps again, blowing out the candle, I found my way into the large cold orderly office, with its big table and its maps, from which Colonel Brandon superintended the running of his property. It was so bleak, so dull, and yet it gave me a curious sense of comfort and security. In such a room as this, I thought, I too could run a business and feel useful.

Then, for the second time, I was brought up short.

For on the wall, behind the bare desk, hung two miniature oval portraits, framed in simple twists of gold. The pictures, at first glimpse, appeared to be of the same girl; until one realized that the two had different-coloured hair. One, with a serious countenance, was dark, like the portrait of Marianne Dashwood in the rectory; the other, Titian-coloured, smiling, could have been myself! I gazed at it for many minutes in total astonishment; then swiftly picked out the required maps, shut the business-room door and, trembling, crept away down the sloping drive and back to the parsonage.

There I discovered a most unwonted state of affairs.

Elinor, who for the past few days had risen and dressed herself in the afternoon, but still remained upstairs, had now ventured below and established herself in the parlour. Edward had returned home unusually early from his parish duties, and was with her. And they were in the midst of an argument.

'I tell you, once and for all, I will not countenance it,' I heard him say, coldly and flatly. 'It would be wholly unbecoming. No right-minded person who is in any way connected with a clergyman in holy orders ought to be capable of even entertaining such an improper – such an ambition.'

He stopped short as I came round the screen which I had installed in order to prevent the worst draughts from blowing from the front door straight through the house to the kitchen.

'Oh. It is you. You are back,' he observed needlessly. 'I see that you found the maps; I hope they are the right ones. Mr Grisewood's messenger is waiting in the kitchen. You had best take them to him directly.'

When I came back from doing so, Edward had gone out into the garden, slamming the door behind him, as was his wont. He could be seen through the window, digging with great difficulty in the wet and heavy soil.

I said: 'Cousin Elinor, you are not warmly enough dressed. You are shivering. Wait, and I will fetch you a thicker shawl. And the fire wants mending.'

Edward Ferrars, like most men, was incapable of maintaining a decent blaze. His frugality permitted no more than a handful of smouldering sticks. When I had fetched warmer wrappings (observing with concern that the calico gown Elinor had put on might have been made for somebody twice her girth) and had coaxed the fire into a mild radiance, I said, 'I brought the addresses you asked for.'

She sighed. Her fine, careworn face did not change its expression. After a moment she answered, 'I am afraid it was a wasted errand. Mr Ferrars will not consider such a scheme.'

'*He forbade* you?'

My blood boiled within me. For two pins I would have run out into the garden and launched a furious tirade against the man, as he dug there, doggedly, in the cold wind. What right had he to frustrate his wife's efforts? When they were intended for the benefit of both?

Elinor was going on soberly: 'Edward, you see, has family in London. His mother – a wealthy society lady; his brother, his sister-in-law. They would not care for it to be known that any connection of theirs could be involved in such an activity as writing novels. And he is – he is a man of the cloth –'

'There is nothing wrong in writing a novel! Think of Fanny Burney! She is a lady-in-waiting at Court – so I have heard.'

'That would be no recommendation to Mr Ferrars.'

'You could publish anonymously. "By a lady". Many do that.'

'Yes,' she said doubtfully. 'But how would I convey the novel to the publisher? Or engage in correspondence? And I do not think I could – no, I could not – run flat counter to Edward's wishes.'

'But it is unfair!'

She gave me a long, candid look from her grey eyes, which seemed larger because of the shadowed hollows in which they were deeply sunk.

'All of Edward's life has been so very unfair, Eliza. He was the elder son of a wealthy parent, and yet, because of a wilful, vindictive act by his . . . by a member of his family, he received only a younger son's portion, and a penurious portion at that. If it had not been for Colonel Brandon's bounty, we should be beggars, Edward and I. And – and Edward finds it excessively hard, at any time, to accept favours. *I* do not repine at our situation here in Delaford, because I am so very fond of Marianne. She and I have no secrets from one another, and there can be no envy or rancour between us. Never, never. But Edward and the Colonel have – have little in common, except for a sense of rectitude. It grates on Edward to be obliged, continually, to receive aid and indulgences from the Manor. Just in order to survive.'

And not so many of them, I thought. Now I was sorry that I had not brought that bottle of Constantia wine.

'Indulgence? What indulgence does he receive? He works harder than any bailiff.'

'Eliza, it is no use. I am sorry now that I raised the subject. Let us talk of something else.'

I was longing to ask her who the young man might be – the subject of the portrait hidden between the pages of *Evelina*. But now some scruple prevented me. The handsome young man was Marianne's secret, not mine; I could not betray her confidence.

So I said instead: 'Cousin Elinor, who are the young ladies – one with dark hair, one of them with m-my c-colouring – in the two miniatures that hang on the wall above the desk in Colonel Brandon's business room?'

Elinor appeared startled to death. 'I have never been in that room – ' she began. 'I never had occasion to – when I was at the Manor – ' talking rapidly, I could see, to bridge the gap while her thoughts raced. For it was plain that even if she had not been in the room, had not seen the miniatures, she knew, or could easily make a guess as to whom the subjects of those two portraits must be.

'One of them was s-so like me!' I stammered. 'Cousin Elinor, could she – could she have been my mother? And – if so – who was the other one? Were they sisters?'

There followed a silence. Then she said, 'Eliza, I am sorry. I am not at liberty to answer your questions. You will have to address them to Colonel Brandon.'

'But how can I? He is not here!'

The door slammed. Edward Ferrars had come back into the house. We could hear him impatiently scraping his shoes with the brush by the kitchen door. Then he entered the parlour, wiping the wet off his hair.

'It rains too hard to work outside any more. And there is somebody riding this way along the Bath road.' He frowned. 'It looks like Mrs Jebb's servant Thomas.'

Chapter 7

IN MANY WAYS, I WAS HAPPY ENOUGH TO BE DRIVING BACK TO BATH with Thomas, catching a glimpse here and there of daffodils in cottage gardens, or a clump of primroses budding under a hedge.

Nobody enjoys feeling unwelcome, and I had felt so, more and more, latterly, in the presence of Edward Ferrars. His cold eye was singularly reluctant to meet mine; always a bad sign; I had heard him say several times to Elinor, 'Surely we can manage without her now? You and Mrs Ashcott can surely manage?' when he thought I was out of hearing. Which filled me with impotent rage, because I knew that Elinor would never contradict him, though she was still far from having made a return to complete health. I knew that without my vigilant eye about the house, fires would dwindle and die into ashes, linen would go unwashed, and evil-smelling little dishes of left-over food would begin to proliferate again in the larder, and would reappear on the dining-table as apologies for meals, because nobody in the kitchen had the resolution or the inventiveness to concoct more nourishing fare.

I had grown fond of Elinor, and believed that she deserved better at life's hands than lonely privation shared with a gloomy, disappointed man. Learning that her daughter Nell had travelled south with the Lauderdales, and was again in their mansion in Berkeley Square, I seized the opportunity, when Elinor wrote to her, of enclosing a short note of my own, stating in firm terms that it was Nell's plain duty to come down to Delaford for a period and take some of the burden off her mother's shoulders.

(Meddling in other people's affairs has never yet brought me any advantage – or them either, in general; but I never seem able to remind myself, beforehand, of this melancholy truth.)

In honest fact, I was glad to be leaving Delaford. I had grown very weary of the continual stench of mud, soaked thatch, and rotting vegetables. I had missed my music (the Ferrars' piano, after standing for ten days in half an inch of water, would never be the same again), the singing, the teaching – even my lazy pupils. I had missed Mrs Jebb's tart, hard-headed company, and the friendly gatherings in the kitchen with Mrs Rachel, Pullett and Thomas. Strange as it may seem, I had even missed Pug.

But the tidings of the New King Street household, now imparted by Thomas, filled me with dismay and apprehension.

'Why I made bold for to come and fetch ye, Miss Liza,' he explained as we drove along. 'Missus ain't been her old self, not nohow, since ye went away.—Or, to put it otherly – she *have* been her owd self.'

Thomas always found it difficult to express himself without laborious beating of the air. He had to drop the reins and clench his fists; luckily the horses were old and meek. 'She've been the same way she were before, when she were Took.'

By 'Took' I knew he meant the time when she was committed to Ilchester jail for eight months awaiting trial for theft.

'What was she like then, Thomas?'

'Bad.' He shook his head many times. 'On the loddy. Brandy, too. Mr Jebb, poor gentleman, he couldn't abide it, but there were no way to ease her mind, no way at all, save she kept on with the loddy. And, Lord bless ye! what a deal she did use to take! Two quarts a week, in double-distilled brandy. Made her right dull and dazed-like, I can tell ee, for days on end. Then – after it was brought in Not Guilty – she pulled herself up, like, and come right to rightabouts. But now – and it's a fair trouble to us in the kitchen – she'm back on it agen, Miss Liza. I got to keep fetching her more and more from Mr Watkyns.'

Mr Watkyns was the druggist who kept the pharmacy on the corner of Cheap and Union Streets.

'Oh, the devil, Thomas! Is she dull now, and dazed-like?'

'Terrible, if you'll believe me, Miss. I and Rachel and Pullett just hope that you can someway fetch her out of it.'

Well, I thought, with the confidence of youth, and why not? I had made myself thoroughly useful in Delaford, why not in Bath?

But the first sight of Mrs Jebb was enough to strike chill into my heart. And, previous to that, another trifling occurrence had disconcerted me very much: as I alit from the chaise in New King Street, taking great care not to jolt a basket of eggs I had brought from Delaford, I came face-to-face with Mrs Busby, chief of Mrs Jebb's whist-playing cronies. To my dismay, she drew herself up, turned her face sharply away from me, and puttered hurriedly on down the street.

'What's amiss with her?' I demanded of Thomas.

He looked troubled, but said, 'Pullett'll tell ye, Miss,' leading the horses away to the livery stable.

Pullett said, 'Go and see Missis first, love. And after, I'll tell ye.'

So I went to see Mrs Jebb, who lay on the sofa in her parlour, with the shades pulled half down.

Her greeting was a compound of bitterness and sarcasm.

'Humph. So you've deigned to come back, hey? Grown tired of your virtuous kin? Hey? Or did they show you the door?'

The heavy lids drooped over her eyes – which seemed to have diminished in size, slanting upwards like those of an oriental. Her face was leaden-pale, and her mouth set in a wry twist, as if she were prepared to disbelieve my answer, even before spoken.

I said: 'Ma'am, I am sorry to see you in such poor case. I had hoped to find you out of doors, enjoying this pleasant spring day.'

'Hah! A fine chance of that I'd have, when all my friends give me the go-by. Show myself in the street? You'd think I had the pestilence!'

A dismal suspicion stirred in my breast. During the hard-driven weeks at Delaford, my encounter with Harry ffinch-ffrench and his friends had sunk to the bottom of my mind. Other matters were of greater moment. But was that wretched affair not lost to view, as I had fondly hoped?

'Is all this *my* fault, ma'am?'

She went off at a tangent – as was often her way when she wished to administer a reprimand – launching into a mumbled tirade against cocksure, self-seeking, puffed-up folk who thought of nothing but displaying themselves in public even when their talents were nothing out of the common, and who required fine clothes and bedizenments – vanity, vanity – outrageous vanity. And to what end? For the applause of a lot of old quizzes, Puts, and fud-duds.

I saw that, while she was in this frame, there was no sense in opposing her with rational argument or excuses. She wished to castigate me – well then, let her, if it did her good.

'Ma'am, I believe you are hungry,' I said – for this was often the case, when she fell into this cantankerous mood – 'Let me fetch you a biscuit and a glass of Constantia.'

'Hah! You think to soft-soap me, girl. Well, you won't!' But she drank the wine when Pullett brought it – the biscuit she impatiently waved away – then sank into a sudden heavy sleep, which alarmed me, for she lay so very inert, snoring loudly.

My heart was heavy. This return was not at all what I had anticipated.

And the goodbye to Elinor had been surprisingly painful.

'I shall miss you, Eliza,' she had admitted – rare words from Elinor, who never alluded to her own feelings. 'I wish *you* were my daughter.' And she laid her hand gently on the farewell present I had made her – a muff I had contrived – clumsily enough – from an old remnant of horsehair blanket, with the hair still on the outside, and lined internally with sheepswool from the hedges. It was a poor enough sort of gift, but I had noticed that her hands were always cold; she had a trick of tucking them into her armpits.

'And I wish, very much, Cousin Elinor, that you were my mother.' (But not that Edward Ferrars were my father, I thought. Perhaps it was due to his bleak parentage that Nell had become such a pattern of selfishness and spite?)

'As to your own mother,' Elinor said hurriedly, 'my very best advice to you, Eliza, is not to speculate about her. There can be no profit – none, none! – in any conjectures – rather the reverse. Put her entirely out of your mind. That is my most earnest counsel.

There – I hear Edward calling. Goodbye, child. You have been such a comfort to me – run along.'

She had raised the clumsy muff to cover her shaking mouth.

'Goodbye, Cousin Elinor. I – I hope that we meet again soon.'

But a brief gesture of her head seemed to deny any such possibility.

By the holy mistletoe, I thought furiously, women lead miserable, driven lives. And why? There is poor Elinor, frozen and half-starved all because of the stupid pride and illiberality of that block she chose to marry; and here is Mrs Jebb, who has friends, a house of her own and a comfortable competence, yet cast into such a state of distress, perhaps, by an act of injustice that did not even *happen.*

If that is what had led to her condition?

I sought the company of Pullett, who was in my bedroom putting away my clothes.

'Lord bless ye, Miss Liza, what a state your chemises be in! Anyone can see there was no fine laundress at Delaford.'

'Why, you see, I had to wear one on top of another, in order not to freeze to death. And there was only cold water for washing. But, Pullett, what in the *world* has happened to Mrs Jebb? And where is Pug?'

'Someone smashed his head in with a brick,' said Pullett, tight-lipped. 'My belief, it was that Wetherell from the draper's store.'

'Why? Why would he do such a thing?'

'To put a fright on Missis. He'll not let up on her. He still hopes to prove she took his goods. And – trouble is – she've been in the shop a couple more times – when she can give me or Thomas the slip – to turn over the things on the counter and tease him. She have a fair streak of wickedness, the Missis – there's no denying. And when she's a bit glum-spirited – why, then, the wickedness come out uppermost.'

I found it hard not to sympathize with Mrs Jebb. Wetherell was such a tallowy, bracket-faced fellow. But I could see the provocation on both sides.

'And what about Mrs Busby? Why did she give me the cold shoulder?'

Pullett looked even more troubled. 'Well, Miss, there's been sad tales going around since ye left Bath.'

'About me? Was it that wretched business with Lord Harry and his mates?'

She nodded unhappily. 'Yes, love. Seems that young – well, I won't soil my mouth with the word – seems he went up to London and spread the tale about that he and his cullies had all tumbled ye, in the beeches. And he carried off your shawl to prove it.'

'In London? But who knows or cares about me in London?'

Then, with a sinking heart, I remembered Nell Ferrars and the Lauderdales.

'And the word come back to here. So, I'm feared, Miss,' Pullett went on, with a nod towards the mantelshelf, 'that they won't have ye no more, up at Mrs Haslam's. And Mrs Jebb's friends have all fallen off, too.'

I had not noticed the letter leaning against the candlestick. My hands shook with anger as I opened and read the single page.

'Yes; you are right. This is my quittance from Miss Orrincourt. What a fool I was, to think it would all blow over so readily. But why should Mrs Jebb's friends fall away because of me? I can leave her house – I will do so directly – why should she suffer for my errors?'

'No, no, don't leave her, love. That'd be as much as to say the story was true. Besides, Rachel and Thomas and me, we just about reckon as how you be madam's only hope.'

'Oh, no, Pullett! Don't say so! She wasn't at all happy to see me.'

'Nay, that scolding's only her way, Miss. She missed ye sore. If *you* can't get her off the laudanum, Miss Liza, nobody can.'

Pullett gathered up an armful of bedraggled muslins and left me.

I went over dejectedly to the sill, and looked out. Beechen Cliff, the scene of my reputed defloration, looked green and verdant. A thrush sang loud trills in a garden nearby. If only those gossips knew half the real truth about me, I thought sourly. How much more ammunition they would have for their spiteful onslaughts. I looked over towards the distant hills where Byblow Bottom lay, and remembered my first arrival in Bath, when I had sorrowed and yearned for Triz and Lady Hariot and Mr Bill and Mr Sam. Where were those friends now? Lost! Irretrievably lost!

I remembered lines by Mr Bill:

> Poor Outcast! return; to receive thee once more
> The house of thy father will open its door
> And thou once again in thy plain russet gown
> May'st hear the thrush sing from a tree of its own.

If only my father's house *might* open its doors to me, I thought, how gladly would I dart between them and disembarrass my friends of my inconvenient presence. But where was that house?

No: that was the wish of a coward. Pullett and Rachel were placing their dependence on me. They hoped that I could restore Mrs Jebb's spirits.—But to what end, poor woman? Her friends had deserted her, Mr Wetherell was persecuting her; it seemed to me that she had fair justification for wishing to dull her senses with laudanum. Why try to drag her back to a sharper awareness of all these ills?

Squaring my shoulders, I walked downstairs.

Life in New King Street for the next three weeks was decidedly odd. I spent most of my time playing cribbage with Mrs Jebb. Going out of doors during the hours of daylight was not advisable. It was too uncomfortable. So many people in Bath – from the school, from the concerts – knew me well that I could not go as far as the chemist's shop on the corner without encountering a raised eyebrow, a hastily unfurled fan, an averted profile or an open sneer. What irked me more than all was the need to maintain control, not to retaliate in kind, not to hurl a Byblow Bottom expletive after these credulous scandal-carriers.

But that would only injure Mrs Jebb. As to myself, I cared little. The very moment that she was back on her feet, I intended to shake the dust of Bath off my own. My next destination remained for the moment uncertain; perhaps to Plymouth, to sell soap to sailors; or to Lisbon, to seek out little Triz and Lady Hariot; or, possibly, to London-town, to follow my fortune. Hoby was there; he had done poorly in some Tripos examination at Cambridge, and his father had accordingly found him a post in a government office.

'Failure in scholarship seems the best recomentation for such work,' he wrote cheerfully – spelling had never been Hoby's strong suit – 'two-thirds of the other fellows in the office have arrived by the same path.'

No wonder our country seemed in imminent danger of being captured by the French!

Mrs Jebb slowly clawed her way back to her usual state of pallid but rational inactivity and dour cynicism. Her own obstinacy and some bullying by myself were the main factors in this partial recovery.

'I have beaten you three times running at cribbage, ma'am; you are not concentrating on the game,' was the sharpest weapon in my arsenal. She could not concentrate with her brain dulled by laudanum. And she could not bear to be beaten, specially by me. So by degrees the doses were lowered, from two quarts to a pint, from a pint to a dram or two.

I began to have hopes. And Mrs Jebb began to make plans.

'I shall sell this house – which I have never liked above half – and we shall transport ourselves elsewhere. But where? – that's the question, as Hamlet kept on saying.'

By now I had a possible answer.

'Oh, ma'am! Let us go to Portugal!'

'To Portugal, child? Why, in the name of goodness?'

'I have some good friends there. And it is said that the climate is very healthy. And – and – and the wine is very agreeable. And the ways of society are free and friendly.'

'*English* society? I am not, at my age, about to learn that barbaric Portuguese tongue.'

'No, no, very many English families live out there. Because of the port-wine trade.'

'Well – well –' she said. 'It may be worth considering.' A faint gleam came into her eye. She added, 'I will consult Penwith about it.' Penwith was her lawyer. By now I knew that Mrs Jebb lived on an annuity which, with her usual sense, she had bought with the final remnants of her husband's estate.

My thoughts began to range, hopefully, around a midsummer removal to Oporto. We could get a ship from Bristol. I began to make notes of sailings.

Pullett and Rachel were quite in favour of the scheme.

'Missis needs a change of air,' said Pullett. 'Bath never did suit her above half.' 'I always did want to see some foreign place,' said Rachel. 'And Miss's hand shows a removal overseas, plain as plain. Haven't I allus said so? And the tea-leaves likewise.'

Only Thomas was doubtful. 'Learn that lingo? Never!' he said.

Matters were in this train when I encountered Mrs Jeffereys, née Partridge.

I had not forgotten her letter. But at Delaford there had been no opportunity to answer it. And now that I was in disgrace, elected by popular accord to be the Black Sheep of Bath, I could not imagine that she would wish to initiate an acquaintance with such a person. So I had not answered her communication. (Though I hugely regretted the loss of a chance to learn, perhaps, something about my mother, I judged it unfair to Mrs Jebb to lay open any more possible avenues of scandal and gossip.)

However one evening when I had slipped out, after dusk, for a breath of fresh air, I heard myself accosted by a voice, an eager whisper.

'Miss FitzWilliam! Oh, Miss FitzWilliam!'

I had made for the river and was walking on the quayside, immersed in reflections about boats, and sailors, and the voyage to Portugal.

'*Miss FitzWilliam!*'

I turned and saw a smallish female figure tripping rapidly after me. When she came up, I fancied that her face was someway familiar; I must have seen it, several times, perhaps, in the Pump Room or at the Assembly Rooms. Twenty years ago it must have been ravishingly pretty: round-eyed, neat, and pink; the black curls were still assembled in girlish clusters over the brow and beside the cheeks. And she dressed, as ladies will who as yet strive after their lost youth, in a pink mantle with rosebuds peeping coquettishly under the brim of her hat. A gauze scarf did little to veil her features. She carried a pink parasol.

'Oh, dear! I have had such ado to follow you! How very fast you walk! I thought that I should never catch up! It is Miss FitzWilliam, is it not? I could not mistake?'

Her voice had a Welsh lilt. Not strong, but perceptible. Very appealing.

'Yes, I am Eliza FitzWilliam.'

'Clara Jeffereys,' she panted. 'Partridge that was. My husband – Mr Jeffereys – he keeps the big ironmonger's store in Cheap Street – you must know it – and my mother – Mrs Partridge – lets rooms in Edgards Buildings – *very* select rooms, and to ladies only; any lady who goes into public under the auspices of my mother is sure of meeting very superior society.'

I was happy to hear it, but not certain how any of this applied to me.

'Mrs Jeffereys – I am not certain if you are aware that – I am under something of a cloud, at present, here in Bath? In fact you may be courting social ruin merely by speaking to me here in the street.'

'Oh, such stuff! As if I cared!' Though in fact she took a careful glance up and down the quay, which was, at that hour, deserted. 'It is true that Mr Jeffereys did not think – which is why I hoped to encounter you some day, in the street – but it is all great nonsense, and I daresay will blow over soon enough – though most vexing for you naturally – and I can see how the story about your poor mama – if *that* should be revived – would, most unfortunately, incline people to believe the worst.'

'Mrs Jeffereys!' I cried. 'What *is* the story about my poor mama? Nobody will tell me. Nobody answers my questions. Who *was* my mother? What *happened* to her? Do you know? Can you tell me? All I know of her is that she died at the age of seventeen!'

Mrs Jeffereys looked very astonished.

'Why, who in the world ever told you that? What stuff!'

'You mean – she is still alive?'

'When I last heard – dear, oh dear, how long ago was that?' She counted on her fingers. 'Ten or twelve years ago, perhaps. She chanced to be passing through Bath, with Lord – with a friend – and they stayed at the White Hart – and she sent me a note – and we met – of course I did not dare to let Mr Jeffereys know, but very fortunately he was away visiting his elder sister in Taunton. Oh, we had *such* a gossip over old days! We were at school together, you see, your mama and I, here in Bath – not Mrs Haslam's, but another, very select school. And then – you see – Colonel Brandon took her away, but he permitted her to come back here for a visit to my family – my dear papa was still alive then, of course. And Eliza and I had such charming walks and talks together.'

This recital left me quite breathless.

'Wait a minute, ma'am – you say that my mother was in Bath *a few years ago*?'

'Yes, yes – that was later on, of course. Eliza said she had called in at the place where you were brought up – Nether Hinton, was it? – but there had been no chance to see you.'

'Did she leave me a fan?'

'That I cannot tell you, dear, but it is very probable. Eliza always had the kindest, sweetest disposition; indeed, that has, so many times, led her into difficulties, for people will so often take advantage of her good nature –'

'You are telling me that my mother is still alive?'

'But that is what I am wishful to ask *yow!*' Halted in her flow, Mrs Jeffereys stared at me, round-eyed. 'That was why I have been so anxious to seek you out! I made sure you must be her daughter – you are so very alike in feature and colour – I thought you would be certain to have knowledge of her whereabouts.'

'But I have always understood that she was dead.'

She bit her lip. 'I suppose – people are so – and then, Colonel Brandon – a kind man, but strait-laced. Yes, I see how it must have been. Well, and the Colonel had his troubles too. Eliza's mother – she was the Colonel's own cousin – she *did* die, in horrid straits, I believe, and the Colonel, by all accounts, he himself reared little Eliza, *my* Eliza, you know – by hand, as you might say. She was his godchild.'

'Not his daughter?'

'Oh, no, my love. Nobody knew who her father was. Her mother had been married to the Colonel's elder brother, you see, dear – but then, she ran away from him – he was a monstrous brute, by all accounts. And he died – very fortunately – so the Colonel inherited the estate and came back from India, and sought out Eliza – he had loved her himself, you see, to distraction – but he was only the younger brother so might not marry her – but it was too late and by the time he found her, she died. And so he reared her child – your mother.'

'Colonel Brandon loved my grandmother and she died? And he brought up her daughter?'

'I'm *telling* you, dear! So then, the daughter – *my* Eliza – fell in love with Willoughby.'

The name struck my heart like a gong.

Willoughby. W.

Willoughby.

'Did he have black hair?'

'Oh, like a raven! I think he was the handsomest man I ever saw in my entire life!'

'Where did she meet him?'

'Why, here, in Bath. When she was staying with my family. Willoughby came from a place in Somerset, Allenham – he used to stay there with his aunt. Some day it would be his, he said. He met us at the Pump Room. That was after Eliza and I had left school. Oh, he was so charming! So spirited! So full of elegance, and wit, and humour, and poetry. And address! To see him and your mother together – why it was like – it was like –' Mrs Jeffereys sought about for a simile, but in vain. At last she said simply, 'Well, there was never *anything* like it.'

'So, what happened?'

'Well,' Mrs Jeffereys said. She furled and unfurled her parasol once or twice. 'In the end, he persuaded her to run off with him – to Gretna Green, he *said* they were going; but I am afraid they never did reach Gretna – and I am afraid he never did marry her, for a year or two later I read in the paper that he married a Miss Grey, a lady of property, up in London – it was said she had fifty thousand pounds. Ah, he had a fickle nature, I fear. And no money of his own. By that time I myself was engaged to be married – to Mr Jeffereys, you know – and Papa was very – so I never did discover, at that time, what had become of my poor dear unfortunate friend.

But I believe that the Colonel called Willoughby out, and that shots were exchanged.'

And much good that did my poor mother, I thought.

'Do you know anything about the lady the Colonel married? Miss Marianne Dashwood?'

'Ay, that I do!' she said readily. 'For my cousin Alice, who is a milliner in Clerkenwell, has a friend who was in service to a wealthy lady, a Mrs Jennings. The Dashwood ladies were staying with Mrs Jennings in London at the time when Willougby got married to Miss Grey. Poor Miss Marianne – ah, and a beauty *she* was, by all accounts! – she was the one that Willoughby left my poor deceived Eliza for. And no wonder! if she was one-half as good-looking as they say. But she had no portion, either, poor thing, so he stayed at her side barely three months, and then, dear, it was off and away to Miss Grey and her fifty thousand. Poor Miss Marianne nearly died of grief, they say. And I fear my poor Eliza must have had her heart broke likewise – besides being left in the family way, you know. All men are black villains at heart, if you will believe me, dear.—All except Mr Jeffereys,' she added generously.

'So Marianne Dashwood was also jilted by Willoughby, and married the Colonel.' And hid Willoughby's portrait in a book, I thought. 'Poor girl.'

'Still, before that she was spoken for by another fellow, but she would have none of him, so then he went after her sister and married her,' Mrs Jeffereys told me, as if to show that Marianne, though disappointed of Willoughby, at least had her fair share of offers.

'Indeed?' I cried with lively curiosity. 'Who could that have been?'

But that she did not know.

'Mrs Jeffereys – are you quite sure that you have no clue as to my mother's whereabouts?'

'Dearie – I'd tell you if I did. You are *so* like her, you know,' she exclaimed again, wiping her eyes unaffectedly. 'I knew you must be hers, the very first minute I caught a glimpse of you.'

'But the last time you saw my mother she was well – and – and happy?'

'Yes, my love. The time I'm telling you of, when she came and stayed at the White Hart.'

'With whom was she staying at that time?'

Mrs Jeffereys gave me a shrewd, careful look.

'Well, my love – not to put too fine a point on it – with some lord. She never told me his name. But she told me she had a plan – when Eliza and I were at school together she was always feather-witted enough, but I could see that since those days she had learned to keep a weather-eye out for herself; she had a plan to start up an establishment in London. As soon as she had some money saved, she said.'

'An establishment! What kind of an establishment?'

'A gaming house. Many of those, you know,' quickly explained Mrs Jeffereys, 'many of them are *perfectly* respectable.'

Dazed with all this information, I said, 'Mrs Jeffereys, two gentlemen are walking along the quay in this direction. If you would rather not be seen talking to me –'

'Oh, thank you, my love, that is thoughtful.—Yes, well, I'm afraid Mr Jeffereys would be greatly – anyway, you will let me know, dear, will you not, if ever you have news of dear Eliza? I should be so happy to hear –'

With fluttering gestures of her parasol and hasty steps, Mrs Jeffereys fled off up Avon Street, and I took my own slow and thoughtful course homewards to New King Street.

I felt almost stupefied. As if I had dislodged a pebble and fetched down an avalanche.

Chapter 8

I SAID NOTHING TO MRS JEBB THAT NIGHT. THESE DAYS SHE retired early, was often abed when I went out. Several times I had offered to play and sing to her, but she said, 'No, child, no. Music is for company. Not for solitude – ' looking about her uneasily at the empty room. And I could not withhold a shiver, recalling how cheerfully in the old days the sound of talk and laughter and song was used to ring across New King Street from her parlour windows.

I need hardly say that after my encounter with Mrs Jeffereys I had retired to my own bed with my head in a whirl.

To have believed for so many years – all my life indeed – that my mother was no more, and then to discover so lightly, so casually, that far from having perished she was very probably, at this time, established in London, either directing the affairs of a gaming house, on the one hand, or leading a life of comfort and dishonour, on the other, in the keeping of a rich nobleman: this, indeed, was enough to turn all my considerations upside down.

What had she been doing all these years? (Had Colonel Brandon ever supported her? Or did he too believe her dead?) Why had she visited me only the one time? (Had the Colonel forbidden her to do so?) What was she *like,* my mother?

In appearance, it was very plain, she and I could have been a pair of mirror-images; but that did not of course mean that we were alike in character. Ardently, I wished to know more about her. And surely, if I succeeded in locating her, if I managed to introduce myself, she would not then repulse me? But perhaps she had given a promise to the Colonel – in return for his having undertaken my support? – or to her protector – by whom, perhaps in the meantime she might have borne other children? – not to approach me?

And where, in this new, dark, confused and tangled panorama of connections, did my father, did Willoughby, take his place? All I knew about him was that he had married a Miss Grey with fifty thousand pounds, and that he expected to inherit a small estate in Somerset – what was the name? Allingham? Annington? Which was, possibly, not too far distant from Delaford?

Vaguely, from three years back, came the echo of a remark made by Edward Ferrars when he thought I was out of earshot. Elinor had said, 'You think there might be talk?' and he had answered, '*He* might come to hear. There is such a strong resemblance.'

A resemblance not to Willoughby, I now understood, but to my mother. Whom Willoughby had abandoned. As he had also abandoned the unfortunate Marianne Dashwood. And how many others, before fixing on Miss Grey and her fifty thousand? Not an estimable character, this Willoughby, my father, with his handsome dazzling appearance, his fire, his wit, his poetry, his address. 'All men are black villains at heart,' had said Mrs Jeffereys. And this was certainly the general view held in Byblow Bottom, where so many legacies of their carefree villainy lay scattered and unclaimed, like eggs at an Easter festival.

How many males could I number among my acquaintances who were not black villains? Well: there was Edward Ferrars, that pillar of rectitude; there was the Colonel; there was Thomas; there were, of course, dear Mr Bill and Mr Sam – but what did I truly know about those two? Mr Sam had a wife, Mr Bill, a sister; but were they kind, were they supportive to those ladies? If they had children, did they maintain them?

Would it be possible for me to write to Blank Willoughby Esquire, Allingham or Ammingham, Somerset: 'Dear Sir, I am given to believe that I am your daughter. I should be delighted to make your acquaintance and would be much obliged if you felt inclined to let me know my mother's address and contribute towards my support.' (But probably, in view of his former way of life, he had run through Miss Grey's fifty thousand by now. And what about his wife, the erstwhile Miss Grey? *She* would probably not be at all pleased to make my acquaintance.)

In the midst of such confused and contradictory thoughts as these, I finally drifted off to sleep.

Next morning, bursting with news, I sought the presence of Mrs Jebb.

These days she did not quit her couch until noon, or later; I found her, pale and listless, still in bed, wrapped in a fleecy shawl (for the spring mornings continued frosty and sharp; anxiously I wondered how Elinor Ferrars might be faring, and if Mrs Ashcott still remembered to leave the oatmeal to simmer overnight). Mrs Jebb was drinking cocoa with a look of gloomy distaste. Scattered correspondence lay over the counterpane.

'Ma'am, only listen! I have made *such* a discovery!'

Ignoring my remark, she said, 'Look at this!' and thrust a paper at me.

It was a letter in the handwriting of Edward Ferrars. It said:

Dear Madam,

I regret to be obliged to inform you that Information of a most Regrettable and Scandalous nature has come to us from a Reputable Source, regarding the young Person at present residing with you, the young Person known as Miss FitzWilliam; news which makes it wholly out of the question for me ever again to receive her under this roof. And I strongly recommend that you yourself should lose no time in expelling this Creature from your own Premises. I regret to say that her conduct has been completely Incompatible with Morals or Decency.

I have the Honour to Remain, dear Madam with respectful compliments, your friend,

Edward Ferrars.

'A reputable source!' cried I in high indignation. 'I'll lay his reputable source is none other than that spiteful tattletale, Nell Ferrars!'

Now, of course, I repented my note urging Nell to come home and take care of her mother. For plainly this must be the fruit of it.

'It is because I told her she should come back to Delaford. Of course she would far sooner remain in Berkeley Square, currying favour with Lady Helen. But, ma'am, listen, my news could not be more timely – '

Eagerly, without reflection, I now poured out the tale of my encounter with Mrs Jeffereys. Mrs Jebb listened in silence.

I concluded: 'And so you see, ma'am, I need not be a charge upon you any longer – or a disgrace under your roof – for, surely, once I have left this house, surely your friends will all return to you – I can go and seek my mother –'

'B-b-b - b-b-but - '

Her stammer took me by surprise. She had turned even paler – leaden-pale.

'But what, ma'am?'

'We were to go to P-p-p-p – to P-p-port –'

Mrs Jebb fell forward, heavily, on to the breakfast tray.

Pullett came running in at the sound of the crash.

'Oh – Miss *Liza!* What in the world did you *say* to her?'

Gulping, I explained to Pullett as we ran for warm water and towels, and I wiped Mrs Jebb's face and laid her back comfortably while Thomas went off at a gallop for the doctor.

'You said you were going to London to seek for your mother? Oh, but Miss Liza – Missis was looking forward *so much* to going to Portugal – she spoke of it so often – "When we and Miss Liza go off on the gad to Lisbon – ' she'd say, "we'll do such-and-such – "'

We stared at one another in horrified silence, and I wished that I had never been born.

❧

The doctor said that it was a stroke, and that Mrs Jebb might rally.

'But I fear that her constitution has been gravely undermined by the pints of laudanum – in brandy furthermore – that she has been imbibing during the past few weeks.'

It had been undermined, too, we concluded, by all the threatening letters she had been receiving from Sydney Wetherell.

'Pay £50 or I will lay an information and bring witnesses who will attest to seeing you purloin two handkerchiefs and a yard of satin ribbon on January 15 last . . .'

There were half a dozen in the same vein, concealed in her reticule.

'Oh, my poor mistress!' wept Pullett. 'Why did she never tell me about them? And she must have been paying him off, too . . . no wonder she has been skimping so, lately, on the housekeeping. No wonder she wishes to sail to Portugal and get away from the bloodsucker.'

But Mrs Jebb was not destined to sail to Portugal.

She did rally to the extent that she was able to talk a little, to consume a spoonful or two of food. But her heart was not in recovery; she paid little heed to us as we came and went, addressed her, pestered her with food or with services; her eyes, her thoughts, were elsewhere.

Once she said to me vaguely, 'Who did you say your father was, child?'

'Willoughby, ma'am.'

'Do I know him?' even more vaguely.

'I have no idea, ma'am.'

'No – I do not think I know him. And I don't think Mr Jebb knew him.'

Mr Jebb was much in her mind. She referred to him very often, as if she thought that he was in the house and would soon enter the room.

Another time she said, slowly and haltingly, 'I wish you to have my rubies, Eliza.'

'Oh, *ma'am*!'

They were an exceedingly handsome and valuable set: old-fashioned table-cut stones, comprising a double choker necklace, bracelets, earrings and two huge circular brooches; she sometimes wore the lot, her lips puffed out in self-derision, to add lustre to a humdrum evening while playing whist with her friends. Latterly, she had not worn them.

I said, half laughing, 'But, Mrs Jebb, you have always told me that the rubies were not for me – because they would clash so hideously with my hair.'

'Never – mind – that. Worth – handsome sum. Set – up – in business.'

'But, ma'am, what about those poor Ferrars? Elinor's need is so much greater than mine.'

'Not – your affair!' she snapped. 'Dispose – rubies – where I choose.'

'Yes, yes, ma'am – of course,' I soothed.

'Don't owe *them* – any good turn. Forbade you – house. Leave – rubies – where I choose,' she repeated, and I forbore to point out that a verbal disposition of property had no legal binding.

She went further though, summoned Rachel and Thomas, made Pullett fetch the stones from the mahogany wardrobe (relic of a much larger house) and take them out of their case.

'Give – to – Liza. Put – in her hands,' she croaked. 'Now – bear witness – you two – Rachel! – Thomas!'

'But, Missis,' said Rachel doubtfully – her face was all wrinkled up with distress, 'there must something in writing. You must put it in writing. And Thomas says the same.'

He nodded with vigour.

Mrs Jebb could not write. All she could produce was some spidery streaks on the paper.

'We should fetch in the lawyer – Mr Penwith – I daresay he can make an affidavit – or some such thing, tomorrow.'

Mrs Jebb nodded slowly. 'Tomorrow. Rubies – for – Eliza,' she repeated.

But in the night she died.

I was with her at the time, for Pullett, who had been sitting at her bedside, grew anxious about her breathing and fetched me. We raised her up and I suggested a little brandy, which always seemed to ease her. Pullett had gone for it when Mrs Jebb opened both eyes and gave me a slow smile – her old, quirky smile, mocking at both of us.

'Ma'am?' I said softly. 'Did you really take that lace?'

One eye slowly closed. And remained shut. The other followed suit. Neither re-opened. After a moment – I had been holding her – I laid her back on the pillows.

Pullett, returning with the brandy, let out a long, low wail.

Of course I did not get the rubies. Mr Penwith, the lawyer, though perfectly civil, was quite scandalized at the idea. In vain did Pullett, Rachel and Thomas assure him that Mrs Jebb's intentions had been completely clear, that they were all witnesses; he made nothing of this.

'My dear good people – anybody could *say* anything! Signed and sealed *must* be signed and sealed. And here – in her will – it states with perfect clarity that they are to go to Mrs Busby. I will take care of them.' And he did so forthwith, tucking them under his arm.

Mrs Jebb's will left five hundred pounds to her cousin Mrs Elinor Ferrars – I was glad of that, though I feared Elinor's husband would appropriate every penny of it for parish purposes – some other trinkets besides the rubies were distributed among her forsworn perfidious friends, and the house in New King Street 'to my faithful servants Rachel and Thomas Kennet'. One hundred pounds to Pullett. Nothing to me, except for a strange codicil, 'I bequeath my dear Pullett and Miss Eliza FitzWilliam to each other.'

'Most untoward – most unorthodox,' said Mr Penwith crossly. 'I told Mrs Jebb so but she would have it; she would pay no attention to my counsel. It means nothing, of course – nothing at all!'

Mrs Jebb left very little cash. The sale of furniture and effects would just about cover the legacies.

I was happy for Thomas and Rachel, who declared their intention of keeping the house and taking in lodgers, in Bath always a most profitable livelihood.

'And you shall be our first lodger, Miss Liza, and for nothing, and for as long as you please. For Missis was that fond of ye, we know she'd a wished it.'

'But, Rachel, I brought her nothing but harm. I am sorry that I ever crossed her path.'

'Stuff and nonsense, miss. She loved ye. This last pair o' years she've been happier and brisker than since Master died.'

Now that it was too late, I wished vehemently that I had asked Mrs Jebb more questions about her husband, about her childhood; about their early life together. Alas, the young are ever so; they think time is unlimited; they expect their elders to go on for ever. The moment for asking questions is always postponed.

But I did not plan to continue in Bath, I told Thomas and Rachel. There was nothing here for me now.

'I am going to London, to look for my mother.'

'And I'll come with ye,' declared Pullett.

Truth to tell, though I was touched by this offer, it did not rejoice me. I felt that Pullett would be a decided anxiety, an encumbrance. A fetter.

'No, no, Pullett; you must stop here in Bath with your friends. How do I know that I shall be able to support both of us? It is hardly even likely that I can support myself.'

'Nay, but I'll help ye,' said Pullett. 'I can work – I can sew – I can take in washing. And it's not respectable for a young lady to be off on her own.'

What she meant, of course, was: just now you are going to need all the respectability you can scrape together.

Not one of Mrs Jebb's friends appeared at her funeral. Thomas, Rachel, Pullett and I were the sole mourners at the grave-side, and walked home in silence leaving her all alone in her coffin, under the wet earth, under the lashing rain. I hoped that she would be reunited with Mr Jebb. And I hoped that the rubies would raise blisters on the wrinkled neck of white-haired, acid-tongued Mrs Busby.

Pullett and I travelled up to London on the stage. Urged by Thomas, Rachel and myself, she had lodged her hundred pounds in the bank. So we had very little money between us. I had nearly run through my last earnings from Mrs Haslam's school, and Mrs Jebb had not paid her servants their last week's wages. I sold a few books, which I had acquired during my sojourn in Bath. Rachel and Thomas sold Mrs Jebb's piano ('which we shan't want,' said they) and insisted on giving us the money.

I wrote a cautious note to Mrs Jeffereys informing her of my intention and, in return, she sent me the address of her cousin,

Mrs Widdence, the milliner in Clerkenwell who she said often took lodgers on her attic floor at a very modest rental.

So, at least, in London we had an address to make for.

'*I'll* take charge of that, and the money,' declared Pullett firmly, tucking the slip of paper with Mrs Widdence's address into her purse. While we were packing she clucked over me like a hen, casting me into transports of irritation. Poor Pullett! She was so proud of her new responsibility.

'Missis knew what she was about, all right, adding that piece in her testament!' she kept repeating. 'Missis knew ye're a harum-scarum young mawther yet, Miss Liza, and want careful watching.'

Accordingly we travelled from Bath to London together in outward amity. But this belied my inner feelings which were in a state of resentment that my great adventure must be thus reduced . . .

Reaching London after dark, we were set down at Paddington Green, where there had been an Easter Fair and a large crowd was still slowly dispersing. People shouted and ran about; crackers exploded.

'What'll we do now, Miss?'

Pullett looked about her fearfully. Her confidence suddenly evaporated.

'Find a hackney coach to carry us to Clerkenwell. You stay there with the bundles while I look for the nearest coach stand.'

'Don't be long!' she cried.

By the time I returned with the conveyance, she was already in a high state of panic. 'I thought I'd never see ye more! The crowds are so dreadsome!' And we had not been driving in the hackney for more than ten minutes when she let out an agonized wail.

'The money! It's gone! My purse! Someone must 'a slit the strings of my pocket!'

Frenziedly she clutched herself all over, trying to prove herself wrong; but no: the purse with all our resources had indubitably been snatched.

'Oh – *Miss Liza*! What'll we do? What *shall* we do?'

'What's amiss?' suspiciously demanded the jarvey, hearing her lamentations, and he pulled up his horse. When he heard what had happened he refused to take us a step farther and evicted us, summarily, with our belongings, into the street. Whipping up, he wished us an obscene fate and was soon out of sight.

'Oh, do stop howling, Pullett! You only make people stare at us.'

We seemed to have arrived in a fashionable, populous area; I looked up at the well-lit street signs and found that we were on the corner of the Oxford Road and Bond Street.

'Sit on the bundles, Pullett, so that somebody doesn't take those, and spread out your shawl; I am going to sing.'

Inspired with this notion by Pullett's wails, which had attracted considerable attention from passers-by, I began my song recital with a long and extremely loud halloo; it was the sound with which in Byblow Bottom we young ones were used to summon one another if anything good was giving away, or if some sport was in prospect:

'Oh, hoooo! Oh hooo, oh, *hooo*!'

It was sung, or shouted, on three notes and, at the full pitch of my voice, it carried amazingly, even through the London hubbub.

Many people turned to gaze at me.

Then, without more ado, I launched into some of the ballads which we had been used to sing back in Somerset; not the polite ones, and the operatic airs which had been considered suitable for the Bath audiences, but rougher, wilder songs, with sprightly melodies that would catch the fancy of the foot passengers and soon have them repeating the choruses. So it proved. A crowd swiftly gathered. And in a short time I had them all humming, tapping their toes and nodding their heads.

A few pennies fell on the shawl, which Pullett had nervously spread out; then a few more; then a silver coin or two; then quite a shower. I caught the glint of gold, even.

All at once a constable appeared, very scandalized. 'Here, push off, young woman!' (Only these were not the precise terms he employed.) 'You can't do that here! This is a respectable street! You are causing an obstruction!'

I replied in my most genteel Queen Square accents – Miss Orrincourt would have been proud to hear me, 'I am so very sorry, Officer, but all our money was stolen in a crowd at Paddington and we require a cab to take us to Clerkenwell. Have we enough money for the fare now, do you think?'

And I swiftly scooped up the cash from the ground and displayed it to him, contriving to slip a crown piece into his hand.

'Eh, well – in that case,' he said, 'I'll find ye a cab, Missie. Only don't ye go for to sing any more! For 'tis an offence and I'd be obliged to take ye up. Move along, now, move along, move along,' he urged the crowd, which began most regretfully to drift away. The constable disappeared in search of a cab.

'Upon my soul, madam!' exclaimed a fashionably dressed man who, during my recital, had been giving me a number of exceed-ingly broad stares. ''Pon my soul, *you* certainly know how to bawl out the old ballads! I fancied I was back at Eton! Tee hee! You've a voice on you that would gladden a herring-merchant. 'Pon my soul, you have! I'd hire you for a glee-party directly, if ever I planned to give one. 'Pon my soul, I would!'

He spoke with a kind of drawling affectation, peering at me through a glass set in the top of his walking-cane, and simpering as if he intended to quiz me. I said, 'Thank you; sir,' coolly, and busied myself with folding Pullett's shawl and handing it to her; the money I had tied up in my handkerchief.

'Oh, come along, my love, for gracious sakes!' exclaimed a lady, jerking at the arm of my interlocutor. She was very smartly dressed, and handsome in a sharp-featured way, but evidently in no mind to be civil to *me*. The glance she cast at me comprehensively analysed and dismissed my shabby gown, worn bonnet and untidy hair tumbling out from under the straw brim. 'Come along, Robert, do!' she repeated. 'We shall be late at your mother's!' and she drew him away. He followed, but slowly, as if to assert his independence, casting many glances back at me.

Now a cab drew up. And I urged Pullett to get into it, and handed her the bundles.

'But we don't know the address!' she wailed. 'We don't know the address in Clerkenwell!'

'Well, we must just ask our way when we arrive there. It is a Mrs Alice Widdence,' I told the driver, 'and she lets out rooms over a milliner's establishment. I think the number might be fifteen.' He nodded, evidently accustomed to such vague directions.

I thanked the friendly constable, and was about to climb into the cab myself when an elderly gentleman stepped up to me.

'Excuse me, madam,' he said courteously, 'but are you a professional?'

'Professional, sir?' I gave him a wary glance.

'Musician.'

'I – yes – I teach music and singing.'

'Remarkable,' he murmured. 'Remarkable. Allow me to give you my card.'

And he handed me a slip of pasteboard, which I tucked into the handkerchief along with the coins.

Chapter 9

Mrs Alice Widdence was a plump, soft-voiced, soft-faced lady with a profusion of ringlets which owed their golden hue to the friseur's art, not to nature; she was light on her feet, quick-moving and had an eye like an Italian dagger. Not a single action of her work-people went unnoticed – and in the establishment at Clerkenwell there must have been at least thirty assistants and ten improvers, not to speak of little 'prentice girls, day hands, porters, footmen and various showroom ladies. Much work was sent out: the skirts of all dresses, no matter how grand or how costly the fabric, were dispatched as soon as cut, borne by little ragged urchins to poor needlewomen living like starlings, half-a-dozen to a tenement, in narrow lanes to the northwards. In the shop, work was carried on at top speed with hardly a break; the work-girls were lucky if they snatched as much as four hours' sleep a night, for Mrs Widdence and her creations stood in the van of fashion, her gowns, cloaks and pelisses were in demand by all the ladies of the ton; nevertheless she lived in daily dread that some of her trade might be pirated or leak away to another business house.

We had not the slightest difficulty in finding our way to her premises, for they were extensive: on the north side of Clerkenwell Road she owned three houses which had all been thrown together; downstairs at street level were the showrooms, which had large handsome windows with a brass bar across them over which hung samples of her merchandise – an elegant gauze shift embroidered with poppies, a lace peignoir, a silk vest. Upstairs were the large workrooms, furnished with long deal tables, where sat the assistants and apprentices, sewing away as if their life depended upon it. Some of the attics on the top floor were sleeping quarters for the workers – when they had any time for sleep; some were let off to lodgers like ourselves. And the cellars were used for storage.

'But there's a bad smell about this place!' said Pullett, wrinkling her nose with disapproval. 'I shouldn't wonder but what there's a cesspit under those cellars, Miss Liza; this ain't a healthy spot, if you ask *me*.'

Pullett, having brought us so near calamity with the loss of the purse, was anxious to re-establish her credit by reminding me of her supernatural powers. Later, in fact, we heard that her diagnosis had been correct; a cesspit *was* discovered under the cellars and, furthermore, there were several bodies in it, of girls who had unaccountably disappeared.

My first object when we had established our credentials with Mrs Widdence, and paid her four shillings apiece weekly lodging in advance, was to ask if she knew anything about my mother. But here I was disappointed. Mrs Widdence had heard of no such person; no lady called Miss Williams had opened a gaming house in London, nor did anybody owning such an establishment answer to my mother's description. And it certainly seemed that, from her multifarious connections, Mrs Widdence would be bound to have access to any such information. However, from her affiliations as former housekeeper to Mrs Jennings, our landlady could, and lavishly did, supply a considerable amount of information about other characters in the Dashwood and Ferrars families.

Mrs Jennings herself – the kind, rich old lady at whose mansion in Berkeley Street the Dashwood sisters had been staying at the time when Willoughby jilted Marianne – Mrs Jennings had died of a dropsy two years since. (And had left a handsome legacy to her housekeeper.) Mrs Palmer, younger daughter of Mrs Jennings, no longer came to London, but resided at Cleveland, her husband's property near Bristol. Likewise Mr John Dashwood, elder brother to Elinor Ferrars, was seldom seen these days in the metropolis, but busied himself in continual improvements to his manor house, Norland, in Sussex. But old Mrs Ferrars, Edward's mother, still remained in Wimpole Street, and her younger son Robert, who had married Miss Lucy Steele, lived close by in Hanover Square, and visited the old lady every single day. The elder Miss Steele had never married, but had returned to relatives in Plymouth. Sir John Middleton, who had married Mrs Jennings' elder daughter, kept his house in Conduit Street and passed such time in London as could be spared from sporting activities. But his first wife had died, and he had married again, a much younger lady.

None of this – relating as it did to persons completely unknown to me – did I find of signal interest, until Mrs Widdence added: 'She buys a deal of gowns here – does Lady Middleton – generous to a fault he is, Sir John, grudges his lady nothing she fancies. And Miss Dashwood often comes along with her, and sometimes the old lady, when she's not too astray in her wits. And they also patronize my other establishment in the West End.'

Aha! thought I. So perhaps there may be a chance for me to see Margaret Dashwood again. Now that I know all about Willoughby, she can hardly withhold such information as she possesses. And perhaps she may know where he now is.

'What about Miss Nell Ferrars – Miss Dashwood's niece? The one who has been staying in town with Lady Helen Lauderdale?'

'Oh, la, *they* never come here! They are far too genteel and great to visit this part of town. But it is true they do come to the Bond Street showroom, and that Lady Helen, she's a free spender. Not Miss Ferrars; she don't buy; Lord bless you, she has not five pennies to rub together. Sometimes Lady Helen will buy her a shift, or a pair of stockings. There is talk, though, that Miss Nell has netted herself a suitor. That may alter matters.'

Poor devil, thought I. Surely he cannot guess what a flint-heart he aspires to take in hand? If he did he'd be off as fast as his legs could carry him. Unless he is some tough old tartar . . .

'A wealthy India merchant, much older than the lady,' Mrs Widdence went on, confirming my guess. 'Mr Joseph Sedgwick. He wears out wives at a great rate. Miss Ferrars will be his third. Depend upon it, she plans to be a widow before too long. But to my mind 'tis just as likely the boot will be upon the other foot – ' She glanced down the room and sent her voice like a blade of lightning: '*Miss Smith*! You are cutting that bodice far too long – I can see from here! Careless, wasteful girl!'

The assistant turned perfectly white, and ducked her head over her work.

As our quarters were very tiny, Pullett and I spent a fair amount of time in the large downstairs showroom; to this Mrs Widdence made no objection. Indeed, the place was almost like a club or assembly room, with its wide glittering floor and red velvet curtains. The polished mahogany counters lay to the rear and so did not impede the continual throng of customers, would-be customers and their friends, who daily filled the space, talking, strolling, inspecting the merchandise and ogling the sales-people.

'I don't like Mrs Widdence above half, Miss Eliza,' repeated Pullett earnestly, at night, in our attic. 'She've a real nasty ring about her, red-purple, 'tis the colour of raw liver, a very ugly colour, if you'll believe me, Miss; and if you ask me this *shop,* as they call it, is little better than a bawdy-house; there's nasty goings-on in some of these attics, and the poor little 'prentices is just worked to death, *and* beyond; my dad once wished to put me into the needlework trade, what they call "under-the-bed" workers, but my mam had it over him that I was to go into house service, and I'm truly thankful she did. Miss Eliza, I don't believe we should stay here; no good will come of it. Besides, how in the world are we to keep ourselves?'

I had put up a sign in a book-and-pamphlet shop in the Strand advertising voice, piano and harp lessons, but so far had received no inquiries; probably, as Pullett said, the neighbour-hood was not genteel enough; nobody in this part of London wished for music lessons.

But I was still absorbed and engrossed by the daily panorama of London citizens, their wives and daughters, friends and lovers, who came and went in the big showroom; I felt foolishly certain that, sooner or later, if only I was able to scrutinize their faces long enough, I would be able to find the two that I sought. Just now I was deeply occupied in wondering about my parents: both of them, it seemed, were still in the world *somewhere* – but where?

'We'll stay just a week or two, Pullett dear, and look about us. Now I know the trick of it, I can always sing a few songs in the street and make a little money.'

'*Never!*' cried Pullett, utterly scandalized. 'I'll not allow it! What would your friends say?'

'What friends? What can it matter what I do?'

The loss of both Mrs Jebb and Elinor Ferrars had made a strange vacancy on my mental horizon.

And yet Pullett had some arguments on her side, as shall be heard.

The attic where we slept was dark and fusty enough, and Clerkenwell Road, though busy, was rather a narrow and dingy thoroughfare; glad therefore of an excuse to make an excursion to an airier, more spacious neighbourhood, I suggested to Pullett that we walk over to Mrs Widdence's other establishment in Bond Street (I now having procured a map and discovered that it was no great distance, probably not above an hour's walk).

Pullett was no walker, however. 'You go, if you wish, Miss Liza, but don't go getting into trouble, now; keep your eyes sharp about you. And no singing in the street, mind! I'll just stay here and mend your worked muslin, which is sadly worn; and maybe lend a hand to one or two of the poor little 'prentice girls.'

So, with a light heart and step, relieved at finding myself alone for once (for, unused to constant company and supervision, I found it decidedly irksome), I set off westwards. Mild spring was turning to warm summer; the streets were dry and dusty, odours of food and horse-dung battled with fresher scent from cowslips and wallflowers on the costers' barrows. A familiar ache moved in my heart as I recalled the kingcups and cowslips along the brook at Byblow Bottom, and the honeysuckle in the hedges; still, I found London a fine, lively town, decidedly more open and airy than Bath; I felt less confined here.

Mrs Widdence's Bond Street dress emporium rejoiced in the name Florinda, done out over the doorway in trailing brass letters; and the showroom itself went under the grand appellation of *'premier magazin'*. Here there were vast looking-glasses from floor to ceiling, set between the panels in the walls. The floor was thickly (and hideously) carpeted in colours of violet and amber, the window curtains were of rich dark green velvet. Small spindly chairs stood against the walls.

Fortunately I was already acquainted with the footman who opened the door; he was from Clerkenwell and gave me a friendly nod. I passed in, attracting little notice from the crowd of fashionably dressed shoppers who assumed, no doubt, that I was a chamberwoman come on some errand for my mistress.

I found a quiet corner, where counter met wall, and fell to my usual occupation of scanning faces.

Snatches of talk came my way: 'Nine shillings a yard is far too dear.' 'But for a cravat?' 'Five shillings would be ample.' 'But the striped one will fray. I am certain that it will fray.' 'And what colour trimmings?' 'I must get some sandal ribbons for my black shoes.' 'A dreadful hole in my Mechlin – I do not know if it can be mended.' 'Excuse me, sir – you are standing on my gown!'

The customers here were of a decidedly superior class to those in the Clerkenwell establishment, I was thinking, when my ears were startled – pierced, indeed – by a loud, familiar voice.

'Lizzie! Lizzie Lubber-fist, as I live and breathe! I heard a rumour you was in town, but gave it small credit – but now I see 'twas true!'

A broad smiling countenance shone, radiated before me; light-brown curls were clustered round this spacious face; and beneath it was a form to match, broad and beamy as a coal-barge, but fashionably attired in a walking dress of olive-striped crape and topped with a tremendously feathered bonnet.

'Well I never did! I thought you was fixed in Bath for ever and a day! So Hoby would have it. But here you are, large as life, in Bond Street!'

'Fanny! Fanny Huskisson! How – how v-very surprising to see you – '

'You never wrote!' she said reproachfully. 'You said you would write to me. But I heard about you nevertheless – from Hoby. Ah ha! my dear, you were a more faithful correspondent to him than ever you were to your friend Fanny! But come – have you made your purchase? Then let us come out of this hurly-burly and have a cup of coffee at Grillons. I want to hear all about you – and not just what you choose to relate. I can tell you, I have heard some scandalous tales!'

She swept me out of the door and round the corner into Albemarle Street. At Grillons – a most superior hotel, plainly patronized for the most part by the nobility – if not royalty itself – I noticed that Fanny was greeted with respect, and we were led to a small cushioned alcove.

'I keep a hotel myself, you see,' explained Fanny. 'Oh, no, not so grand as this! It is in Bedford Row – a coffee house and tavern. But' – she gave me a wink – 'we in the business all know one another.— A pot of *Cafe Talleyrand,* Sam,' she said to the smiling waiter. Her French accent was straight from Byblow Bottom.

The coffee, when it came, I found to be liberally laced with brandy.

'Why Talleyrand?' I asked.

'How should I know? I suppose he liked it that way. But now, come! Tell your tale!'

So I told it, somewhat abridged. At different points she nodded her feathered head.

'Ay, they were a wild, godforsaken troop, those Bath Bucks. But I've heard misfortune's overtaken 'em – iss, fay!' (She still had a West Country accent.) 'Taken up for debt, your friend Harry ffinch-french, *and* his friend Ned – stuck in the Marshalsea, both of 'em, now, till Turpentine Sunday, I daresay; their fine kin have grown tired of bailing them out.—But what are you doing in town, my love?'

'Looking for my parents.'

'But why?' She was bewildered. 'What difference can it make to you if you find them? I never had the least inkling as to who my mother might have been. Does that ever trouble me? Not a whit!'

'But you do at least know your father? He set you up in your tavern?'

Fanny's father, like Hoby's, I gathered, was a government minister, a high-up official in the Board of Trade. While not officially acknowledging his love-child, he was on friendly terms with her and frequently visited her establishment.

'Come in with me, Liza – do!' she offered cordially. 'I am planning to open a coffee shop; in Jermyn Street, probably. You could manage it for me! That would be better than teaching music to a parcel of whining schoolgirls and getting yourself tumbled in the Bath woods by a troop of nasty macaronis.'

'But, Fanny – I told you –'

'Yes, well – ' She brushed my denial aside. 'And, pray, where's the sense in wasting time searching for your pa and ma? If they had wished to seek you out, they would have done so. Now, here's my direction – ' She handed me a card. 'Think it over, love, if you must, but don't delay too long. Come and see me. I promise you, there's no future for you in music, *or* in teaching – not a jot, not a sop. No one will hire you now, not after the Bath affair. And we females from Byblow, you know, can have no hope of ever being accepted by the Nobs – we have to manage as best we can. And we get along not too badly, I assure you!'

'I daresay you are right,' I agreed sadly as she surged to her feet, round, cheerful, buxom and vulgar. I tucked away her card and in doing so found another which, up to this moment, I had forgotten, folded into my waist pocket. Bringing this out, I studied it.

'Dr Giovanni Fantini. Do you know this name, Fanny?'

'Why yes – I've heard it,' she said vaguely. 'He is some musical fellow.'

'White's Club, where is that?'

'Oh, it is one of the grand clubs. In St James's. Where all the old gagers foregather. Do you know, Liza, how I first guessed that you were in town? One of the girls who works for me – little Sue Scrope – do you remember her? She swore up and down that she'd heard your voice one night – singing in Bond Street. Pho, pho, my love, I told her, Liza would never demean herself to do such a thing. (For if you wish to ruin yourself, once and for *all,* my dear, that is the way to go about it.) And you have now to be extra careful because of the Bath Bucks, besides coming from you-know-where.—Now, my love, do not stay a day beyond your week with old Madam Widdence – do you know what *her* nickname is? The Scarlet Pimperness! – but join up with me, and we shall have such larks! Lassy me, is that the time? I must flit directly! Sam, can you fetch me a hack?'

Off she bounced. I took my way back up Albemarle Street and returned, presently, to Florinda's, since my wish to survey the patrons of those premises was not yet appeased.

And Fortune smiled on me. After an hour or so, in walked the very person I hoped to see: Miss Margaret Dashwood. She was with another lady who took her way upstairs, apparently to be fitted for a gown; Miss Dashwood rather wistfully scrutinized some ribbons and trimmings, but not as if she had any intention of buying.

'Miss Dashwood,' I said in her ear.

She spun round as if stung.

'Miss FitzWilliam!' she gasped. 'Good heavens! How – how very amazing. I had – had no idea that – that you were here – in town.'

She glanced about her apprehensively, as if terrified that some of her acquaintance might see her talking to me.

'Miss Dashwood – may I speak to you for five minutes? May we go outside?'

She looked in a hunted, nervous way up the stairs; but the lady still had not returned.

'Wh – why, yes, certainly; that's of course.'

Twittering, she accompanied me into Hanover Square, just a step away.

'Miss Dashwood, I wish you would tell me anything – anything at all – about my father. Willoughby. Because – after all – you did know him quite well – did you not?'

'Oh,' she said breathlessly. 'Well, you must understand, I was just a child – only thirteen or fourteen – when he, when he was making up to my sister Marianne. He really – he really did seem then as if he loved her. He seemed quite besotted about her. And Marianne doted on him. Indeed, we thought it would kill her when he gave her the go-by. He was so very handsome. And attentive! Only of course afterwards we feared it was all a take-in, because just a few months before that he had, it seemed, been so very thick with

Miss Wil – with your mother. And then, only a few weeks *after,* proposed to Miss Grey!'

'But your sister – was she happy with Colonel Brandon?'

'It was like weak tea after strong liquor,' said Margaret Dashwood unexpectedly. 'For her. Nothing would ever be the same. That was why she would never consent to have Brandon's child. That was why she would never see *you.*' I gasped. She went on, 'Oh, I was supposed to know nothing of all this. I am an unmarried lady – not fit for my ears.' She laughed angrily. 'Of course, we all knew that the Colonel was paying for your upkeep in Somerset. But Marianne refused most vehemently ever to have you at Delaford. Or visit you. Or even permit the Colonel to visit you.'

'And my mother? Where was she meanwhile?'

Miss Dashwood shrugged. 'Who knows? Died in some spunging-house, doubtless – like *her* mother before her.'

She gave me a sharp look. Life had dealt Miss Dashwood various knocks, I thought, in the few years since she had taught at Mrs Haslam's school. Her escape from that institution had not been all freedom and frolic.

'And Willoughby?' I asked.

'If I were you, Miss FitzWilliam – ' she began. Then her eyes widened, looking over my shoulder. 'Oh, mercy – ' she breathed.

An oddly familiar drawling voice behind me said, 'Why, demme! If it ain't my charming sister-in-law. Mag! Mag Dashwood! Looking as guilty as if she'd been caught with her fingers in the church collection plate! And holding a confidential ladies-together yarn with – why, 'pon my soul! If it ain't the Sweet Singer of Bond Street! The Mayfair nightingale! Was anything ever so fortunate!' He peered at me with languid impertinence. 'Here was I – and my dear lady the other night – all agog to know your name – so that if we should chance to hold a musical party, you might be the chief performer –'

'Not I!' interrupted his dear lady, who had also been scanning me in a decidedly shrewish manner. 'I beg you won't include me in your schemes, Mr Ferrars! For I've not the least wish to be connected with this person, not in any way whatsoever. And I'm mightily surprised at you, Miss Dashwood, that you should lend yourself to converse with such a creature!'

But Margaret Dashwood, affrighted, had flitted away from us and hurried off round the corner. I coolly made my excuses, in spite of his calls of 'Hem! Hem! Excuse me, ma'am! Your servant!' and walked away eastwards, very much annoyed at the interruption, and that I had got so little good out of Margaret Dashwood.

If that impertinent fellow was her brother-in-law, then he must be Robert Ferrars, Edward's younger brother, who had superseded Edward in his mother's affections. But what a contrast between the two brothers! I was not fond of Edward – who could be? – but he was decidedly superior to Robert.

Chapter 10

NEXT DAY MRS WIDDENCE CAME UP TO ME IN A MOST AFFABLE, insinuating and smiling manner to say that she had heard tell that I had a beautiful voice, melodious as any nightingale. As to that, said I, opinions might differ, but I had a *trained* voice and could sing, and had given public recitals in Bath.

I waited for her to divulge her purpose in approaching me.

'Well,' explained Mrs Widdence, 'in that very ungenteel, low-class establishment as calls itself Tivoli, run by a woman who has the sauce to style herself Madame Deloraine, though to my certain knowledge she's no more Madame and no more Deloraine than that spittoon; plain Jane Higgs she was born in Hackney – '

She paused to catch her breath. I recalled a very superior-looking modiste which I had passed in Bond Street the previous afternoon. Tivoli was the name on the gilded sign.

'– In that place,' continued Mrs Widdence, 'they gives musical entertainments. Young ladies playing on the harp and fiddle. To amuse the customers, you know, and 'tice folk in from the street.'

Now, of course, I could see whither she was steering, but chose to remain politely blank until she had explained herself further.

'I was a-wondering, now, Miss FitzWilliam, if you might see your way to giving us a song or two – of an afternoon, you know – in the Bond Street saloon, of course, not here – if you've no other pressing engagements, that is . . . ?'

Her inquisitive eyes raked me and my unimpressive attire. Plainly, she was dying to know why I spent so much time in her premises, studying the customers.

'Nothing too lively or – or skittish, you know, Miss FitzWilliam, but just a few elegant ballads, now and then – I esteem as how that would be a very superior class of entertainment to offer the clients. Don't you agree?'

'And what would you think of paying me, Mrs Widdence?'

At this she looked rather blank, and said after a moment or two, 'But it would be a 'tisement of you, Miss Fitz, make your name known among the Nobs. I'd no thought that you'd expect *payment* for it –'

I mentioned the sum that I was paid for those concerts in Bath. Mrs Widdence seemed even more shaken.

'As to that – I don't know –' she demurred. 'Seeing as how you pass so many hours in the showroom already. It's not as if –'

'Ah but, you see, Mrs Widdence, I have my reputation to consider.'

At which she threw me a very sharp look and said touchily, 'Might I ask what there would be besmirching to your reputation about entertaining my clients, who are drawn, I'd have you know, from the very highest circles?'

'Oh, I say nothing against your clients, Mrs Widdence, but I must not make myself too – too available, you know.'

'Well, well,' she began, a little placated.

'I tell you!' I said, as if the idea had just come into my head. 'I will give a recital for your Bond Street customers in return for three weeks' free lodging for myself and Pullett. How would that be?'

'Humph!' she said. 'You're a young lady as has her two sides screwed tight together, I can see, Miss Fitz! You strike a hard bargain. Well – we'll give it a try. Now – as to what you will wear – '

She wanted me to wear one of her creations – some atrocious bronze-green satin confection. But I was adamant.

'I'd not be able to sing a note, Mrs Widdence, wearing a robe that was not mine and not paid for. It would shred my voice all to ribbons. And the gown too, like as not!'

She agreed to my terms, though dissatisfied.

'It'll be no 'tisement of my goods, Miss Fitz, none at all, if they see ye sing looking like a plucked gosling.'

'I will find something suitable, Mrs Widdence. Pullett shall furbish up one of my evening gowns and make it presentable.'

With that she had to be content. It was agreed that my first recital should take place on the following Saturday, and Pullett spent some of the intervening time in mending the black-and-white muslin that I had worn for the Bath concerts. Very disapprovingly – she did not like this scheme at all.

Mrs Widdence's *magazinière,* a tall, willowy lady, magnificently done out in a violet silk gown and lace streamers (and who happened to be really French, escaped years before from bloody doings in Paris), announced to the customers in ringing tones that a musical performance was about to begin.

'*Mesdames, mesdemoiselles, messieurs! Silence! Écoutez, s'il vous plaît!*'

A few heads turned, curiously.

I took a deep breath and began.

I had asked if I could sit on the counter, but Mrs Widdence did not at all approve of that suggestion.

'It would give a touch of informality and – and licence to the proceedings, which I do not care for, Miss Fitz. Like some – some creature in a bar! No – you had best stand with your back to the counter – you may have a chair in front of you, so that the clients will not jostle you.'

With that I had to be content.

And it was far harder – immensely harder – than the Bath recitals, where at least we performers were set apart from the audience, on a dais; harder, even, than my desperate venture in the public street, where I was comfortably anonymous, and the passers-by were free to loiter or walk away as they chose.

But here I could sense a kind of annoyance – resentment – affront – as people who had come in simply to buy a pair of gloves – or study colours of ribbons, or to ogle the saleswomen – found themselves willy-nilly exposed to a douche of song.

I sang 'Where the bee sucks' to Mr Arne's setting – unexceptionable, I thought – and another Shakespeare ditty, 'Sigh no more ladies,' by Mr Smith. Then, as I felt I was barely holding my audience, who seemed indifferent, if not positively scornful, I broke into the ballad 'O, she looked out of the window', which had been so successful in Bath. Here, at least, it caused the listeners to stand still for a few moments and slightly abate their chatter – and I ended with a melancholy ballad, 'The maid betray'd', which happened just then to come into my head.

The reason that this song had been running through my mind was because I had passed several of the preceding days in searching through all the spunging-houses of the city, on a vain search for my mother. *Her* mother, as I now knew, had been discovered by Colonel Brandon in such a place, having been abandoned by husband and lover both, and reduced to her last extremities. And it seemed mournfully possible that, since she was not to be heard of in any other locality, my own mother too might have sunk to a similar condition. Her plans for setting up her own gaming-house might never have come to fruition.

But I had not found her; nor had I encountered anybody who knew anything of her history. I had, though, listened to a sufficient number of other histories – wretched, heartbreaking tales of poor girls enticed to the city on false promises, sunk in a morass of debts which they had no possible means of paying off – since the sale of their own persons, which at first had seemed a simple way out of the difficulty, had proved merely a vicious spiral, yielding continually less and less as their freshness faded, and incurring, as well, the hazard of danger and disease.

I sang the ballad with anger and sorrow, thinking of these helpless women, and my own helplessness to do anything for them.

'Pssst! Sing 'em something *cheerful* now!' whispered Mrs Widdence sharply.

But I said, 'No, that's enough. I am out of practice. My voice is tired.'

In any case, I could see the customers were not in a mood to be sung to. There was a scatter of indifferent applause, and some titters and boos, as a spate of conversation broke out, unchecked.

Mrs Widdence looked both discontented and angry.

And a tall young man forced his way towards me through the crowd.

He was strongly built, pale and extremely well dressed. With an eye made critical after so many days passed in sartorial premises, I scanned his superbly cut jacket of dark grey superfine, his close-fitting dove-grey pantaloons, highly polished Hessian boots, his snowy neckwear. His hair was russet-fair, his countenance covered in freckles. And very, very familiar.

'*Hoby!*' I cried out in unaffected delight. 'What joy to see you! How very – how very grown up you look!'

He looked not only grown up, but masterful and authoritative, not to say severe. His countenance had lengthened somewhat with the years; also filled out, firmed and matured.

He showed no equal joy at the sight of me.

'This is no place to talk – ' were his opening words – and he gave a frowning glance about the showroom.

'Mrs Widdence,' said I – she was still glooming at my shoulder, wholly dissatisfied at the outcome of her ventures. 'Mrs Widdence, here is an old friend of mine, Mr – Mr Robert Hobart, whom I have not seen for many years. May we step aside into your office to talk over old times for a few moments?'

With an ill grace, she agreed.

It seemed to me that she already knew Hoby. And certainly she eyed him with respect.

On the way to the office, whom should we encounter but Nell Ferrars and the Lady Helen.

'Well, Eliza!' said Nell coldly. 'I suppose we all expected that you would disgrace yourself in some way, sooner or later, but I am sorry indeed that you take such a public way of advertising your ruin to everybody in the Polite World.'

Lady Helen said nothing at all, but lifted her chin and turned her head aside. On the whole, I thought it best not to make any reply.

As soon as Hoby and I had arrived at the comparative privacy of Mrs Widdence's little business room – where stood stacks of big wicker baskets lined with oil-skin, and a table piled high with bills – we fell to quarrelling bitterly.

'Liza, how could you be such a fool? You know – you should know, coming from Othery – you have to keep your reputation wholly white, wholly unblemished. Not a single whisper must sully it. I had believed that you were safe – established in a very respectable, unexceptionable way down there in Bath – and what happens? First you get yourself into a devil of an imbroglio with those high-playing, foul-tongued riff-raff – as that Friday-faced female says – and now all the Polite World knows of your downfall –'

'It is not true! It is all a pack of lies! And – in any case – why should the p-p-perditioned Polite World be interested in what happens to me?'

'Because it makes a lively story!' said Hoby furiously. 'And then – to put the cap on it – you have to sing that dismal ballad about the maid betray'd – and the other one about never changing your maiden name – have you no sense of discretion at all? Do you *want* everybody to spit on you and point the finger of scorn at you? Why in the world did you ever have to leave Bath and come up here?'

'Mrs Jebb died. And I lost my post at the school because – because of what happened.'

'Well, there! You see! What did you expect to happen, if you make a fool of yourself? And what the devil do you expect to do in London?'

'I came to look for my mother. And father.'

'Oh,' he said blankly.

'Do you know, Hoby – have you ever heard – what became of Willoughby?'

He continued to look at me as if I had taken leave of my senses. I felt like an exhausted runner who has to keep running or he will fall.

'I have a strong wish to find my parents,' I muttered. 'It is all very fine for you, Hoby – your father is the President of the Board of Fisheries' – I had read this in the newspaper – 'and I daresay he has found you some fine public position – what *do* you do, by the by?'

'I act as assistant for Mr Nash at his public works. On the Regent Canal. And designing a new street to run northwards from Piccadilly,' he answered mechanically.

'Just as I thought! And a very engrossing occupation, I dare swear! But what can I do? No one has offered me the occupation of digging a canal.'

'You have your music.'

'Hah! You see where that gets me. I've a good mind to accept Fanny Huskisson's offer.'

'That trollop! I forbid you! I absolutely forbid you! Whatever she offers can only be thoroughly discreditable.'

'What right in the world, Hoby, what right have you to tell me what I shall do or shall not do? Why-why,' I stammered furiously, 'you d-d-did not even answer my letters! Or at least only one in five!'

'And as for setting up to live with this terrible old madam, Mrs Widdence, who, as everybody knows, has procured girls for half the peerage –' he was storming on, when Mrs Widdence herself walked into the small room.

'Mr Hobart,' she said coldly, 'I must ask you to quit this chamber. It – it ain't befitting for you to be closeted with the young lady here any longer.—*Out* you go! Anyhow, there's another gentleman wishes to speak to miss. So kindly give us the benefit of your displacement.'

With a last angry glare at me, Hoby – decidedly high-coloured around the cheekbones – strode out of the door.

'Well there!' said Mrs Widdence indignantly. 'Fine sort of *friends* you have, Miss! But anyway, here's the Signior, wishful to speak to ye – and I hope ye'll be a bit more ladylike and refined with him, as 'is own chapelmaster to His Grace the Duke of Cumbria!'

After which with a frown, a grimace and a meaning wink, she left us together.

The Signior was the same elderly gentleman who had accosted me before in Bond Street.

'I gave you my card, Signorina,' he reproached me. 'Why did you never write to me? Here have I been, searching through all the inns and hotels of London for you –'

His English was fluent and correct, but heavily accented.

'Sir, I must apologize. But I have been very much occupied.'

He glanced around the little room with dissatisfaction.

'This place will not do. You shall accompany me, if you please.'

'But to where? I have a friend – in Clerkenwell – who will very shortly be expecting me – '

Pullett had refused to come to Bond Street to hear me sing. She said it was not respectable, and no good would come of it.

'Ah, I shall not detain you long, at this present,' Dr Fantini said. 'But I wish to show you something which will perhaps enjoin you to listen to what I have – I have to propose, relating to your future.'

Very doubtful and hesitant indeed, I was yet thankful for any excuse to leave Mrs Widdence's showroom. I made her a brief explanation, which she accepted curtly, and followed the white-haired gentleman through the crowd and out to the street, attracting various stares and comments, a few favourable, many detrimental or sneering, on my way to the door. Outside, I was led to a carriage, among the many which blocked the way, and noticed that it bore a coat of arms on the panel and was driven by a very superior-looking coachman.

'Sir, where are we going?'

'Only to Grosvenor Square,' Dr Fantini assured me. 'Then you shall be conveyed onwards to your place of lodgement, if you so wish.'

The ride to Grosvenor Square was brief and performed in silence.

We drew up before a handsome mansion on the south side of the square, and I was escorted by my companion into the house – ushered through the door by a bowing servant – and taken up a flight of stairs into a morning room.

'Now,' said Dr Fantini, 'I must ask you to look at that portrait on the wall.'

It was a life-sized head, very beautifully painted. The signature was Thomas Lawrence. And it was a portrait of my mother – done when she was perhaps five years older than my own age at that time.

'Good heavens,' I said faintly. And again, 'Good heavens!'

Mechanically, I pulled up a chair, sat down upon it and continued to study the portrait. Dr Fantini allowed me to do so in peace for many minutes. Then he said quietly, 'Now, my dear Miss, will you allow me to have my say?'

'Of course, sir.'

'Your mother was a lady named Elizabeth Williams. Am I right? And you were born around the year 1793?'

'To the best of my knowledge, sir, yes.'

'Your mother left you in the care – as she had promised to do – of Colonel John Brandon. And she herself chose to go to London to – ah – pursue a career in opera. She, like you, had a voice of remarkable power and – ah – range. But she happened to be heard, singing the part of Elena in *Elena e Paride* by my employer, the Duke of Cumbria, who was so greatly taken with her voice and – ah – appearance and demeanour, that he – that he invited her to become part of his household.'

'Made her his mistress?' I suggested.

Dr Fantini gave me a severe look.

'My dear Miss, my master the Duke is not – is not a man to be trifled with. He is a man of strong character and integrity. At that time he was twenty-seven years older than Miss Williams, he had for many years been unhappily married and lived separated from his wife and from their three children. He was greatly occupied in government affairs, being, at that time, Chancellor of the Exchequer. He became deeply, deeply devoted to Miss Williams and remained so. He preferred to have her always with him – whether down at his house, Much Zoyland at Alderbrooke in Wiltshire, or at this house in London. He could not bear to be apart from her for more than a day.'

'Sir! Please tell me! Where is my mother now?'

'Your own birth, Miss Eliza, had put your mother in peril of her life. She was told by her medical attendant that to have another child would certainly kill her. This was a great sorrow to her, as she felt a deep obligation and love to my master and would have wished to bear him a child. But it was not to be. He forbade it. He cherished her, he told her, more than any child.—However in the end she was allowed to have her way. Two years ago it was found that she was increasing.—And the prediction was right. She died in childbirth, and the child died also.'

After a moment I said faintly, 'Where is she buried?'

'At Much Zoyland. Would you wish to visit her grave?'

'Of *course* I wish it! Of *course*!' I burst out, and then – I could not help it, too many blows had been struck at me during this dreadful day – I fell into a passion of crying and flung myself down flat on the richly carpeted floor.

Dr Fantini behaved with compassion. In silence, he allowed me to have my cry out, then raised me up and escorted me to a bedchamber where, behind a closed door, with napkins and lavender water, I could repair the ravages to my eyes and complexion.

When I emerged, Dr Fantini was waiting for me with a glass of strong, sweet wine.

'What is this?' I asked, sipping it warily.

'It is port. The Duke – like Mr Pitt – prefers port to claret. Also, he owns a vineyard in Portugal. Now, Miss – are you feeling more the thing?'

I said that I was.

'My offer from the Duke is to take you back to Much Zoyland. There, if – if you are both of a mind to such a scheme – he undertakes to provide for you, have you educated, your voice trained –'

'It has already been trained,' I objected.

'Ye-es,' Dr Fantini rejoined distastefully, ' – not very *well* trained, Miss.'

'Oh.' Could I, I wondered, endure the prospect of *more* training, *more* education? Still, I did wish to see my mother's grave. And to meet somebody who had loved her so much. I could talk to the Duke about her. And – who knows? – he might have tidings of Willoughby.

Besides, I could always leave Much Zoyland, if the Duke and I did not agree.

'The Duke knows about my – my reputation? And where I come from?'

'The Duke is exceedingly well-informed about almost everything.'

'I shall tell him all my history.'

'Very good, Signorina.'

'Another thing – I have a friend, maid, companion – whom I shall wish to have with me.'

'By all means,' Dr Fantini said graciously. 'That will be most conformable.'

So matters were arranged.

Chapter 11

The Duke of Cumbria always dressed in a full suit of old-fashioned clothes. He wore a bulky horsehair wig, which must have weighed several pounds. His coat bore great cuffs and massive buttons, and was stiff so that the skirts stood out; his ruffles were long and always dazzling white. The heels of his shoes were higher than is now common – for the Duke was not a tall man, though at all times a most impressive figure; and the shoes were ornamented with silver buckles, very polished. His face was much seamed and grooved, with care, and grief, and age, his skin somewhat pale; but the black eyebrows above his deepset eyes exceeded in size any that I have ever seen. His voice was very thunderous, though never harsh.

When my mother had first known him she was eighteen, and he forty-five; and they had been together for about fifteen years when she was carried off untimely. So he was now more than sixty, but looked older; he moved slowly, with a stoop, except when on horseback. He played no instrument himself, except the kettledrums; but he loved to hear playing and singing, and took care to ensure that the people about his household should be proficient in the musical arts. His private secretary, Solomon Mayhew, played the piano with brilliance; his steward was a gifted fiddler; even the little page-boys were encouraged to sing and whistle.

Much Zoyland, the Duke's favourite seat in Wiltshire, was a huge old rambling house, built in the reign of Queen Elizabeth on the ruins of an abbey. It was spacious, with wide grassy courts, but also with small cosy low-ceilinged rooms; with great draughty halls, and also narrow passageways. Some of its doorways were so wide that a chaise-and-pair could have driven through; others so narrow that a thin person had to turn sideways to pass between the door-posts.

I grew to love it dearly.

'This is something like!' said Pullett, looking about her with approving eyes, as we drove up the long avenue and had glimpses of formal gardens with bright beds and clipped hedges. 'This is the kind of place I can settle in.'

Her responses to the Duke were in the same favourable spirit. 'He've got a mighty queer ring, but it's a good one; blue and grey mixed; like the sky before sun-up, when you don't yet know, will it be fine or driply.'

Before going to Zoyland I had an assignation that I was obliged to keep, though with no great eagerness for it.

On Sunday I went, with Pullett in reluctant attendance, to see Nell Ferrars in Kensington Gardens. I had written a note appointing a meeting there.

'She'll never, never come,' said Pullett, who had known Nell – and thought very little of her – since early childhood. 'You think that one would bestir herself to leave her great connections and come to see you? – not after what happened!'

For I had given Pullett a pretty clear idea of my ill-success in Bond Street. And, to do her justice, she had not said 'I told you so.'

I said, 'I think Nell may come. She may even bring her great connections with her. To jeer, perhaps. Or simply out of curiosity.'

I had written in my note to Nell: 'I would like to speak to you for a few minutes on a matter of great import concerning your mother. I hope very strongly that you can spare the time for this meeting.'

'Well, I'll *be*!' exclaimed Pullett, after we had taken a couple of turns up and down the Broad Walk. 'There she does come, to be sure!'

'And she's brought some of her great friends with her.'

To my great despondency, she had with her Uncle Robert Ferrars and his wife the shrewish Lucy.

'Odso, Mistress Fitz,' drawled out Robert Ferrars, as the trio came up to us, 'I fancy, don't you know, you had best return to Bath and the young ladies' school; ecod, you had indeed; a London audience seems to find you a trifle lacking in *coloratura,* hey?'

'Don't be a fool, Robert,' stated his better half. 'The young ladies' school won't have her back.'

'Miss Ferrars. I should like to speak to you privately,' I said to Nell.

'Zooks, here's a fine coil! What's so woundily exclusive that *we* can't hear it?'

'If Miss Nell wishes to tell you later, that is entirely her own affair. But she may prefer to keep the matter to herself.'

– 'I'm sure I don't care,' said Mrs Ferrars sharply. 'Come, Robert!'

Affronted, they dropped a few yards behind, while Pullett walked on ahead.

'Well? What is this private communication?' Nell sourly demanded.

I pulled a letter out of my reticule and handed it to her. It was from the publishers John Murray at Number Twelve Albemarle Street.

It said, 'Dear Madam, at your request, knowing that you do not propose a long visit to the Metropolis, we have read your friend's novel with much greater celerity than our normal office procedure permits us, and we are now happily in the position of being able to tell you that we are entirely of your opinion about the Work. We, like you, think it a most delightful and captivating tale, and that it will be sure to take the public fancy. We are pleased to offer these terms for its publication' (terms were here stated) 'and wish you will now favour us with your friend's address, so that we may be in communication with her personally. You informed us on your visit last week that she had a number of other novels already written. My partner and I shall be most eager to peruse those also, and hope that we may be in a position to make her an offer for them as well, following what we are certain will be the success of this one.'

'What *is* all this about?' demanded Nell, handing the paper back to me. She sounded puzzled and impatient. 'I know nothing about writing novels. Why should you show this to me?'

'The novel is by your mother,' I said. 'And she has five others hidden away in her bedroom chest.'

'So?'

'So she may be in a position to derive a handsome income from her writing. Life at Delaford Parsonage may in future not be on quite such a level of grinding poverty.—Provided, of course, that your father may be brought to accept the situation.'

'That is not my affair,' said Nell, even more impatient. 'They must settle it for themselves.'

'Don't you *want* your mother to be a little more comfortable?'

'What business, pray, is this of yours?' she demanded.

'Listen, Nell. You know that your grandmother is touched in her wits?'

'Tiresome old biddy,' muttered Nell. 'What of it?'

'Elinor – your mother – has a presentiment that she finds in herself signs of the same disorder. I do not know if she is correct in her guess. But she fears it, *deeply*. If she can profitably dispose of those six novels that she has written – with such labour, in secret – if she can do that, then she will be comfortably provided for, against – against such a dreadful contingency. There will be enough money for nurses, kind capable people to live in the house and take care of her. She need not fear a terrible old age of hardship and possible ill-usage. Do you see?'

Nell looked hunted. She said, 'My aunt Marianne would help. She would be there. And Uncle Brandon.'

'I doubt that. It is not known where they are at present. They might never come back to England. And you know that your father – is not a solicitous husband. Is out all day on parish affairs.'

'Oh –!' She looked even more harassed. 'So, what am I supposed to do?'

'You could go home and stand by your mother – if your father tried to raise objections to her novels being brought out.'

'But I am engaged to be married!'

'Yes, Nell, and I am going to tell you something about marriage. And about your husband-to-be. And about the death of his last wife.'

'What can you *possibly* mean? What can *you* have to tell *me*?

She stared at me, red with outrage.

'Listen, Nell, I was battling my way in the world while you were still a babe in the cradle. Now pay attention.'

I told her what I had heard from Mrs Widdence about Joseph Smethwick, about how his last wife had died. And the one before. And about what men can do to women whom they have at their mercy.

'I don't believe you!' she declared obstinately. 'It is all a pack of ill-natured gossip.'

I could see, though, that I had greatly shaken her.

'By the by,' I said, turning to summon Pullett. 'Just before I left Delaford, Ralph Mortimer was asking for you. He had sold out of the army, it seems, and is now managing his father's estate.'

'What is that to me?'

But she looked decidedly thoughtful and I saw her standing still, for several minutes, poking at the ground with her parasol, in no particular haste to rejoin her companions.

***

I will not deny that my initial glimpse of the Duke of Cumbria gave me a stab of icy, hideous fright, taking me back in time, fifteen years or more, to the days when I used to patter along the village street, halfpenny in hand, to the vicarage and the ministrations of Dr Moultrie. What Dr Moultrie did at that time I have never mentioned, and never shall; this narrative, as I have stated before, is intended for no more than a partial record of such events as I choose to recount.

Suffice it to say that most speedily did I come to understand that His Grace in no way (save that of most superficial appearance) resembled Dr Moultrie but, on the contrary, was a most upright, affable, high-principled and pleasant-humoured gentleman. Indeed I have never met his like.

It was inevitable that I should feel nervous and ill-at-ease during the opening moments of my first dinner, tête-à-tête with the Duke – which was also our first encounter. He had courteously given me time to rest, before we met, and to remedy the effects of the two-day drive from London. And at dinner he appeared in full ceremonial evening apparel, satin knee-breeches and velvet jacket, with a great smouldering emerald among the folds of his neck-cloth. I could have wished for Mrs Jebb's rubies, old fashioned and table-cut as they were.

However a very few minutes sufficed to set me completely at my ease.

The Duke's first appraisal of me was enough to set tears a-rolling down his cheeks.

'Don't mind me, my dear,' he said, unaffectedly mopping his eyes with his table-napkin, 'but you are so very like your dear mother that your appearance has been quite a shock to me. Indeed, I should have known you if I had met you in Zanzibar! No wonder Fantini was so excited when he saw you in Bond Street. Oh, good gracious me, it is such a great, great pity that you could not have been placed with your mother from the very start. What a deal of sorrow and trouble that would have avoided. What a zany poor Brandon was not to have permitted it. But he had some starched-up notion that, as your mother was his cousin and you therefore his cousin also, family tradition, family pride, whatever, required that you not be brought up by a fallen woman. So, what happens? He leaves you to your own courses and – inevitably – you fall too!'

'Well, sir, as to that, I –'

'– I believe, to his credit, Brandon had some notion at first of taking you into his own household later on. But Mrs Marianne put a stop to that, tiresome creature, with her romantic notions and fidgety prejudices. And then, of course, they went abroad.'

'Have you met Colonel and Mrs Brandon, sir?'

'No, my dear, but I have a great friend and neighbour, Sir John Middleton – he will be dropping in to take his mutton with us one of these days – I see him very often – who knows them well.

'Now, my child, I don't wish you to be under any anxiety or misapprehension about my intentions towards you,' the Duke continued, passing me a dish of duckling with olives – we were dining very informally. 'I shall not be making any amorous approaches towards you – that, indeed, I should regard almost as incest; (not but what it might be very agreeable,' he added in parenthesis. 'You are so *very* like your dear mother, you know). But, latterly, you see, she and I – such a relation, alas, was not possible betwixt us, for, as the result of a most unfortunate toss I took over a double oxer, my proclivities in that respect were wholly trammelled; in fact,' he explained, 'with the best will in the world, *I can't get it up*. So you may regard me simply in the light of your kind old father-in-law, my dear; and – more's the pity – that was the way in which, latterly, your dear mama also regarded me.'

'But, sir – ' a host of questions immediately rushed through my head. Did I dare to utter them? But the Duke having opened on such a comfortable, cordial basis, I thought that I did dare.

'Well, my dear? What shall I call you? I cannot call you Eliza, like *her*; that would touch too tender a vein. I shall call you Lizzie – if you have no objection?'

'None, sir, in the world. But – about my mother – I was given to understand by Dr Fantini that her sad death was caused by a disastrous childbirth; how – in the circumstances you mention – could this come about?'

'Why, it was this way – the silly, silly girl,' he said, hastily refilling both our glasses. 'She thought to do me a good turn – make me a kind *of present,* you see. This house is not entailed, and I have often bemoaned the fact that I have not a son I can leave it to; I am fond of the old place, you see. And Stannisbrooke, my official heir by the Duchess, is such a dull, prosy lump of a fellow! I can't stand to think of him here. Well, let that flea stick! I had a favourite nephew, my younger brother's son, Michael Ravensworth, who used to visit us; a captain in the navy he was, dear fellow – '

'Is he no more, sir?' I asked gently, as the Duke wiped his eyes again.

'No, the poor devil lost his life in that ill-fated Walcheren expedition. Sad waste! Sad waste! He was worth ten of my own son. I had far rather he had been my heir. But, this is how it was; he and Eliza put their heads together, and thought it would please me to know that she was increasing – that there would be a child about the house again – and, no question, it *did* please me, I was as happy as could be –'

'But – good heavens,' I said faintly, thinking that 'put their heads together' was hardly an accurate description, 'the *risk* that she took – that they took – ' And several different kinds of risk, I thought. For were they really so philanthropic in their motives, simply seeking to give the Duke an inheritor for his mansion? Or did they in fact love one another, was it an affair of the heart, rather than pure disinterested benevolence? For the Duke was, after all, twenty-seven years my mother's senior, and Michael Ravensworth no doubt a handsome young captain, a dashing and romantic figure? Well, I should never know. Certainly not from the Duke, who had loved them both equally and seemed sincerely grieved. Perhaps – I could not help

thinking – matters had turned out well for the Duke – though trag-
ically enough for the younger pair – all of them being spared sad
discord and disillusion in later days.

'Did you ever meet my father, sir – Mr Willoughby?'

No, he said, he had not.

'But my friend Sir John knew him well; Sir John will tell you
anything you wish to know. Ah, he was a sad scapegrace, I fear. But
still, as he is your parent, my dear Lizzie, we will not disparage him
too much. As to his whereabouts now, I know nothing; but perhaps
Sir John will be better informed.'

In the meantime it was strange – most strange and ghostly – to
live in the great house at Zoyland where my mother, whom I had
never met – not to remember at least – had contrived to leave such
an imprint of her personality. There were dogs she had reared,
birds she had tended – for Eliza, it appeared, was devoted to
animals; she had owned parrots, monkeys, even a tortoise, a grass-
snake and a hare; some of these, in the interim, had died of natural
causes; some – the monkeys, for instance – had been found too
poignant or too tiresome a reminder and had been dispatched to
other homes; but a great red-and-grey parrot still sat on a perch in
the morning room and once in a long while would raise its heavy
head and scritch out, *'Good day, Eliza!'* in a harsh voice that never
failed to send a freezing shiver down my spine. An old spaniel,
which had been her favourite, would sometimes come and sit with
its head upon my knee.

In a drawer of her bureau, in the little room that she used as her
study, I found papers – notes, jottings, household reminders – in a

hand strangely like my own – a list of suggested gifts for the domestics at Christmas-time. And a footnote to the list: 'But what shall I ever give *him*? So good – so universally kind – but already so amply supplied with all his needs – except the one – oh, me!'

And on a loose page at the end of this collection, I found some handwritten lines under the superscription, *Willoughby*:

> In vain ye woo me to your harmless joys
> Ye pleasant bowers, remote from strife and noise;
> Your shades, the witnesses of many a vow
> Breathed forth in happier days, are irksome now
> Denied that smile 'twas once my heaven to see
> Such scenes, such pleasures, are all past to me.

Poor Eliza! Sadly, sympathetically, I wondered how long my mother had continued to entertain such feelings for her faithless lover – and was mildly relieved, when I discovered, some months later, that she had not composed the lines herself, but merely copied them from the works of Cowper.

I visited her grave very regularly – sometimes with the Duke, sometimes alone. He, almost daily, brought fresh flowers to it – generally of a violet hue if it could be managed, for that, he said, was her favourite colour. The grave lay at the farthest end of the little churchyard which adjoined the pleasure gardens of Much Zoyland house, so that to reach it one need only cross the lawn and pass through a lych-gate.

'I can see the stone from my bedroom window,' the Duke told me fondly. 'So, I think she cannot be lonely there. And it is a solace to me to see the stone.'

On it he had inscribed *My dearly loved Eliza,* and the date of her death.

Tucked into the volume of Cowper's verses (in which I found the foregoing lines) I later discovered another piece of handwritten verse which touched me deeply:

To my Daughter

> Dear Child! I cannot hear thee cry
> I cannot see thy face
> For us, all life must saunter by
> And yield no meeting place.

> Yet through Death's final Gate, I trust
> Thy countenance to see
> That Doom, which turns us all to dust
> Can hold no fears for me.

These lines I have found nowhere else, so concluded that they must be Eliza's own.

Besides these things there were countless cushions that she had embroidered, tapestries that she had stitched, views and landscapes framed upon the walls that she had painted in water-colours or in crayons. There was a whole drawer full of fans – silk, ivory, lace, parchment, plumes – to which, sorrowfully, I added the one she had given me. There were her books – novels, chiefly, but also some volumes of essays and poetry – shelved in an alcove.

It was strange indeed, thus slowly to become acquainted with her.

There was even an old hack that she had been used to ride, out to grass in a paddock. I had never learned to ride in proper fashion

– though, of course, with the boys, I had from time to time scrambled bareback over the moors on rough Exmoor ponies – so riding lessons now took their place on my timetable, along with singing and music lessons, languages and literature.

Although I had myself been a teacher at Mrs Haslam's school, I was soon – though in the most kindly and considerate manner – made to understand that there were grave gaps and deficiencies in my education.

'But sir – to what end is all this?' I said to the Duke one day, when he handed me a volume of memoirs which he said would enlarge my knowledge of European history.

'Education, my dear Lizzie, is an end in itself. You are already a young person of considerable parts; you have intelligence and a mind of your own; that mind requires to be fed; with learning at your command you need never be at a loss. You will have resources, you can entertain yourself. And,' he added, 'those about you.'

'If I could be trained for some post or position,' I said, thinking of Hoby and his waterways.

'Ah; that, my dear, I am afraid is out of the question.'

The Duke spoke with kind finality, and went off on his own concerns.

While riding about the park at Zoyland, while dutifully following my mother's example in stitchery (but without her proficiency), while practising my piano and taking voice lessons from Dr Fantini, a most exacting teacher – I had ample time to think and reflect and remember.

I thought of Mrs Jebb a great deal, and related her story to the Duke.

He, as always, displayed the liveliest interest in my narration. 'You have such a knack of depicting character, my dearest Liz! I can almost fancy she were here in person. I am sure I should have taken great pleasure in her company.'

'I am sure that you would, sir; and she in yours. But, to this day, I cannot determine whether she really did steal that first piece of lace or not. The gloves I know she took, but I am fairly certain that was just to tease the shopkeeper, who had been pestering her. But if she did it, what was her reason? Her motive? She commanded a comfortable income. She had no need to steal.'

'I would hazard the guess,' said the Duke, 'that she was bored, and needed the fillip of danger to enliven her days. Ladies, as well as men, need these stimulants, I believe. In my time I have known members of the fair sex who were wild gamblers. Or who followed the hunt like Valkyries.'

I looked at him in astonishment. His explanation was so simple, so obvious! And it occurred to me that the same explanation might account for my mother hazarding her life, taking her terrible chance.

And yet it never struck the Duke that the same conditions, the same constraints, might apply to me also . . .

'Do sing your new canzonet, my dear,' said the Duke. 'I like it so much. And then we will fetch in Solomon, and you and he shall play those Haydn duets.'

Music was the Duke's greatest passion. He was in ecstasies, listening, and was happy to sit for hours, beating time upon his buckskinned thighs – or on his kettledrum – and singing out loud whenever the music presented a theme that *could* be sung.

Naturally, as it was not yet July, and the Houses of Parliament were still in session, the Duke departed at intervals for his London mansion to take part in debates.

'Later on I shall be wishful to bring you up to town with me, my dear Liz,' he told me, 'to bear me company as your lamented mother always did. Indeed I could hardly bear to pass a day without her! And I am growing to feel the same about you. But I must not be selfish, and you are better employed at this present in learning your books and singing your scales here at Zoyland.'

To tell truth, I wondered a little whether his wish for female company, my mother's and now mine, was motivated in part to prove something about himself to the Polite World: that he could still command the affections of an elegant, accomplished young person. Or was it from pure affection? Affection, without doubt, played its part; I missed his company – always good-tempered, always well-informed and lively – when he was up in town. But it gave me more time to read, think and be myself.

'This is a *good* berth,' said Pullett. 'This is the best berth I ever was in. Or you, for sure, Miss Liza. Mind you never do anything to offend His Grace.'

Pullett had struck up a cordial relationship with Mrs Budgen, the housekeeper at Zoyland; and the two ladies spent hours together, mulling over the talents, propensities and defects of my mother, and deciding which of my qualities descended from her.

'That hand, now! Wherever can she have had it from? Her mother's was the same. But we don't know who *her* father was.'

'Some gypsy, for sure.'

They nodded their heads sagely together.

The Duke, surveying my hands with concern, though without the least repulsion, told me that if I wished he would pay for the best surgeon in Europe to operate on both hands, reduce my number of fingers to the norm and alter the large hand to ordinary dimensions. I thanked him most sincerely, and said I would give the matter a great deal of thought before coming to any decision, an attitude of which he approved.

Pullett was against tampering. 'Leave matters be, Miss Liza,' she said. 'As ye were made, so should ye remain. Doubtless Providence had some end in view.'

Another counsellor of the same opinion was Tark, the head groom, who used to accompany me on rides when the Duke was in London.

'Never touch that elf-hand, Missie,' he said. ''Twould be fell unlucky. And so I'll tell His Grace, if you wish it.'

'Why, Tark? I believe you, but why?'

'Ah,' he said. 'My old grandma had gypsy blood. From Savernake Forest she come, where there was a big tribe of 'em, those days. And she'd say that a hand like yours, with six fingers, was mighty lucky, and a sign that, soon or late, it'd win ye your heart's desire – some such thing.'

'I see. Well, it has been lucky once already,' I said, remembering the rescue of Triz. What a long time ago that seemed!

I told the Duke about my friendship with Mr Bill and Mr Sam, and he was deeply interested.

'I have all their verses, of course. And I believe your Mr Sam comes sometimes to lecture in Bristol. Would you wish to hear him, if he does so again?'

'Oh, *sir*! Could I? *Could* I?'

'No reason in the world why not.'

Indeed, in the autumn of that year, I do not recall whether it was October or November, the Duke was kind enough to take me, as he had promised, on a special excursion to Bristol, to hear Mr Sam speak on literature at Mangeons' Hotel. The Duke had lately been suffering somewhat from the gout, and thought a course of treatment at Bristol Hot-Wells would not come amiss; so thither we proceeded with both objects in view.

I will not conceal that to leave Zoyland for a few days now and then, to tread the streets of a city, visit shops and circulating libraries, was no great hardship for me. The Duke hired a house in Dowry Square and sent servants and linen ahead to make sure that all would be comfortable, since the weather was sharpening and setting in for what later became a memorably cold winter. Meanwhile, over on the continent of Europe, Napoleon's empire was collapsing into ruins.

And I sometimes wondered if, now that the fighting was as good as over, Colonel Brandon and his lady would return to England – though, even if they were to do so, as matters now stood it did not seem likely that this event would affect me in any way.

In Bristol – despite the attractions of Hot-Wells, the Pump Room, the shops, the coffee houses and the excellent public library – I was, of course, devoured, possessed with one expectation, one feeling only – the thrilling knowledge that soon I was to see my dear Mr Sam again.

The Duke cautioned me, very kindly, very solicitously.

'I am afraid, my dear, that you may find him sadly changed. I have heard from several sources that he is not a well man; he drinks intemperately and, they say, takes a deal too much laudanum. Eh, bless me! These poetical fellows, they do drive themselves with a cruel spur.'

On the night of the lecture, the Duke's agent procured for us excellent seats in the front row of the ballroom at Mangeons' Hotel, so that I was able to see only too well the sad changes in my dear Mr Sam.

He arrived late, with no apology for this, and proceeded to talk with terrific speed and intensity. His subject was Shakespeare.

The very moment he began speaking, I forgot all about his changed appearance – he had grown stouter since I saw him last, and therefore looked shorter; his face was plumper and flushed, and his hair somewhat thinning, lighter and greyer in colour than I remembered; his eyes remained exactly the same, large, dark, soft and dreamy; his clothing was decidedly soiled and unkempt, neckerchief disordered, and his right leg greatly swollen.

But his voice carried me straight back into the past. He spoke without notes and, as I say, very rapidly, yet each word came clear as a hunting horn. Listening, I was transported in a flash to the bridge over the Ashe River. He seemed to be speaking directly to me.

He was talking about Hamlet. 'Compare the easy language of common life in which this drama opens, with the wild wayward lyric of the opening of Macbeth . . . Then the shivery feeling, at such a time, with two eye-witnesses, of sitting down to hear a story of a ghost . . . O heaven! words are *wasted,* to those that feel and to those who do not feel the *exquisite* judgment of Shakespeare!'

I listened, rapt, as the words poured out of him in precisely the manner that I remembered – a wonderful, exhilarating, sparkling spate. This man is a genius, I thought. No question about it. He is a genius.

At the close of the lecture there was tumultuous applause. Mr Sam hardly heeded it. He gave a perfunctory sort of bow, making for the door, stumbling somewhat.

'Do you wish to step up and speak to him, my dear?' said the Duke kindly. 'Let us go round to the back of the stage.'

But, by the time we had done so, Mr Sam was making for the lobby of the hotel.

We pursued, and caught him close by the entrance.

'Sir!' said the Duke. 'Mr Coleridge! My ward, here, Miss FitzWilliam, wishes to recall herself to you.'

Mr Sam looked at me vaguely. His eyes, I saw, were darkly blood-shot and their black pupils reduced very small. He was sweating and pale as lard. His hair was lank with the sweat and greatly disordered.

'*Sir! Mr Sam!* Don't you remember me? Back in Somerset? At Ashett? At St Lucy's church? How you and Mr Bill used to take me for walks?'

'Ashett?' he mumbled. 'Ashett? – No, no, I do not remember. Excuse me –' and he pushed hastily past us, and out into the gusty cold rain which was falling.

I was *quenched* with shock and disappointment. The transition from the nobility and brilliance of the lecture to abrupt, ugly reality was too severe; I held tight on to the Duke's arm, almost fainting from pain and grief.

Fortunately the Duke's coach was close at hand – he was always well served in such matters; he and Tark helped me to my place and we were soon back at the house in Dowry Square, where fires were burning, and the Duke obliged me to drink a glass of warm wine.

'You must not blame him too much, my poor child; I have talked with his doctor, who informs me that he is suffering terribly from rheumatic heart disease and erysipelatous inflammation – not to mention the atrocious quantity of laudanum and brandy that he regularly imbibes. We should rather wonder that, in such a case, he is able to deliver a lecture *at all* – let alone such a one as we have just been privileged to hear! Bless me! How the sparks did fly. Poor fellow! Poor fellow! They say he is all to pieces. Even his friend Mr Wordsworth did not scruple to describe him as a rotten drunkard and an absolute nuisance.'

I could not sleep all that night, but tossed and turned, soaking my pillow with tears, and came to breakfast so heavy-eyed that although we had planned to stay in Bristol and hear the other seven lectures the Duke counselled against it.

'You will only distress yourself all over again, my child. Rather return to our own library and read over the man's poetry to yourself; that, after all, still remains and will always be his monument, when he is long underground.'

'I daresay you are right, sir,' I said faintly. And so we returned to Zoyland. (In fact, as we heard afterwards, several of the later lectures were cancelled, due to Mr Sam's ill-health.)

'And I do not believe that the Hot-Wells have had any good effect on my gout, whatsoever,' said the Duke.

Not long after this, Sir John Middleton came over to Zoyland, bringing with him his cousin the elderly Mrs Dashwood – even skinnier, vaguer, paler, more fly-away as to white hair and untidy raiment than she had been when I had seen her at Delaford; but still, it seemed, clinging tenaciously to life.

'Bless her, she likes an outing,' said Sir John comfortably – he was a burly, cheerful, red-faced man, who looked as if he would be more at ease striding through a pheasant copse than sitting in somebody's drawing room being offered sherry and biscuits. 'And to tell truth, m'wife sometimes finds her a trifle fatiguing – m'wife's mighty close to her confinement, now, y'know, so small matters become irksome which, at an easier time, would never trouble her.

Some of the old lady's little ways – her habit of talking to houses, about birds, y'know.'

'Oh, yes, I remember,' said I. 'When she was at Delaford –'

'Just so! Just so!'

Mrs Dashwood was wandering about the room, ignoring the glass of ratafia which had been poured for her, crooning to herself and sometimes murmuring a few words.

'But we hear cheerful news from my cousin Elinor,' Sir John went on, once assured that his elderly relative was doing no harm. 'Elinor, it seems – believe it or not – has writ a book! And found some publisher fellow prepared to print it! And sport the blunt to the tune of one hundred and ten pounds! Pretty hand-some, hey? And they, the publishers, are prepared, as well, to take on *five other books* that she has been scribbling away at all this time – why, bless my soul, Elinor was always such a quiet, civil-spoken lass; who would ever have expected so much inventiveness to have been fermenting away inside her head? Now, if it had been Miss Marianne, always up in the boughs over something – But Elinor! You could have knocked me down with a feather when the news came. And, if the books *take* – and these pub-lisher fellows appear to think it altogether probable – that will make a most advantageous change in the circumstances at Delaford Rectory – which, I venture to say, have been pretty straitened. Cousin Elinor writ a very pretty letter to m'wife to say they would soon be happy to have the old lady back with them again. Young Nell's home, it seems.'

I sighed, thinking that to have Mrs Dashwood back would place yet one more burden on Elinor's shoulders. Yet she was fond of her mother; no question of that.

'Did she say – did you gather – how *Mr* Ferrars had taken the news of his wife's authorship?' I inquired.

Sir John gave me a broad, conspiratorial grin. 'Now *there's* a pompous, puritanical, touchy, self-regarding fellow if ever I met one,' he said. 'Reading between the lines, y'know, I fancy he didn't like it above half. But some friend of theirs had shown the book to the printer-fellow – *not* Elinor herself, it seems – so he couldn't blame *her*. And the blunt will come in mighty handy – no question of that. Since Brandon and Mrs Marianne are still away, the Lord only knows where.'

'My ward wishes to know, Sir John,' said the Duke, 'whether you have any recent knowledge as to the whereabouts of her father, Willoughby, you know.'

'Why, bless me, yes!' said Sir John. 'Had a letter from Willoughby not above two months back. Poor devil! Poor Willoughby! Such a pleasant, good-humoured neighbour he used to be, and had the nicest little black bitch of a pointer as ever I saw.'

'Why, sir, what has become of him?' cried I.

'Ah, well, you see, he outran the barber, got himself gazetted, had to sell up. Came to a complete smash, and if he'd not left the country pretty smartly would have found himself in Newgate. At the last he borrowed £250 from me, but I don't regard it; I doubt I shall ever see it again,' he added to the Duke in a low voice.

'Oh, how dreadful!' said I. 'But what became of Miss Grey, his wife?'

'Ah, she died, some while since. By all accounts, he didn't grieve overmuch. No, poor fellow, 'twas a false scent – full cry in the wrong direction – all his heart, all his regrets, were fixed on Miss Marianne. 'If only I'd stayed with her,' he was wont to say to me, 'I should be a better man now.' Mind you, I always held that to be a load of fustian; for Miss Marianne was *not* a lady to live on bread and scrape. They would have been in the basket just as soon, or even sooner, with his gaming ways, and she with no fortune to bring him.'

'So what country is he in now, sir?'

'Why, in the letter he writ me he said he was off to Portugal – Lisbon, I daresay. Living is cheap there, I understand, now the French have been rompé'd; and the poor deluded fellow – having picked up from some piece of gossip that Brandon and his lady proposed making a stay in Portugal on their way back from India – I truly believe that Willoughby goes there in hopes he might gain a glimpse of Mrs Marianne; though, for the matter of that, I fancy Brandon would as soon send a bullet through his chops as not. Ay, the two of them did stand up together once, to my knowledge. Fegs, Brandon has a touch of steel in him, withal he's such a quiet, mumchance sort of fellow.—And damme, after all, *he* paid to rear the other fellow's daughter all those years!'

'Myself, Sir John!' I reminded him.

'Ay, bless me, so you are; begging your pardon, my dear! You've no look of Willoughby, that's why I forget; Willoughby was such a black-haired, black-avised romantical sort of fellow, all the young ladies were setting their caps at him. But you, now, I dare swear, take after your mother.'

'Yes, she is the image of her mother,' said the Duke, smiling at me fondly.

'I always had a notion,' went on Sir John, who seldom listened to what other people said if it was more than two or three words in extent, 'that Brandon and his lady went abroad because of Willoughby. There he was, you see, only forty miles off at Combe Magna, making it known to all and sundry that he still hankered for Mrs Marianne; what is a poor husband to do in such a case? No, depend upon it, if they knew that Willoughby had gone overseas, Brandon would bring her back in the bounce of a cracker.'

Presently the Duke took Sir John off to look at his coverts – and to converse, no doubt, in a more masculine and confidential manner; I was left to entertain Mrs Dashwood.

She was still wandering, prowling, fidgeting and gazing at my mother's water-colours.

'There's a bird in this house,' she remarked.

'Several, ma'am,' I said. 'A parrot, two canaries, a goldfinch –'

'No, no, a bird, a bird. A bird.'

She had said the same thing at Delaford, I remembered. Where there was no bird.

'What kind of a bird, ma'am?'

'A caged bird, a prisoner bird.' She looked at me very intently, frowningly, and yet I felt she hardly saw me at all. It seemed as if she searched for something buried deep down in my very essence.

'My daughter Elinor, my daughter Marianne, my daughter Margaret – where are they now? Where are they? Are they well?'

'Your daughter Elinor is well – you will surely see her soon,' I soothed the poor lady. 'She has written a book.'

'A book, a book?'

I picked up a volume of *Camilla* from a small table.

'A book like this. It is called *Charlotte*. It will be published.'

She nodded, thoughtfully. I could not tell whether she understood or not. But she seemed to take in *some* intelligence.

'And Margaret?'

'Up in London. Enjoying the pleasures of society,' I said, though I doubted if this was the case.

'And Marianne? My beautiful Marianne?' Her voice trembled.

'She is with her husband – Colonel Brandon,' I said quickly. I hoped that what I said was true. 'You remember Colonel Brandon – so kind, so good?'

Sometimes I felt as if I were in a play, the only human character acting among a cast of puppets – Brandon, Marianne, Willoughby, Eliza – puppets or masked characters, whom I was never to be permitted to meet.

I persuaded Mrs Dashwood to come into the small dining room – as the men still remained out-of-doors – to eat a nuncheon of cold fowl, fruit and cake. Then, with Pullett's assistance, she was induced to lie down upon a day-bed in a cool chamber and rest.

But still she kept casting anxious glances about her and crying pitifully, 'There is a bird, a bird, a *bird* in this house. Please let it fly away! House, house, answer me! Where is that bird? Why will you never let it go free?'

Chapter 12

After a year at Zoyland, as my voice had greatly improved under the tutelage of Dr Fantini – or, so said Dr Fantini – the Duke began to invite professionals down from London, musicians and singers, and to hold performances of operas and oratorios, *Armide, Orfeo, Jephtha* and so forth, in which I sang the lead parts. And he would give house parties on these occasions.

It was understood, at such times, that though I sang in the performances and sat at the Duke's table during mealtimes, I was not to be spoken to by his guests. It might be all very well, was the Duke's view, on informal occasions, if such old friends and connections of the family as Sir John Middleton should come visiting, for me to engage in conversation with them; but on no account was there to be any social intercourse between myself and persons of the ton, of Polite Society.

Particularly, of course, with ladies.

Indeed on one such occasion, when Mrs Marsonby, the wife of the Bishop of Bath and Wells, happened to sit opposite me at dinner and so far forgot herself as to lean across the table and say to me, 'My dear, you sang the aria "Hush ye pretty warbling quire" with the most exquisite sensibility! It was all I could do to keep the tears from flowing!' the Duke was quietly outraged, and later took the Bishop on one side to tell him that his wife had transgressed the unseen but acknowledged boundary line that existed in his establishment, and that another such trespass 'might occasion the overthrow of our pleasant musical evenings'. The Bishop apologized for his lady and promised that such a *faux pas* would not occur again.

Some may inquire, why should I remain passively in a situation of such ambivalence, not to say indignity? And the answers are manifold and complicated.

First, I sincerely loved the Duke, and he on his side seemed deeply attached to me. He had loved my mother; and I was her replacement. He was like a relative. I never relaxed the formality of my demeanour towards him, calling him always 'Sir' or 'Your Grace' but none the less there existed a warm, teasing friendship in our relations, which were delineated by invisible frontier lines and transacted with as much grace as a minuet or passacaglia. Nobody had ever loved me before – except for Triz – how could I resist such a lure?

– Nor, to be truthful, did I feel any great deprivation in being excluded from intercourse with persons of the ton; as I have mentioned before, I found their elaborate, cultured, structured conversation excessively tedious, and had no particular wish to take part in it. If the talk related to matters on which I was informed, books the Duke had brought me to read, music that I knew, political issues with which I was familiar – then, to be sure, I listened eagerly and drew my own conclusions as to the knowledge and wit of the speakers. And afterwards, with the Duke, I would often exchange comments and impressions. But I was never tempted into expressing opinions publicly, or wishing to play a part in such exchanges. I saw no need for that.

Then, in all material ways, my situation was one of great comfort and self-respect. I lived in much luxury and was treated with deference – and, I may add, with affection – by all the people in the Duke's household, who deferred to me as their mistress and brought me all the small problems that were considered too trivial for the Duke's own ears, yet required some practical solution.

I accompanied him on his visits to the house in Grosvenor Square and met a number of his political friends. I went with him to the picture gallery in Pall Mall and to the Royal Academy, to Covent Garden and Drury Lane where I was able to see works by Shakespeare, Sheridan and many another; even a play called *Remorse* – not a very good play, I thought – by my Mr Sam. The Duke and I passed some weeks in London during the notably cold winter of 1814, when the Thames froze for weeks on end and, for the duration of the period, a great Frost Fair was set up on the frozen river (christened Freezeland Street) with stalls where one could purchase oysters, cockles, gingerbread and brandy-balls. But the Duke caught a severe cold at this time, which worsened to a congestion confining him to his bed for several weeks; and though he made a good recovery, he was somewhat aged by the severity of the indisposition, thereafter spending less time in town and more at Zoyland.

It was during this period that I met Hoby again.

I had been pained and angered – very much so – by the encounter with Hoby at Mrs Widdence's showroom in Bond Street. I have not alluded to these feelings in my narrative before, because they went too deep. That he who, when we were younger, had been so much my friend and ally, in his rough and carefree way, who had so often taken my part and shielded me from trouble should, when we met again after so long a period, have no kind greeting, no kind remembrances – nothing but anger and cold, critical reproof – this vexed, this chagrined me beyond measure. I had hoped that he might afterwards repent of his harshness and write some note, make some attempt to meet or some gesture towards reconciliation – but he had not done so. And my removal to Zoyland shortly afterwards had effectively nullified the hope of any future such understanding.

It took me many, many months to digest the pain that meeting had occasioned.

Therefore I was no little taken aback when the Duke informed me that he had invited Mr John Nash and his young assistant, a Mr Robert Hobart, to come and pass a few days at Zoyland, in order to advise him about digging a canal.

I had long since recounted to the Duke many tales about my early days at Nether Othery – or such parts of it as I considered suitable for disclosure – and he had of course learned from other sources details regarding the subsequent histories of some of my childhood acquaintances – such as Fanny Huskisson, and the numerous progeny of Lord S——— who now, mostly grown, were leading variegated lives in the Metropolis, some received into Polite Society, others not. Hoby's name, however, had never been mentioned between us, though I had sometimes descried it in *The Times* or the *Morning Post* when these journals carried articles relating to work on the new Regent Street or Regent Canal. And I had – I cannot deny – sighed over the social ordinances which permitted Hoby to make his way respectably in the world, but denied the same right to me.

Now I told the Duke that I had known Hoby as a child, and I tried to express to him some of my views on society's unfairness. He shook his head indulgently. 'Ay, but you see it ain't the same, my dear, it ain't a parallel case for men and women. For a man it don't greatly signify if he be a bastard or not. Many bastards have made great names in the world. Why! William of Normandy was one. And look at all the dukes who are descended from side-slips of Charles II! But the ladies, bless their hearts, have to mind their reputations – else where should we all be? You may think it unfair, my child, and doubtless to some degree it is; but, on the other hand, the fair sex do have compensations, in that they can expect to be provided for and looked after.'

A flood of argument swept into my mind: that many women were *not* provided for but, on the contrary, lived wretched lives; and further, that many women who moved in the highest circles bore reputations that were far from unblemished – consider Lady Melbourne, for instance, who was thought to have borne several of her six children to fathers other than her husband. But I forbore to argue. The Duke tired easily these days, and I had come to recognize the gestures that denoted this fatigue: he would rub and rub at his forehead with a silk handkerchief, as if hoping to clear his brain.

And it ill behoved me to argue with him on the latter point, since I myself was so cherished, all my slightest wishes considered. (It was only my deepest wishes that went unregarded.)

When Hoby and Mr Nash came down to Zoyland I saw little of them at first, save at supper-time, for they were out with the Duke all day, riding over his demesnes, debating suitable sites for water-courses. But on the third day the work was concluded, and they came home early.

I arranged for a nuncheon to be served and, at the Duke's request, kept them company in the room he called his observatory, for it ended in a glass-walled greenhouse, and here he kept his great brass telescope with which on a fine night he would walk outside and study the planets.

I sat somewhat apart and occupied myself with knitting a silk cravat for the Duke, when suddenly he said to me: 'Liz, my dear, did I not hear you, some time since, express a wish for a water-garden?'

'Why, yes, sir, I did – but it was of no great consequence; just an idle fancy.'

'A fig for your idle fancies! Here we have a young fellow who is as skilled with a dowsing-rod as Patrick the steward with his fiddle-bow; let us walk out and find you a suitable spot while we have this expert help at command.'

It was a fine, balmy May afternoon, so we all strolled out through the wide glass doors on to the green lawn beyond, which extended for some three hundred yards to the foot of a gentle rise, where narcissi were just giving way to bluebells and orchises.

'Now then, young Hobart, let Miss here have a demonstration of your virtuosity,' said the Duke, who had plainly taken a huge fancy to Hoby. I, meanwhile, had taken (or chosen to take) an equal fancy to Mr John Nash, who had a round, creased, humorous face, a smiling mouth and two tilted eyebrows which shot up and down with great velocity. He would I suppose at this time have been about sixty – but very brisk and active. He was describing to me the huge hall that he was in course of building for the Regent behind Carlton House in which the latter was to entertain the Tsar of Russia, the King of Prussia, and other European dignitaries during the summer celebrations.—For, thank heaven, the Continental war was now as good as over.

I told Mr Nash with sincerity that, considering all his notable public works, it was amiable of him to spare time to come down and give my guardian the benefit of his advice and experience.

'My dear, it is a great treat for me to get out of London once in a way and come to so beautiful a spot. Especially just now when the city is so abominably crowded. And it is a joy to spend time in the company of the Duke, who is one of the best-natured and most intelligent men of my acquaintance.'

'Come here, my dear Liz,' called the Duke. 'Come and try your hand at Mr Hobart's contraption.'

For the past three days I had been keeping as far distant from Hoby as was compatible with the requirements of hostessly politeness; I had avoided falling into talk with him, or even meeting his eye; but now it seemed there was no help for it.

I walked across the grass and took the forked hazel twig he was extending in my direction.

'You must hold it in your hands – so – with the two prongs pointing towards you and the single prong pointing ahead,' he explained in a careful, colourless tone. 'Turn your palms upward, and let your thumbs point back.'

None of which was news to me, since I, with Hoby, Will and Jonathan, had on several occasions watched old Gathercole dowsing for a well when the village source had dried up.

But the unexpected sensation of Hoby's hands on mine – the live, rough, active warmth as he laid firm hold of my wrists and, with professional care, adjusted my fingers on the hazel wand – that was very startling indeed and, in a flash, swept me back to a distant time that I had believed was long buried and gone out of mind.

Also I could see – from his startled look of recollection – that Hoby had, in the interim, forgotten about my elf-hand. It formed, for him, a reminder of the same kind. His own hands shook as he relinquished the rod to me.

'Come then, Liz, my dear!' called the Duke cheerfully. 'Let us see if you can strike water from the rock, like Moses with the waters of Meribah!'

'You must pace backwards and forwards over the grass,' Hoby instructed me, still in the same level, dispassionate tone. 'Don't try to move the fork at all; only hold it steady. And try to empty your mind of thought or expectation; let the stick do the work for you.'

So I walked.

'Don't look at the stick!' called Hoby again.

So I kept my eyes up, looking at the gentle green hill, or the old, rose-red house with its trees around it, or the three men who stood smiling in the sunshine as they watched me. At least Mr Nash and the Duke were smiling; Hoby's face remained very grave. He had fewer freckles now, I noticed, though still a fair sprinkling over his nose and cheekbones; he was dressed with great neatness and propriety in a well-cut riding jacket and buckskins; he was uncommonly pale. I wondered what kind of a life he led in London these days; did he have a wife? Children? A house? A mistress? Was he ambitious? Did his manner of life satisfy him? It seemed very singular indeed to me that, in one way, I knew him so *very* well – I could have made a map of all the scars on his thighs and stomach where he had fallen down the rock face of Growly Head and gashed himself so badly – yet, on the other hand, I had no clue, no clue at all, as to what was passing through his head.

The hazel twig suddenly sprang violently downwards, thrusting itself away from me so that, taken completely by surprise, I dropped it on the ground.

'Rabbit me! Look at that! I believe she's got it!' exclaimed the Duke, utterly astonished.

'Why – I do believe she has!' cried Mr Nash, equally startled.

'Try it again,' said Hoby quietly. And he picked up the fork and handed it back, settling my hands on the two prongs, as before.

I do not know if his hands were trembling this time. Mine certainly were.

'Go back to where you were before, and walk from that spot.'

So I walked the same track again, and the stick behaved in the same way, violently wriggling, twisting itself out of my grasp.

'Well, well!' cried Mr Nash. 'It seems as if Miss has the gift, Your Grace. Bless me! You need never trouble to hire us professionals again, you have the talent residing here in your own household! – Now *you* make an essay, Robert; see if the rod agrees in your hands with what Miss has told us.'

I was trembling, almost sobbing.

'Why, my dear, sure you are not cold?' said the Duke. He patted my shoulder, wiped my eyes solicitously with his own kerchief. 'There, there! It was just the surprise! Who would have dreamed that you have such a talent? Though indeed, my love, you possess such a multiplicity of parts, I am sure it is not to be wondered at.'

While he thus soothed me, he kept his gaze on Hoby who, walking over the same course that I had taken, secured the same result; the stick sprang from his hands and bounced on the turf.

'So! So! Now Miss can have her water-garden as wet as she pleases,' said Mr Nash. 'That is, of course, if your Grace don't mind carving up your bowling-green!'

'Miss knows she can have whatever she wants,' said the Duke. 'Lilies and kingcups and dab-chicks all over the grass, if that is the way her fancy takes her.'

'Th-thank you, sir,' said I, half laughing, half crying. 'You are by far too good to me. I must go into the house, I believe – I believe that stick has given me the head-ache!'

'It was the shock to her,' I heard the Duke saying, as I ran away from them, feeling Hoby's grave eyes still on me. 'Normally, Lizzie never has the head-ache!'

That evening, their last, the Duke invited a few neighbours to dinner to meet Mr Nash and his assistant. The Bishop and his wife were of the number, also Lord Giles Trevelyan, the Lord Lieutenant, and his lady. Pleading my head-ache, I asked if I might be excused from the meal.

The Duke, of course, excused me – he was never exigent; but later a message was sent, asking if I felt recovered enough to sing to the company. I did not wish to be churlish, so put on an evening gown, went down to the music room and entertained the guests with airs by Handel, Arne and Bononcini. The Duke bustled about, fondly and kindly, supplying me with wine and asking if I were entirely recovered. I answered yes; (in fact the head-ache had been nothing but a diplomatic evasion).

Afterwards – as the air was exceedingly balmy and the moon shone bright – the guests all wandered out on to the terrace.

'Ay, Mr Hobart, that's right, you take Miss out for a breath of air,' said the Duke, who was obliged to escort the Bishop's lady. 'It will be sure to do her good.'

So Hoby took me out. We went farther afield than the other guests, into the cherry orchard, which was shedding a snowfall of white blossoms.

'*How can you bear it?*' said Hoby violently. 'How can you bear your position here? A plaything – a toy – permitted to converse with none other than Cumbria – or such others only as he sees fit – as if you were a sultan's woman in a zenana – indeed, I see no difference! *You* – who were used to be such a wild, free girl, Liza – what makes you remain at Zoyland for a single day? You are not a pauper, after all – you have resources – you have your voice – you could, I dare say, find work of some kind on the stage –'

'I am greatly obliged to you!' I returned, shaking with anger. 'I may tell you that last time we were in London I had an offer from an operatic management – yes! – from the management of Covent Garden Opera House – of three thousand pounds and a benefit performance, if I would sing for them for a season.'

'Then why in the *world* did you not take it? Are you mad?'

'The Duke was not at all well at the time – he would have hated it – it would have seemed so dastardly ungrateful to him –'

'*Ungrateful?* For heaven's sake, Liza! He has completely devoured your life – wholly demolished your good name –'

Conveniently, Hoby chose to forget that on our previous encounter, before I had even met the Duke, he had told me that my good name was already destroyed beyond recall after the incident with the Bath Beaux, not to mention my impudent and vulgar song recital in Mrs Widdence's showroom.

I pointed this out to him. 'And *he* didn't care about that! The Duke didn't! He took me in – cared for me – had me educated – instructed me in the ways of polite society –'

'To what end? If you are never to enter society? You might as well be a leper – untouchable –'

'But he is *good* to me, Hoby! He has been so kind. Everything within his power he has done for me – even to this water-garden. *You* just went off – '

Suddenly it was all too much for me: the thought of the kind, considerate, affectionate old man, still in his heart sorrowing for my mother, but solicitous to provide me with any indulgence that lay within his power. And this thought merged, in my mind, with recollections of all the other unappeased longing there was in the world – Willoughby's for Marianne, hers for him, my mother's lines to her lost love, Mrs Jebb calling out to her long-dead husband, who had spent eight months in jail for her sake.

'Oh, what is the purpose of it all? Oh, where will it all end?' I muttered, and, stumbling to a stone bench that stood by a great thickset hedge at the end of the orchard, I dropped down wearily upon it and hid my face in my hands.

Next moment Hoby had wrapped his arms around me and, with his cheek against mine, was murmuring urgent phrases of comfort into my ear.

'Liza-loo!' (That had been his name for me in the old days.) 'Little one! Dear one! Don't! Don't cry so! Hush! Listen! *Don't* carry on so! I didn't mean to be unkind. It's just – I can't stand to see you, like an apple on a tree, so far out of reach! It's no use, I love you – I love you – always have, I do believe. Ever since the old days. That's why – that's why – oh, please try to stop crying!'

Like the Duke, he fetched out a kerchief and tried to mop my face.
'I am not crying!' I gasped. 'I never cry. Perhaps I am laughing.'

Indeed, for one moment, I almost could have laughed from sheer
astonishment. It felt so comfortable, so familiar, to sit thus, enclosed
in the circle of Hoby's arms; I leaned against him, thinking we might
be up on the moor in a clump of heather, or snug under my wind-
break on Growly Head.

But we were not.

Soon I pulled myself out of his arms, stood, drew in a deep breath
and shook myself to rights.

'No, dear Hoby, we mustn't do this. It is wrong. We don't
belong to each other any more. I have my place here. You have
yours in London –'

'But listen, Liza! You are not *married* to old Cumbria, there is no
binding legal tie –'

'Oh, don't be so – so nonsensical! Of course there is no legal tie.
But there are a thousand other ties of – of affection, gratitude,
respect – duty –'

'But it is unnatural. He is more than twice your age –'

'And what is so unusual about that? There are more disparate
marriages made every day.'

'If you come away to London with me –'

I said: 'Are you asking me to marry you, Hoby?'

There was a long silence. And then he said, 'It would not be
possible to do that, Liza. Not at this time. My career, you see, is just
commencing to make good progress – I have many first-rate connections – commissions – thanks to Mr Nash; I am invited to great
houses and consulted by people who, three years ago, would not
even have known my name – it is all beginning to move so fast –'

'Yes, I quite understand,' I said politely. 'There would not in this dazzling scene be space enough for a wife who was a duke's leavings, who had been rolled on Beechen Cliff by the Bath Beaux; who had come in the first place from Byblow Bottom.'

I began to walk away from him.

He ran quickly after me, and now he sounded most urgent, even heartsick. 'But, Liza, I love you! I hardly understood how much, until now! Don't you remember those old days at all? You must! You loved me then – I swear you did! Lord, how we used to go it! Don't you remember?'

'What I remember is of no consequence.'

'Please don't go in, Liza! Don't leave me yet!'

But I did leave him, and walked indoors to where the Duke was bidding goodbye to his guests. As was customary on such occasions, I stood a pace or two behind him and curtseyed silently to them, receiving silent bows and a few smiles in return.

Next morning I kept to my room until Mr Nash and his assistant had departed. The Duke seemed a little disappointed that I had not come out to breakfast with them and bid them farewell.

'I thought, my dear, that you would have more to say to Mr Hobart, your old playmate. Such a conversable, agreeable young fellow! Didn't you have a fine time with him talking over the old days in Byblow Bottom?'

The Duke was always entertained by tales of that disorderly place.

But I said, 'No, well, you see, sir, Mr Hobart has grown so very respectable now, that it is best not to remind him of those times.'

'What a pity! And what about your water-garden? Shall I call in McPhee and give him orders about it?'

'No, my dear sir, I have thought carefully about it, and I do not believe that it is worth breaking up your beautiful turf. So I have changed my mind. Instead I would prefer that you take me up to London for a few days; Mr Nash told me that the ladies' shops are now full of wonderful French fashions, brought over from Paris.'

Chapter 13

THAT SUMMER OF 1814, WHEN THE WHOLE POPULATION OF England seemed to be singing, dancing, letting off fireworks, entertaining foreigners, or departing to visit the continent, which had been for so long out of reach, found me listless, disenchanted and forlorn. When the Duke visited London to observe the junketings, I had no wish to accompany him and most often remained at Zoyland.

'What is the matter, my dear?' he asked me, over and over. 'What is it that you lack? What can I do for you?'

'Nothing, my dear sir, thank you, nothing at all. You are kindness itself, and I have everything in this world that I can possibly ask for.'

Except, I could have said, the things that money cannot purchase: my childhood restored to me, with some alterations; my friends returned, my lost loved ones replaced, all the cracks and chasms in my life mended and refilled.

On one occasion when I was alone, the Duke being away in London making a speech in the House of Lords, I took a foolish toss while riding somewhat recklessly in the park at Zoyland and was obliged to lie abed for a few days with a cracked collarbone. The

Duke came anxiously hastening back from London, and consulted over me with the faithful Dr Swinton, who had been his private medical attendant for the last twenty years, and who had looked after my mother also.

The two men remained in muttered conference at the far end of my bedroom for a long and tedious time, while Pullett fidgeted about, folding towels and unfolding them again, moving articles from one place to another, in order to have an excuse to pass near them and overhear what they were saying to one another.

'Imagine it! His Grace is asking the doctor whether you might have thrown yourself down a-purpose!' she reported indignantly.

'How ridiculous! As if I would ever do such a thing!'

In any case, thought I to myself, if ever I wished to put a period to my existence, I would certainly never arrange to do it in such a hit-or-miss fashion.

'And now they are talking about your mother,' she reported, bringing me a piece of lemon peel to rub on my fingers.

'My mother! What in the world has she to do with my falling off a horse?'

This the Duke told me, after the doctor had gone, in forthright terms (for which I was thankful, as Dr Swinton, though a skilled practitioner, was always so embarrassed when attempting to explain himself to a female that he sank into a morass of unintelligible euphemisms).

'It seems, my dear, that the good doctor took the opportunity to examine you thoroughly while you were unconscious from your tumble. He feared, you see, that you might have done yourself a mischief in the lumbar region – or, possibly, that you might suffer from the same disability as your poor dear mother, so that it would be dangerous for you to give birth to an infant.'

I stared at the Duke, dumbstruck.

'But,' he went on, 'although Swinton tells me that you are somewhat *narrow* in that area – so that due care and precautions should certainly be taken – he sees no inherent impossibility.'

'Very obliging of him to concern himself,' said I. 'But the contingency seems a remote one; I do not precisely understand its relevance to my cracked collarbone.'

'Why, my dear,' the Duke said simply, 'the good doctor and I are not blind, you see, and we can neither of us help noticing that you have been decidedly moped these last months; have pined, gone off your oats, grown somewhat peakish and mumchance. And we put our heads together, do you know, and wondered if it might not be possible to kill two birds with one well-aimed stone.'

Now I continued silent, half out of sheer puzzlement, half because I had a grisly guess as to what might be coming.

'No use beating about the bush,' went on the Duke. 'Life you lead here ain't really natural for a gel of your age. Can't deny it. And here am I, unable to supply your needs but still, dammit! eager and wishful to secure an heir for this estate, so that it need not fall into the hands of that *devilish* bore, Stannisbrooke.'

'But, sir –'

'Let me finish, my dear,' said he, holding up a hand. 'Very attached to you – and I know that you are fond of me, any dunce could see that – but still, a nod's as good as a wink to a blind horse. —What I mean is, I would not take it amiss if you felt inclined to kick over the traces, just a trifle, and supply me with a little counterpart – ideally a *boy*, don't you see – who might be just the thing to content us both; give me a successor for this house, which I dearly love, and you an occupation, someone else to care for and tend – hey?'

His rolling magisterial tones came to a stop, and he peered at me from under his bushy eyebrows.

'But *who,* my dear sir,' said I, after a careful pause, 'who is to be – whom are you casting as the progenitor of – of this useful little person? I see many snags to your plan, but the first one is that so few – ahem – potential fathers come our way, here at Zoyland.'

And not a single one that I care a fig for, I added internally.

The Duke looked a little confused. 'Well, my dear, I did wonder about that personable young spark who travelled down with Nash and gave you instruction in water-divining – hum? After all, he's an old acquaintance of yours, you said that you had known him since childhood, it's not as if he was a stranger – d'ye see? Old friends, you are. There need be no great delicacy in the matter.'

'But – good God, sir – there are two sides to such a proposition. Quite apart from *my* feelings – which we will not at present enter into – Mr Hobart might not see his way –'

'Hem!' said the Duke. 'As to that – not to put too fine a point upon it – I believe Mr Hobart might be persuadable. Indeed yes.'

My tongue clove to the roof of my mouth. No words came to me.

'Make substantial provision, naturally,' said the Duke. 'All drawn up legally and shipshape. Remain in Zoyland for your lifetime – goes without saying. Of course there will be a heavy sum to pay for the tax, since there is no kinship involved, but that would be no bar to your child inheriting –'

He beamed at me, quite rosy with enthusiasm over his plan.

'Your dear mother would be so pleased!'

'You asked Mr Hobart? You put this scheme to Mr Hobart?'

'Over a glass of claret at White's,' nodded the Duke.

'And he said?'

'Surprised at first – to be sure – a trifle confused – but – yes – though properly diffident, *quite* properly so – I believe he might be persuadable.' The Duke added, after a moment's thought, 'He is a young man of very correct sentiments. Very correct. He talked about this house – about Zoyland – in a most discerning manner. He has an eye for beauty.'

As well he might, thought I.

'I do not believe there would be any especial hindrance in that quarter,' the Duke concluded.

Keeping my tone severely neutral, I replied, 'No, my dear sir, I fear that the insuperable difficulty lies here – ' and I pointed at my own breast.

'Eh? My dear?' cried the Duke, greatly disconcerted. 'Can you not fancy the young fellow, then? I quite thought – I understood – I believed –'

'I would prefer not to conjecture what you believed, sir,' said I.

'Coming from Othery – as you do – and then, you know, that other little escapade in Bath?' pursued the Duke, now in rather a melancholy manner as if he felt ill-used. 'I thought, you know, that you might find yourself in a more complaisant, accommodating frame – hey? It's not, after all, as if you was one of those starchy, touch-me-not young ladies that one used to be obliged to take on to the floor at Almack's – thank the Lord!'

'I am truly sorry to disoblige you, my dear sir. But I cannot see my way to it.'

He seemed really cast down; made as if to speak several times, then checked himself; rubbed furiously at his brow with a silk handkerchief.

'Curse me! And I had been so certain that this scheme would suit everybody,' he muttered, looking like a forlorn child who has had the promise of a toy inexplicably and arbitrarily withdrawn. He wandered out of my boudoir to his own bookroom, where for two hours after he was to be seen, through the open door, furiously scratching away on paper with a quill pen, apparently crossing out as much as he wrote, crumpling the paper and throwing it down. I wondered if he were attempting to draft a letter to Hoby, informing him that the scheme to provide an heir for Zoyland had come to naught. And – I will not deny – I felt sorry for the Duke, and almost wished it within my power to further his design; but it was not within my power.

That evening, I noticed the Duke stumble when we walked across the hall to supper; and he seemed, once or twice, hesitating in his speech, as if words jostled in his mind like flood wreckage piled against a bridge in the Ashe River; but next morning he appeared his old self again, kindly and solicitous, watchful of my welfare as always.

'That matter we spoke of yesterday, my dear,' he said, when we were strolling in the lime avenue, 'we'll not speak of it again – hey? Unless, of course, at any time, you see fit to come to another conclusion – in one way or another? Then, you know, you have only to indicate your wishes. Just tip me the nod, and I'll have the young fellow down before you can say hopscotch.'

'Thank you, sir. You are very kind to me, always. But I believe I must abide by my decision.'

I sighed; and so did he; and we walked on for many yards in silence.

A month later I received a letter from Lady Hariot Vexford.

It was written from Amarante, in Portugal, and had taken, I realized, almost a year to reach me. It had been addressed to me in care of the lawyers at Dorchester (so evidently a letter written by me to Lady Hariot and Triz from Bath, giving Mrs Jebb's address, had failed to reach them). The lawyers had readdressed the letter to Mrs Haslam's school, who had passed it to Edward Ferrars who in turn had sent it on to Mrs Jebb's house in Bath. And from there an uneducated hand (doubtless Mrs Rachel's) had dispatched it to Mrs Widdence in London, who, amazingly, had directed it to me at Zoyland. (Perhaps she hoped for my custom, now that I lived under such august patronage.)

Dated from the autumn of the preceding year, the letter said:

My dear Eliza,

I write this appeal to you since you are now, I truly believe, the only hope left for my unfortunate daughter, to whom, I know, you once felt a genuine and deep attachment. So well do I remember how kindly, how patiently you helped her with her lessons, sang to her, told her stories, took part in her infant games and fancies, and supplied her with daily companionship in the nurseries and gardens of Kinn Hall. My heart aches almost unbearably when I recall those days which, at the time, seemed anxious and lacking in hope or security; but oh! how peaceful and prosperous they now appear, in comparison with what has befallen us since.

When we first arrived in Portugal we made our home, as I believe I informed you (supposing that my communication ever reached you) with my sister (Lady Anna Foliot) in Lisbon. Her husband was attached to the British Embassy there, but most unfortunately for us he was shortly thereafter transferred to Brazil. My daughter Thérèse had suffered acutely on the voyage out to Portugal; in fact at one point I despaired of her even surviving the sea-passage; so it was out of the question for her to attempt the long and hazardous voyage across the storm-tossed Atlantic Ocean. A Portuguese friend of my sister's offered us house-room in Oporto; we therefore removed to that town, where I was able to support us (though precariously) by giving lessons in English grammar and literature and the Classics. When the French invaders arrived we were obliged to flee, but were given asylum by a kindly group of nuns from the Convent of Santa Clara who had betaken themselves to the inhospitable shelter of a ruined monastery in the mountains to the north of the Douro river. This refuge also we were obliged to leave, after Sir Arthur Wellesley, with wonderful intrepidity, flung his troops across the Douro on barges and drove the French northwards out of the city. We and the holy sisters were likewise driven northwards by the tide of battle and on many occasions barely escaped with our lives.

All that was four years ago. It had been, of course, our intention to return to Porto, as the Portuguese call it, once the invaders had been driven out of the city; but for a long time this was not possible, since the country was utterly wasted; there was no transport; all the horses and mules had been taken off, either by one army or another.

The retreating French were *monsters*. They fired farms and villages, destroyed crops, hanged poor peasants, put priests to death. For months we lived, if you will believe me, on crows stewed in vinegar, black bread and a little rice. There was no way to go southwards through the mountains except on foot. And my poor child was not equal to that. So we remained, with some of the nuns, in a deserted village where the houses were in ruins. For two years we stayed there, gradually effecting improvements in our situation, spinning and weaving goats' wool, cultivating gardens, rescuing the shattered vines, growing a little maize by the brook sides, reclaiming pigs that had run wild in the pine woods. At last I was able to send a message to a Mr Croft in Porto (whose daughter I had taught Latin) asking for a loan to enable us to return to the city.

But during this period there were still troops of brigands and freebooters roaming the devastated country: some of them deserters from the defeated French armies, others merely the ruffians of all kinds that war throws up. A band of such vile creatures came to our hamlet. They were possessed by the mad notion that the retreating French army had hidden an earthen pot containing two hundred milreis in gold and silver coins and diamonds from Brazil somewhere in our humble mountain refuge. We could not persuade them otherwise. They dug up all our carefully tended vegetables, tore apart the walls that we had so painfully built and, when they found nothing, vented their fury and disappointment on our small colony of helpless women. Two they bayoneted outright. Perhaps they were the lucky ones. No doubt they are now in Paradise. Me, they did not dare maltreat. Such wretches are highly superstitious and possibly they believed, because of my cast eye, that I was under the protection of the Evil One. They merely tied me with ox-hide ropes to our own loom in the dovecote, where I was obliged, for hours, to listen to the screams of their victims. Among whom was my daughter. Then they left, first setting fire to some of the buildings. Luckily a mountain thunderstorm extinguished those fires, and after hours of struggle I was able to free myself and go to the help of the survivors. Thérèse I found cut, bruised, battered, almost entirely drained of blood. It was a wonder she still lived. The others, hardly in better case. Two died. Slowly, in the following weeks, they made some recovery. But my child has never recovered. She is palsied from the waist down, and cannot move her legs. Also mute. She does not speak, only tears pour from her eyes.

Using money Mr Croft sent, I was able to have her transported by litter as far as Amarante, where we now are. We hope to go on to Vila Real, where there is said to be a doctor. But she was so enfeebled by the first part of the journey that I again feared for her life. A priest in this town tells me that in his opinion the extremity of terror and pain suffered by Thérèse has locked her into a kind of catalepsy from which only profound surprise or joy can release her. I believe that he is right. So far, no expedient that I can contrive has proved of any use.

Now, my dear Eliza, I know this is asking a great deal; perhaps asking something that may not be in your power to grant. For all I know, you may now be a married woman, or engaged in some pursuit that will not permit you to strike camp at short notice, pick up your skirts and sail for Portugal. But oh! if you *could* come, I think, I truly believe, that your arrival might be the only event that would have the power to deliver my child from her dreadful prison. And I do beg you, if it is within your power, to make this effort, to come.

How can I be certain that you will even receive this letter? Or that it will not take so long finding you that my daughter's bondage may have been unlocked by death? I cannot be certain, of course. But I do have such a great faith in your attachment to Thérèse that I believe, if it is at all possible for you to do so, you will come, and that if you come you may be able to help her.

We move next to Vila Real. Should we for some reason leave that place, make your inquiries of the nuns in Oporto; the various convents are in communication and will know where foreigners are lodged. If you ask for 'the Englishwoman and her afflicted daughter Teresa' anybody will be sure to tell you.

Ever your friend,
Hariot Vexford.

I read this letter sitting in the Duke's rose garden, on a sultry afternoon in July. The drowsy scent of full-blown roses, catnip and hot flagstones enveloped me like a quilt, and a sleepy whirring came from the grasshoppers in the meadow beyond.

We have been at war, I thought, this country has been at war with the French ever since I was a child, but what do I myself know about war? Battles are fought, Trafalgar, Vitoria, Salamanca, ships are sunk, sailors drowned, soldiers cut down by cannon fire – all to protect this island; but how am I, Eliza Williams, affected by such happenings? I hear about them as if they were in a play by Shakespeare or Sophocles. But these people, my friends, Lady Hariot, Triz – they have met war face to face. And I went on to think about Colonel Brandon and Marianne; I had at times been critical of them in my mind, for paying me so little heed as they moved about India, or travelled from India to Portugal; but how could I know what cares they might have had, what dangers faced them?

As soon as I had read the letter I longed to show it to the Duke; but he was in London, attending the great fete in Carlton House (in the special pavilion designed by Mr Nash) given in honour of Sir Arthur Wellesley, who had been created Duke of Wellington.

The Duke returned to Zoyland the following day, tired and, for him, out of humour.

'London is nothing but a bedlam,' he peevishly said. 'They have covered Hyde Park with oriental temples, pagodas, bridges and towers. There is no milk to be had, the cows are all banished from the parks; and it is impossible even to get clothes washed, all the laundry-women are devoting themselves to princes and foreign visitors.'

'Oh, sir! Pray – pray – read this letter!'

He read, frowning, his lips pursed in a silent whistle, eyes eclipsed under the bushy canopies of eyebrow.

Having reached the end he at first made no comment, but puffed his cheeks out in a long sigh. Then he went through it again, slowly and carefully.

'You realize that by this time the poor thing may be no more?' he said at last, turning the sheet around to study the date.

'Yes . . .'

'But I suppose you are none the less bent on running off to the rescue. Hey? The clement heart of Miss never yet permitted such an appeal to go unanswered. As I am well aware! Mendicants, cadgers, barkers, touters – every guttersnipe and gypsy in the country comes cap in hand to you for alms.'

'Well,' I said, 'I know what it is to be alone and friendless – '

'Humph! And I suppose the chance of seeing Mrs Marianne constitutes no added inducement?'

'I beg your pardon, sir?'

'This post-scriptum – '

I had not noticed the post-scriptum, tucked in one corner. It said, 'I understand that Mrs Marianne Brandon, the widow, I suppose, of your guardian is staying at present with the nuns of the Santa Clara Convent in Oporto.'

'Good heavens!' I stared at the Duke. 'Then, that must mean – I suppose – that Colonel Brandon has met his end.'

'Died in some battle, doubtless, poor fellow.'

'No wonder he never returned to Delaford.'

''Tis to be hoped that Mrs Marianne has informed the lawyers,' the Duke said drily. 'But now, my dear – if, as I surmise, you are eager to be off to Portugal on this wild-goose mission, I have but one stipulation.'

'Of course, my dear sir,' I replied, somewhat inattentively, for my mind was astir with speculation about Marianne Brandon. Did she intend to remain in Oporto, or would she come back to England? Had Willoughby – had my father – ever succeeded in his aim of seeking her out? Might they – if Colonel Brandon was no more – might they be reunited?

The Duke went on. 'My stipulation, child, is this. I shall accompany you to Portugal myself. My ship, the *Miranda,* sails from Bristol in ten days' time with a cargo of cod and dry-goods – most fortunately as it turns out – so you are assured of a satisfactory passage. And we can reside at the Factory House in Porto, while you make your inquiries. My steward, Bliven, shall accompany us; he can make all the needful arrangements. And Enrique Morton, my agent out there, can put inquiries in train for you.'

'But, sir – '

I must confess that I was somewhat aghast at the Duke's plan. The prospect of travelling thus, with all the consequence and consideration that his presence was bound to entail, did not at all enliven my spirits; to speak the truth, I had hoped to be off on my own, in solitude and freedom.

'I had been planning to send Bliven over,' the Duke went on comfortably, 'in order to find out how the *quinta* was recovering from the effects of the French ravages. But he has always proffered some reason why such a trip would not be convenient. Now I shall go myself, and that will be much better. I shall enjoy a stroll down the Rua Nova des Inglezes. Porto is a pleasing town.'

I did not voice any of my many objections. And, later, I was glad that I had not. For Dr Swinton issued a most vehement veto against his noble patient undertaking any such excursion.

'Your Grace has been looking fatigued, and of late I have noticed you stumble several times. It would be highly injudicious – unthinkable – out of the question.'

'But a sea voyage might be the thing to set me back on my feet,' objected the Duke.

'*Not* across the Bay of Biscay in August, my dear sir! When gales may be expected daily! It would be folly – arrant, irredeemable folly!'

The Duke would have argued further but, that very day as it chanced, he stumbled again, on the terrace steps, and might have fallen and injured himself severely had not Lamb, his devoted valet, leapt forward and caught him just in time.

'Oh, bless me! I am growing to be a clumsy, infirm old dotard,' the poor Duke lamented. 'None of my friends will wish to come near me, soon.'

Seeing that he was really cast down, I teased him gently.

'Indeed they will not, sir! Since you are so bad-tempered and irritable, and entertain them so stingily, and so completely fail to see the point of any joke they may tell you.'

'Minx!' He pulled my ear. 'Well: I see how it is. You must go on your errand of mercy without me. But I do implore you most urgently not to dilly-dally any longer than you need over there, but, once your mission is accomplished, hurry back to your poor old friend in Zoyland.'

'Of course, sir. That's of course,' I said helplessly, my heart bleeding a little. How could I make any such promise? How could I tell what the case might be, when I found Lady Hariot and Triz? But it was no use to say those things.

'In the meantime, before you set to your packing,' went on the Duke more cheerfully, 'I want you to order a goose, or some capons, or a few quail, for I have Mr Nash coming down again tomorrow, and Sir John Middleton said that he would step over to meet him, now his lady is safely brought to bed.—Oh, and, by the by, Mr Nash's young helper will be accompanying him.'

This was news to me, and not particularly agreeable news. But I smiled and curtseyed, and went off to give the necessary house-keeping instructions.

'So!' said Pullett, as I changed my dress for dinner. 'So! You're off to Portugal, it seems? And not a word to *me* about it! A fine thing, to keep your plans from them as is most closely concerned.'

'I was going to tell you,' I said, twining feathers into my hair. 'It seems that gossip runs in this house faster than heath-fires. I would have told you.'

'Well, I'm coming with you.' She set her lips ferociously.

'*Oh no!*'

'Oh, yes!'

'But you dread going in a ship! And they all say the Bay of Biscay is the most terrible water in the world.'

'Just the same, I'm a-coming. I'm not having you getting up to mischief alone in foreign parts. Dear knows what you'd be doing. And why you can't stay and marry that nice young Mr Hobart, I *can't* conceive.'

I accidentally dug a hairpin into my scalp and clenched my teeth. 'Marriage with him is not in question. He hasn't asked me.'

'He would, soon enough, if you hit him hard enough. And he has a *good* ring – a good, clear yellow. Then His Grace would leave him Zoyland, and we'd all be in clover.'

'Will you kindly hold your hush, and hand me that hairbrush and go away.'

She went off with a flounce.

❦

Hoby was much more subdued on this visit. The pretext for it was some summerhouse, or maze, or gazebo that the Duke wanted Mr Nash to design for him, and the three men were off, conferring about it and its possible site for a large part of the first day. And Sir John Middleton came over to dinner that evening, very full of his new baby.

'Smiling little fellow, worth a dozen of his prune-faced elder brother, who is the spit-image of my first wife. Devilish bad luck, I call it, that a man's constricted by this cursed entail, and can't bequeath his property where he chooses. If I could help it, I'd not leave a groat to the progeny of that Friday-faced female, my first wife.'

The Duke sighed in agreement, and drank off a large goblet of claret.

'Sir, sir!' besought Dr Swinton. 'You *promised* me that you would be very abstemious with your liquor.'

'Oh, deuce take it! Not allowed above a mouthful of wine – and Lizzie going off on a wild-goose chase to Portugal – and McPhee tells me that caterpillars have got into the succession houses so that we shan't have any apricots – '

I caught Hoby's eye fixed on me anxiously.

After the meal, when the elder men were still at their port, he came into the drawing room where he found me playing Cimarosa sonatas.

'Why are you going to Portugal? And when?' he demanded without ceremony.

'Do you remember Lady Hariot? And Triz?'

'Of course I do.'

I told him about Lady Hariot's letter.

'But this is folly,' he said. 'Complete folly! Firstly, how will you ever find them? Secondly – if the letter took so long in reaching you, it is odds but the poor girl has died long since. How old is she?'

'I suppose, sixteen or seventeen.'

'She will have died, you may be certain, and your trip will have been for nothing. And you yourself may be in considerable danger out there – the country still upheaved from the effects of war and French occupation, swarming with lawless men – you don't speak the language – you have never been abroad before – why should you do this? Lady Hariot never did so much for *you*, that I recall –'

'She was as kind to me as a mother –'

'And I've heard it said that Boney is not safely confined in Elba, that he might escape and the French would rise up again in support of him – Liza, you *must* think again. This is a most ill-considered caper.'

I said coldly, 'The Duke himself raised no objections to my going. I must ask you, Mr Hobart, to confine your advice to those over whom you have some authority. Over me, you have none.'

And, as he still stood lowering at me, I rose up from the piano and walked towards the door.

'Since you and the Duke have become such fast friends,' I added as I left the room, 'you might come down and visit him while I am away.'

PARTING FROM THE DUKE PROVED A SEVERE, AN UNANTICIPATED ordeal. It was little short of agony, indeed. He looked up at me from his chair like some sad old dog who cannot understand why he is not permitted to accompany his owner for a walk. His eyes, under the bushy brows, were brimming with tears. He could not speak.

'I will come back to you as soon as I possibly can, sir, I promise. Truly, *truly.*' The words came from me, though I had not intended saying any such thing. But his look smote me to the heart. Why, I wondered, why are human beings obliged continually to give one another so much pain?

And quitting Zoyland was very bad. The domestics were downcast to see me go, and many besought me not to make any prolonged sojourn in Portugal, but to hurry back without too much delay. 'Indeed, we and His Grace can't spare ye, Missie,' said old Tark.

Pullett had sunk into a gloom for days beforehand. Her glances of farewell, as we drove away, at every bush, every tree, every turn of the road, each seemed intended to convey a reproach. To make matters worse, the sea voyage, on the ship *Miranda*, was wretched from start to finish. The only thing for which I was thankful was that the Duke himself had not carried out his intention of accompanying me.

We were over a fortnight at sea, with contrary gales, and the waves in the Bay of Biscay so raging and mountainous that even the sailors were sick, and poor Pullett more dead than alive, weak as a ghost, unable for six days to take any nourishment apart from cold water, since her stomach was in such a condition of irritation that it rejected even a crumb of bread.

Thus befell a most distressing occurrence. One evening Pullett left our cabin (a tiny, cramped compartment, not much larger than a dog kennel) complaining that the air stifled her, she could not breathe; and crept out on deck.

I, unlike everybody else on the ship, had not been taken sick, but was utterly exhausted from unceasing care of Pullett for the last six days. I wearily inserted myself into my hammock – a process akin to mounting a fretful horse – with the intention of resting for ten minutes and then going to see after Pullett. Instead, I fell into a profound slumber which lasted until daybreak. To my horror, when I next awoke, Pullett had not returned to the cabin and, when I scrambled out on deck, nobody could tell me where she was; or had even laid eyes on her. The storm was still raging, and it became dismally plain that the unfortunate woman must, in her weakness and disability, have been swept overboard during the hours of dark. She could not swim, I knew; there seemed not the slightest possibility of her having survived.

If *only* I had accompanied her on deck, I thought, again and again, this dreadfully sudden end could have been averted, and she would probably have continued to live for many more years. I had no idea of Pullett's age; she might have been in her late fifties, but, wiry and healthy, she often boasted that she had never felt a day's illness in her life. She had no family, no friends but Rachel and Thomas.—Her untimely death lay, a heavy weight on my conscience, for a great while thereafter; the heavier because, in the past, I had often found her self-appointed authority over me decidedly irksome and uncalled-for, annoying rather than amusing or touching. But now, more than I could have believed possible, I missed her tart, admonishing, censorious guardianship.

And oh, how I missed the Duke's fond, easy, uncritical company!

At last the ship changed her course eastwards and we made our way up the river Douro (dodging the dangerous sand-bar at its mouth) and came to Oporto, which, as the Duke had told me, is a fine, precipitous old town, with steep streets, roofs and spires rising up in layers, very grandly, on either side of the river. In many ways it is not unlike Bristol; or so I thought. We tied up near the *armazem,* or warehouse, from which the Duke's wine was shipped to England, and at last I was able to step ashore into a new world.

I ought to have felt as free as a bird. And, indeed, I was deeply interested in all around me. I liked to observe the short, compact, but graceful women, mostly pale-faced and black-eyed, with close-fitting bodices over white linen shirts, serge petticoats, muslin kerchiefs under heavy black hats, ornaments of gold and floss silk, black lace shawls and parasols to shield them from the sun. The men wore broad-brimmed hats, short jackets, and tight-fitting trousers to the calf. Both men and women mostly had wooden-soled slippers. And some peasants wore cloaks made of rushes. The air jangled with the sound of bells – goat bells, church bells, mule bells; and was rich with the smells of fish and dung. The streets were amazingly filthy. Pullett would have been scandalized.

Bliven, the Duke's manager, a rather surly man, who plainly regretted the necessity of putting himself out on my behalf, led me from the region of warehouses, mostly belonging to English port-wine shippers, to the English Factory House, a handsome granite building which had been abandoned and somewhat damaged during the French occupation, but was now restored to its former use.

Here Enrique Morton, the Duke's local agent, a black-haired man, half-Portuguese, was able to arrange for my accommodation overnight in a hostel, and for my transport up the Douro river next day, should I wish it, in a *barco rabelo,* the flat-bottomed boats which are employed for the transportation of wine casks from the numerous vineyards farther up the river. There were many of these to be seen, plying back and forth over the water. They have square sails and oar-shaped rudders worked by three men, and are capacious, being able to carry from twenty to eighty pipes of port at one time. The roads in this country are extremely bad (as I was soon to discover for myself) and almost all the wine transport is conducted by water.

Having, therefore, a day to spend in Oporto, I resolved to go directly to the Convent of Santa Clara and make inquiries there, in case by good fortune Lady Hariot and her daughter had succeeded in removing thither in the period since Lady Hariot's letter had been written.

Accordingly I purchased a black hat (so as not to stand out too conspicuously from other women in the streets) and inquired my way to the convent which, I discovered, lay not too far from the wharves and the English Factory Building. The Portuguese tongue was so very guttural as, at first, to be almost wholly incomprehensible to me but, by a mixture of French and Spanish acquired at school and from the Duke's tutors, I was able to make myself understood. I learned that there were two religious establishments, one for monks and one for nuns. To the latter I made my way and found it situated on top of a high hill-brow, with magnificent views over-looking the wide, curving Douro. Seeing the whole town thus laid out before me, I found it even harder to conceive how the intrepid Sir Arthur Wellesley had cast his troops over this swift-flowing stream under the guns of the French on the northern bank.

Had Colonel Brandon taken part in that engagement? I wondered.

Arrived at the convent, I stated my business to a portress at a little grille, and was sent to wait in a small parlour with whitewashed walls, sparsely furnished with a few oaken stools.

I had asked for an English-speaking sister, if possible, and was presently rewarded by a soft voice from behind yet another grille, which first administered a blessing on me in Portuguese and then added, 'Spik Inglizh.'

I inquired if she was able to tell me the whereabouts of an English lady and her afflicted daughter.

She would ask, she said, and vanished again. After a longish interval she returned and informed me that when last heard of – but that was not recently – the lady and her daughter were lodged at the convent in Vila Real.

'A que distania?'

About twenty leagues, perhaps.

I thanked her wholeheartedly for this useful clue, and left an offering for the convent. (The Duke had been lavish with travelling money. 'If go you must, it will ease my mind at least to know that you are comfortably provided for,' he said.)

As I retraced my steps past the portress's lodge, a tall Englishman was making inquiries there. Voice, build and costume were all decided indications of the Anglo-Saxon race.

'Are you certain that you have no information?' he was saying. 'Ask once more.'

'Very well, I will inquire again, Senhor.'

The stranger wore a long, caped travelling cloak and a black hat pulled down low. I had but a glimpse of a portion of his face. His glance passed over me incuriously for I wore black like any Portuguese female and furthermore had my hat pulled down to screen my countenance; and he for his part was wholly intent on his business. I had an instantaneous impression of deep-set dark eyes, grizzled locks, and a visage harshly scored by marks of illness, grief or dissipation. Bad temper, too. He tapped his cane impatiently on the stone floor of the lodge as if he were a person unaccustomed to be kept waiting in draughty ante-rooms. Yet his clothes had been shabby, I thought as I walked off down the hill, and his shoes dusty.

The Duke had warned me about the discomfort of Portuguese lodgings, and his gloomy predictions were amply fulfilled. As I tossed, flea-bitten, on a hard bed that night, and listened to the rain lashing against the ill-fitting casement, my brief glimpse of the stranger's face returned to me several times.

And, amid confused wonderings at the Portuguese – how could they display such charming taste in adorning so many of their buildings with façades of blue-and-white pictorial tiles, while allowing rats to roam freely in their streets and so many villainous insects to bite their visitors? – I tried to decide of whom the strange Englishman had reminded me so forcibly.

– No, dear reader, it was not Mr Sam; though the flashing dark eyes bore a superficial resemblance to that lost hero; it was somebody very much more familiar, somebody that I had seen recently and frequently; who could it possibly be?

Weary of such useless conundrums I at last fell asleep, but not for long; church bells clanging far and wide woke me to a day of torrential rain. The Duke had warned me of this also.

'Portugal is the doorstep to the Atlantic ocean,' he said. 'Doubtless all those Atlantic gales have their part in the production of such noble wine as is shipped from the Douro; that, and the soil, and the climate, which is hot in summer, very cold in winter; indeed the vines of the Douro region have not their equal anywhere in the world. Or such is my opinion. It was a fortunate conjunction of talent and circumstance which brought the English there, a couple of centuries ago, to trade Newfoundland cod for wine.'

Myself not at all grateful for the weather, being no imbiber of port-wine, I rose, ate a breakfast of hard bread, tea and preserve (made, I think, from pumpkins), then Mr Morton came to escort me to the boat.

When I had told him that I wished to travel to Vila Real, he said that would be no problem, as the Duke's vineyards lay to the east of a village on the Douro called Peso da Régua, and the *barco* would take me as far as that place, from where I could arrange for mule transport through the mountains (the Trás-os-Montes) to my destination.

The Duke had kindly supplied me with all kinds of equipment for my journey, a mahogany box containing metal plates, a pot for boiling water, spoons, knives, packets of dry biscuits, raisins, a lead-lined box of tea and a waterproof cloak. Having observed the meagre space allotted me on the *barco rabelo,* I ungratefully consigned all these things (except the waterproof cloak) to the keeping of the porter at the Factory House, having little doubt in my mind that anybody who grew up in Byblow Bottom could make her way through the mountains of Portugal without such appurtenances.

Certainly it would have been hard to find a place for them on the *barco,* which was piled high with empty wine casks ready for the vintage, which, Morton told me, would start shortly in early September.

'It varies from one vineyard to another; the Duke's place, Quinta dos Rosas, lies on a very warm, sheltered slope and is ahead of some of the others. You will wish to see the vintage, I daresay,' he added disapprovingly, and seemed relieved when I told him that depended on whether my search for Lady Hariot proved successful, in which case I would no doubt remain with her.

'What happens at the vintage?'

'We hire a number of Spanish itinerant workers, *gallegos,* a kind of gypsy, who migrate southwards at this season. They tread the grapes in the *lagares,* which are great stone tanks. It is punishing work, fit only for the strongest men; the first spell of treading lasts uninterruptedly for eighteen hours; so the men who come to do it are rough, dirty and wild.'

'*Why* does the first shift last so long?'

This idle question from a female he thought proper not to answer, but declared, firmly, 'It is a scene not suitable for ladies. They sing very obscene songs as they tread, also.'

I could see that he, like Bliven, thought it was very inconsiderate and tiresome of me to come, needing assistance, to the Douro valley at this season. Or, indeed, at all.

The passage up the river lasted for several days. We were favoured with a following west wind, but the current is a swift one, and oars were required as well as sails for the *barco* to make any progress. At night we received hospitality from *quintas* along the river. The weather continued dismal. I could tell that the scenery must be magnificent, but often it was almost invisible. High, green, terraced hillsides rose on either hand, glimpsed in a ghostly manner through veils of gliding mist and rain. Some were striped in vertical lines, some horizontally, according to the vine-grower's taste. The landscape was a most curious combination of wild grandeur and mathematical neatness, wholly unlike anything I had ever seen before.

Sadly, I wondered what Mr Sam would have made of it.

'Mr Morton, I wish to relieve myself,' I said on the first day. 'What arrangements are made for that?'

'None,' he said shortly.

'Then be so good as to ask the boatmen to turn their eyes away from me.'

He plainly thought this was tedious and finical of me; the sailors had shown no such delicacy when answering the call of nature.

At noon a meal of black bread, *bacalhau* (which is dried salted fish), olives and wine was available to the boatmen as they went about their work, and to me as I perched on a crate of sardines doing my best to keep my feet from being trodden on as the men moved about.

Huddling under the Duke's waterproof cloak, I resolved to write him a letter, as soon as I was able, to inform him how invaluable this garment was proving.—But I would not tell him, yet, about the death of Pullett; that would make him too sad and anxious.

The food became sodden as we ate, but since the black bread was hard, and the dried cod fiercely salty, having it rinsed with rain was no disadvantage.

At dusk on the third day, we reached Peso da Régua, a fair-sized village scattered for half a mile along the steeply sloping bank. Many vineyards have warehouses and lodges here, since there is a good anchorage. Our *barco* was tied up and Mr Morton escorted me to a *pousada,* which was far from luxurious; my bedroom was a garret with a baked clay floor, the bed was a wooden plank, and the goatskin blanket so scanty and verminous that I was glad, again, to wrap myself in the Duke's waterproof cloak. The rafters, too, were swarming with bugs. Supper was not bad, however: a soup composed of chicken, bacon, rice, beans, bread and I know not what other ingredients. I would have liked to explore the village but, as the rain continued to lash down, thought it best to retire, Mr Morton having promised to arrange mule transport for me to Vila Real early on the following morning.

❧

'One mule and *two* men?' I inquired doubtfully after breakfast (black bread and a drink of milk). 'And that mule looks fit only for the knacker's. And why do I need two guides? Surely one would be sufficient?'

'Mules are still in very short supply,' Morton said sourly. Today the note of irritation was even more noticeable in his tone. Plainly he longed to be rid of me. 'During the French wars, both mules and oxen vanished entirely. And it is better you have two guides, for defence. You may encounter bands of *gallegos* travelling south. They are wild, lawless beings. These men are there to protect you. Their names are Manuel and João.'

'Very well. Thank you,' I said, not troubling to mention that the two escorts looked fully as capable of villainy as any *gallegos*. 'Do they know the way to Vila Real?'

'Of course! It is about seven leagues, but the ways are very mountainous and un-posted. You should reach your destination before dark, however.'

'Thank you,' I said again, set my foot in the wooden stirrup and mounted. The two guides held each a stirrup on either side and trotted, keeping pace easily enough with the mule, which maintained a kind of steady shamble, half walk, half trot.

Our road at first climbed steeply zig-zag up the hillside between vineyards. The rain had ceased and the day at last was glorious; I could not forbear a lifting of the heart, as I surveyed the immense prospect of mountains, deep river valley and terraced hillsides that lay about me all glittering and new-washed.

The roads, it is true, were amazingly bad, little better than goat-tracks, and, once we reached the rolling country high above the river valley, they were very confusing, running hither and thither in all directions. I could see that in misty or rainy weather, without the sun as a guide, it would be easy to lose oneself.

Manuel and João were a laconic, not to say surly, pair, exchanging no more than a couple of syllables every half hour or so. But, when the sun stood overhead, Manuel said, 'It is time to eat' – or, at least, that is what I assumed he meant.

By now we had long left the Douro valley and were in a high, mountainous region, very sparsely populated. A few of the fields were cultivated, but the houses, if any, were mostly in ruins, where the French armies had passed, laying waste. Pine woods grew on some of the slopes, and the ravines were thickly grown with chestnut trees.

I reined in the mule and dismounted.

Morton had provided us with a bundle of food, fastened to the crupper. I untied this, and passed bread and smoked sausage to the two men, then sat on a rock – we were in a kind of glen, near the foot of a cliff – to eat my own share of food.

The guides bolted down their portions; then the one called João moved away (to relieve himself, I assumed); absently watching his companion, I noticed his eyes widen and his lips compress; then he made a kind of gesture, to attract my notice, and suddenly called out: *'Senhora —'*

Following the direction of his eyes, which were *not* on me, I flung myself to one side, almost in time – but not quite – to avoid a heavy glancing blow from the rear, which fell on the side of my head. João had stolen up behind me, intending to dash out my brains with a rock.

I had a long knife concealed in my high riding-boot. I plucked it out, and stabbed him with all my strength in the chest.

'Jesus-Maria!' he gasped, and fell bleeding to the ground.

Manuel, meanwhile, had snatched up my waterproof cloak (which I had earlier discarded as too hot). He made for the mule, but I anticipated him, grabbing the reins, and threatening him with the knife, although my head still sang from the blow and my heart was pounding fiercely.

But Manuel on his own offered little threat. Abandoning his comrade, he fled off, clutching my cloak, scrambled round the corner of the cliff and was soon out of sight.

About to remount the mule, I hesitated, debating within myself what I ought to do about João. The region here was a desolate one; so far we had encountered not a single soul; if I left him here, would he bleed to death?

Holding the reins, I cautiously approached him and found, to my shocked astonishment, that he was dead; my knife must have penetrated his heart. (It was indeed extremely sharp; it had been another journey-gift from the Duke, along with the handsome pair of boots which had been made with great ingenuity to hold, in one boot a weapon, in the other, a purse.)

While I was thoughtfully resheathing my blade and considering with some gravity and bewilderment the fact that I had killed a man, had in one single moment deprived a fellow-creature of his life for ever, I was startled almost to fainting-point to hear a voice address me.

'*Hola, Señora!* It seems that you made a bad choice of travelling companions!'

Looking past the mule, and the dead body, I saw two strangers regarding me. Both were large, swarthy, untidy men, with black ringlets, velveteen breeches and wide-brimmed, dusty hats.

'We were witnesses to what happened,' said one. 'We were up there, on top of the crag, we saw that vermin there pick up the rock to smash in your head – *Dios!* – what a blow *that* would have been! And we saw you, Señora, spring aside and finish him off with as neat a lunge as any matador, *brava!* – and then we saw the other cowardly rogue make off. And good riddance to him! But what of this one?'

'He is dead,' said I. 'But I did not mean to kill him.'

'*Morra!* Let him go. He is no loss to the world. But you, Señora, you are not Portuguese, surely?'

'No, I am English. And you are not Portuguese either, I think?'

'No, lady, we are wine-treaders from Spain, come south to earn a few honest reales. At home we are charcoal-burners.'

They beamed at me with great goodwill.

'You are *gallegos*? But I thought they always travel in troops?'

'So we are a troop. But we left our companions at the top of the cliff to come to your assistance.'

'That was very chivalrous of you! And now you can add to your kindness by telling me if I am on the right track to Vila Real?'

'Quite right,' said they. 'Just continue on with the sun behind you, and you should be there in three hours. But would you wish us to accompany you?'

'No, no, that is kind and courteous of you, but I shall do very well.'

'*Bueno*! As the Señora wishes. What shall we do with this rubbish?' pointing to the dead João.

'I don't know. Drop him in a ditch, perhaps.'

There was a crevice below the cliff, where gorse and brambles grew. They stowed him in there, out of sight, first prudently going through his pockets, which yielded a few silver coins. These they shared out scrupulously – first having offered them to me. But I refused with horror.

'Evidently the Señora is not used to war. The winner takes the spoils.'

'No,' I said, 'I am not used to war. I would prefer for you to have the money. And I am very glad you came by when you did.'

Indeed I was. Their friendly presence had lightened that bleak moment when I must face the fact that I had committed murder.

'The Señora will be lucky in her life, I think,' said one of them, looking in a calm, uncommiserating manner at my right hand still grasping the mule's rein. 'She is a *d********.*' And he used a Spanish term that was unfamiliar to me.

'Just the same, she should be on her guard,' said the other. 'The peasants around here – who, I may say, are a barbarous, backward race – many of them believe that a person with such hands as the Señora's must be a *l*****.*'

Another unfamiliar word.

'What is that?'

'One who is a man or woman by day, but at night becomes a wild beast and runs about devouring sheep or children.'

'Oh, a werewolf. Perhaps that is why those two guides thought it best to make away with me.'

'Not so! They simply acted according to their natures. If we encounter the other rogue, we will cut his liver out. Now, Señora, is there anything else, any other service we can render you? Would you wish to meet our companions? They are very good sort of men.' He beamed at me again. Indeed, both of them, rough-looking as they were, seemed very good-hearted and well-disposed, not at all the way the *gallegos* had been described to me.

I thanked them heartily, but said I had an urgent errand to seek out a sick friend and must be on my way.

'*Adios,* Señora, then. *Vaya con Dios.*'

'*Vaya con Dios* to you also.'

And so we parted. I shall remember them all my life.

Considerably cheered by this encounter I continued on my way, keeping the sun behind me as recommended, and presently, in the distance, over a few wooded ridges, I saw the spires of what must be the town of Vila Real, the Royal City.

The mule was plodding along more and more slowly. I would sell it in Vila Real, I decided, and if possible buy another. It was indeed fortunate, I thought, that João and Manuel had not known how much money I carried, or they would have made a much more determined attempt to murder me. My hat, in which I had constructed a false crown of black leather, was lined with banknotes, as well as my travel documents. And the left-hand boot held enough gold moidores to buy a vineyard. Thanks to the Duke.

One day, I thought, I would tell the Duke about the death of João. Nobody else. And not in a letter.

As the mule slowly trudged on its way, I meditated on the death I had caused, trying to teach myself, as I knew I must, how to give this happening a place in my mind without excessive horror or needless guilt. Oddly, what I most felt was a wish that I had known the man better. His death seemed – *was* – so much that of a random stranger. If only he had been Dr Moultrie! Or Squire Vexford! Or his brother! Or one of the Bath Beaux. I could then have felt there had been a purpose and a value in removing him from the human race. But about this man I knew nothing, not even if he had a wife . . .

Vila Real is a largish shabby town, with large shabby houses and wide streets, and a feeling of being perched high up on a wide and windy plain. It seemed quiet and subdued; the elderly men all walked about wrapped in shawls. I inquired my way to the nunnery and there learned, with some exasperation, that Lady Hariot and her afflicted child had indeed stayed there with the nuns, for some considerable time – *'Eu! la doenta!'* – but that, seizing the chance when a train of merchants went by with supplies, they had transferred – or planned to do so – to Lamego, a city south of the Douro, where there was a famous church, Nossa Senhora dos Remédios, approached by a great many steps, where miraculous cures were performed; or were said to be performed. Doubtless, the nuns said hopefully, by now the poor little one had recovered the use of her limbs.

The Holy Sisters were delighted to offer me a bed for the night. I was accommodated in a cell, whitewashed and spotless, where I slept on a rush pallet – or, at least, tried to sleep; the image of Manuel's face, his eyes twitching aside to watch his comrade pick up the rock, the instantaneous knowledge that my life depended on rapid movement, getting away – these things kept me awake, or plagued me with fearful dreams, from which I woke gasping to find that I had hurled myself off the mattress on to the floor.

In the morning, studying myself in the tiny glass (no bigger than a crown piece) which Pullett had given me for a last Christmas gift (ah, poor Pullett!), I discovered that the crack on the head which João had dealt me had left its legacy in the shape of two notable black eyes, glossy and contused, from which my own bleary optics peered out painfully.

'Ay, ay!' cried the sisters in horror. 'What *happened* to you?'

I explained that a rock had fallen upon me, which satisfied them.

'Such things are not uncommon in the mountains.'

But they persuaded me to remain in Vila Real for several days, which in truth I was glad enough to do, since I felt shaky and weak and my head ached amazingly.

'And then, it is very fortunate, Father Soeiro will be travelling to Lamego, and you can travel with him.'

Peering again into the little mirror, at my blackened visage, I now realized who it was that the strange Englishman in Oporto had resembled: it was myself!

Chapter 15

FATHER SOEIRO WAS A REMARKABLY CHEERFUL, CHATTY companion. He travelled in comfort, with an escort of two mounted manservants and a baggage mule. Evidently when it came to procuring four-legged transport, the good father had better connections than Enrique Morton. Through his helpful offices I too was enabled to exchange my sorry mount for a healthier beast, and we made our way back to Peso da Régua at a much more rapid pace than I had achieved on my outward journey.

When we reached the spot at which the man João had met his sudden end I kept my gaze firmly away from the cleft in the rock where his body lay; Father Soeiro noticed nothing, but continued his disquisition on the English: a most extraordinary race, he found them, large, fair, mad, fond of pursuing hares and disgracefully given to adulterating their port-wine with elderberry juice. 'But we Portuguese have passed edicts forbidding them to do that!' he cried triumphantly.

I said, 'I am very sure my guardian the Duke of Cumbria permits no such practices in his vineyards.'

'Well, let us hope not; but it must be said,' the Father allowed with a sigh, 'that the English are excellent fighters. Ah, that

Wellington!' He pronounced it Velington. 'What a man! I have seen him, wearing a plain grey frock-coat. *Nosso Grande Lorde!* He sent a thousand carts with guns up the breakneck hill from the Douro valley to Lamego. That was before the siege of Ciudad Rodrigo. Wait until you see that hill! You will be amazed. He had three armies, and he swept them all secretly together and drove the French eastwards. And when he crossed the river where it marks the frontier with Spain he rose in his stirrups and shouted, "Farewell, Portugal!" Ah, what a man!'

Father Soeiro wore a dark blue cloak and a slouched hat. If ever we passed a charcoal-burner collecting pine cones in a basket, or a peasant ploughing his field with a crooked broken branch, or a fisherman casting his line over a trout stream, they would fall on their knees as we went by and greet him: *'Bom dia, Senhor Padre!'* and he always replied with a blessing: 'Praised be Jesus Christ our Lord!' to which the reply was: 'And praised for ever and ever!'

His arrangements had all been made in advance. When we reached Peso da Régua there was a narrow boat, a *saveira,* waiting to ferry us across the river. *'Agua de Douro, caldo de pollas,'* quoted Father Soeiro fondly, looking down into the swirling waters – by which he intimated that the water was as full of fish as chicken broth of meat.

Across on the opposite bank from Régua more mules were standing ready.

'Nada, nada!' said the good father when I offered to pay my share. 'Give the money instead to the church of Nossa Senhora.'

I had glanced cautiously about the streets of Régua, wondering if I might set eyes on Manuel – or Mr Morton. Had there been any previous connection between Morton and the two guides, I wondered. Or had he merely – annoyed with this tiresome female wished on him by his employer – fobbed me off with the first two vagabonds and the first sorry nag that came to hand?

I saw neither of them. Morton, doubtless, was preparing for the vintage.

I wondered what Father Soeiro would say if I told him that I had killed a man; but I had not the least intention of telling him any such thing.

In fact, I thought sadly, there was nobody now Pullett was gone, except the Duke, to whom I could impart such a tale. To Mrs Jebb I could have told it, once upon a time. She would have received it dispassionately. Elinor Ferrars? No, no, not possible. She would feel in duty bound to pass it on to her husband.

Recalling Elinor, I fell to wondering about her sister Marianne. Was it conceivable that I might encounter her in my wanderings about Portugal – this strange country where the roads were no better than mule-tracks, even though English, French and Spanish armies had galloped along them, only three years before, where the towns were so small, so isolated, so widely scattered apart? At what refuge in this land, I wondered, had Marianne Brandon come to rest? And her husband, Colonel Brandon? Was he really dead? And – most teasing, tantalizing question of all, where now was Willoughby?

During the two days of inactivity passed at Vila Real, my first wild speculative supposition had hardened into a certainty. The man I had seen in Oporto at the convent, asking questions, must be Willoughby; my father. That one lightning impression I had of him remained with me still, as a single glimpse of a brightly lit scene lingers imprinted on the closed eyelid.

His face – I now realized – was exactly the same shape as mine. His eyes were set like mine; they differed only in being black. His voice – rather harsh and resonant – that was mine too. I hoped that my face might never set into such lines of grief or discontent – but that was not impossible. No wonder he had seemed familiar. I saw his face in my mirror every day.

He was searching for somebody, making inquiries at convents. And so was I. We might well meet again.

Lamego lies high in the mountains south of the river Douro. Conspicuous on the summit of a hill, as you approach the city, is the church of Our Lady of Remedies, at the top of its daunting flight of steps. True pilgrims climb the steps on their knees, reciting a prayer on every step. For the lazy or unbelieving there is a track which winds around the hillside. In the town down below there is also a handsome cathedral, various noble mansions, and other churches, besides the remains of a 500-year-old castle.

All my hopes and thoughts, however, were centred on the convent, which lay behind the Church of Nossa Senhora. It is famous for its medical offices.

I said goodbye to kind Father Soeiro, who was bound for the bishop's palace, and he wished me godspeed. Then I urged my mule up the track which ascended Our Lady's hill. At the top there were groves of pine trees. I left the mule tethered to a tree and made my way to the portress's lodge of the convent. There I knocked and asked my usual question.

'A lady and her sick daughter? Meninha Teresa?'

Ah, yes, said the portress, they were indeed here. In fact, on a fine day such as this, they would be taking the air in the convent gardens. If the Senhora cared to follow the path to the right, and then to the left, and then to the left again, and proceed through the orange grove, she would most likely find the ladies out on the terrace, where the air was freshest . . .

Carefully following these instructions, I passed through a vegetable garden, where two Sisters were hard at work among cabbages, pumpkins, artichokes and tomatoes; then a flower garden, fragrant with roses and geraniums; then through the orchard; and came out from its shade into the glare of a wide cobbled terrace overlooking the impressive panorama of the town's roofs and spires down below, and the vine-covered country beyond.

They would hardly sit here, I thought, in this blazing sun. But then I realized that there was an immense pine at the far end of the terrace, casting a patch of shade as big as a ballroom; and against the trunk of the pine two figures were sitting, one on a stone bench and one in some kind of basket-chair.

Suddenly my heart felt as huge as the pumpkins the Sisters had been cultivating. It beat so strongly in my chest that I had no room to breathe. Slowly I walked the length of the terrace and approached the two figures.

And they were Lady Hariot and Triz.

But so changed.

Of course, I recognized them. They were unmistakable. But Lady Hariot reminded me of the crooked branch I had seen a peasant ploughing with earlier in the day: she was so thin, she was so dry, she was so brown, she was so bent. Her eyes, though, were exactly as I remembered, one looking severely in my direction, the other gazing obliquely at some distant scene, visible to her alone.

And Triz. Could this be Triz? My little, pretty playfellow? This wan, dry, twisted creature, bundled in the basket-chair, with stick-like limbs dangling limply, mouth awry, staring eyes fixed on something dreadful? My heart turned over with horror at the mere sight of her.

And yet she knew me.

I had thought at first that perhaps she was mad – her face was so vacant and lacking in response to anything about her.

But when she saw me slowly approach, she started and her hands gripped the arms of the chair. She let out a little cry, then babbled a soft stream of words that were incomprehensible to me. The poor lopsided mouth curved into a smile. By degrees, I began to take in the meaning of what she said.

'Alize!' she was saying. *'Alize! Alize!* Alize.*'*

'Oh, Triz! Oh, my dear little Triz!'

I knelt down beside her, gave her a hug, and kissed her poor twisted face. And yet – I hate to say it, but it is true – I had to suppress a severe shudder of repulsion to do so. She was so horribly different from my little fair-haired charge and companion. She looked like a changeling indeed – some strange wizened elf-being left behind by the hill-people in place of the human babe they have stolen. She looked sick, vacant, deranged. Spoiled. Dreadfully spoiled.

But now Lady Hariot was gripping my hands – with her old, remembered strength – and her voice, warm, vibrating, full of intelligence, transported me at once back to Kinn Hall, to Growly Head, to the gardens dropping down in terraces above Byblow Bottom.

'Eliza! My dearest child! You came! You found us! Oh, that was so good of you! See, Thérèse knows you! She recognizes you! Even in your Portuguese hat! Do, please, take it off, and let us have a thorough look at you!'

So I removed my hat and kerchief, placing the hat (with all my wealth inside) carefully under the stone bench.

'No, you have not changed in the very slightest,' declared Lady Hariot. 'Unlike us! And, look, Thérèse thinks the same. I believe that is what she is trying to say.'

Triz was babbling away, eagerly, incomprehensibly, her thin hands clasping and unclasping, her eyes intently fixed on mine.

'Do you know,' Lady Hariot murmured to me, 'she has not spoken – *at all* – since *then*. I really do believe that your coming here may be – may be the – ' Her mouth shook, and she clapped her hand over it. I flung my arms around her.

'Dearest Lady Hariot! I am so *very* glad to have found you.'

'I do hope,' she said after a moment, taking firm control of herself again, quietly stroking Triz's dry, straw-like hair. 'I do hope, dear Eliza, that leaving England, that making your way here, did not prove too much of a difficulty?' She spoke absently, her eyes were back on her daughter. Or one of them was. The other was on the horizon.

I thought of the Duke, piteous, his eyes swimming in tears. I thought of Pullett lost in the Bay of Biscay; and the startling smoothness and ease with which my knife had slipped between João's ribs.

'Not too difficult,' I said.

'I do *hope* that you can remain here with us for a long time. I do believe that – with your help – now she has moved, now she has spoken – you will be able to bring Thérèse back to life again. She – look! – she even moved her knee a little.'

'Alize,' said Triz again. And then, 'Carthur, Carthur.'

'What can she mean?' said Lady Hariot, puzzled. 'Carthur? What is it, my love?'

'I think it is a game that she and I used to play. King Arthur and Sir Bedivere.'

'Bedvir, Bedvir,' agreed Triz joyfully. Her dull eyes opened wide. And then, of a sudden, she yawned and nodded, and the eyes closed. I looked in alarm at Lady Hariot, but she was unperturbed.

'She does that. She grows tired and falls asleep quite suddenly. It is partly that – we have to feed her on pap – she can hardly swallow – and I think the nuns mix in a little poppy juice with her food to keep her tranquil; otherwise, at first, she used to go into frenzies, which were quite terrifying.'

'Oh, Lady Hariot. What you have been *through*. For you, it must have been worst of all. Even worse than for her.'

'How can we judge? But now,' she said, 'I believe it is going to be better.'

A handsome blue-robed Sister approached us along the terrace.

'This is Sister Euphrasia, the Sister Superior,' Lady Hariot said to me in French. 'She has been our good angel. Sister Euphrasia, see, here is my friend, my daughter's old playmate, come all the way to us from England! And my daughter knew her! She spoke! Now, I do believe that Thérèse may get better!'

Sister Euphrasia smiled at me very kindly. 'You are most welcome to everything in our House. And now we shall redouble our prayers for this poor little one, for we can be sure that we have the ear of God.'

A younger Sister came hurrying along, crying, 'It is time for the little one's supper. Shall I take her in for you, Senhora?'

'Oh, thank you, Sister Luisinha, you are very kind. And now for ten minutes I and Senhora Eliza can have a happy time talking over the old days.—You must tell me, Eliza, everything, every single thing that has happened to you since last we saw one another.'

I cast my mind back to the last time I had seen her, dejectedly climbing on board the Spanish ship at Ashett.

What a great deal had happened to me since that day. Rather too much to tell, really.

'Oh, by the by,' said Lady Hariot. 'Now, this *will* be of interest to you. There is another English lady who has recently come to this convent. In fact she is thinking of entering here as a religious. But she has not yet made up her mind, has not yet taken final vows. And she is a connection of yours, Eliza.'

'Indeed?' I said. 'What is her name?'

'She is Mrs Marianne Brandon. Her husband was your guardian – was he not? I understand that he died at the siege of Ciudad Rodrigo.'

Mrs Marianne Brandon was a most elegant lady. She wore what seemed at first sight to be the habit of a religious, but if you looked closely you saw that the wimple and stole were made of dark blue silk, so dark as to be almost black; that the silver cross around her neck was slung on a chain of sapphires large as peas.

We met just before supper. The guests at the convent – of which there were a dozen or so – ate at a separate table with Sister Euphrasia. She herself ate nothing but peas and rice, but the guests were served superior fare: baked mutton, meat with rice, mullet, hake, cucumber salad, quince and roseleaf jelly, small cakes and biscuits.

'We are proud of our kitchen,' smiled Sister Euphrasia, seeing my surprise.—'And here, dear Senhora Brandon, is another young compatriot of yours, Meninha Eliza Williams.'

Mrs Brandon turned chalk-white. Her soup spoon fell from her hand. I thought she might faint.

But Lady Hariot, who sat next to her, picked up her glass of cloudy vinho verde and said, in a low voice, 'Quick, take a pull of this. It will do you good.'

And pull yourself together, woman, was implicit in her voice.

'How do you do,' said Mrs Brandon to me, coldly.

I said politely that I was well and added – since something had to be done to fill this silence – that some years before I had the pleasure of meeting her sister Elinor Ferrars (I did not mention that I had nursed her after the fever) and I was happy to be able to report that five of her novels were to be published shortly.

'Five?' said Mrs Brandon faintly. 'Novels? *Elinor?*'

'Why yes . . . It seemed that she had been writing them, unknown to anybody, for some time. Perhaps she began after you and – and your husband – travelled abroad? And in the end – in the end they were submitted to a publisher. And he liked them very much indeed.'

'Edward – Mr Ferrars – he permitted this?' Marianne still spoke in little more than a thread of a voice. But luckily, now, some of the other guests had begun a conversation among themselves.

'I understand,' I said temperately, 'that he was not too favourable at first, but since the publisher's opinion was so very enthusiastic – and affairs at Delaford somewhat – somewhat straitened – especially since the flood – '

'Flood?' said Marianne vaguely. 'Was there a flood?'

'Well, that was two or three years ago now.'

'I am afraid,' she said, 'that our English mail does not always catch up with us. And when it does, it is so old that I do not much regard it. And my husband – latterly – was greatly occupied with his military duties . . . '

Her voice trailed off. She still regarded me as if I were some venomous reptile which had found its way into her boudoir.

Marianne Brandon was a handsome woman. Once, she must have been extremely beautiful. Her complexion was brown, but transparent, her features remarkably regular, and her large dark eyes still retained some of the brilliancy they must have held when she captivated the younger Willoughby and beguiled him away from my mother.

She, in outward appearance at least, was far less altered than my father. If it *had* been my father.

But something – it seemed to me – was lost, that must once have been in her countenance: a fire, a spirit. I remembered accounts I had heard of her – the lively, passionate, poetic girl – from Sir John, from Mrs Jebb, from cottagers in Delaford. 'Ay, ay,' had said Sir John, 'she was a witch, a girl in a thousand, no other could hold a candle to her. She was like a candle herself – a whole handful of candles.' And he burst into hearty laughter, astonished at his own poetic imagery.

But now the candle was extinguished. And the spark, the spirit that lit the flame, had been withdrawn. She was a handsome, well-cared-for woman, but the hunger for experience, the eagerness in pursuit of knowledge, the hope, the awareness, had left her. How old would she be? Barely forty, surely. But she looked and behaved like somebody long settled into middle age, someone who for years had been accustomed to have all her wishes catered for. Whereas I noticed that Lady Hariot accepted no services from the nuns that she could not perform herself, and was evidently accustomed to undertake the most menial tasks for her child, Marianne Brandon sat enthroned like a dowager, and expected all the world to revolve around her.

Me she plainly disliked, and wished to have as few dealings with as possible. I had thought of mentioning that I had recently seen her mother, old Mrs Dashwood, but concluded that, in the circumstances, this would not be tactful, since the old lady was somewhat unhinged; a reminder of so gloomy a fact would be no recommendation.

After supper I left the other guests and sat with Triz in the room that she shared with her mother: a cool, stone-paved ground-floor chamber with a door opening on to an enclosed herb garden. The little nun, Sister Luisinha, was with her carefully administering drops of medicine; she smiled at me and said, 'Here, *cara crianca*, is someone you love as well as your dear mother!' and the poor lost eyes looked at me, and brightened, the poor twisted mouth faltered out sounds of greeting.

'I have come to play cat's-cradle,' I said. 'Do you remember, Triz, how we used to do that? If Sister Luisinha will be so good as to provide us with a piece of string.'

This the good nun was happy to do, and for an hour or so I manipulated the feeble fingers, which were stiff and thin as chicken-bones, while chatting on cheerfully about the games we had been used to play, the gardens at Kinn Hall, the nursery, her pony, the groom Jeff Diswoody and the poems and stories I used to tell her.

'Do you remember the *Ancient Mariner*, Triz? Do you remember how "Ice, mast-high, came floating by, As green as emerald"?'

It was like watching the wind blow over water; the response was there instantly, the ripple of recognition; but then it faded again. And, as before, she suddenly fell asleep.

During our talk Lady Hariot had come quietly into the room. After she had settled her daughter for the night – 'Come into the orchard, Eliza,' she said. 'It is early yet, a warm, balmy evening, and the other guests will be all in the visitors' parlour; we can talk more freely in the open air.'

So we strolled at leisure under the trees. Lady Hariot walked limpingly, with a stick; the years had been hard on her.

'This Atlantic climate is not the best for my rheumatic bones,' she said laughing. 'And being tied up to that devilish loom for twelve hours left me permanently out of shape. But Thérèse and I come from a tough stock, I fear; we survive.'

It seemed to me that Lady Hariot had survived much better than Marianne Brandon; not in health but in spirit.

'Tell me about Mrs Brandon,' I said, presently.

'Oh, I have talked to her very little. She is not wishful to communicate with strangers. But I know that she was very angry at the death of her husband (he was in command of that band, you know, at the siege of Ciudad Rodrigo that the French called *"les Enfants Perdus"* because they were sent in, as a forlorn hope, in order to draw the first fire and cause the French to set off their mines prematurely; they were all volunteers, and Colonel Brandon, it seems, was one also, though as a man of senior rank it was not required of him). His wife cannot forgive him, or Fate, for this. I think it has soured her.'

'She was very devoted to her husband, I conclude?'

'Well,' said Lady Hariot after a pause for thought, 'I am not certain that I could say so. My cousin Bess met the couple in Lisbon (he was invalided home, you know, after a wound received in the East, and decided to spend his sick leave in Portugal); Bess knew them tolerably well and she told me that Mrs Brandon was a very sharp, autocratic wife; he was quite slavishly devoted to her, gave in to her every whim. It was she who chose not to return to England, Bess said; he would have been glad to go back to his manor – in Dorset, was it? – and sell out. But then the French invaded. And so he returned to active service under his old commander.'

So, after all, I was wrong, I thought. My notion of Marianne, homesick for peaceful hours with her sister in the room overlooking the walled garden had not been a true picture.

'Perhaps he grew tired of being her slave and went back to war as a kind of escape?'

'Perhaps. And now he has escaped for ever.'

'And she feels defrauded.'

However, she has another string to her bow, I thought; her former suitor, Willoughby. But is she aware that he is eagerly seeking and inquiring for her? Does she know that? Willoughby, it is true, is now a bankrupt *émigré;* not such an attractive catch as he once was; but would that weigh with her? If she truly loved him? After all, she herself must be very comfortably provided for.

'Colonel Brandon was a wealthy man, surely? She inherits his fortune?'

She and Willoughby could live well enough on that, I thought.

'Not all of it, I believe,' said Lady Hariot. 'There is some closer relative who comes in for the manor and English estates. Sister Euphrasia told me that Mrs Brandon has money, invested in the Funds, which she would bring to the convent as her dowry, but no land or property. I think that Sister Euphrasia . . . does not consider Mrs Brandon . . . a very promising candidate for the cloister.'

'I can see that – if she is so filled with bitterness. I wonder *why* she was so angry? If she was not especially fond of her husband.'

'Oh . . . lost opportunities, perhaps. But now, Eliza – tell me more about yourself.'

So I gave her an account – a partial account – of my activities.

For some weeks, life at the Convent of Nossa Senhora settled into a smooth rhythm. Two or three times a day I sat with Triz for an hour or two, talked, played, joked, tried to warm her poor wits back to a pattern that she could sustain without reminding her of the hideous thing that had happened to her.

And I thought a great deal, at these times and between them, of men, and the violence that they do to each other – and to women – and wondered why the Almighty saw fit to combine in them these damaging, dangerous impulses, along with the ability to write sublime poetry, perform heroic acts of self-sacrifice and create the concept of a benevolent Maker.

Was He indeed so benevolent? I wondered. To me, his creation sometimes seemed frighteningly close to an act of malice.

I was cheered, though, by the Sisters. Busy, broad-hearted, they never paused to trouble their heads with such questions, but went continually about their work of healing the sick and helping the poor. Nossa Senhora had an impressive reputation throughout Portugal and Spain for the excellence of the healing work that was carried on there; and, from watching the activities of the nuns, I was able to gather a vast deal of useful information. If ever, I thought, I happen to be faced again with a situation such as the aftermath of the flood in Delaford, I would be very much better equipped to deal with it.

One thing I did observe here that might be improved: a great deal of the water used in their various decoctions and medicaments was drawn from a great tank filled in part with rain-water, in part from a muddy brook that meandered its way down from a slight rise to the south. This water was not over-clean.

Diffidently I asked Sister Euphrasia if I might be permitted to try my skill at hunting for a spring on their own property, which might supply them with fresher, purer water? She thought, gave gracious permission, and asked where I would search? In the orchard, perhaps, said I, as that lay somewhat uphill from the convent and its cloister.

Half a dozen of the younger nuns cheerfully assembled to watch me make the essay, along with Lady Hariot, who brought Triz along in her basket-chair and established her in the fragrant shade of a lemon tree.

I had cut myself a forked stick (privily, beforehand, in order not to display my formidable knife) and now began systematically pacing through the orchard, section by section. For a long time nothing happened, and Sister Euphrasia, who had come out between duties to cast an amiable eye over the proceedings, said kindly, 'After all, it would be wonderful if there were water here that had not already been discovered by the Moors! For they were in this region until the twelfth century; and the Moors had a special genius for discovering and making use of water.'

This I acknowledged politely, though it seemed to me possible that a spring might have shifted its location, or been covered up during six centuries. And so indeed it proved; after Sister Euphrasia had smilingly paced away, back to her administrative duties (her gait reminded me a little of Mrs Jebb) the wooden prong in my hands suddenly, as that day at Zoyland, took a decisive plunge downwards. I retraced my steps; it happened again; and again; and again.

Fortunately it was in a space between four trees.

'*Ay, ola!*' cried the nuns. 'It is as if the finger of Our Lady herself had pointed. Now, what happens?'

'Now, we dig,' I said stoutly. Though my confident manner concealed a certain anxiety, for supposing we dug and dug and nothing resulted?

The gardening nuns fell to with a will, and so did I; Lady Hariot offered to help, but I told her that it would be too much for her injured back. She had loved gardening at Kinn, I remembered, and so had Triz; we gave Triz a handful of wet earth to roll and knead in her fingers, and she murmured and babbled happily over the warm gluey wetness.—For very soon the earth, as we dug, began to grow wetter and wetter; a pool of muddy water collected at the bottom of our hole. Now the old man, Jorge, who helped in the nuns' vineyard, came and took over: 'It will be a fine well,' he said, hissing with approval. 'We shall make a fine big pool, and face it with stone, and set in a spout in the side wall. Indeed, I do remember that there was a spring spoken of hereabouts in the days of my great-grandfather; I suppose it will have been blocked up at the time of the terrible earthquake.'

'The earthquake was felt here, then, as well as at Lisbon?'

'Oh, yes, though not so severe.'

Sister Euphrasia reappeared, full of cordial praise.

'We shall sing a special chant of thanksgiving tonight after evening prayer! Now there will be no more water disputes with the vine-growers farther up the valley. You have done us a most useful service, Meninha Liza.'

Marianne Brandon had wandered into the orchard, attracted, I suppose, by the commotion, to see what was going on. But when she saw that I had some hand in the business, her lip curled and she walked away again. I saw her at a distance, in the pine grove, pacing to and fro (limping slightly, I noticed); as she walked she read and reread a letter, plainly with dissatisfaction, for in the end she crumpled it in her hand and threw it on the ground.

'*Pai dios!* Look at that child!' cried Sister Luisinha, for Triz had by now completely lathered herself with mud, and was smiling like a happy nixie. She was wheeled away, and the nuns followed.

I, ever curious, went over to the pine grove, which Marianne had now quitted, and picked up the paper which she had thrown down.

'My Adored Marianne,' it said, 'for so you will always be, though well I understand that I have no shadow of a right or claim upon you. I know that I once did you an irreparable injury, I know that to you I must seem the greatest villain upon earth. I left you – I callously abandoned you, to marry a rich woman for whom I had no regard, then, or ever. It was you – you – that I always loved. Yours is the image that has been constantly before me. I have been in continual agony since that parting. O God! what a hard-hearted rascal I was. There is nothing to be said in my defence. Yet I beg you – I beseech you – to consider my misery and my penitence. I have heard that you are now free again – that your excellent husband who, I am aware, deserved you as I never did – that he is no more. Can you ever consider returning to one who, likewise free, thinks of you continually, mourns you, longs for nothing but your company? I understand that you are contemplating a permanent retirement to the cloister; that you are at present in retreat at Nossa Senhora dos Remedios. O pray, pray think again before taking leave of the world! Remember one who loves you would be overjoyed to spend the rest of his days in your service. W.'

'Post Scriptum. A letter in care of the English Factory at Oporto will find me and bring me speedily to your side.'

Well! What a thing to find lying crumpled on the pine needles of a quiet and God-fearing community of nuns! And, also, what an expostulation, what an outpouring to find from one's *own father!* I read and reread the missive in astonishment, wondering how *I* should feel if somebody ever addressed such a cry to me. (I tried to imagine Hoby penning such sentences, but wholly failed.) I wondered if Marianne would ever find it in her heart to soften her resentment against this man; judging from her reception of this letter it seemed unlikely. Did I blame her? I cannot say that I did. After all, he had used my own mother even worse; had never made any inquiry after her at all (so far as I knew) or any attempt to save her from the results of his careless seduction. It was entirely due to her own efforts – and the good fortune of attracting the Duke's attention and affection – that my mother had passed the latter portion of her days in some comfort and security. While, as for myself – when had Willoughby ever displayed the least concern for *my* welfare?

Here it occurred to me to reflect that, in fact, for the somewhat dismal circumstances of my own upbringing, Mrs Marianne Brandon was rather more blameworthy than Willoughby. True, he had never sought me out; but then quite possibly he was never even informed of my existence. But Marianne Brandon, jealous of my mother – though Heaven knew she had no need – had actively worked against the Colonel ever coming to visit me, or taking any but the barest interest in my concerns. And if letters about my school fees, or about the needs of the people at Delaford, had gone unanswered, it was to Marianne's account that this must be laid. Probably the Colonel, busy at Salamanca or Ciudad Rodrigo, had never even heard of these matters.

I went in to pass an hour with Triz (now rid of mud); rather absently I sang to her, and drew her pictures of sheep and oxen and men digging. She seized the pencil from me and herself drew more pictures, of men on horseback. At first, with an icy heart, I thought they might be portraits of her ravishers; but then, smiling, she explained them:

'Carthur – Gal-had – Bidvere.'

'Yes, darling. King Arthur, Galahad, Bedivere. Beautifully drawn.'

'I wish we had a few more drawing materials,' said Sister Luisinha. 'I think it is a very remedial activity for her to portray events and men, like this, on paper.'

I had a brilliant idea. 'Why should I not take a boat to Oporto and there purchase a packet of papers and paints and brushes? I should be happy to present them to the convent. And then other sick people could use them as well. I could go and return very quickly – in a very few days.'

The Sister was enthusiastic. 'Yes! And there are other commissions that we could lay on you – several! I will inform Sister Euphrasia; she is always saying what a pity it is that we have nobody to spare for these errands. Silk thread for the altar frontals – medicines – needles – it is true the little Teresa will miss you, but it need not be for more than a few days, as you say.'

'Do you think she will ever recover, Sister?' I asked. (Lady Hariot was not in the room.)

She looked at me gravely. 'No, Meninha,' she said. 'You are doing her immense good. Her mind is clearing of the poisons that were in it. And that is the best that we can hope for. She is no longer living in a cloud of horror. But that she may ever be restored to full, normal living – this I do not believe. I think she was always something a little different from such a person as you or I – weaker in body. Perhaps closer to the Eternal Spirit.'

A changeling.

'Yes, Sister, I believe you are right.'

'Of course I am right.'

'Well, I will go to Oporto and get some paints.' But first, I thought, I will write to the Duke.

And I retired to my cell and did so. I wrote him a long, loving letter, giving a fairly full account of all that had befallen me, explaining that it might still be weeks, perhaps months, before I would feel free of my commitment to Lady Hariot and Triz – unless the Duke might feel inclined to offer them hospitality at Zoyland? Which, of course, could prove a most happy solution for all concerned. And I was, ever and always, his loving ward, Lizzie.

At supper that night Sister Euphrasia had a lengthy list of commissions for me to undertake in Oporto. Lady Hariot asked for some muslin kerchiefs. She had used all hers for mopping and band-aging. Innocently I inquired of Mrs Brandon if there were any errands or messages that I could perform for her? I would be visiting the English Factory, I added. No, she said coldly, she thanked me, but there was nothing. She looked as sour as the vinegary wine we were drinking.

'You have to excuse her,' said Sister Luisinha to me later. 'She receives considerable pain from her ulcerated leg.'

'Oh, poor lady. I did not know. Was she wounded in battle, then?'

'Oh, no, nothing like that. I think she hurt her leg when a mule she was riding ran up against a rock. For some reason the gash will not heal. She has had it for a long time.'

Now the convent vintage was in full swing. I passed the yard, as I rode down to the Douro, where, in the great granite *lagar* about seventy men, in rows of ten, each with their arms over the shoulders of the row in front, were tramping and chanting out, left! right! left! right! interspersing their shouts with wild cries and shrieks.

'They will go on like that for many hours,' said the overseer.

I looked to see if, by any chance, my friendly rescuers were among the *lagares*. But it was impossible to tell, they were all so locked together. Then they began bawling out a song to a very catchy refrain. I could see that the words must be very bawdy; my guide hurried me away with a face full of disapproval.

At this time of the year there was continual traffic up and down the river, of dinghies, canoes, caiques, and boats like gondolas. The convent *barco* was about to set off, and I had a rapid passage to Oporto, both wind and current being favourable. We reached the town before dusk fell on the following day, and I was able to perform at least half my errands and leave my bundles, bespeaking myself a bed (on Sister Euphrasia's recommendation) at the Convent of Santa Clara.

Here, the portress – the same who had, on my former visit, declared herself unable to furnish Willoughby with news of Mrs Brandon's whereabouts – on hearing my name, uttered a soft exclamation, and begged me to give myself the inconvenience of waiting a moment or two while she went in search of the English-speaking sister. This person, soon making her appearance, gliding up to me at speed in her felt-soled slippers, ejaculated: 'Ah, it is so fortunate that you have returned to us, Meninha! For we have, a few days since, received tidings concerning a friend of yours – or so we believe. A poor lady was picked up (doubtless by the especial intervention of Sant Iago himself), rescued half-drowned from the waves –'

'*No!*' I exclaimed in utter astonishment. 'Not Senhora Pullett?'

'But yes, but yes! That was the name.'

'Is she here? Can I see her?'

'No, no. She is in Spain. Many leagues distant from here. At our sister convent, in the holy city of Santiago de Compostela. But, as soon as the poor thing was sensible and could make herself understood – which, we were told, was not for some little while – she was most urgent that you should be told of her whereabouts. She told the Sisters there that you were travelling to Porto, so messages were sent here. And we were not certain where you now were –'

'She is really alive – really, really alive?'

What a weight off my heart!

'Indeed, yes! Picked up by sardine fishers – so we were told – and taken to the Holy Sisters at Santiago. But now, at this present, still very feeble, very frail. She is mending, though, the Sister Infirmarian wrote. And her one hope is that you will come, as soon as you are able, to fetch her away.'

'May I write to her? Can a letter be sent to Santiago?'

'But certainly.'

So I wrote Pullett a joyful note, describing how I had finally found Lady Hariot and Triz (I skirted over my experiences prior to this), explaining that I could not immediately abandon them, but had plans for them, involving the Duke, which I hoped to put into effect as soon as possible, when Triz should be a little further amended in health. Meanwhile I besought Pullett to be patient, reiterated my great delight that she was still in the world, urged to her learn Spanish and embroidery from the Sisters, and promised that, as soon as lay within my power, I would return to England, calling at the port of La Coruña – or wherever was most convenient – to pick her up.

The English-speaking Sister undertook that my letter should be dispatched with their next budget of convent business to Compostela.

Now, with a huge expansion of spirit and a belief that, as all seemed in such propitious train just now, Fate might continue to smile on my enterprises, I made my way to the English Factory, handed in my letter for the Duke, which I was assured would go with the following day's packet, and inquired for the address of a Mr Willoughby.

'Certainly, Senhora. He lives in the Rua dos Flores, among the silversmiths.'

I was given the directions, which involved climbing up and down a great many steps and traversing many of the narrow *ilhas,* or alleys, which thread between the greater thoroughfares of this steeply pitched city.

I found the door. I knocked at it. And thought of various probabilities: that the man I sought would have gone off to Lamego to be closer to Marianne; that he would *not* be the man I sought; or that he would simply not be at home.

But he was at home, and he was the man I sought. It was the same shaggy-locked, haggard-faced man whom I had seen making his inquiries at the convent. Only now he was not wearing hat or cloak, but simply indoor dress of shirt, velvet waistcoat and pantaloons, all decidedly shabby. His face, full of hope and delight as he pulled open the door, lit up momentarily – even more when I first pushed back my hat – then closed into a mask of disappointment as he realized I was not the person he expected.

'Senhora – I think there must be some mistake. I am not expecting anybody.'

And that's a lie, I thought.

He began to close the door.

He had spoken in Portuguese. I replied in English.

'No, sir, there is no mistake. You were not expecting me, but allow me to introduce myself. I am your daughter, Eliza Williams.— Or, I suppose I might say, Eliza Willoughby.'

Chapter 16

I AM YOUR DAUGHTER,' I REPEATED TO THE MAN WHO STOOD silent in the doorway.

'I don't believe you,' he snapped. 'I don't understand! What is this? Go away! Go to the devil!'

But I said, 'I have not travelled all this way in order to be shooed off so easily. You may as well allow me ten minutes of your time. Besides' – I produced the crumpled sheet of paper which I had picked up in the pine grove – 'I have come from the Convent of Nossa Senhora. I can tell you – if you like – about the reception of *that.*'

He snatched the paper, glaring at me. His eyes, I saw, were red and bloodshot.

'What did she say – *what did she say?* Have you a message?'

'Let me in,' I said.

So – ungraciously – he retreated and I followed him into a large shabby room with a worn grass carpet, a wooden ceiling, walls papered in dark red, a table with a soiled red damask cloth, two chairs and very little else. Some papers and a few books were strewn on the table. There was a bottle of wine and a glass, a plate with a lump of hard bread and a slice of sausage.

The room smelt stale, of smoke and dirt.

I sat down on one of the chairs.

'I am your daughter,' I repeated.

'What is *that* to the purpose?' He looked hastily at the letter, then, as if it stung him, flung it into a charcoal brazier where it flamed up, adding to the acrid smells in the room. 'What do you want of me? Do you want money? I haven't got any.'

'Of course I don't want money!' I shouted angrily. 'If I did, I certainly would not come to *you*! I just wished to see you – to meet you – is that so strange?'

Apparently it seemed so to him.

'What is your purpose in coming here? – Did, did *she* send you? M-Marianne?'

'No, *indeed* she did not. If the truth must be told, I think she detests us both equally. You, I suppose, for leaving her; me, for being your daughter by another woman.'

'Did your mother send you then?' he said suspiciously. 'Eliza, was it?'

'No!' I almost spat at him. 'My mother is dead! How or where she died is no concern of yours. I am sorry, now, that I came to find you. *Nobody* sent me. I just wished – wished to make the acquaintance of my father. But now I see that it was a wasted errand. I am glad' – I was almost choking with rage and disappointment, though Heaven knows by this time I should have been prepared for disappointment – 'I am glad that I have good friends, friends of my own.'

And how brightly they shone in this dismal atmosphere: the Duke, Lady Hariot, even Hoby and poor little Triz.

Willoughby seemed to me like a man dried up, a husk, with no juice or meaning left in him. The same thing had happened to him, I thought, as to Marianne: the vital spark had ebbed away and left them.

Now he seemed a degree less antagonistic. He sat down, rubbed his forehead, and addressed me, rather hopelessly, 'She did not answer my letter? There was no message? None?'

'She threw the letter away. I picked it up. But I think,' I said scrupulously, 'that she is very unhappy. She is not well. Perhaps, if you waited a while, and tried again –'

'How can I?' he muttered. 'Already I owe rent on this place – twenty milreis. Wretched as it is, I can't afford it. I must leave Oporto and find some cabin in the mountains. She was my final hope.'

'You are courting her simply because she has money now? Is a rich widow?'

'No! Damn you! Get out! May the fiend fly away with you.'

He sprang up, so full of rage that I instinctively dropped my hand to the hilt of the knife in my boot. But then he sank down on his chair again, muttering wretchedly, 'Oh, what does it matter what you think? Only go. I have nothing for you, nothing at all.'

'No,' I said coldly. 'I can see that very plainly. But perhaps *I* have something for *you*.'

And I laid forty milreis on the table, before letting myself out of the door.

Outside in the street I was not particularly surprised to observe a man leaning against the wall; a man who looked as if he had been waiting and listening there for some time. But I was dismayed when he slunk up to me and said: 'Aha! It is the young Senhora who killed my friend João! And now, what will you give me, Meninha, not to inform the authorities and lead them to the spot where you concealed the body?'

At another time I might have been alarmed by this threat.

But the man, Manuel – now I recognized him – was such a small, unimpressive, ratlike character, and I was worked up into such a wrathy passion from the recent interview with Willoughby, that I simply thrust my right hand menacingly under his nose.

'Do you see that hand, friend? Do you know what it means? It means that I have the power to change myself into a wild beast at night! I can tell you, now, that if you "inform the authorities" about me, you will never have an easy night in your bed again. Never! For I shall come, one night, in the dark, and get you with my teeth and claws; I shall come and deal with you as I dealt with your friend João.'

And I showed him all my teeth and thrust my face towards his.

He turned white as chalk, gave a lamentable cry, and scuttled away down the dirty alleyway.

I walked wearily uphill, feeling no triumph at all; and climbed the steps towards my hard narrow bed at the Convent of Santa Clara. Not until I was undressed and lying down did I remember that I had eaten nothing. But at that time I could not have taken any supper. It would have choked me.

❧

Next morning, having performed what remained of the various commissions for Sister Euphrasia, I returned to the English Factory to pick up my other purchases. There I was greeted cordially by the manager, who, on hearing my name, exclaimed that he was holding letters from England for me.

'Why, thank you, sir! I am greatly obliged to you. I will read them on the boat.'

I had bespoken a boat the day before, and was wild to be on my way. I wished that I had never come to Porto.

I waited until we were clear of the city, battling our way upstream between the huge terraced hillsides, before opening my letters.

One was from the Duke's doctor.

My dear Miss Williams

This will be sad news for you, I fear. I must break it at once. His Grace is no more. He fell into a melancholy after you had gone, from which it proved impossible to rouse him. He seemed to have a premonition that you would not return. 'I shall never see her again,' he kept repeating. And, alas! this proved to be true.

But pray do not blame yourself, dear Miss Williams. I had been apprehensive of his failing ever since the spasm that he suffered prior to your departure. I think that your leaving only hastened an inevitable outcome. And, be assured, his end was an easy one; he simply fell asleep one evening and, the next morning, failed to wake.

He spoke of you a great deal – almost continually.

He has left you – as the men of business will inform you – amply provided for in funds and jointures.

I had rather expected that he would leave you Zoyland – since he knew that you are greatly attached to the house; but instead he has, rather oddly to my way of thinking, left the house to young Mr Hobart, with a proviso that you, during your lifetime, are always to have the use of your own apartments there.

Doubtless you will be hearing also from Mr Hobart and his own lawyers about this. (I fancy the Duke cherished some matrimonial hopes in regard to you and Mr Hobart – since he was most deeply attached to you both – and planned by this means to further such a scheme.) He had Mr Hobart frequently with him before he died.

I send my best regards to you and Miss Pullett, and hope that your business in Portugal has prospered and is within sight of a happy conclusion. All the staff at Zoyland join me in good wishes and strong hopes of seeing you back here within the not too distant future.

Yr obdt srvnt

Elijah Swinton.

The second letter was from Hoby . . .

This one irritated me *so much* that I crumpled it and threw it over the side of the *barco*. And was visited, as I did so, by a sudden sympathy for Marianne Brandon, pacing in the pine grove as she read Willoughby's appeal for help. What *do* they take us for? Parcels, to be picked up and unwrapped at will?

But these thoughts were superseded by a heavy, a wretched, an overmastering grief for my old friend, my kind guardian and companion, so that I sat, for the remaining days of the journey, stricken, with my head in my hands, regardless of the churning current, the fresh, following wind, the animated scenes on the hillsides where grapes were gathering and oxcarts plied to and fro.

For the vintage was now well under way.

Sister Euphrasia had promised to send a pair of mules to meet me, with all my packages; present also at the anchorage, to my no small surprise, was little Sister Luisinha, who bore a pale and troubled countenance.

'You have heard already then?' she exclaimed, when she saw my tear-swollen eyes. 'But no – how could you?'

'Heard what, Sister?' said I with a mournful premonitory lurch of the heart. But how could there be worse tidings than what I had already received?

It seems there could.

'The little one – the little Teresa – she has left us. She has gone to the Holy Mother.'

'Left you? What do you mean?' I repeated stupidly. 'Died? But she seemed quite well – quite especially so, when I took my leave the other day. Did she have a seizure? What happened?'

'It was yesterday afternoon,' Sister Luisinha said, unaffectedly wiping her eyes with her veil as we rode slowly up the steep zig-zag hill. 'The weather was fine so we took her, as so often, to the pool in the orchard; that was always her favourite place, ever since you discovered it. And there she sat, humming to herself in the way she does – did; old Sister Maria, who was with her, went to speak to Jorge about the vines, and Lady Hariot was coming over the grass, not too far away, when the Little One suddenly rose up and walked – *walked* – took several steps – which she had never done before, all the time she has been at Nossa Senhora – and she fell, poor child, into the pool. But before that she said something – Lady Hariot will tell you. Sister Maria ran back, and Lady Hariot was there, and they had her out of the water directly; she was in it no longer than the stroke of a bell; but that was enough to stop her heart which, you know, was enfeebled by what she had suffered before. She died instantly.'

'Oh, *poor* Lady Hariot . . . '

'Lady Hariot has a strong spirit,' said Sister Luisinha. 'She bends like the bough of an ash tree; she will not break.'

I saw that this was so when I went to Lady Hariot's room where Triz lay, lapped in cloudy muslin and white roses, on her narrow bed. Lady Hariot rose from where she was kneeling and came to envelop me in a strong embrace, which I returned.

'Oh, Lady Hariot! – *Why* was I not with you when it happened?'

I felt the greater guilt, because my errand to Oporto had been so full of self-interest; I had wanted to see Willoughby; my other errands had been trivial pretexts contrived to give an air of virtue to the mission.

But Lady Hariot said: 'Listen, Eliza. You are not to reproach yourself. I think – I believe – that Thérèse wished to go. You had roused her mind from the slough where it had floundered for so long; enough so that she could see there was a way ahead for her. Out of this life into another. But – and do not take this hard, my dear girl – so long as *you* were with her, she did not like to leave you. It would have seemed ungrateful. Listen and I will tell you how she went. I was only a few yards away, coming towards her, and I saw her *stand up* – she, who had not moved from her chair for three years – she stood, she walked forwards, holding out her hands as if she saw something ahead, and she called out, quite clearly, 'Come again, my dear Lord King Arthur, come again!' And then she fell headlong into the pool. I and Sister Maria were with her immediately and pulled her out, but I believe her heart had stopped before she ever fell.'

I received this in silence and remained so for a long time, looking down at the pale, motionless face which, now freed from its premature lines of suffering, looked like the ivory carving of some stern young angel.

'Come again, my dear Lord King Arthur! It was the game we used to play.'

How clearly I could remember little Triz, in the garden at Kinn Hall, saying, 'I wonder what Sir Bedivere did after that? I wonder if he ever *did* see King Arthur again?'

On the boat, coming up the Douro, my sorrow for the Duke had been tainted by anger and frustration, because I had hoped and planned to bring Lady Hariot and Triz back with me to Zoyland, where I was sure the Duke would receive them kindly. Now, with Hoby as owner, I felt this plan would not be possible. Would be out of the question.

But the death of Triz showed me, in a flash, how idle it is to engender such plans and contrivances; Fate tosses them aside, like leaves in autumn gales.

'Thérèse will be buried here, in the Sisters' graveyard,' said Lady Hariot, blowing her nose. 'They hold her funeral tomorrow.'

'I will ask Sister Euphrasia if I may sing with the choir.'

'Of course . . . how queer. I had forgotten about your voice.'

'What will you do, where will you go now, Lady Hariot?'

'I shall have to see,' she said doubtfully. 'My sister is still far away in Brazil. The Portuguese royal family seem so comfortably established there, they show no signs of returning to Lisbon. I am really not certain where I shall go. Back to Porto, perhaps.'

I sang a Gloria at the funeral service. And afterwards Marianne Brandon approached me. Up to that moment I had not seen her for a couple of days; I supposed she was keeping to her apartment until the service. The Sisters had no organ in their small chapel, only a piano. Marianne played for the service – very beautifully. I realized that compared with her I was no musician at all.

'Will you accompany me into the orchard for a few minutes?' Marianne said to me as we left the chapel.

'Yes, of course.'

I followed her, a little puzzled, noticing that she limped even more heavily. I wondered whether or not to tell her about Willoughby.

She made for the bench by the wall overlooking the huge view down across the city of Lamego, and we sat there for several minutes in silence.

Then Marianne said: 'Death clears one's mind. Do you find that? It puts our own small doings in perspective.'

I sighed, thinking of my dear Duke, and she went on musingly:

> 'Even such is Man, whose life is spun
> Drawn out and cut, and so is done:
> The rose withers, the blossom blasteth,
> The flower fades, the morning hasteth,
> The sun sets, the shadow flies
> The gourd consumes, and Man, he dies.

'Do you know those lines?'

I did not, and looked at her with quick interest: to hear poetry coming from the elegant Mrs Brandon was something unexpected. But then I remembered those books in the boudoir at Delaford.

Now she surprised me anew.

'I owe you an apology,' she said. 'I have been angry with you for a long time – as perhaps you guessed.'

It needed no acute intelligence to guess that, I thought, but remained silent.

'From the start, I bitterly begrudged my husband's interest in you,' she said. 'The more, as I was childless. I made it a policy to prevent him visiting you, or bringing you over to Delaford.

'And therefore I was thunderstruck – *outraged* – mortified and infuriated beyond bearing – when I learned, after his death, that he had left you the Manor in his will.—Oh, I have been provided for – financially – I have no reasonable cause for complaint; but to lose that house – the groves, the gardens – the mulberry tree –'

For a moment she remained without speaking, choked, I thought, by emotion; she muttered something about 'Norland' which I did not comprehend.

I, meanwhile, as may be readily understood, was wholly dumb-struck with incredulity.

'Left me the Manor?' I muttered stupidly after a while. 'You mean, Delaford?'

'Yes. Did you not know?'

'How should I?'

'Well, I suppose there is a lawyer's letter awaiting you somewhere. Perhaps they did not know where to find you.'

I said hoarsely, 'That bequest seems to me utterly unjust. The Manor was *your* house – you had furnished it, you cared for it, you lived there – you loved it –'

I thought of the pleasant room overlooking the rose garden; the books on the shelf, pictures on the walls, the portrait of Willoughby hidden away between the pages.

'Oh, no,' said Marianne. '*Men* build these houses. Women only occupy them for a short space. We come and go, my dear girl, like swallows. Delaford Manor was there before me, and will outlast me.'

The same was true of Zoyland, I thought. It was built in the reign of Elizabeth; I could claim, at best, no more than temporary tenancy.

And now I did not even need to do that.

A new feeling, unfamiliar, came to startle me. Could this be happiness? Or at least a kind of wry appreciation. For such a neat, symmetrical pattern. One home is withdrawn, another provided.

'Mrs Brandon: if the Manor has really been left to me – which seems to me utterly astounding and improbable – then, please believe me, you must always regard it as your home. That room – your books, your pictures –'

'Oh? You have been there, in the house?' said Marianne. She seemed rather surprised, not best pleased. 'I did not know.'

'Once – on an errand for your brother-in-law.'

And another bubble of amusement burst inside me. Was Edward Ferrars going to have to swallow his chagrin and be obliged to receive me as a neighbour? As the Lady of the Manor?

'You are generous,' said Marianne. 'You show more generosity than I have shown you; but' – she exhaled a long breath – 'I am informed that I had better make my peace with God and order my affairs. This cankered leg that I am plagued with does not respond to treatment. I am not to expect any extended future.'

'Oh – *poor Willoughby!*' I exclaimed.

She looked up in amazed inquiry.

'*You have seen him?* Here, in Portugal?'

'Yesterday. I went – I have always wanted – ' At a loss for explanations, I mumbled, 'He is my father, after all.'

With a faint smile, she said, 'A fairly non-doing one, I collect?'

'I had never met him in my whole life, so I did wish to see him, just once. And,' after some thought, I added, 'perhaps I am glad that I did. Otherwise it would always have been a question. Now, at least, I know him, what he is like.—He is like somebody who died years ago.'

Sighing, Marianne rose and began to limp back towards the cloister. As she walked away, she remarked, 'I only hope that knowing Willoughby does not put you off the male sex for ever. He was different when he was young, I assure you.'

For a moment I considered trying to plead his case; but what would be the purpose? She was not for him, and never would be.

Over her shoulder she added drily, 'I shall probably make it my business to see, however, that he does not go hungry.'

And I grinned, thinking of the forty milreis that I had deposited on the table. Women, it appeared, would always see that Willoughby did not go hungry.

I went indoors and sought out Lady Hariot.

'Listen, dear Lady Hariot, it seems that I have inherited a house. Will you come and share it with me? It is by far too large for one single woman.'

'But – Good Heavens, my dearest child! – You will, for sure, find some man to fulfil that office – '

'I am not at all certain about that,' said I. 'In any case I am going to take my time about coming to any such decision. And there are many considerations which make my future marriage most unlikely. And Delaford is not too far from the country that you love – not too distant from Ashett and Growly Head. And one of the plans I have – for I am an heiress, I shall be wealthy – one of my schemes for the future is to oversee the children of Byblow Bottom, make sure they are properly treated and not left to the usage of people like Hannah Wellcome. And Dr Moultrie,' I added, after a moment.

'In that case,' said Lady Hariot, 'if such is your plan, I will come with you, and gladly. I do not care to be idle.'

'There will be plenty to do.'

I thought that I would wait a while, yet, perhaps for the solitary intimacy of the sea voyage, while we sailed up the coast to Coruña to pick up Pullett, before telling Lady Hariot my other piece of news: that, in the course of the next year, I was to bear a child.

No, dear reader, I do not propose to tell you *whose*; that you may – if so disposed – try to puzzle out for yourself; I leave such unimportant matters to provide for the diversion of the idle-minded.

But I can tell you this. My child will be a child of the wild. All she will derive – all she will *need* – from her father, will be freedom. And that freedom in her I will defend, so long as it lies within my power, from society's jealousies, ambitions and rancours.

I hope that the child will be a girl. I think it will be. And will have my hands. As the gypsy and Pullett told me, my hand has brought me luck. But, girl or boy, which ever it be, I shall nurse it and care for it myself. No child of mine shall be consigned to Byblow Bottom.

And no, again, reader, I shall not marry Hoby. He has lost his chance.

Perhaps I shall take to writing novels, like Cousin Elinor.
Perhaps this is one of them.

About the Author

The late Joan Aiken was a scholar and a prolific author of children's books and Jane Austen sequels and continuations. She is the author of *Emma Watson*, which completes Jane Austen's posthumously published fragment *The Watsons*, and of *Mansfield Park Revisited*, a sequel to *Mansfield Park*.

.